STAR WARS®

THE NEW ESSENTIAL GUIDE TO ALIEN SPECIES

THE STAR WARS LIBRARY
PUBLISHED BY DEL REY BOOKS

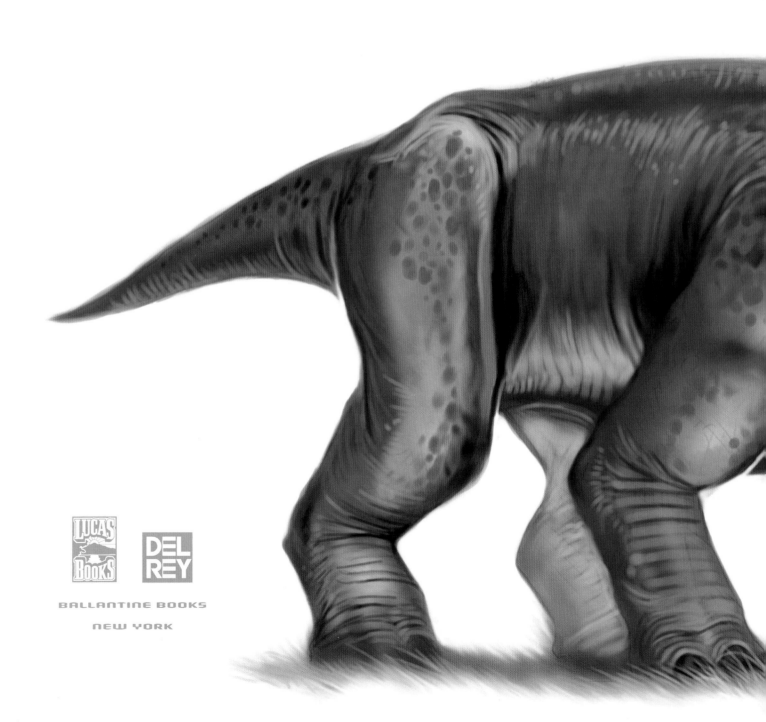

LUCAS
BOOKS

DEL
REY

BALLANTINE BOOKS

NEW YORK

STAR WARS®

THE NEW ESSENTIAL GUIDE TO ALIEN SPECIES

Text by Ann Margaret Lewis and Helen Keier

Illustrations by Chris Trevas
and William O'Connor

For my son Raymond, who wanted me to play
with him instead of write; my husband, Joseph,
for his love, patience, and support; and for Helen,
who deserves this and a whole lot more
—*Ann Margaret Lewis*

For my son, Vince, for thinking I am the coolest
mom on the planet because I play video games
and love *Star Wars;* for my mother, Cynthia, for
her lifelong reminders that I could accomplish
anything if I set my mind to it; and for Ann, for
giving me the opportunity to do this with her
—*Helen Keier*

And for the fans . . .
—*Both of us*

A Del Rey Trade Paperback Original

Copyright © 2006 by Lucasfilm Ltd. & ® or ™ where indicated.
All Rights Reserved. Used Under Authorization.

Published in the United States by Del Rey Books, an imprint of The Random House Publishing
Group, a division of Random House, Inc., New York.

DEL REY is a registered trademark and the Del Rey colophon is a trademark of Random House, Inc.

ISBN 0-345-47760-X

Printed in the United States of America

www.starwars.com
www.delreybooks.com

2 4 6 8 9 7 5 3 1

Interior design by Foltz Design

This book could never have happened if not for the help and support of so many people:

Sue Rostoni, Jonathan Rinzler, and Leland Chee of Lucasfilm for giving us the opportunity and the invaluable assistance necessary to see this project to its completion.

Del Rey editors Steve Saffel for his generosity and Keith Clayton for his enthusiasm and patience. Also production manager Erich Schoeneweiss, another kindred spirit when it comes to the world of *Star Wars.*

All the Bantam and Del Rey *Star Wars* authors whose imaginations made these creatures come alive.

The comic-book artists and writers from Dark Horse and Marvel who made them incarnate in imagery.

The Wizards of the Coast Games authors and game designers who created an incredible wealth of amazing material.

Daniel Wallace and Abel Pena, our personal gurus of *Star Wars* wisdom. The depth of your knowledge is absolutely astounding. This book never would have been finished without you.

To all the creators at ILM and Lucasfilm who with their incredible imaginations created a good number of these creatures out of clay, plastic, paint, and rubber, then made them dance on screen.

Ann: A special thanks to my husband, Joseph, for giving me love and support through this entire process; my mother, Mary Ann, and my sister, Karen, for their encouragement; and to Helen—I cannot even begin to thank you enough for easing my stress and giving me hope. You are the absolute best.

Helen: My special thanks go to my son, Vince Skrapits; to the friends whose faith in me sustains me on a daily basis: Sonja Vanihel, Kay Silverwood Hilgendorf, Elizabeth Davidson, Matt Gladden, Glen and David Oliver, Sean Reiser, Gary Tucker, and the LeMaire family; to Ben Harper, Aaron Allston, and more than a few people I won't name in the interest of space but who know who they are, for all their encouragement; and last but not least, my thanks go to Ann. We said to each other when we met several years ago that we should write together someday, and to my great pleasure, now we have.

And especially to Mr. George Lucas for giving us the never-ending gift of *Star Wars.*

CONTENTS

INTRODUCTION

"A Vurk, a Gungan, and a Chevin walk into a bar. The bartender says . . ."

In this *New Essential Guide to Alien Species,* we cover the species that make the watering holes of scum and villainy come to life in that great "galaxy far, far away." We also give you in-depth dossiers of the many alien players that populate George Lucas's ever-expanding universe. Whether they were invented by the designers of the ILM Monster Shop, the novelists, comic-book writers and illustrators, or game developers, this book provides you with the details on the most pivotal species in the *Star Wars* galaxy.

The species in this book were selected because they met one or more of the following criteria: they appeared in at least one of the films, they were important to a major story line, or they were members of a species that begged for further exploration. While we've done our best to select as many as possible of the species fans would like to see, as a second edition there are many that were not included that may have been in the first edition. As with all of the *Essential Guides,* the goal was to provide a valuable and representative overview of the vastness of the *Star Wars* universe, taking into account all the favorites and introducing you to a few new faces you may not have met before.

While our perceptions of a given species are often based on only a few of its members, the truth is not all members of a given species are truly identical—even the clones and animals. Among creatures and persons, there is a great deal of variety in values, traditions, and appearance. So while each entry herein may note the shared characteristics exhibited by a given species, there will come events that lead any individual from that group to "break the rules." As our inspiration Senior Anthropologist Hoole once said, "In this galaxy, when you've seen one, don't assume you've seen them all." Words to the wise as you set off on your journey to meet the players in this colorful, sometimes frightening, but always thrilling galaxy of our dreams.

In the course of your own visits to the cantinas, spaceports, and gambling clubs of the Galaxy Far, Far Away, may the Force be with you, and with all creatures great, small, wild, and wonderful.

ABOUT THE ENTRIES

In our last edition, Senior Anthropologist Hoole provided much of the observational material for the species he studied. Following the good senior anthropologist's recent retirement, he left his notes and volumes of research materials for us to use for this new guide. These detailed texts, along with our own observational notes, have helped us put together our entries and provide the following information. Please note that survey teams have not been able to reach all the worlds affected by the Yuuzhan Vong invasion, so the status of some species in the wake of that event has not yet been determined. If the present status of a species is known, it will be given in the body of the entry.

DESIGNATION

Each species is designated as *sentient, semi-sentient,* or *nonsentient.* Usually this is based on a species' ability to reason, use tools, and communicate. A panel of multicultural scientists determines the designations only after a government-approved research team has conducted a field study or has made some significant finding regarding the sentience of any given species. The designations are defined as follows:

Sentient: When a species is given the *sentient* designation, it is considered able to reason and understand abstract concepts and ideas, make and use tools, and communicate with written or spoken language. Most primitive tribal species have this designation; it does not imply that a species is civilized to the point of space travel.

Semi-sentient: The *semi-sentient* designation implies that a race has some reasoning ability, but cannot grasp elevated or abstract concepts. In many cases, it has not yet formed a written or spoken language. These species are considered to be in evolutionary stages—on their way to achieving sentience. Under the Empire, these species were not entitled to landownership, but this has been undergoing reconsideration in the Galactic Federation of Free Alliances.

Nonsentient: A *nonsentient* species is one that does not reason at all, surviving only on its natural instincts.

HOMEWORLD

Most alien species have a homeworld or system. Some, like the bantha, are found in many systems, and still others, such as the Hutts, have transplanted themselves to a new home. The primary locations of a given species within the galaxy will be listed here, and its present home will be likewise indicated.

AVERAGE HEIGHT

The average size of adult members of a given species is provided in meters.

PRONUNCIATION

The pronunciation of the species' name is provided in Basic. For the pronunciation key, please see page 218.

NOTABLE APPEARANCE

We provide one of the noteworthy appearances of each species in book, film, or comics.

GLOSSARY OF DESCRIPTIVE TERMS

The following terms are used to describe the species in this book. Many of the varieties covered in this volume belong to one or more of these classifications. Given the unique evolutionary conditions found on each planet, it is impossible to fit every species into a neat classification. These are broad terms useful in describing an unfamiliar species to one's colleagues.

Amphibious: A creature that can live both in water and on land, or has two stages of life, one that is completely water-based, the other land-based. Some are born as tadpoles possessing gills, and develop lungs to breathe air, while others have compound lungs that allow them to breathe underwater and on land.

Arboreal: A species that lives among forests and trees, and is specially adapted to tree living.

Avian: A species bearing the characteristics of birds or flying mammals.

Canine: A species that possesses some characteristics of the dog family, including a pronounced muzzle, sharp teeth, advanced hunting and tracking instincts, heightened hearing, sight, and smell, sharp teeth, claws, padded feet, and a tail.

Cephalopod: A species that bears the traits inherent in most squid and octopi, namely water-based or amphibious creatures with tentacles.

Cetacean: Any species of aquatic or marine mammals, usually typified by a predominance of the following: a hairless or nearly hairless body, anterior flipper-like limbs, vestigial posterior limbs, and a flat, notched tail.

Crustacean: Aquatic lobster-like arthropods or shellfish that usually have a segmented body, a chitinous exoskeleton, and paired, jointed limbs.

Cyborg: Any species that has been enhanced with technological implants.

Feline: A species that carries some characteristics of the cat family, such as extremely flexible body, sharp teeth, slit-pupiled eyes, a tail, hunting and tracking instincts, heightened hearing, sight, and smell, and padded, clawed hands and feet.

Gastropod: A species that has no true skeletal frame and moves by means of a wide muscular foot, or whose whole body acts as one large foot.

Humanoid: Those species that, while not related genetically to humans, possess characteristics similar to humans, such as two arms with hands, fingers, and an opposable thumb, two legs, a torso, and a single head.

Insectoid: Any species that has the characteristics of insects, which may include a chitinous shell, multiple legs, antennae, and multifaceted eyes.

Mammal: This classification usually refers to warm-blooded vertebrates that grow fur and usually bear live young (although not always, as some have been known to lay eggs). Regardless of the birth process, a female mammal nurses her young.

Near-human: These species are genetically related to humans, and are usually classified as humans. Only four near-human species are represented in this book.

Pachydermoid: A species with characteristics attributed to pachyderms, usually including baggy, leathery skin, a trunk, and steady, thick legs and feet.

Plant-based: A species that reproduces itself and roots like most plant life, usually feeding through photosynthesis. Some plant-based species resemble animal species, depending on evolution.

Porcine: A species bearing the characteristic of a pig, sometimes including a blunt-ended nose, tusks, hooves, and large physical size.

Primate: Mammalian species exhibiting the characteristics of monkeys or apes, including fur, fingers, and opposable thumbs. They are often referred to as humanoids because of their similarity to human physiology, but this depends on their sentience designation.

Proboscidian: A species that has a long trunk or feeds through a proboscis, such as the Anzati. Some proboscidians are also pachydermoids (see *Pachydermoid*).

Reptavian: A flying reptile.

Reptilian: A species with the characteristics of a reptile or snake, usually including leather-like skin, claws, slit-pupiled eyes, and a forked tongue. They reproduce by laying fertilized eggs. Some can change color to match their environment. Trandoshans, Barabels, Yevetha, and Falleen are all reptilian races.

Reptomammal: A reptile that reproduces through live birth rather than laying eggs.

Rodent: A species that carries characteristics of mice or rats, or gnawing or nibbling mammals that have continuously growing incisors.

Saurian: See *Reptilian*.

Ungulate: A species that has hooves, or whose claws evolved from hooves, and sometimes chews its cud.

Vacuumbreather: A species that can survive in a vacuum, including that of outer space, often consuming nutrients from space dust and mineral matter. Mynocks are vacuumbreathers.

STAR WARS®

THE NEW ESSENTIAL GUIDE TO ALIEN SPECIES

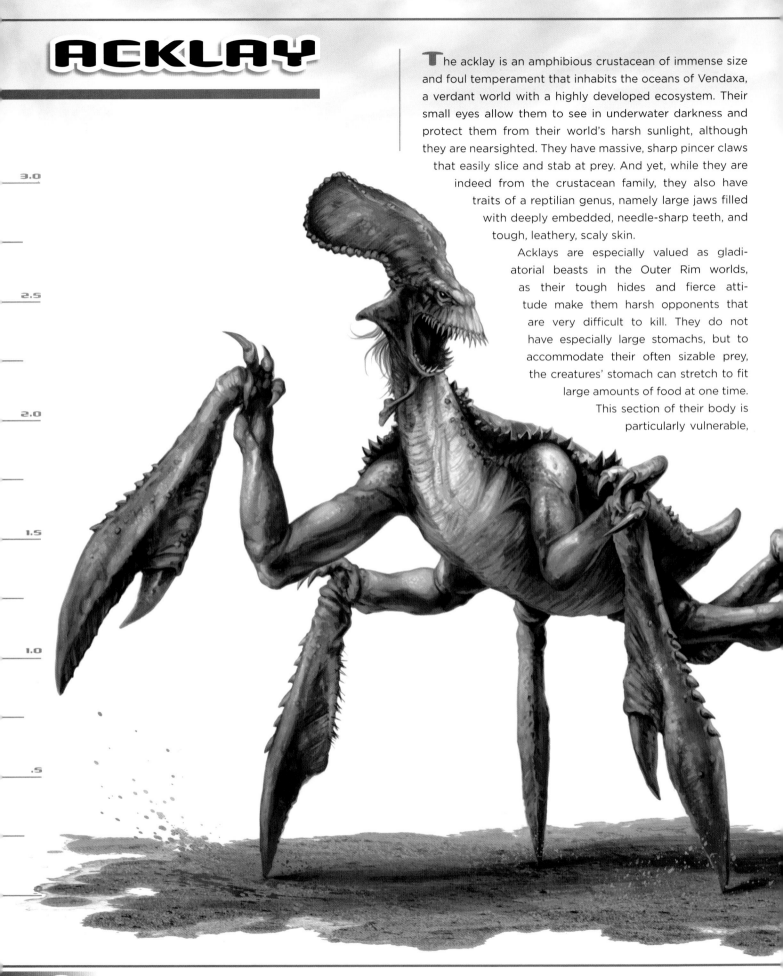

ACKLAY

The acklay is an amphibious crustacean of immense size and foul temperament that inhabits the oceans of Vendaxa, a verdant world with a highly developed ecosystem. Their small eyes allow them to see in underwater darkness and protect them from their world's harsh sunlight, although they are nearsighted. They have massive, sharp pincer claws that easily slice and stab at prey. And yet, while they are indeed from the crustacean family, they also have traits of a reptilian genus, namely large jaws filled with deeply embedded, needle-sharp teeth, and tough, leathery, scaly skin.

Acklays are especially valued as gladiatorial beasts in the Outer Rim worlds, as their tough hides and fierce attitude make them harsh opponents that are very difficult to kill. They do not have especially large stomachs, but to accommodate their often sizable prey, the creatures' stomach can stretch to fit large amounts of food at one time. This section of their body is particularly vulnerable,

3.0

2.5

2.0

1.5

1.0

.5

as the flesh covering is not as tough as the rest of their hide. Acklays have an extremely high metabolism for creatures their size, giving them a lot of energy—but they starve quickly if not fed frequently throughout the day. In gladiatorial environments, this can prompt them to have an appetite for many unfortunate arena victims, and it also makes their upkeep expensive for owners, who must frequently run them in the arena to satiate their appetites.

Like some reptilian species, acklays have a bony neck plate that they display to intimidate opponents. This also protects the acklay from overhead neck attacks. In addition, acklays can use this plate as a type of weapon, by bucking and weaving their heads to and fro to strike an opponent.

Acklays walk on the tips of their claws, seeming to glide on toe point like dancers. Yet these claws are lethal for an acklay's adversary. During combat, the acklay uses its claws like hatchets, waving them about to slice its opponents to bits—or to pinion its prey to the ground like a skewer weighing several tons. An acklay's claws are long enough to enable the beast to attack at a safe distance from its victim. These hardened appendages have little to no feeling, but rising from the joint of the main talons is an additional claw that is somewhat sensitive. Sensory hairs or cilia lining the surface of the exoskeleton claw allow an acklay the sense of touch. It is also able to sense its prey's body electricity with its cilia.

In their native habitat, these ferocious creatures hunt the plains during the day for the leathery-shelled lemnai, which, being nocturnal, are usually asleep in their dens. At night, acklays return to their lairs onshore to rest. Under the ocean surface, they feed on schools of fish that they can suck into their gaping, toothy maws.

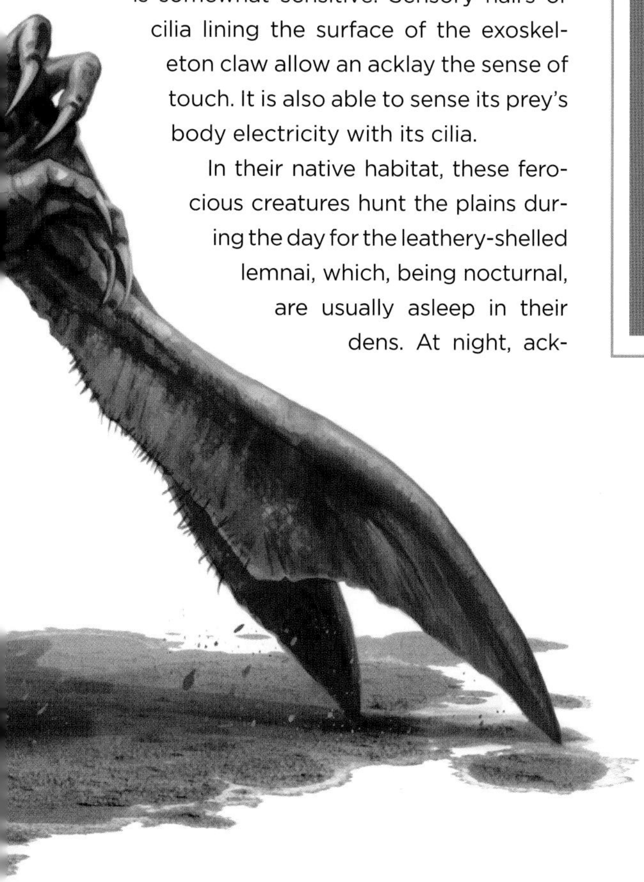

On Geonosis, acklays have only one natural predator: the merdeth. Enormous carnivores larger than star freighters, merdeths are armored insects with hundreds of small legs and masses of barbed tentacles that emerge from underneath their heads. Slow-moving creatures, merdeths often attack acklay dens, trapping the acklays inside and eating them.

While the acklay is originally from Vendaxa, the species also has a thriving population on Geonosis. Largely renowned for its droid technology, Geonosis also became well known as a hive of gladiatorial gaming and executions. One of the most popular species transferred to Geonosis was the acklay, which was then bred for arena entertainment.

A new mutant subspecies of acklay has appeared, larger and fiercer than its genetic relatives, a result of the chemical pollution contained in its habitat in the Golbah Pit of Geonosis. This new subspecies is different from the primary acklay in that its outer shell is a glossy black. The mutant acklay has heavier claws than its relative, and it is even able to hunt successfully in the dark, murky waters of the Ebon Sea. In addition, the mutant acklay can breathe underwater and is a highly skilled swimmer, allowing it to prey upon creatures not typically hunted by acklays. Overall, the mutant acklay is larger and tougher than its cousins, and will absorb considerably more damage before it is brought down.

Acklays may have been exported to worlds other than their traditional habitats to serve as live weapons during the Clone Wars. Records of the 501st Legion indicate that the unit was attacked by packs of acklays in the wilds of the Outer Rim planet of Felucia, then under Commerce Guild control. It is possible that the Confederacy of Independent Systems was able to move acklays from one loyal world to another without drawing attention to the shift within the scientific community. This theory has some support due to the fact that initial clone reports were unable to name the creatures, where as if the acklay had been native to or expected on a planet, the clones would have been briefed on them. At present, there are no indications that acklays remain on Felucia, perhaps a testament to the 501st's effectiveness.

DESIGNATION
Nonsentient

HOMEWORLD
Vendaxa/Geonosis

AVERAGE HEIGHT
3.05 meters

PRONUNCIATION
Ăk'-lā

NOTABLE APPEARANCE
Episode II: Attack of the Clones

AIWHA

The aiwha is an eight- to ten-meter-long aquatic mammal that flies on massive wings spanning twenty to thirty meters. Xenobiologists claim that aiwhas originated on Naboo, though a large population is also found on the planet Kamino. On both Naboo and Kamino, their primary habitats are the planets' oceans, and many have also been domesticated for use as riding mounts by Gungans and Kaminoans.

Aiwhas are strong creatures, using their muscular wings and pectoral muscles to create thrust for gliding in the air and swimming underwater. By building up momentum in the cresting waves, they can launch themselves into the sky to soar above the water. Aiwhas are able to propel themselves by shifting ballast, which they manage by utilizing two particular physical attributes. First, their skulls are porous and contain several buoyancy chambers, which fill with water when they dive under the surface. When aiwhas want to launch above the waves, they blow water from these cham-

bers in a fashion akin to the way most cetaceans use a blowhole. Aiwhas also have a special vascular system that enables them to shift body density. Their spongy, porous body tissue absorbs hundreds of kilograms of water, and when they soar into the air, they expel the liquid from their tissue to make themselves lighter. During flight, aiwhas release high-pitched whistling sounds. These sounds are used by the animal as internal sonar for underwater navigation, and as radar for night flying.

Although certain parts of their bodies allow for the intake and release of ocean water as mentioned above, aiwha skin is smooth, flexible, and virtually waterproof. This reduces air drag for the aiwhas when flying, while also allowing them to cut easily through the currents and retain body heat in cold seas. Aiwhas use their tails to aid in propelling themselves in and out of the water, either as rudders or for thrust. In addition, aiwhas have small, strong hind legs that are of limited use on land. They strongly prefer the seas over dry land, and do not walk very often on hard ground. Aiwhas also possess sharp teeth that they use to capture and hold prey.

Aiwhas make homes in nest-like "pods" on the ocean surface, and, like most cetacean mammals, they bear their young live. Unlike many of their genus, however, they will usually give birth to more than one calf at a time. Because up

to three or four aiwha families will nest together in one pod, they can often have clutches of eight to two dozen young in a grouping. While these creatures have been bred for docility, they are fierce when their pods are threatened, and will fight with an intense rage that is incongruous with their normally peaceful temperament. Conversely, domesticated aiwhas are very protective of their riding masters, seeing them as family in lieu of their podmates.

Aiwhas feed primarily on shallow-swimming krill and fish—filtering their sustenance, as most cetaceans do, through sieve plates in their baleen. By using high-pitched underwater sounds similar to the ones they utilize to navigate, aiwhas will corral their prey into a grouping and then suck them into their opened maw. However, aiwhas are omnivorous, unlike other cetaceans found throughout the galaxy. They will consume seaweed, kelp, and other plants found on the ocean floor as well as vitamin-laden grass from wetlands.

Creatures of the same genus as aiwhas can be found in several systems throughout the galaxy, including the planets Naboo and Kamino. Historical records indicate that the aiwha was brought to Kamino from Naboo, and that the Kaminoans cloned the present population from that stock to serve their needs. Despite their aquatic nature, the Kaminoan breed of aiwha is resistant to electrical shock. This makes them impervious to the dangerous electrical storms that often rage on the planet's surface. The Naboo breed, meanwhile, is not immune to such an attack. Xenobiologists believe that since aiwhas are probably a relatively recent addition to the Kaminoan environment, this trait was most likely added to their species during the cloning process. Even so, the Kaminoan aiwha prefers to go underwater during these storms; flying through them is highly unpleasant.

Kaminoans find the aiwha to be the most efficient means of traveling from one of their stilt-cities to another. They also use aiwhas to make religious pilgrimages to the ancient Kaminoan cities that lie at the bottom of their oceans (land-based Kaminoan culture was destroyed when the entire planet was flooded at the conclusion of a planetary ice age). Aiwhas provide a peaceful, spiritual means of transportation to the remnants of their ancient heritage, where the Kaminoans honor their ancestors rather than engage in archaeological exploration.

Gungans, on the other hand, use aiwhas for private mounted transportation, but also find them especially useful as bombers for aerial warfare and reconnaissance in the Gungan army. These military aiwhas are specially trained not to use their radar or make other sounds when flying for reconnaissance, but instead to rely on direction from their riders, although Gungan army aiwha riders can command their mounts to use their screech as a weapon when necessary. Because of this, aiwha-riding Gungans often wear earplugs when an attack is imminent, communicating with one another and their animals through hand signals and gestures initially developed for reconnaissance use. Military-trained aiwhas extend their loyalty just as any domesticated aiwhas do, often sensing when their riders are injured or incapacitated and need to be removed from battle. Among Gungans, stories abound of aiwhas saving the lives of their riders with a well-timed retreat.

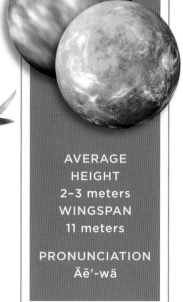

DESIGNATION
Nonsentient

HOMEWORLD
Kamino / Naboo

AVERAGE HEIGHT
2–3 meters
WINGSPAN
11 meters

PRONUNCIATION
Äē'-wä

NOTABLE APPEARANCE
Episode II: Attack of the Clones

AMANI
(Amanaman)

The Amanin (often referred to as Amanaman) are a primitive tribal hunter-gatherer species native to the planet Maridun, a world of large forests and grassy plains located in the Outer Rim. They are a sentient planarian species (i.e., of a worm genus), and they serve throughout the galaxy as laborers, scouts, and sometimes bounty hunters. Amanin are quiet, introspective beings who often converse in deep, low voices. Although they tower over many races, even Wookiees, they prefer to remain unnoticed as befitting their predatory nature. Unavoidably, however, their striking appearance in size, color, and decoration often has the opposite effect. For example, Amanin are known to carry at all times a staff from which the skulls of vanquished enemies hang. This has earned the Amanin the nickname Head Hunters.

Amanin are very tall, thin, mostly yellow-skinned arboreal beings who gain their height from long arms, which they use to travel from branch to branch. They have short, thick legs with extremely large feet, and while their bodies may appear awkward, Amanin are actually quite deft in movement. When on the ground, they walk slowly, but are able to curl themselves into a ball and roll at speeds ranging from forty-five to fifty kilometers per hour. Although it is difficult for them to perceive their surroundings well when traveling in this manner, Amanin are able to use their rolling momentum as a form of attack. They will speed past an opponent and unfurl their bodies to lash out with claws or clubs, often instantly killing their unsuspecting victim with the controlled force of impact.

By contrast, the placement of Amanin internal organs aids them in avoiding fatal injuries. As in other worm species, their organs, including their brains, are spread throughout their entire form. Moreover, they possess multiple copies of each primary organ, further enhancing their ability to survive wounds that would kill many species. This duplication of functional parts has led scientists to believe that Amanin can actually regenerate lost or damaged organs and limbs, and it is theorized that it is possible for an Amani to be cut fully in half without being killed. In such an event, however, it is thought the individual's regrowth may actually spawn two identical Amanin. Male and female are indistinguishable in this species, and it is believed, though as yet unproven, that they are hermaphrodites.

Amanin skin is moist, but susceptible to drying, so they prefer to make their shelter in humid environments, particularly rain forests. Their yellow-and-green coloring helps them blend in with their forest and grassland environments to avoid being detected by other predators. In addition, the coloration signals the poisonous properties of the slime that is secreted by their bodies to keep their skin damp and to fend off most of the carnivorous creatures found in the forests of Maridun. This slime deters all local predators save the charnoq, the only creature the Amanin fear.

Amanin have tiny eyes that can see clearly in Maridun's dim light, as well as little mouths that open surprisingly wide for engulfing raw game. As with other worm species, Amanin expel their biological waste through their mouths, although after having experienced interaction with other species, they mostly do this in private, as they have come to learn how it disturbs others. They also have a sense of smell so keen that they can detect strangers in their midst from more than ten kilometers away.

The Amanin have a simple, warrior tribal culture. Each tribe controls a forest region on Maridun, typically surrounded by grasslands. Amanin refer to all nonforested areas with the same term: gruntak. When an Amanin tribe's population grows too large, the extra youth of that tribe cross the gruntak regions to find a new section of forest to inhabit. This flight can result in battles over land rights with other Amanin, called takitals. The tribal leader or shaman, known as the lorekeeper, keeps stories of these struggles in a history that he often recites at special events.

During Palpatine's rule, Maridun was occupied by Imperial forces, setting in motion a series of events that changed the world and its people forever. A careless Imperial general led his troops across sacred Amanin grounds, and in retaliation, the local Amanin tribe waged a takital against the Empire.

DESIGNATION
Sentient

HOMEWORLD
Maridun

AVERAGE
HEIGHT
2–3 meters

PRONUNCIATION
Ăm-an'-ē

Janek Sunbar, an Imperial officer, distinguished himself during the takital, opening the door for an accord with the Amanin leader. Unfortunately, the price of peace was high. In the agreement, the tribal leader would turn over to the Empire any Amanin prisoners taken during takitals, and in return the Empire would stay clear of their lands. A similar arrangement was soon made with lorekeepers of other Amanin tribes. As a result, many captured Amanin were used as free labor in the mines of Maridun or scattered as slaves throughout the galaxy, forced to work at other Imperial facilities.

After the Empire shifted its attention away from Maridun, smuggling bands took over the spaceports and mining operations that the Empire abandoned, and Maridun is now run mostly by organized crime. Many Amanin have moved to the spaceports from their forest homes. Some travel offworld to conduct takitals against humans, viewing it as a form of retribution for what the Empire did to their kind. Traditional lorekeepers see this behavior as a corruption of their traditions, and do their best to train youngsters not to follow such a path. Other lorekeepers moved to the cities with their youth to sell blessings and native memorabilia to offworlders stopping at their spaceports. And similar to the way rural Amanin brought their culture to the cities, there are Amanin who have taken sophisticated technology, specifically blasters, back to their traditional communities for use in conquering new tribal lands in the takitals.

Amanin, as a whole, prefer to remain ignorant of galactic politics. While Amanin slaves have been known to temporarily take sides, usually it is to participate in a takital to win their freedom, or in obedience to their masters, with whom they've formed a lorekeeper bond. The best way to persuade Amanin to join a cause is to convince them that their tribal honor is at stake while showing great enthusiasm for their tales of prowess.

In person, Amanin are quiet and thoughtful, although they love exchanging stories. They develop fiercely loyal relationships with any leadership figures whom they consider lorekeepers, even when those people may not have their best interests in mind—mob bosses, employers, even slave owners. In several cases, Amanin have refused to leave slavery when given the opportunity because their loyalty to their masters was so intense—a trait that made the species extremely useful to the Empire.

NOTABLE APPEARANCE
Episode VI: Return of the Jedi

ANZAT

The Anzati are one of the deadliest and most mysterious species in the galaxy. Because Anzati are roamers, they are often considered mythical, and for a long period of time the true location of their homeworld was a mystery. Scientists who traveled to the world reputed to be Anzat simply disappeared without a trace, although some reports place it on the outskirts of the Mid Rim, near the Perlemian Trade Route. Believed to be one of the first of the spacefaring races, they are human in appearance, ranging in height from 1.5 to 1.7 meters with grayish-hued skin and bulbous noses. While scientists have had little opportunity to study Anzati, the sketchy medical reports found on the species seem to indicate that they have no natural biorhythm—no pulse. Given that fact, it is a complete enigma as to how their circulatory system functions.

Being natural predators, Anzati prefer to hunt sentient races of all shapes and sizes, and they possess two prehensile proboscises that they keep coiled in their cheek pockets for feeding on unsuspecting victims in a rather unique way. Jedi who have encountered the species have suggested that Anzati mind control is a type of Force manipulation; they can sense the Force and use it to bewitch their victims in a way akin to the famous Jedi mind trick. To lure in unsuspecting targets, Anzati mesmerize them with this form of telepathic control that strengthens at close range. Once a subject is in their power, Anzati will uncoil their proboscises from their cheek pouches and insert them into a victim's nostrils to suck out brain matter. They call this meal "soup," "luck," or the "Sea of Memory"; in their tradition, the term refers to the life essence, or spiritual power, of the victim. It is reputed that Anzati can keep victims alive for several feedings, enjoying the fear and terror their prey feels throughout the ordeal. Some Anzati believe feeding on living vessels in this way gives them eternal youth and energy. This belief can be traced to the Silent Voices, luminescent bands of gases that glow in the Anzat atmosphere at night, and which ancient Anzati thought were the life essences of their ancestors. Although such a possibility is not scientifically viable, it illustrates the level of importance that "soup" plays in Anzati culture, mores, and belief structures.

According to anecdotal evidence offered by sentients lucky

enough to survive their encounters with Anzati, they are loners who wander throughout the galaxy, returning to Anzat only to find a mate and reproduce, and in some cases to train with Anzati master assassins. They reproduce infrequently and usually live for many centuries. Parents do not typically give their children names, instead allowing them to seek names that best blend in with their chosen prey. Youthful Anzati reach puberty at approximately one hundred standard years of age, and leave Anzat to hunt for "soup" to continue their "eternal" existence.

Studies of different galactic creation myths contain no information about Anzati, though some tales say they have existed longer than any other species. They often act as patrons of the arts, but few have actually contributed with works of their own. Because they are a long-lived species, they tend to view mastering an art as a pointless goal since all other competitors die before they do.

One art that does fuel their interest enough to participate in, though, is stealth. Anzati are master hunters, incredibly sly and crafty, and difficult to capture. Because of their secrecy, hunting skills, and training, Anzati are often employed by organized crime factions as assassins. Anonymity is used to their advantage, so they rarely, if ever, work in groups. It is only in the capacity of a bounty hunter that they will abandon their lonely ways and band together to form a corporation or guild. On these exceptionally rare occasions, they will sometimes share prey and the financial rewards of their hunts. These corporations are temporary, often existing for only one hunt, as they end up killing each other to eliminate competition for a very "soupy" victim.

The constant drive to hunt for "soup" seems to be the central factor of Anzati life; one could almost consider them an addicted people. Once they begin the hunt, they think of nothing else but to satisfy this hunger, which grows stronger with each passing year. Anzati have been reported to view all other peoples as livestock to be harvested to fulfill their needs, although some have been known to try to stave off the craving for as long as possible between feedings. Either way, because the hunger grows as they age, they end up becoming more and more isolated in their need. The older the Anzati, the more unstable and obsessive they become, often to the point of insanity. They lose focus on the world around them and in many cases will make a crucial mistake, leading to their ultimate destruction.

Although the Anzati as a species are isolationists, essential reports have surfaced of at least three significant events that brought the species into open conflict with the Jedi—

DESIGNATION
Sentient

HOMEWORLD
Anzat

AVERAGE
HEIGHT
1.7 meters

PRONUNCIATION
Än'-zät

incidents that propelled them into the galactic spotlight for a short time.

The first episode began roughly a thousand years before the Clone Wars. A rare Anzati Jedi named Volfe Karkko who had never tasted "soup" believed himself above the instinct shared by the rest of his species. Unfortunately, this same arrogance led Karkko to think he could control his inbred nature, and he fed—a mistake that in turn resulted in Karkko succumbing to the dark side. Karkko was captured and held in stasis for a millennium on the prison world of Kiffex. During his imprisonment, however, his mind remained active, and he was able to draw numerous followers. Over time, his legend grew among the Anzati on Kiffex, who worshipped him as "the Dreamer," converting his resting place into a sacred temple. Karkko fed his followers' baser instincts, turning them feral and causing them to prey on the residents and inmates of Kiffex with a ferocity striking even for Anzati. Jedi Master Tholme and Aayla Secura ultimately defeated Karkko, who had struck out against the Jedi.

Later, during the Clone Wars, a group of Anzati master assassins took on contracts to work for the Separatists under Count Dooku, training a secret society of Nikto warriors known as the Morgukai. The Morgukai had been thought to be extinct, but were being reproduced by the Separatists through cloning techniques. The Jedi Master Tholme and his Padawan, Aayla Secura, were able to thwart this potentially devastating source of soldiers.

A second Anzati Jedi, Nikkos Tyris, was responsible for founding a competing order of Force-users during the Clone Wars called the Saarai-kaar, later known as the Jensaarai. Fortunately, the Jensaarai did not pose significant harm to others, never rising to influence much beyond their homeworld and only seeking to serve as protectors. Because their initial leaders were not corrupted by the dark side, the Jensaarai actually served the light side of the Force, despite their reverence for Sith traditions.

NOTABLE APPEARANCE
Episode IV: A New Hope

AQUALISH

The Aqualish are bulky, tusked humanoids known for hair-trigger tempers that can flare without cause or reason. Most anthropologists feel that the streak of anger and rage carried by Aqualish harks back to the early years of the species' evolution.

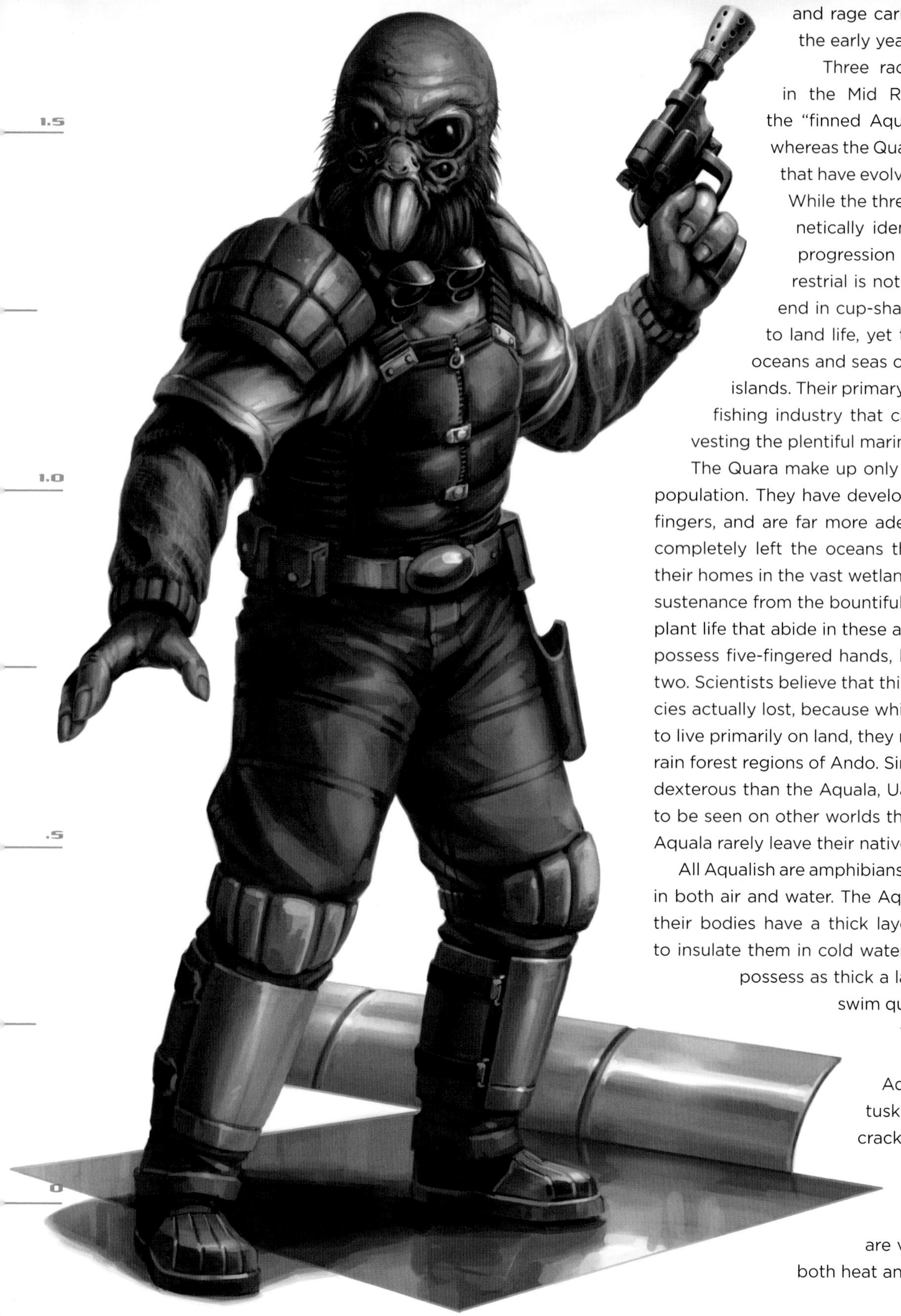

Three races of Aqualish inhabit Ando, in the Mid Rim. The Aquala, often called the "finned Aqualish," is the baseline species, whereas the Quara and Ualaq are minority races that have evolved from their Aquala ancestors. While the three Aqualish races are nearly genetically identical, the Aquala evolutionary progression from aquatic mammal to terrestrial is not yet complete, and their hands end in cup-shaped fins. Aquala have adapted to land life, yet they prefer to live close to the oceans and seas on floating cities, ships, or small islands. Their primary source of food is the extensive fishing industry that casts nets kilometers long, harvesting the plentiful marine life from Ando's waters.

The Quara make up only one-tenth of the overall world population. They have developed humanoid hands with five fingers, and are far more adept in fine motor skills. Having completely left the oceans through evolution, Quara make their homes in the vast wetland areas of Ando, gleaning their sustenance from the bountiful waterfowl, land creatures, and plant life that abide in these areas. The Ualaq, like the Quara, possess five-fingered hands, but have four eyes rather than two. Scientists believe that this is one trait the other two species actually lost, because while the Ualaq developed fingers to live primarily on land, they mainly reside in caves and dark rain forest regions of Ando. Since their appendages are more dexterous than the Aquala, Ualaq and Quara are more likely to be seen on other worlds throughout the galaxy, while the Aquala rarely leave their native home.

All Aqualish are amphibians of a sort, being able to breathe in both air and water. The Aquala are better swimmers, and their bodies have a thick layer of blubber under their skin to insulate them in cold water. The Quara and Ualaq do not possess as thick a layer of blubber, as they do not swim quite as often and tend to stay in warmer waters.

Common to all three of the Aqualish races are large, thick tusks. These tusks are useful in cracking open shellfish or burrowing into swampy loam to dig out marshy plant life for sustenance. Aqualish tusks are very sensitive, and receptive to both heat and cold, as their enamel surface

1.5

1.0

.5

0

contains a dense layer of nerve cells. As a result, Aqualish can be seen rubbing their tusks on wooden surfaces. They find this activity pleasurable rather than painful, akin to giving themselves a massage. This sensitivity can also help them determine the texture of their food before chewing. Unfortunately, the heightened responsiveness can also produce extreme pain if their tusks are chipped or broken, and a damaged tusk can sometimes result in enough pain to immobilize an Aqualish for weeks.

The complexion of the three Aqualish races varies. The Aquala tend to have skin that ranges in color from dark blue to dark green, probably to keep them camouflaged while underwater. The Ualaq and Quara are often more gray or black, though they, too, usually have a hint of blue or green in their grayish pallor.

The Aqualish are endowed with large, glassy black eyes that allow for keen vision underwater. Their eyes are not built for bright light, accounting for a preference for darker environments when Aqualish are offworld. On brighter planets, they tend to gravitate to dark bars or dens, even sleeping during the day then venturing out at night—particularly the Ualaq, whose four eyes are even more sensitive than their counterparts'.

In all three Aqualish cultures, strength is held in high regard. Aqualish show open disdain and hostility to those who appear weak, and when first meeting another individual will often act aggressive and confrontational. If the other person doesn't respond in kind or defend him- or herself, the Aqualish will assume that the other is weak and continue the harassment.

Because of this combative behavior, Aqualish history is fraught with conflict. Before the Republic formed, the Aquala faced a drop in their food supply from overfishing marine populations. Since they tend to be an unreasonable people, they blamed the Quara and Ualaq for the lack of ocean life. This disagreement escalated to an all-out war that could have destroyed all the Aqualish races, were it not for a timely, otherworldly occurrence.

A spaceship arrived on Ando. Various legends hold that the visitors were from Corellia, while others assert they were from Duro. The Aqualish were not yet spacefarers, and they reacted to the visitors with fear and rage, directing their ire for one another onto these "invaders from the sky." They attacked and killed the ship's crew, but left the vessel in perfect condition for study. A truce was reached among the warring parties, who forged an alliance to examine the craft and build one of their own.

DESIGNATION
Sentient

HOMEWORLD
Ando

AVERAGE HEIGHT
1.7 meters

PRONUNCIATION
Äk'-wä-lĭsh

Not long afterward, the Aqualish peoples were roaming the galaxy. Their first stop was a neighboring world, which they decimated with their war-like rage. However, their capacity to truly conquer other worlds was hampered by their limited abilities to adapt foreign technologies. When they encountered new devices, they linked them to their own—but they could not develop original designs or mesh the differing technologies seamlessly. As a result, their machines were often slipshod and patched together. They could not compete with other beings whose technology was more innovative, streamlined, and adaptive.

During its expansion, the Republic sent envoys to many different worlds, inviting them to join the new galactic government. The Aqualish, of course, rebuffed the invitation and instead fired upon the first Republic vessel they encountered. The Republic, having superior technology, soundly defeated the Aqualish, and this began a short yet violent conflict that so overwhelmed the volatile Aqualish that they had to surrender. As a term of concession, the Republic demanded that the Aqualish dismantle all offensive weaponry on their hyperspace vessels. The government of Ando would also have to heed the direction of Republic teachers and advisers, and Ando would become a ward of the Republic until it could earn full citizenship. Realizing they could not overcome the more advanced firepower of the Republic, the Aqualish acquiesced.

While the agreement was a bit restrictive at first, culture and government eventually grew and developed for the better under the guidance of the Republic. With the assistance of Republic scientists, the Aqualish were able to discover the problem that had led to the decrease in marine life and repair that ecosystem. Today, their fishing product is their primary export, and is considered some of the finest seafood in the Galactic Core. It should be noted, however, that during the Clone Wars, the Andoan Senator briefly seceded from the Republic, allying himself and the worlds he represented with the Confederacy of Independent Systems.

Ando chafed under later Imperial rule. Constant insurrection led the Empire to impose martial law, turning Ando into a police state. As a result, the Aqualish despised the Empire, but preferred to fight on their own rather than join the Rebel Alliance. More recently, Ando has been left to its own devices as the Galactic Federation of Free Alliances struggles to keep itself together.

NOTABLE APPEARANCE
Episode IV: A New Hope

ARCONA

The Arcona are tall, cold-blooded, serpent-like reptilian humanoids, with triangular heads and bulbous sensory organs that sit between two large, glittering eyes. They hail from the planet Cona, a hot, desert Inner Rim world with an atmosphere that consists of nitrogen, hydrogen, and ammonia. Their skin, which ranges in color from an ebony gray-black to a deep brown-red, has the density and texture of fibrous tree bark.

The planet Cona orbits a blue giant star known as Teke Ro. Possessing no axial tilt, Cona's unusual circular orbit results in a world with no seasons, and it remains hot throughout the year. However, the insulating atmosphere also causes a cycling of warm and cool airs across the planet surface, making separate parts of the world one even temperature.

While ammonia vapor is plentiful on Cona, the planet is completely lacking in freestanding water. As a result, Cona plant life is very complex and able to enact an amazing chemical reaction that produces water for sustenance. Some of the more advanced plants secrete an acid to bore into the bedrock for oxygen, which they gather in gastric pods at their roots. Meanwhile, the plants will bring in ammonia through their leaves, which they then break down into its elements of hydrogen and nitrogen. The hydrogen adheres to the oxygen and produces water, which the plants also hold in their gastric pods before releasing the excess nitrogen back into the atmosphere.

Needing more water than Cona's atmosphere could provide, the Arcona long ago discovered this hidden botanical source of nourishment. They use their thick, sharp claws to dig into the ground and rip up the roots of these water-bearing plants. Some vegetation grows so deep and large that the Arcona will dig "mines" to harvest the water pods from plant roots. They have developed a system in which they avoid picking the roots completely bare, allowing the plants to maintain their own nutrition and grow new pods. This provides the Arcona with a steady supply of water.

Everything the Arcona eat contains trace amounts of ammonia from the planet's atmosphere. Thus, the Arcona have a high tolerance for ammonia; in fact, as a by-product of their evolution, the gas creates enzymes that enable their bodies to function properly. Ammonia is also utilized by their supplemental circulatory system, which eliminates waste products from the Arcona's bodies, equalizes their overall temperature, and carries nutrients to their skin. When traveling offworld, Arcona imbibe ammonia supplements to maintain the appropriate levels of these natural enzymes in their systems.

Despite their large, sparkling eyes, the Arcona actually have poor eyesight. Much like an insect, their eyes are made up of thousands of tiny photoreceptors, each of which sees a specific color. These photoreceptors also detect movement, but they cannot read fine, distinct shapes. Consequently, an Arcona's entire field of vision is a colorful blur.

To assist their poor vision, Arcona possess a bulbous, diamond-shaped sensory organ that sits between their eyes. Most observers believe this to be a nose, but in reality, the organ detects heat patterns emitted by other living creatures, enabling the Arcona to bring their environment into better focus. They can distinguish most galactic species by their heat signature.

As with most reptiles, Arcona have olfactory organs located in their constantly flicking tongues. When Arcona have difficulty distinguishing objects in their environment, they flicker their tongues to find their way. Their sense of smell is quite keen, and they use it, along with their heat-sensing organ, to determine the moods of those they encounter.

Arcona society is largely and strongly communal, valuing the needs of a collective group over those of an individual. Therefore, they lack a sense of individuality and rarely speak of themselves in the first person, using the pronoun *we* instead. While they generally have strong familial ties, males usually raise Arcona children, as females are considered more reckless and irresponsible. Even so, males of the species take a great deal of time and care in selecting their mates, often making their decision to court a female after months or even years of researching possible candidates. Arcona regard a commitment to marry as a commitment to parent. Small communities or "nests" revolve around parenting, as the safety of the young on such a dangerous world is paramount.

Most family communities make their nests within twenty kilometers of the "Grand Nest," where representative adults of surroundings communities meet every twenty days. An elected Nest Leader conducts meetings and handles business much as a city mayor would, resolving disputes and putting forward community works.

The Arcona trail the galaxy in terms of scientific and

technological development because their primary focus is on community life and the raising of their families. Not many dedicate their time to the study of the hard sciences, and most who live on Cona are teachers or laborers.

The planet is rich in precious metals. Before the Clone Wars, prospectors arrived on Cona and traded mineral rights for water, building impressive spaceports and developing imposing cities around their operation. Soon, however, the mining corporations learned that Arcona natives are easily addicted to sodium chloride—salt. Since salt is easier to transport, the corporations began to trade salt for prospecting rights.

In an Arcona's body, salt acts as a hallucinogen, interfering with the optic nerves to create an intoxicating display of color. Its ultimate effect is deadly, though, in that it causes an Arcona's pancreatic organ, which changes ammonia into water, to fail. More visibly, it changes an Arcona's eye color from green to gold. Once addicted, an Arcona craves about twenty-five grams of salt a day before withdrawal begins. Since female Arcona are more free-spirited and less homebound, they make up the bulk of the Arcona addicts—driven to feed their need at all costs.

Because this addiction is a family- and community-destroying plague, non-addicts will not hesitate to attack and kill anyone discovered to be selling salt on Cona. The Republic enacted strict laws to curtail the transport of salt to the system, and the Arcona, too, have their own laws prohibiting the sale or importation of salt to their world. Still, this has done little to stop its trade on the black market.

Despite the Arcona's tendency to adhere strictly to tradition, when scouts from the Old Republic first made contact with the species, many members were extremely enthusiastic about exploring the galaxy. Entire communities sought employment with corporations that came to mine and build on Cona, hoping for the chance to travel offworld. As a consequence, in the civilized areas of the galaxy, Arcona colonies are common—with whole families traveling together. Presently, they travel a good deal around the galaxy, using technology developed by other species. They can now be seen in every major spaceport, either as tourists or employees of vast multiplanetary corporations.

DESIGNATION
Sentient

HOMEWORLD
Cona

AVERAGE HEIGHT
2 meters

PRONUNCIATION
Är-kōn'-ä

NOTABLE APPEARANCE
Episode IV: A New Hope

BALOSAR

Balosars are a humanoid species native to the Balosar system, located in the Core Worlds. Notorious for their corruption, Balosars are common throughout the galactic underworld. They resemble humans, except for two antennaepalps that rise from their skull. Balosars can retract these antennaepalps, hiding them within their thick, coarse head of hair, giving them an even more human appearance, to the point that they can often pass for humans if they are trying to escape detection. They usually appear more frail and sickly than the average human, however, due to a polluted home environment.

Balosars' antennae are unique in the galaxy. Not only can they improve Balosars' hearing, enabling them to listen into the subsonic range, but the antennae also give the species a very slight psychic intuition, which some Jedi liken to a Force sensitivity, though it cannot necessarily be classified as such. They can pick up spikes in emotion—particularly negative intent—from those around them, giving them a sort of "danger sense." They depend on their antenna abilities to survive, employing them quite frequently on their crime-ridden homeworld.

Another distinctive Balosar physical trait is their resistance to toxins. Because they hail from a contaminated world, most Balosars grow up exposed to practically every industrial poison in the known galaxy. As a result, they are practically impervious to poisoning, despite their otherwise frail physiques.

As well as suffering from a high pollution rate, the planet Balosar is also impaired by a dangerously depleted economy. Interstellar corporations commonly bribe Balosar politicians in order to buy inexpensive real estate and build sweatshop factories that employ many underpaid natives. These factories have so destroyed the environment that little sunlight reaches the surface, and the atmosphere is barely breathable. The highly industrialized Balosar has often been a primary focus of galactic relief agencies, which find it difficult to operate there because of the political corruption.

Balosars are typically stereotyped as spineless, weak-willed, and selfish—but these traits are primarily due to the condition of their society. Research studies published in the *Journal of Personality and Galactic Psychology* do not indicate such innate or genetic pathology unique to the species. Many live in poverty and suffer from ill health because of their environment, leading to severe depression. Others have developed an overly grim outlook on life that they express with pointed sarcasm. As with many species, Balosars often leave their homeworld hoping for a better existence, only to encounter the hardships associated with resettling in a foreign environment. They are frequently perceived by others as self-absorbed, but in reality are more bent on survival—a focus that skews their moral perceptions. Most have difficulty determining right from wrong, and it is common for Balosars living offplanet to have criminal records as a result.

Compounding the environmental influences on Balosar life, their corrupt government has allowed the educational system to become severely underfunded. Balosars wishing to receive an education must go offworld, and the earlier in their educational careers, the better. Research strongly suggests that the younger a child is when they leave Balosar, the better the potential is for academic success. Moreover, health outcomes are markedly improved for these youngsters. A strong and persistent positive correlation has been demonstrated between the age of departure and educational failure. The older students are when they depart Balosar, the more likely they are to drop out before completing their education. These unsuccessful students often return home to Balosar, and to the same bleak prospects they left behind. Thus, it is not uncommon for Balosar parents to send their children to primary schools on other worlds when scholarships are available.

The fraudulent Balosar government is intricately embroiled with the galactic underworld in the illicit trade of death sticks. The primary ingredient of these drugs is Ixetal cilona extract, distilled from balo mushrooms that are grown on Balosar in great quantities in underground farms. Death sticks are extremely addictive and highly toxic, leading to certain death for most species, frequently over just a short period of use. And yet the users don't seem to mind. Many addicts end up hopelessly hooked after simply giving it a try, savoring the death stick's sweet, alluring flavor and the feeling of instant euphoria that the drug brings. The death stick's toxicity affects addicts' brain function, causing them to slip into bleak depression when they are not consuming the drug. Addicts find themselves craving more and more death sticks in order to hold on to the sense of happiness they receive during the short amount of time it takes to smoke one.

The use of this product by the Balosars themselves has further contributed to the pollution found on their homeworld, and while Balosars are immune to the toxicity of the death stick, they are not safe from its addictive properties. Desperate Balosars can be seen in busy spaceports throughout the galaxy hawking death sticks to earn whatever credits they can. Some, if not most, are addicted to their own product and sell the death sticks to support their own habits.

DESIGNATION
Sentient

HOMEWORLD
Balosar

AVERAGE HEIGHT
1.6 meters

PRONUNCIATION
Băl'-ō-sär

During the time of the Old Republic, illegal trade in death sticks became the greatest competition to the addictive spice from Ryloth called ryll. This rivalry resulted in a deep-seated dislike between Balosars and Twi'leks that continues to this day. Death sticks were easy to produce in mass quantities due to the prolific growth of balo mushrooms—which, unlike ryll, were an easily renewable resource. Ryll needed to be mined in rather dangerous conditions, and was also most potent when combined with glitterstim to create the synthetic spice called glitteryll. Additionally, the ryll supply was tightly guarded at times, and regulated for use in the manufacture of several medicines. Thus, for a brief time, death sticks dominated the illegal drug trade, but this was not to last. Twi'lek drug lords were not pleased at the reduction in their income, and gang wars erupted. The Balosars defiantly peddled their wares when able, although it proved necessary to become more discreet about it. However, by the dawn of the New Republic, the Balosar environment did what the Twi'leks could not. The pollution choking the planet made its way into the underground balo mushroom farms, killing a massive amount of the crop and severely damaging the spore stock, and the Twi'leks used this opportunity to seize complete control of the spice market. Many Balosar drug merchants were reduced to joining forces with the Twi'leks as middlemen and low-level, unimportant runners.

At the end of the New Republic era, Balosar was briefly in the attack path of the Yuuzhan Vong during their march toward Coruscant. At the time, Balosar was not bound by diplomatic treaties to the New Republic and therefore not formally protected by her military. However, the planet managed to escape invasion and Yuuzhan Vong terraforming when the tide of war took the aggressors elsewhere.

NOTABLE APPEARANCE
Episode II: Attack of the Clones

BANTHA

Herds of woolly banthas inhabit the desert wastes of Tatooine in the Outer Rim, as well as the grasslands and plains of other worlds throughout the galaxy. Since banthas are found in such a large number of agricultural systems, it is believed that early space settlers transported the species to new worlds. Although largely domesticated, on some planets wild herds can still be found. There are several known varieties of banthas in existence, including the common bantha (*Banta majorus*), the smaller, shy dwarf bantha, and the rangier, slender dune bantha. One specific subtype of bantha is the Kashyyyk greyclimber, which differs from its Tatooine cousin in that the greyclimber has massive cranial bone plates in place of horns; it has also adapted to climbing through the evolution of articulated toes that can grip wroshyr trees. The common bantha is by far the most numerous, but as banthas are found on a multitude of worlds, more subspecies may yet be discovered.

Generally used as beasts of burden, the tall, gentle creatures are intelligent, dependable, and trustworthy. They are extremely strong, able to carry up to five hundred kilos of cargo, or five human-sized passengers, including a driver. Because of their rocking gait, many first-time bantha riders have been known to complain of motion sickness. Although banthas prefer to move at a slow pace, they can run at great speeds when necessary, and stories of bantha stampedes are commonplace on all the worlds they inhabit.

Banthas are extremely adaptable, abiding comfortably in all sorts of climates, able to survive for weeks without food or water. From world to world, bantha subspecies vary in size, coloration, social grouping, behavior, and metabolic specifics, but one commonality is that surprisingly, these mostly gentle giants are herbivores. On Tatooine, banthas live on meager sand lichen mats found either in protected hollows or just under the sand. Due to their size and internal stores, they can live for nearly a month without sustenance.

In addition to being beasts of burden, banthas are a valuable source of nourishment for many cultures. Bantha meat is edible, and their skin and long, thick fur can be used for clothing. Bantha-skin goods such as boots and luggage are expensive luxuries on some planets. Furthermore, Bantha bones and horns are carved by members of several cultures to make tools, ornaments, and toys.

Banthas exhibit many of the traits typical of herd animals. Wild banthas have been known to gather their dead in bantha graveyards. When attacked, they usually flee, and most bantha species will only fight in defense of the herd and their young. In the event that they are trapped, or when young banthas must be defended, male banthas will form a circle around their calves and cows, using their large tapering horns and three-meter-wide size to protect the herd. They strike by lowering their heads and ramming their large spiral horns into an attacker. Some cultures have taken advantage of the bantha's horns and bulk by using domesticated breeds as beasts of war, spurring them to charge at foes and trample them underfoot.

On Tatooine, woolly banthas have been left to roam free in the harsh desert climate, and the species has flourished. They are the transportation of choice for the native Tusken Raiders, who have a special and unique relationship with their mounts. Upon reaching the age of five, a Tusken Raider is teamed up with a young bantha, and the two develop an emotional bond that lasts a lifetime. If its master dies, a "widowed" bantha will often fly into a suicidal rage. The tribe then waits until the bantha tires of its rampage, afterward turning it out into the wilderness to survive on its own. Usually, the unfortunate bantha dies of grief and dehydration.

Likewise, if the bantha mount is the first to perish, the Tusken Raider to whom it was bonded will become inconsolable to the point of ruthlessly attacking others in the clan, or even taking his or her own life. If such Tusken Raiders do not die from their despair, they are sent out into the desert on a vision quest, to contact the spirit of their fallen bantha partner. If their bantha companion guides them to the afterlife, they will expire in the barren wastelands of Tatooine. If, however, their former mount wishes them to live, it will guide them to a new, riderless bantha, which then becomes their new companion. Tusken Raiders who return with a fresh mount are given high honor in their communities.

DESIGNATION
Nonsentient

HOMEWORLD
Tatooine

AVERAGE HEIGHT
2.5 meters

PRONUNCIATION
Băn'-thä

NOTABLE APPEARANCE
Episode IV: A New Hope

BARABEL

Barabels are a vicious, reptilian race native to the Outer Rim planet Barab I, a world of murky darkness in the orbit of a dim red dwarf star. During the day, most living creatures dwell belowground to protect themselves from the intense heat and radiation cast by the red dwarf. When evening arrives, the environment cools enough for the denizens of Barab I to go to the surface and hunt.

The physique of a Barabel is designed for nocturnal hunting and fighting. Their entire form, from head to tail, is covered with spiked scales of tough keratin that darken from purple-green to black as they age. These scales not only help camouflage Barabels, but also protect them from heavy blows or low-power blasterfire. This external protection is further insulated by a layer of blubber that helps the species retain heat during the cold nights on Barab I.

Barabels are natural hunters who kill with strength and efficiency. Their mouths are filled with needle-sharp teeth up to five centimeters in length, perfect for crushing the bodies of even the toughest-skinned prey. Beyond this, they can also use their huge claws for efficiently rending flesh. Since Barabels hunt primarily in the darkness, their eyes possess slit pupils that read the electromagnetic spectrum of light from infrared to yellow. However, they are unable to see green, blue, or violet light, which puts them at a disadvantage on planets with brighter suns.

Barabels often work as bounty hunters and mercenaries, channeling their natural love of the hunt into a means of earning credits. They are known for having an explosive temperament, but unlike some other violent races, they value both intelligence and wisdom, often focusing on these traits in order to control their aggressive nature. They can be cooperative to attain a common goal, and they are efficient when working in teams, making them particularly valuable in a military environment. Extremely loyal to their spouses, family members, and hatchmates, Barabels are genuinely loving and gregarious in such a community setting. While they have been known to extend this loyalty to non-Barabels with whom they feel close, outsiders or strangers are more commonly met with belligerence and hostility.

Barab I orbits the red dwarf Barab at a distance of less than 125 million kilometers. As a result, the planet is scorched during its six-standard-hour day, exposed to high-intensity ultraviolet, gamma, and infrared radiation. Water rapidly evaporates from the surface, leaving the world in a humid haze, and most of Barab I's plant and animal life must live in caves or rock crevices and canyons in order to thrive. Those species that remain out during the day survive by closing up in protective cocoons or possess reflective skin or hair that protects them from the damaging rays.

At night when the heat dissipates, the natives of Barab I leave their shelters to feed in a sudden frenzy. They move quickly to avoid a nightly torrential downpour that occurs as a result of the day's water evaporation and the subsequent planetary cooling.

This wild cycle of lethargy and feeding has contributed to the largely primitive nature of Barab I and its resident Barabels. The world was discovered by an Imperial charter called Planetary Safaris, which brought expeditions to Barab I to hunt Barabels. Because members of the species are mostly solitary, preferring to roam the surface alone, they were more susceptible to these Imperial hunting parties. This also placed them at a disadvantage when the Yuuzhan Vong eventually conquered Barab I, although on a one-on-one basis they made formidable opponents to the invaders—more so than many other species.

Before the Yuuzhan Vong invasion, however, one brilliant Barabel named Shaka-ka managed to unite fellow members of her species into armies to destroy Planetary Safari ships and decimate their hunting parties. The local Imperial governor, shocked at the loss of both vessels and tourists, sent a Star Destroyer to investigate. After learning of the origins of the uprising, the Imperial captain Alater determined Barabels to be a sentient species and gave them the full protection of Imperial law.

Upon their entrance into the Empire, Shaka-ka once again enlisted other Barabels, this time to build what would become the one permanent city and spaceport on their world: Alater-ka, named for the captain who recognized their sentience. This underground city consists of numerous tunnels and caverns that are interlocked around the central spaceport. Although Alater-ka remains a crude city with primitive resources, it is not wanting for tourist attention, as an agreement was eventually reached with Planetary Safaris to reinstate expeditions on Barab I, allowing parties to hunt some of the dangerous resident wildlife, with Barabels now acting as guides. Barab I is also a popular haven for galactic criminals, smugglers, pirates, and the like, who are willing to take a chance with the harsh environment in order to escape from law enforcement.

After Barab I was liberated from Imperial rule, the Barabels

DESIGNATION
Sentient

HOMEWORLD
Barab I

AVERAGE HEIGHT
2 meters

PRONUNCIATION
Bär'-ä-bĕl

nearly started a war with an insectoid species known as the Verpine. They briefly made arrangements to sell frozen Verpine body parts to the Kubaz to be eaten as a delicacy. To this day, there remain some tense relations between these two species.

Even though Barabels' "official" history began with their discovery by Planetary Safaris, it is believed that these Imperial hunters were not the first galactic visitors to Barab I. Barabel legend tells of a war that erupted among Barabel factions over prime hunting grounds. Family units, all motivated by common interest, banded together to form two armies that were each bent on the ultimate destruction of their enemies. The final battle was defused, though, by the arrival of a Jedi Knight who managed to resolve the dispute. The legend speaks highly of the "great warrior from beyond the clouds" who prevented them from killing one another.

Barabels therefore, commonly show Jedi both great reverence and deference. In the years after Palpatine's demise, a stranded Jedi took a Barabel apprentice named Saba Sebatyne. An ensuing surprise appearance by Saba Sebatyne, who emerged with her own Jedi students and hatchlings to assist during the Yuuzhan Vong War, seems to be hard evidence that the Jedi influence on Barabels was no myth.

Other than this tale, though, most Barabels are fairly ignorant of their culture's history, and they seem to prefer to remain that way. They have no inclination to create an overarching civilization, choosing to remain in their small family units and acting as solitary hunters in the Barab I night. Although they hold no technology of their own to speak of, those few Barabels who have departed Barab I manage to use the technology of other races with great efficiency, and a few are known to have become ace pilots. Frequently, Barabels seen offworld are functioning as bounty hunters, trackers, or mercenaries. Only Barabels who travel to other systems are recognized as capable of speaking or understanding Basic, as those who remain on Barab I mainly do not bother to master any language other than Barabel, which consists of hisses, growls, and snarls.

While the Yuuzhan Vong saw fit to conquer Barab I in their quest to dominate the galaxy, the planet was not destroyed. Many Barabels, masters at stealth, managed to go into hiding in caves and underground hovels until the threat had passed. While their numbers diminished, the species managed to survive the slaughter with their wits and tenacity.

NOTABLE APPEARANCE
Dark Force Rising (novel)

BESALISK

Besalisks are large, stocky, flightless avian humanoids who hail from the planet Ojom, located in the Deep Core. They have thick bodies with multiple brawny arms, a bony headcrest surrounded by feathers, and a wide mouth from which hangs a large flexible sac.

Male Besalisks have four arms, while females can possess as many as eight. But despite such multiple appendages, each Besalisk has only one primary hand, much the same as humans are right- or left-handed. Their brains are not sufficiently complex to provide greater limb coordination. A Besalisk can hold items in all of her hands, but cannot use more than four of them to do specific tasks at a time. For instance, a female using all eight of her arms can have four arms working independently, but the other four must work in concert with one another. This characteristic particularly comes into play when Besalisks are engaged in hand-to-hand combat, as they are not able to wield weapons independently in all of their arms. Most Besalisks will simply carry one or two (although females may sport three), with their most effective weapon being grasped in their primary hand.

Sadly, Besalisks are the subject of many misconceptions. To begin with, while they are descended from birds, casual observers will frequently mistake them for a reptilian species. Whereas Besalisks have a skin pouch hanging from their chins that is similar to the ones often seen on both birds and reptiles, their thick, scaly skin is the source of the perception that they are members of the latter group, as are their toothy mouths and sharp-clawed hands. Also, since they typically possess bulky, fleshy frames, Besalisks are sometimes viewed as gluttonous by other races, but in reality they store food and water in their bodies for weeks, allowing them to go for an extended period of time without eating or drinking. It is also common for Besalisks to sweat a great deal, giving the impression that they are nervous or in ill health. However, their bodies are merely accustomed to the frigid environment of Ojom and do not react well to warmer climates.

As with most birds, Besalisk young are hatched from eggs that females lay during the warm season. A female will usually bear a clutch of two eggs at a time, at which point the male will take over the duty of keeping them in his brood patch—an area of the male's abdominal skin that falls down over the eggs and hugs them close to his body for warmth. During this time, the females will care for the home and earn the family living.

Besalisks are monogamous, and they will mate for life following a long courtship in which the female chooses, and sometimes fights for, the male of her preference. Such competitions can get violent the longer the search for a mate continues. The quest for males can take place at any time during Ojom's solar year, but each commune will hold events specifically to meet and choose mates during the warmer months. Ojom is a frightfully cold world, covered in massive glaciers that roam the planet's ocean surface. The Besalisks live in sparsely populated communal groupings on each of these glaciers. These communes are made up of at least a thousand nuclear families, and are in turn governed by an elected leader who acts as an arbiter in any disputes. When the population grows over a specific number, the leaders solicit volunteers from families to start a new commune, in an attempt to keep all such groupings at relatively the same size.

Other than their communal arbiters, the Besalisk people have no overall government in place, and for this reason they never had any representation in the Old Republic Senate. They seem to prefer their autonomy, allowing other species to handle galactic political affairs. And yet their independence has come at a price. During the period of Imperial domination, the Besalisks were threatened with enslavement. To avoid that fate, many individual communes made deals with underworld criminals, and have since been indebted to them, particularly the Hutts.

On Ojom, all interstellar traffic is handled through orbiting space stations, which are more welcoming to offworld visitors than is the planet itself. Most Besalisk business dealings are carried out on these space stations, particularly those of a nefarious nature. However, other species, not Besalisks, commit most of the violent crimes on these stations. Even when wrapped up in underworld affairs, Besalisks remain relatively peaceful, preferring to find thrills through self-fulfillment rather than harming or stealing from others.

On the whole, Besalisks are a quick-witted, generous, and sociable people. They form strong and lasting friendships with members of all species, and can be extremely loyal once they grant an individual their trust. A keen attention to detail allows Besalisks to adapt easily into other cultures and utilize their technologies, although they create none of their own. They do have a tendency to be unreliable dreamers, however, and Besalisks can often be flighty, out for amusement and adventure that involves little concern for their own welfare. They do not fear danger, a concept that normally doesn't occur to them until they're in the middle of it. Exceptions to this rule certainly exist, although there are not many, and those few that are atypical of their species often use the common perceptions held them to pass off as fearless anyway. As a result of this intrepid nature, many offworld Besalisks are entangled in underworld operations such as smuggling, gambling, and organized crime—generally without realizing the gravity of what they're doing.

Besalisks can also be gregarious and chatty, taking pleasure in talking about others, gabbing and gossiping simply for the joy of conversation. Since they are very observant, taking in details quickly and without thinking, this, combined with their willingness to strike up conversations, makes them excellent sources for valuable information. In addition, to the utter frustration of their underworld employers, they seem to have a habit of occasionally walking off the job in an attempt to find other ways to amuse and enrich themselves. Consequently, many a Besalisk has ended up on underworld hit lists, repeatedly putting them among the most wanted species in the galaxy at any given time.

DESIGNATION
Sentient

HOMEWORLD
Ojom

AVERAGE HEIGHT
1.8 meters

PRONUNCIATION
Bĕs'-ä-lĭsk

NOTABLE APPEARANCE
Episode II: Attack of the Clones

BITH

The Bith are a highly evolved, humanoid species native to Clak'dor VII, a planet that is part of the Colu system in the Outer Rim. Their tall craniums house immensely oversized brains, the result of years of calculated breeding. Bith are known for their contributions to the arts and sciences and are considered some of the greatest thinkers in the galaxy. Calm, peaceful, thoughtful, and introverted, Bith are consummate pacifists—a trait that comes not only from their learned history, but also from their planned physiology as well.

The Bith are biologically developed to be suited for complex work. Scientists have been unable to determine the ultimate origin of their species, since they have evolved so completely that they most likely retain none of the attributes of their evolutionary ancestry. The areas of their brains that handle abstract thinking skills, such as language, deductive reasoning, logic, mathematics, and music, are enormously large and highly developed compared with those of other sentient species. Those brain regions that control most instinctual behaviors—fear, aggression, and so forth—are much smaller, making them pacifistic by nature. Scientists theorize that they have lived in a highly structured civilization for so long that they have completely lost the ability to function on an instinctual or irrational level.

Bith possess five-fingered hands with opposable thumbs, making them well suited for doing detailed handiwork. They are extremely adept at constructing tools, as well as developing and using technology to suit their needs.

The Bith's large eyes are ideal for such a high-tech lifestyle, as they allow the species to perceive minuscule details, or study complicated microcircuitry for long periods of time. The Bith have also developed beyond a need for sleep, instead meditating for short periods of time in order to provide their bodies with an appropriate amount of rest. The fact that they no longer require traditional sleep has resulted in the Bith losing their eyelids through evolution; a hard, translucent shell protects their eyes from injury or dust abrasion.

The most fascinating aspect of Bith physiology is perhaps their streamlined respiratory system. Their tiny nose serves only as an air intake. From there, oxygen flows to a single lung, where it is transferred directly to the bloodstream. Waste gases are exuded through the skin, but only after every last molecule of oxygen has been used.

Due to this specialized respiratory system, Bith olfactory senses are located in folds of skin on their cheeks, rather than in their noses. Their sense of smell is exceptionally sensitive, enabling them to perceive the slightest chemical changes in the atmosphere around them. Phereoreceptors situated in the skin folds send a detailed chemical analysis of each scent to the brain, allowing a Bith to recognize even the faintest of smells in microseconds.

Bith rely on technology to handle nearly every aspect of their lives, including reproduction. Prospective parents take a sample of their DNA to a computer mating service (CMS), which then matches it up with other samples provided by members of the opposite sex. The CMS projects the outcomes of various pairings, or child patterns (CPs), and offers these potential outcomes to the future parent. After selecting a CP that meets his or her qualifications, the Bith is introduced to the mate, and the two negotiate the number of offspring that they will produce, and how many each parent will raise. Upon arriving at an agreement, they deliver cells to a Reproduction Center, and a year later their children are delivered to their door. As they've reproduced in this manner for so long, Bith have actually lost the ability to produce offspring naturally, and what began as a matter of preference is now a matter of necessity.

Although technology does serve many of the Bith's needs on their world, it was, at one time, nearly the cause of their society's demise. Almost one hundred standard years before the dawn of the Empire, two cities on Clak'dor VII—Nozho and Weogar—were embroiled in a competition to secure patent rights on a new stardrive that the cities' leaders hoped to sell to other worlds. As was traditional in Bith society, each city submitted its patent claim to a neutral arbitrator.

The agent representing Nozho, however, happened to discover some unfavorable information on this arbitrator, and blackmailed him into giving Nozho the patent preference. When the mayor of Weogar heard of this, he refused to accept the arbitrator's decision, and both cities began production on the stardrive, setting off a cutthroat rivalry that ultimately led to wholesale war. After a full standard year of bloodletting, Nozho finally unleashed a chemical weapon that eradicated 90 percent of the population of the opposing city. The remaining occupants of Weogar retaliated with biological weapons of their own, causing a massive evolutionary degeneration and destroying most of the life on the planet. Their world, which had once been a garden paradise, was now a poisoned wasteland of genetically mutated, toxic plants and vicious creatures. In order to survive, the remaining Bith were forced to build giant domed cities, where they've lived ever since.

As a consequence of this devastating war, Bith technology has not progressed for many years. Their own natural resources exhausted, they have come to rely on the commodities of other worlds. Their chief export is their intellect, and various agencies and companies galaxywide employ Bith as scientists, mathematicians, artisans, accountants, and musicians. Bith are a principal source of innovative ideas throughout the galaxy, and are often highly paid to participate in corporate and governmental think tanks on many of the Core Worlds.

On Clak'dor VII, the Bith political structure is highly organized and dependent, again, on technology. Leaders are chosen through a computer analysis of a candidate's heritage, intelligence, accomplishments, and career. These selected leaders, who form a type of committee, retain ultimate authority over the Bith people through a complex system of laws that keeps the committee's activities under close scrutiny.

On the galactic political stage, the Bith were active in the Old Republic, and helped develop and negotiate many of the treaties for planetary entrance to the Old Republic Senate. As the Clone Wars erupted, the Bith were outspoken opponents of the conflict, and throughout the reign of the Empire, their government formally withdrew to the Bith homeworld, refusing to give the new, tyrannical regime their support. However, a few members of the Bith government secretly supported the Imperial cause as a logical means of establishing galactic order. They surreptitiously provided the Empire with computer programming and engineering prowess for many Imperial technology designs.

Following the fall of the Empire, the Bith did not reopen communication with the New Republic until the Hapans offered aid to the fledgling galactic government. Encouraged by the Hapan gesture of confidence, the Bith soon established formal relations with the New Republic.

DESIGNATION
Sentient

HOMEWORLD
Clak'dor VII

AVERAGE HEIGHT
1.7 meters

PRONUNCIATION
Bĭth

NOTABLE APPEARANCE
Episode IV: A New Hope

BOTHAN

1.5

1.0

othans are short, furry humanoids native to the planet Bothawui, which is located in the Mid Rim, although they have established colonies on other worlds, such as Kothlis and Torolis. The Bothans evolved long ago from feline progenitors, though they retain only a few attributes that connect them with their ancestral background. They are covered entirely with fur, the color of which can range from milky white to dark brown; the hair on their face tapers downward to form a type of beard. Their fur serves as an additional transmitter for the Bothans' body language, in that undulations in the hairs on the head signify their emotional state, or emphasize important points during a discussion. These subtle changes are usually difficult to decipher by those who are not members of the species, although some outsiders have learned to read these nonverbal cues with great accuracy. Such a knowledge of Bothan behavior is extremely helpful when negotiating with this intelligent and opportunistic people.

Also similar to most cat species, they possess sharp eyes and teeth, as well as five-fingered hands with nails that extend and retract, though they rarely use them unless they find themselves in one-on-one combat. And in Bothan culture this is a rare occurrence, which explains why most outsiders are unaware that they even have this ability.

Bothans express themselves with great eloquence, and mastery of public speaking is an accomplishment that merits prestige in their culture. They are consummate politicians, and as such they are important players in the arena of galactic politics. Well known for their intelligence-gathering abilities, Bothans are considered unsurpassed in that field. Preceding the Battle of Endor, many of them sacrificed their lives to steal the technical schematics for the second Death Star, as well as the information that the Emperor would be present conducting an inspection of the station during the Rebels' planned attack. For this and other reasons, they achieved an influential role in the New Republic government. The New Republic military prided itself on its Bothan members, with Bothans serving in every capacity from pilot to admiral. One Bothan in particular, Borsk Fey'lya, served as Chief of State before uncharacteristically sacrificing himself during the Yuuzhan Vong invasion of Coruscant.

Despite Fey'lya's noble deed, status is almost always the goal of Bothans. The quest for influence and power is at the heart of their culture. By nature, Bothans are greedy for status, often becoming manipulative and opportunistic while seeking the prestige that comes from controlling others. Wealth isn't as important to them as influencing those who have money, and family clans frequently plot ways of gaining resources and strategic positioning. When a Bothan clan desires something, be it information, an object, or a position of power, members will spy on one another, spread rumors, and make convenient alliances. They seldom attack a competitor directly, usually waiting for rivals to make mistakes.

One side effect of these cultural motivations is that Bothans are also habitually paranoid, believing that anyone who's not working for them is working against them. Unfortunately, their paranoia is usually well founded. Layer upon layer of schemes swirl around any clan, and outsiders who associate with Bothans often find themselves unwittingly caught up in the web of intrigue. This paranoia can be taken to extremes against other species, to the extent of xenophobia and prejudice, and can blind Bothans to the genuine, good intentions of others, often to their own detriment. They simply do not attribute a lack of guile to those beings with whom they come into contact.

Bothawui and all the Bothan colonies are locally governed by the Bothan Council, which consists of representatives of each clan and serves as the primary lawmaking and law enforcement body. Each of the member clans is a collection of families who have bonded together in a common tradition or heritage. Currently, approximately six hundred clans are part of the council, and more than fifty others have petitioned for membership. These newer clans are typically from smaller, younger settlements that have formed apart from the established colonies. In order to be accepted for membership, a simple majority of the council must approve a petition, and representatives of new clans are constantly engaged in forming alliances to meet their goal of inclusion.

In order to manage council business, the members elect one of their number to become the Council Chief. All policies are decided by a majority vote, with the Chief holding the tie-breaking call when necessary. Every council member heads up several ministries and committees, and appoints clan leaders to positions of importance. Payoffs and rewards are common, as these clan leaders, in turn, assign others in their retinue to lower-level positions. This centuries-old system of finding favor and gaining power enables Bothans of any clan or background to attain prestige and influence if they manage to play by the right rules. It also allows powerful clans to maintain their established realms of control on Bothawui.

The Bothans have long been a spacefaring race, settling on many planets outside Bothawui, the most notable of which is Kothlis. However, anything that can be found on Bothawui is found on its colonies, though the newer settlements that are still not official members of the Bothan Coun-

cil get less attention in terms of goods and services—all the more motivation for them to use intrigue and stratagem to push their agenda in the council. Thus, Bothans of these upstart colonies can be some of the most ambitious and backstabbing examples of the species that one may encounter.

Set in the heart of Bothan space in the Mid Rim, Bothawui's location has made it a major trading center and hub for shipping convoys. Business thrives there, especially because the low tax rates and governmental bureaucracy are not overly burdensome. Several major galactic banking and financial institutions have sited their corporate headquarters there, employing thousands of Bothans in their operations as well as in the major trading exchanges centered on Bothawui.

While banking and finance appears to be the fastest-growing legitimate business on Bothawui, spying is still the Bothans' main industry. Everyone comes to Bothawui to get information, even though it can often come at a hefty price. The Bothan spynet, an underground system for buying and selling all forms of data, is just as active as it was under the rule of the Empire. Organized crime factions, political leaders, and corporate moguls arrive on the Bothans' world to get an inside scoop.

And yet, for all the Bothans' deceptive nature and quests for self-advancement, Borsk Fey'lya's death is just one example revealing the core of their being. At heart, the majority of Bothans are brave and loyal, and they will serve causes that they believe in to the bitter end. Many other species find Bothans difficult to deal with because they seem to lack selflessness, but in reality, most Bothans ultimately do believe in freedom and sacrifice to achieve a venerable goal. They will take chances and risk much in any conflict that threatens those they love or those to whom they've pledged loyalty.

DESIGNATION
Sentient

HOMEWORLD
Bothawui

AVERAGE
HEIGHT
1.5 meters

PRONUNCIATION
Bŏ'-thăn

NOTABLE MENTION
Episode VI: Return of the Jedi

CAAMASI

The term *Caamasi* means "friend from afar" or "stranger to be trusted" in the languages of many cultures throughout the galaxy, and never did a people have a more appropriate title. The Caamasi are tall, mammalian humanoids with golden down covering their bodies and purple fur that surrounds the eyes; stripes extend around the backs of their heads and shoulders. Their two eyes are set below a strong brow, and their triangular-shaped ears jut outward. Caamasi have only three delicate and gentle fingers on their long hands.

All Caamasi can create lasting, vivid memories called memnii that are shared telepathically with other members of their species. Memnii enable them to actually experience historical, important, or poignant personal events as if they were present. Because all history is valuable, and because these memories can teach others, Caamasi hold recollections of tragic or devastating events as well as happy ones. Clans often intermarry to spread memnii, and the Caamasi can even share memnii with Jedi.

They are a people who mate for life, and when Caamasi choose a companion, they will share specific memnii with their spouse, who hold these memories close to their heart and eventually pass them on to their children. These memnii are usually private moments from their lives, incidents that helped form their consciences and enabled them to grow into who they are. It is reputed, but not confirmed, that some Caamasi couples share such private memnii during the mating process.

Despite their dedication to a solitary spouse, there are reports of some Caamasi debating the introduction of polygamy among their people, most likely to repair a devastation to their population that was caused by Emperor Palpatine after the Clone Wars. As with anything the Caamasi consider, such a concept would clearly be debated and examined from every angle before their society could reach a decision. For them, it would represent an entire cultural shift, and be a particularly difficult and delicate change, as the connections between mates are usually quite singular and special. Most sociologists feel polygamy is antithetical to the Caamasi way of life, and have either dismissed these rumors as hearsay, or decided that the species will ultimately not accept the concept, even if introduced as a means of survival.

By nature, the Caamasi are artistic, wise, and freethinking, and believe in peace through moral strength. According to Caamasi legend, the first Jedi Knights journeyed to their planet ages ago in order to learn the moral use of the Force, although Caamasi Jedi are rare. Considering that the Caamasi way of life has endured unchanged for generations, it is a strong possibility that this is more than a simple fable.

Sadly, while admired for their peaceful wisdom, the Caamasi also managed to acquire the scorn of those who did not appreciate such moral fortitude. In an incident that followed the Clone Wars, Emperor Palpatine engineered the desolation of the planet Caamas in the Core Worlds in order to rid his empire of the peaceful Caamasi. Indeed, heavy bombardment destroyed all the resident vegetation, and most of the Caamasi were killed. Refugees from Caamas traveled to several other worlds, with the bulk of the remaining survivors settling on the ill-fated Alderaan, again suffering at the hands of the Empire. Fortunately, a large Caamasi remnant community endured on Kerilt, and some later relocated to Susevfi.

It was ultimately discovered that a group of Bothans had helped Palpatine's agents sabotage Caamas's shield generators, thus allowing the sudden, violent attack to send firestorms raging across the world. When a copy of the Caamas Document, which detailed Bothan involvement in the tragedy, was revealed on the planet Wayland, it touched off a flood of demands for the Bothans to purchase a new, uninhabited planet for the remaining refugees. The Bothans have yet to fulfill these demands, but even as the few remaining Caamasi calmly and patiently await a permanent home, they continue to work side by side with the Bothans in a fundamental example of forgiveness.

Despite the unfortunate devastation their species has suffered, the Caamasi remain steadfast pacifists. Most are artists, merchants, diplomats, or scholars. Although they will serve governments as ambassadors, they will not serve in the military. The leaders of the galaxy frequently rely on the Caamasi as advisers, especially the members of the new Jedi order, and the species has been particularly helpful in aiding the Jedi to regain some of their lost history and traditions through the sharing of key memnii. They were also instrumental in drafting early incarnations of the New Republic Charter, negotiating agreements among conflicting worlds, species, and institutions, and serving as a voice of

DESIGNATION
Sentient

HOMEWORLD
Kerilt (by way
of Caamas)

**AVERAGE
HEIGHT**
1.8 meters

PRONUNCIATION
Kä-ä-mä'-sē

reason in the growing Senate. Senior Anthropologist Hoole noted that the Caamasi were crucial to the cause of peace in the galaxy, bringing difficult disputes between beings to successful and satisfying conclusions with a calmness and gentleness found in few other species.

Perhaps no Caamasi typifies his people and their dedication to peace better than the late Elegos A'Kla. A'Kla was living a quiet life on Kerilt when he met a human named Corran Horn, then a Jedi apprentice. A'Kla's uncle was a Jedi who had served with Horn's grandfather, and through the information Elegos carried in his memnii, he was able to direct and offer assistance to Horn along his path to Jedi Knighthood.

Following this, A'Kla became trustee of the Caamasi Remnant, and advised the New Republic as a Senator. As part of his duties, A'Kla accompanied Princess Leia Organa Solo to the Outer Rim on a fact-finding mission in the early days of the Yuuzhan Vong invasion. After assisting in evacuations at the battles of Dubrillion and Dantooine, A'Kla volunteered to present himself to the Yuuzhan Vong as an envoy. The Yuuzhan Vong commander Shedao Shai initially appeared to comply with A'Kla's request, but in an act of deception he took the Caamasi's life to demonstrate the invaders' intentions for the galaxy. Shai then returned A'Kla's body to the Republic, having first prepared it for burial according to Yuuzhan Vong traditions. Shai's message was received, and in Corran Horn's grief following his friend's death, the Jedi challenged Shai to a duel with the fate of the planet Ithor hanging in the balance. Although Horn defeated Shai, the Yuuzhan Vong once again failed to honor their agreement, and Ithor was destroyed. It might be thought that A'Kla's sacrifice was for naught, and that he failed in his mission, but his example lived on, a pillar of hope for the rest of the galaxy that the Yuuzhan Vong could not defeat.

NOTABLE APPEARANCE
I, Jedi (novel)

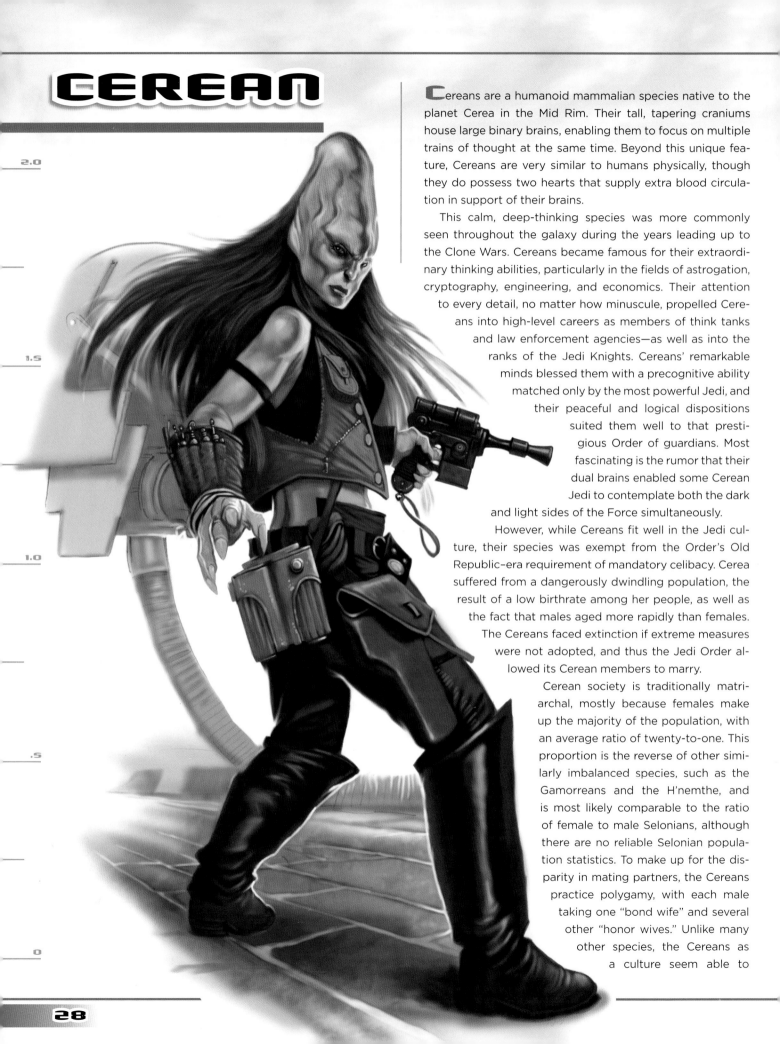

CEREAN

Cereans are a humanoid mammalian species native to the planet Cerea in the Mid Rim. Their tall, tapering craniums house large binary brains, enabling them to focus on multiple trains of thought at the same time. Beyond this unique feature, Cereans are very similar to humans physically, though they do possess two hearts that supply extra blood circulation in support of their brains.

This calm, deep-thinking species was more commonly seen throughout the galaxy during the years leading up to the Clone Wars. Cereans became famous for their extraordinary thinking abilities, particularly in the fields of astrogation, cryptography, engineering, and economics. Their attention to every detail, no matter how minuscule, propelled Cereans into high-level careers as members of think tanks and law enforcement agencies—as well as into the ranks of the Jedi Knights. Cereans' remarkable minds blessed them with a precognitive ability matched only by the most powerful Jedi, and their peaceful and logical dispositions suited them well to that prestigious Order of guardians. Most fascinating is the rumor that their dual brains enabled some Cerean Jedi to contemplate both the dark and light sides of the Force simultaneously.

However, while Cereans fit well in the Jedi culture, their species was exempt from the Order's Old Republic–era requirement of mandatory celibacy. Cerea suffered from a dangerously dwindling population, the result of a low birthrate among her people, as well as the fact that males aged more rapidly than females. The Cereans faced extinction if extreme measures were not adopted, and thus the Jedi Order allowed its Cerean members to marry.

Cerean society is traditionally matriarchal, mostly because females make up the majority of the population, with an average ratio of twenty-to-one. This proportion is the reverse of other similarly imbalanced species, such as the Gamorreans and the H'nemthe, and is most likely comparable to the ratio of female to male Selonians, although there are no reliable Selonian population statistics. To make up for the disparity in mating partners, the Cereans practice polygamy, with each male taking one "bond wife" and several other "honor wives." Unlike many other species, the Cereans as a culture seem able to handle the potential difficulties of polygamy because of their placid temperament.

The planet Cerea is ruled by a president who oversees a Council of Elders—a primarily female team of wise and venerable individuals who consider each side of an issue thoroughly and objectively. They allow for open discussion on political and legal matters, but after the elders have made a decision, the resolution is final and no appeal is permitted. It was this body that prevented Cerea from joining the Republic and the Separatists alike during the Clone Wars, largely in an attempt to preserve the planet's natural resources from greedy Senators who would exploit them.

The world of Cerea is a lush, verdant paradise, and Cerean culture centers on honoring that environment. Cereans value living in harmony with nature, and therefore have set in place stringent laws to protect their surroundings from hazardous waste and technological contamination. By nature, they shun technology and powered transports, although they have consented to the construction of "Outsider Citadels" in certain areas of their planet for beings from more developed worlds to reside. Unfortunately, these citadels have become overcrowded and polluted.

Meditation and contemplation are central to life for all Cereans, not just to those who follow the path of the Jedi. To enhance their focus during these sessions of reflection, Cereans often employ kasha meditation crystals, which have a calming and mind-clearing effect on the user. The crystals are decorated with special etchings created by Cerean artisans to harness their natural harmonic energy.

Cereans also hold an extreme reverence for the ancient traditions of their people. Although a female Cerean typically has only one name, a male has three, the origins of which are derived from those of his father and grandfather. These names are arranged in any order based on cadence and to make the whole name meaningful. A female, meanwhile, will only take an additional name if she becomes a bond-wife, adopting the name of her husband's grandfather for official matters. This is an interesting custom, given the Cerean's matriarchal culture, seeming to indicate that while females are the guiding force driving their society, family lineage is actually passed down through the male line.

An additional display of the importance of tradition in Cerean society can be found in their clothing, as much of their modern garb harks back to garments of old. Elders and

DESIGNATION
Sentient

HOMEWORLD
Cerea

**AVERAGE
HEIGHT**
2 meters

PRONUNCIATION
Sĕr'-ē-ăn

other prestigious members of society prefer to wear a special surcoat, the style of which resembles an ancient mantle of honor. Cereans also retain great enthusiasm for the study of early fighting techniques, especially the art of using a shyarn: a light, arc-edged sword used in honor duels. Cereans send their children to train at shyarn-ado training schools, and masters of this type of swordplay are featured in well-publicized tournaments and demonstrations. Shyarn are notably distinctive in that when they connect in battle, the curved swords become magnetically attached—making for some very physically challenging and sometimes brutal combat. Some say that, as a form of catharsis, Cerean duelers release every bit of aggression that they possess while participating in the sport, which is perhaps why it is so appealing to this normally peaceful people. The shyarn form has also developed into a fine art, as many of its choreographed exercises have become a popular mode of dance expression. Troupes of shyarn dancers travel Cerea, and they have even been seen throughout the galaxy, displaying the majesty of this ancient form of self-defense.

Despite these examples of Cereans respecting time-honored customs, it was the drive for technology and progress that nearly had unfortunate consequences for the young people of Cerea, and possibly the entire planet. During the Clone Wars, many youthful Cereans spent their leisure time in the Outsider Citadels, where they were exposed to the luxuries of other worlds and became desirous of such objects for themselves. They sought to radically change their culture's ways, but in reality this behavior was deviously being encouraged by agents of the Separatists, specifically the Trade Federation, who held these youth as captives. Fortunately for Cerea, the Jedi intervened, and the young hostages were safely returned to their families.

Sadly, the Clone Wars continued to be unkind to Cerea and its people. As the planet chose neutrality during the war, Republic and Separatist armies fought a brutal battle on Cerea to prevent it from allying itself to the other's side. In the process, much of the pristine world was destroyed and many inhabitants lost their lives, including the Cerean president Bo-Ro-Tara, who was assassinated before the Republic could claim a victory. Following the Clone Wars, the Cereans readopted their isolationist stance, and reports from that world are scant to nonexistent.

NOTABLE APPEARANCE
Episode I: The Phantom Menace

CHADRA-FAN

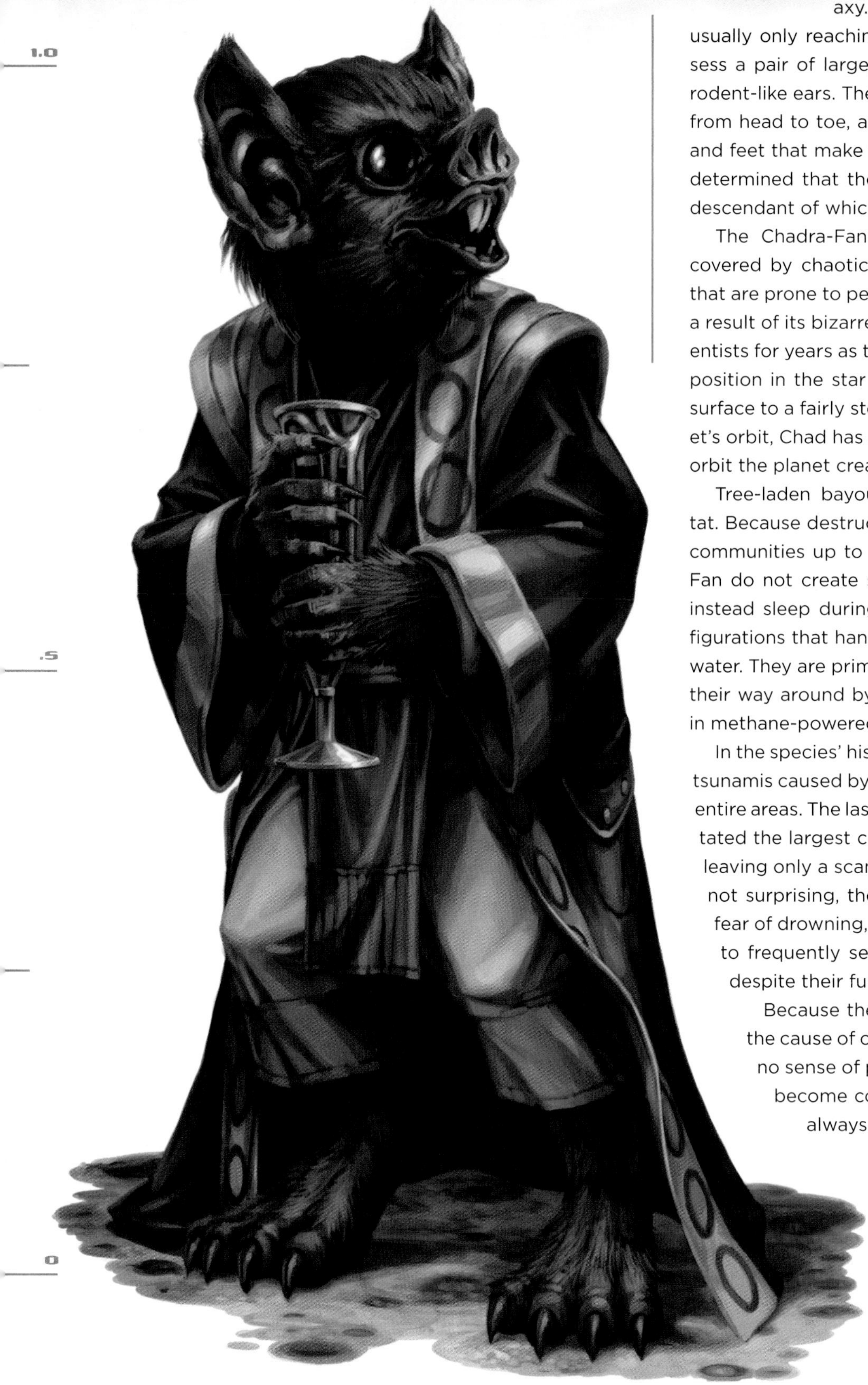

The small, dexterous Chadra-Fan are rodent-like beings who inhabit the world of Chad, located in the Outer Rim of the galaxy. They are petite in stature, with adults usually only reaching about one meter in height, and possess a pair of large, dark eyes, a flat nose, and prominent rodent-like ears. The Chadra-Fan's bodies are covered in fur from head to toe, and they have curiously oversized hands and feet that make them adept at climbing. Scientists have determined that they evolved from nimble tree rodents, a descendant of which still inhabits the treetops of Chad.

The Chadra-Fan's homeworld is three-quarters water, covered by chaotic seas as well as by marshes and bogs that are prone to perpetual flooding. The planet's weather is a result of its bizarre elliptical orbit, which has confused scientists for years as to whether it occupies the third or fourth position in the star system. Chad's star warms the world's surface to a fairly steady temperature, and despite the planet's orbit, Chad has almost no axial tilt. The nine moons that orbit the planet create a regular system of tides.

Tree-laden bayous are the Chadra-Fan's primary habitat. Because destructive tidal waves can sweep across their communities up to three or four times a year, the Chadra-Fan do not create solid structures for their dwellings, but instead sleep during midday in swaying open-walled configurations that hang from the cyperill trees high above the water. They are primarily out during dusk and dawn, making their way around by hopping from tree to tree or traveling in methane-powered, boat-like vehicles.

In the species' history, there are numerous stories of giant tsunamis caused by ocean earthquakes that have wiped out entire areas. The last significant one on record utterly devastated the largest community of Chadra-Fan on the planet, leaving only a scant few alive in that particular region. It is not surprising, then, that Chadra-Fan have an instinctive fear of drowning, and Chadra-Fan traveling offworld tend to frequently seek out planets with arid environments, despite their fur.

Because their world's volatile weather patterns are the cause of constant relocation, the Chadra-Fan have no sense of permanence, a trait that has led many to become consummate thrill- and pleasure-seekers, always on the lookout for a new adventure.

How Chadra-Fan perceive and respond to their fast-paced surroundings is due in part to their biology, not just their environmental experiences. The Chadra-Fan's senses are strangely unique—in particular those of sight and smell. The species' large black eyes can see into the infrared spectrum of light, giving them a marked advantage at night and in poorly lit areas. In addition, their olfactory sense is remarkably distinctive, the result of two sets of nostrils that each serves a separate specific function. The outer pair detect water-soluble scents like most humanoid species, while their inner nostrils control Chadra-Fan's chemoreceptive sense of smell.

In terms of physical appearance, the differences between male and female Chadra-Fan are undetectable to an outsider. The Chadra-Fan determine gender differences through their sense of smell, and they will relay their feelings of attraction through the release of pheromones. Some of these pheromones are released involuntarily, creating an aura of attractiveness as well as relaying their family ancestry to others. Chadra-Fan also purposely release pheromones to transmit emotions, as their faces are not all that expressive—feelings such as anger, fear, arousal, and joy are communicated through olfactory rather than visual perception. These scent-related messages can be very complex, and may even lead to some confusion should their involuntary pheromones combine with their voluntary ones. In addition, they will evaluate non-Chadra-Fan with this unique ability, and those who are familiar with offworlders can frequently determine a particular species simply by assessing their infrared aura and scent.

On top of this scent communication, Chadra-Fan converse verbally in high, squeaking tones, the interpretation of which is dependent upon a keen sense of hearing. If Chadra-Fan are tone deaf, they will not be able to speak, as their speech patterns rely on specific pitches to relay meaning.

Due to their small size and active nature, Chadra-Fan's metabolisms are extremely high, and their mental and physical activities run at a feverish pitch. Mostly sleeping in short two-hour naps during the daylight hours, they will then work the rest of the day gathering food, tinkering, and entertaining themselves at a frenzied pace. As a result of their speedy lifestyle and biological makeup, Chadra-Fan fully mature around age fifteen and usually live no more than forty standard years.

Chadra-Fan society is organized into a clan structure, and the immediate family divisions within each clan are typically impossible to discern. Everyone shares the duty of parenting one another's children, and households are open to anyone at all times. Because Chadra-Fan are so used to having other members of their kind around, they will con-

stantly seek companionship; left on their own, they can die of loneliness within a period of weeks. They never travel unaccompanied, preferring even the companionship of a complete stranger to a lonesome journey by themselves.

With their strong familial ties, children are the center of the Chadra-Fan community. A young Chadra-Fan only leaves his or her clan when wed, or sometimes not at all, as the married couple remains with the clan that has fewer children so that they may increase the group's number.

Within their clan structure, Chadra-Fan have no chosen leaders. Everyone takes a guiding role at one time or another, stepping in where they have expertise and then surrendering the leadership to others who have more experience as a situation warrants. Chadra-Fan work well with partners and in team situations, as they are often either extremely forgiving, or merely ignorant, of team members' failings. For this reason, it is not unusual to see Chadra-Fan in the company of criminals—they are usually so self-absorbed or accommodating that they make loyal, well-received companions and mechanics for the most unsavory members of the galaxy's underworld.

While the Chadra-Fan are generally deemed a technologically primitive people, they do tend to have a compulsion to tinker. They are extremely inventive, able to come up with new tools and learn about technology after only a short time spent studying a piece of equipment. Depending on the complexity of the machinery they have studied, they can frequently pull apart most items and reassemble them in a short time frame. Most Chadra-Fan who travel offplanet end up working as mechanics or in technological research-and-development facilities.

Original Chadra-Fan mechanical creations are actually considered a hot commodity by those who take interest in collecting such things. Each piece is always completely distinct, made by a dedicated craftsman, and often regarded as a piece of art whether it works to specification or not. While Chadra-Fan are competent at mass-producing technical items, they prefer to construct each of their creations individually, and it is an object of pride and artisanship to fashion the most innovative technological designs. And while every singular item created by Chadra-Fan may not operate as anticipated, those that do, function exceptionally well.

DESIGNATION
Sentient

HOMEWORLD
Chad

AVERAGE HEIGHT
1 meter

PRONUNCIATION
Chăd'-rä-Făn

NOTABLE APPEARANCE
Episode IV: A New Hope

CHAGRIAN

Chagrians are tall, powerfully built amphibious humanoids native to the water-covered world of Champala in the Chagri system of the Inner Rim. Early in the species' development, Champala's sun became temporarily unstable and bombarded their world with dangerous amounts of radiation. As a result, Chagrians developed a skin pigmentation that ranges in color from light blue to deep indigo and makes them resistant to most forms of radiation. In addition, Chagrians' eyes grant them the ability to see twice as far as most beings in low- or dim-light conditions, and in such cases they still maintain the ability to distinguish color and detail.

Outside of their distinctive skin, Chagrians' most notable feature is their horns, particularly the lethorns, which protrude downward from the sides of their head, growing and thickening over a Chagrian's lifetime, often to the point of draping over the shoulders and onto the chest. The males of the species also possess a set of regular horns that rise from their skulls upward, often giving them an intimidating appearance. These extra horns were once used by males in underwater duels to acquire mates, charging and impaling their rivals in an effort to eliminate their competition. In recent times, this practice has been made unnecessary and illegal, with arranged marriages becoming the norm among their species, but a male Chagrian's upper horns are still seen as a sign of virility, strength, and, unfortunately, vanity. To prevent their horns from becoming an encumbrance as they grow, they will file down the tips in their daily grooming rituals.

Due to their perpetual exposure to Champala's saltwater oceans, native Chagrians have a weak sense of taste that grows even more inadequate as they age. With their taste glands being subjected to the high content of sodium in Champala's water, all items that enter their mouths taste solely of salt, and by the time they reach adulthood, most Chagrians have no sensation of taste at all. Thus, they frequently have no interest in eating, viewing it as a waste of time, and will often carry nutritional supplements with them to substitute for meals. Also, Chagrians are known to be cautious about food on other planets, analyzing it for nutritional value before consumption. Their tongues are mostly used to detect smells—flickering in and out as among many saurian species.

Born as tadpoles roughly thirty centimeters long, Chagrians develop their legs, arms, and air-breathing lungs as they grow from infancy outside the womb. They are usually born in clutches of three or more, and are cared for in warm, sealable tubs of circulating water in a family's private home. These tubs are closed up at high tide, so the children are not swept away in the waves. Once children's appendages form, they leave the tub, already able to walk on land with little assistance. At this point, their horns will begin to grow, attaining about half of their maximum length by the time a child reaches puberty.

Because they inhabit a world largely immersed in water, Chagrians built their cities along the coastlines in strips of land along small, jungle-covered continents. The architecture of these cities is designed to take in the flowing surges of Champala's oceans at high tide, filling the structures with water. When this happens, Chagrians will swim from building to building and from floor to floor, continuing their lives with little interruption. The spaceports, meanwhile, are the only structures that are on perpetually high and dry land. Fortunately, the many areas of Champala that were damaged and polluted due to mining accidents in the Imperial era have been carefully reclaimed and returned to their previous state by the Galactic Alliance.

In general, Chagrians are a peaceful, law-abiding people, with some members of the species taking the obedient part of their natures to an extreme, often becoming rather stern, stoic, even downright obstinate about following procedure. This isn't the case with all Chagrians, however. Because their society is primarily affluent and the people are rarely wanting, they have no sense of greed and are hardly ever motivated by such base desires. The basic needs of Chagrians are met in abundance, be it for food, shelter, or health care. The educational system is well regarded and many Chagrians pursue advanced university studies, both on- and off-planet.

Their economy primarily centers on tourism, as large numbers of visitors frequently flock to their oceans and beaches, and their accommodating and selfless demeanor makes their homeworld a very popular spot for vacationing. Restorative spas and all-inclusive resorts dominate the cities of Champala, and are popular with all species living in the Inner Rim—not just those from water-based worlds. Chagrians enjoy meeting and interacting with others, preferring to live in urban areas where they can mingle on a regular basis. Although most Champala-based Chagrians do not speak Basic, those who venture offworld learn it eas-

DESIGNATION
Sentient

HOMEWORLD
Champala

AVERAGE HEIGHT
2 meters

PRONUNCIATION
Shäg'-rē-ăn

ily, and often return home to teach it to those in the tourism industry.

One of the most prominent Chagrians in galactic history was Mas Amedda, the Speaker of the Senate during the later years of the Old Republic. Although Amedda lived in a world where politics was ruled by corruption, and he was often forced to trade on that corruption, he began his career believing himself an honest politician with a genuine desire to serve the people. He initially became Speaker during the ill-fated chancellorship of Finis Valorum. Amedda was aware that he did not have the influence to become Chancellor himself and continued to serve as Speaker after Palpatine was elected Chancellor. Based on Palpatine's easygoing interpersonal manner as the Senator from Naboo, Amedda mistakenly believed that Palpatine would be malleable once in office and that he could influence Palpatine for the good of the beings under his care. In fact, during Palpatine's first few years as Chancellor, he appeared open to suggestion as Mas Amedda hoped and enacted several initiatives Amedda put forth. However, Palpatine was actually turning the tables on Amedda, collecting enough information to control him. As a result, Amedda continued to serve, even after learning of Palpatine's secret identity as Sidious, Dark Lord of the Sith. When Palpatine declared himself Emperor, Mas Amedda and Palpatine's other close advisers continued to keep the knowledge of Palpatine's identity as a Sith Lord hidden from the rest of the galaxy. Amedda's Chagrian temperament prevented him from being overly concerned with the thought that this knowledge might someday make him a liability to the Emperor.

After the Emperor rose to power and it was clear that the Empire was a harsh and tyrannical regime, many Chagrians joined the Rebellion. They were particularly important in freeing other water planets from Imperial oppression, including Mon Calamari. Champala was one of the first worlds to join the fledgling Alliance of Free Planets, and later the New Republic, where they remained ardent supporters through the transition to the Galactic Alliance.

NOTABLE APPEARANCE
Episode I: The Phantom Menace

CHEVIN

The Chevin are a technologically advanced, carnivorous, migratory pachydermoid species inhabiting Vinsoth in the Outer Rim, a world of varying temperatures and climates. Because of their protective hides, Chevin can thrive in any of them, although they seem to have a preference for the temperate, semitropical conditions found on the planet's grassy equatorial plains. However, the fact that their population is concentrated in such areas may also be because that is where their culture originated.

According to archaeological and sociological studies conducted on Vinsoth (at great price, as the Chevin charge exorbitant fees for access to their archaeological treasures), the Chevin evolved from giant, thick-boned mammals that lumbered across the plains of Vinsoth. They've retained several characteristics from their forebears—qualities that make them an extremely robust and resilient species.

Chevin present very imposing figures, standing on trunk-like legs that support their large, bulky frames. A trunk-like snout drops from their huge heads nearly to the ground, enabling them to forage while at the same time watching for predators. Their trunks are also the source of an impressive olfactory sense that allows them to locate food without bending over.

Chevin's round black eyes seem to lack pupils, but in reality each eye is one great pupil. Light is filtered through a double-lid system, the first of which appears to simply be clear, but in fact acts as a filtration for damaging light rays and protects the eyes from dirt, wind, and other irritants. The other fleshy lid further shields the pupils with the Chevin's naturally tough hide.

A Chevin's hide is capable of withstanding the impacts of small projectiles and blade attacks, and though small blasterfire can cause their skin to burn, it does not typically cause them much pain. Those who have encountered the Chevin in close combat have observed that it takes a heavy blaster, lightsaber, or other similar high-powered weapon to truly injure one. The thickness and toughness of their hide, however, significantly limits their sense of touch.

Chevin possess long arms, and their three-fingered hands, larger even than their three-toed feet, can touch the ground as they walk at an ambling pace. Though they move slowly, Chevin are quality hunters, circling their prey with precision teamwork until it stumbles into their trap. This finely tuned strategy helped them to dominate and enslave Chevs, a humanoid species also native to their world. The Chevin do treat their slaves relatively well to encourage subservience, allowing Chevs to keep their own cultural heritage and supporting them in all forms of art and expression.

The Chevin are consummate opportunists. For many, their goal is to acquire wealth, power, and status by any means necessary, and thus the galaxy has come to know them as smugglers, gamblers, blackmailers, and gunrunners. As mentioned, Chevin are also slavers, exploiting the humanoid Chev species with whom they share their world. And yet they do not consider themselves evil, instead believing themselves realists—using their wiles to survive or prosper in a merciless galaxy. In their own circles, they are quite honest, and are rarely known to ever double cross a business partner for any reason. But if they themselves are betrayed, Chevin can rank among the most vindictive and brutal adversaries in the galaxy.

Not all Chevin share the same "merciless galaxy" view, however. The scientific and technological communities of Vinsoth focus their interests on new medical discoveries, and on creating greater and better products of engineering. Sadly, these forward-thinking Chevin usually end up working for their more aggressive counterparts. Even so, small breakaway collections of independent-thinking scientists and engineers have formed secret societies to combat the slavery that has been a black mark on their culture for eons. Ending this slavery would give them easier entrance to the Galactic Alliance, something these progressive Chevin desire for worldwide protection as well as economic growth.

The Chevin are a migratory species, traveling the plains searching for wild backshin—herd animals that are their primary source of meat. Their family-centered communities traverse their world in large platform vehicles called lodges. Wealthier groups use repulsorlift vehicles, while others use lodges with wheels, although slaves are almost always forced to walk from campsite to campsite. A pack of as few as forty or as many as 250 lodges will travel together at a time to create a sprawling,

DESIGNATION
Sentient

HOMEWORLD
Vinsoth

AVERAGE HEIGHT
2 meters

PRONUNCIATION
Shĕ'-vĭn

moving village. All the wandering communities, however, stay in contact with one another through electronic communications, so that if one group is threatened, the others can come to its aid. It is unusual for a village to remain in the same place longer than a few standard weeks, unless members find the particular location to be rich in game, or inclement weather forbids travel.

Those Chevin with the resources to do so travel and trade offworld regularly, bringing home the goods, clothing, and cultural influences of other peoples. Before encountering other species, Chevin did not wear clothes at all. Now they enjoy adorning themselves in the richest of robes and jewelry—and flaunt their vestments as a sign of prestige.

Politically, Chevin are monarchists with a dictatorial system of government. A dictator governs each continent while overseeing a panel of self-chosen advisers. These Chevin are some of the very few who do not travel in the moving villages, instead residing in centrally located establishments. These rulers rarely war with each other, though they do tend to compete for land, power, prestige, and trade privileges.

Chevin acquired their initial technical know-how from offplanet sources, and adapted it to their own needs. Unfortunately, much of their other technology is focused on maintaining control of the slave population—one reason a faction of the scientific community wants to end the practice, which is felt to inhibit growth in the field. The Chevin leadership has made profitable use of a lot of the slave-controlling technology by selling it to other worlds to use for security purposes.

During the reign of the Empire, the Chevin supported the Imperial rule of the galaxy, finding it to be a profitable relationship, as they provided the Empire with foodstuffs, slaves, and their unique slave-restraining equipment in return for the offworld goods they desired.

Offworld, Chevin are usually found in expensive casinos, space stations, underworld-controlled pleasure palaces, and high-tech gladiatorial gaming houses. A few of the Chevin working for change on Vinsoth left during the war against the Empire to join the Rebellion. These few work within the Galactic Alliance, encouraging the government to put pressure on their homeworld's leaders to end slavery on Vinsoth. Unfortunately, these valiant individuals often become the targets of bounty hunters and assassins hired by the dictators of Chevin, who see their actions as traitorous.

NOTABLE APPEARANCE
Episode VI: Return of the Jedi

CHISS

Until about ten standard years after the Battle of Endor, little was known of the Chiss, a humanoid species from the frigid world of Csilla in the Unknown Regions, other than the fact that Imperial Grand Admiral Thrawn was one of them. Thrawn, whose real name was Mitth'raw'nuruodo, revealed almost nothing about his species. Despite his exile, Thrawn was secretive regarding his people. However, agents of the New Republic, after conducting analyses of surrendered and captured Imperial logs, found several points of interest. In addition, reports from the University of Sambra that detail investigations of Chiss sites such as Nirauan have yielded reliable information. Very few recorded encounters with the Chiss have been unearthed, although they are reputed to have driven back the Ssi-ruuk, a military threat as fearsome as the Nagai, the Yevetha, and the Yuuzhan Vong. With blue skin, jet-black hair, and glowing red eyes, the Chiss generally command attention in a crowd of other humanoids. Their skin and eye colors are due to a chemical reaction to an oxygen atmosphere, and the more oxygen contained in the air they breathe, the greater the intensity of these two features. In addition, the evolved changes to their eyes have given the Chiss superior visual acuity, even in low-light conditions. Occasionally their black hair will gray with age, especially in females. This is considered a mark of distinction in their culture; among Chiss, it is felt that the child of a parent possessing graying hair will greatly affect society. Other than their distinctive eye and skin color, there is little else to differentiate them physically from standard humans.

The Chiss are typically attractive, intelligent, and private people, and are so protective of their society that they have managed to keep their species' existence largely secret from the rest of the galaxy. This isolationism makes it difficult to form conclusive statements about the Chiss. For example, scientists believe they do not experience an adolescent stage of life, but advance quickly to full maturity. However, this may be the result of societal and cultural influences and demands rather than physical growth, or some combination thereof.

Scientists also believe that the Chiss are descended from an ancient human colony founded in an age predating the Old Republic. However, they are sufficiently different from humans to be considered an independent species, as is the case with Zeltrons. The Chiss are highly evolved, taking great interest in art and science, and maintain a powerful military. In many accounts, they are described as pensive—contemplative, deliberate, and calculating—studying situations from every viewpoint and considering all the alternatives when making a decision.

The Chiss control more than two dozen systems surrounding their homeworld of Csilla, in a political federation known as the Chiss Ascendancy. Their society is regimented, inflexible, and strangely xenophobic, and their colonization and control of neighboring worlds was evidently achieved not for want of power or riches, but instead to establish order over chaotic elements that could ultimately pose a threat to them. Indeed, the Chiss are generally a peaceful species, but when attacked, they fight with efficient, well-planned strategies, and they do not give up the battle until their opponents are destroyed or subjugated. Most, if not all, of the systems they conquered were defeated after their respective leaders attacked the Chiss, as it is against the law for Chiss to engage in preemptive strikes. This is such a moral imperative that Thrawn was exiled when he called for a preemptive strike against an enemy.

The Chiss have no known Force traditions. Moreover, research conducted by the Jedi historian Tionne has identified only one Chiss Force-user, a female Dark-sider named Sev'rance Tann.

Statistically speaking, it is unlikely that Force sensitivity is this rare among an entire species once evidence of its existence has been demonstrated, especially a species so biologically similar to the most widespread Force-users, humans. However, one can hypothesize that Chiss practices and beliefs may have led to such a lack of Force traditions and known Force-users. As the Chiss believe that aggression against a potential enemy is forbidden until that enemy has launched an attack, the power bestowed by Force-sensitivity may be considered by the Chiss as too great a temptation. Thus, hypothetically, if there are unrecorded Force-users among the Chiss, they may work to keep their talents secret. One's family is a paramount concern for Chiss, and a Chiss Force-user may fear bringing shame upon them—worse, exile. A public prohibition against disclosing one's talents in the Force may be so strong that unless Chiss are Force-sensitive themselves, they are unaware the Force exists.

Records uncovered from the remains of Outbound Flight suggest that this ignorance of the Force was initially the case with Thrawn, a condition he was not likely to allow for long. We can surmise that because Thrawn had contact with the galaxy outside the Unknown Regions prior to the Clone Wars, it was most likely Thrawn who brought Tann, and her lover, Vandalor, to the attention of Darth Sidious, whom Thrawn had met during the Outbound Flight crisis. Whether this was an attempt to remove Tann from a difficult and dangerous situation on Csilla or to simply provide Sidious with a soldier and tactician he could rely on, we will never know.

Chiss society is directed by ruling "families" that are not necessarily indicative of bloodline so much as function, and each family is its own branch of the Chiss government or society. Although details are unclear, reports are that the number of ruling families has fluctuated somewhere between three and twelve. Some facts have also been discovered regarding four of the families. The Nuruodo family, which was Thrawn's clan, controls the military and foreign affairs, and the Csapla family administers the use of the Ascendancy's natural and agricultural resources and manages colonial issues. The Sabosen supervise education, justice, and public health, while the Inrokini direct business, communications, civilian technology, and the sciences.

The Chiss are frequently perceived by outsiders as arrogant, calculating, and aloof. It is said that they see every non-Chiss as a potential threat, even when working on a common goal, and as a precautionary measure, they will continuously calculate strategies for protecting their own interests. And if for some reason a Chiss is defeated or humiliated in a venture, he or she will carefully scrutinize what happened to ensure that such a setback does not occur a second time.

Despite this xenophobic mistrust of other species, or perhaps because of it, the Chiss have a heightened interest in the study of the scientific and, in the case of Thrawn, artistic achievements of other beings. Through the analysis of these creations, he came to understand the dangers and weaknesses of their potential enemies.

One difficulty in uncovering further details on the culture of the Chiss is their incredibly complex language, Cheunh. Linguists who have managed to record the language find it to be one of the most intricate and indecipherable of all humanoid dialects in the galaxy. It is theorized that the Chiss prefer it that way, as this complexity makes it that much harder for outsiders to learn about them.

DESIGNATION
Sentient

HOMEWORLD
Csilla

AVERAGE
HEIGHT
1.7 meters

PRONUNCIATION
Chĭss

NOTABLE APPEARANCE
Heir to the Empire (novel)

CLAWDITE

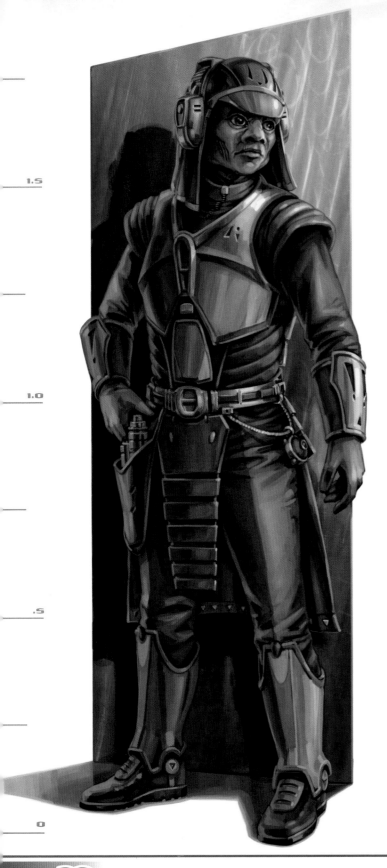

Clawdites are a reptilian humanoid species native to the planet Zolan in the Mid Rim. They are renowned for their shape-changing abilities, although in its natural form, a Clawdite's skin color typically varies from yellow to green. Their large yellowish eyes have black, slit-like pupils, set in a face with almost human features. With their shape-changing skills, Clawdites can alter their appearance drastically to mimic that of other humanoids, even to the point of including the clothing and jewelry they are wearing, as long as those items are worn close to the body. Clawdites treat their skin with special oils to keep it supple and flexible for shape changing and to reduce the possibility of cracks or tears. They are specifically reptomammals and, unlike true reptiles, do not reproduce by laying and hatching eggs, instead giving birth to their offspring in singular pregnancies.

Unlike other shape-changing species such as the Shi'ido, Clawdites' body-altering ability causes them great discomfort. And yet, with practice, they can work past the pain to maintain some startling disguises. Their capability relies heavily upon their concentration, and it is only a well-practiced Clawdite who can rest while in altered form. In addition, Clawdites spend a good deal of time learning meditation and concentration techniques that allow them to maximize their transforming talents. Unlike the Shi'ido, Clawdites cannot, however, alter or add to their mass—they can only mimic species that are humanoid and roughly the same size as themselves. They also cannot match the features of a specific individual, nor can they change their physical form to look like species with drastically different body configurations and postures, such as Mon Calamari or Dugs. Most Clawdites will lose their shape and revert to their natural form if they are distracted, and if they are killed in disguise, they will return to their true appearance.

However, there have been reports that the bounty hunter Zam Wesell, unlike other Clawdite shapeshifters, was able to assume the forms of species with drastically different body masses (most notably that of a Dug). There is no evidence suggesting that this feat has been duplicated, so it is believed that Wesell must have developed her own technique for shapeshifting. On the other hand, there is nothing to suggest that another Clawdite cannot similarly learn how to assume new forms. Although the exact physiological mechanism by which Clawdites assume the form of other beings is not yet understood, and as water makes up most being's bodies, xenobiologists have speculated that Wesell might have been able to alter her body's water content with a finer degree of control than other Clawdites, perhaps through the use of a medical device or injectable substance. Wesell may have been able to expel water to reduce mass, and then, conversely, absorb it to increase mass. This process would be limited by the amount of water her body's cells could expel or contain, perhaps with lower and upper thresholds. In addition, it would have been necessary for her to manipulate any absorbed water in order to create a skeletal system to support her weight.

It is not known whether Zam Wesell's daughter, Sone, shared this ability with her mother, as she disappeared after Wesell's death on Coruscant shortly before the start of the Clone Wars. Recent attempts to test these theories have proven unsuccessful, and for understandable reasons, the Clawdites are not anxious to have their shapeshifting studied with great scrutiny, as they fear negative repercussions and prejudicial treatment.

A Clawdite's ability to change form increases with age. Clawdite children can do little more than change color, a skill that begins as early as infancy, with small babies shifting hues to communicate hunger or discomfort to their parents. Any simple exterior alterations such as this are harmless to most Clawdites—it is only when they actually shift their mass that the process becomes painful. Under their new government, Clawdite schoolchildren attend classes instructing them on how to manage their strengths, which has made a greater number of Clawdites more practiced and efficient with their talents in recent years.

In general, Clawdites are solitary individuals who often shun company unless it is beneficial to their goals. Harsh realists who carry a strong sense of suspicion and mistrust for all they encounter, Clawdites frequently have difficulty forming friendships, and the concept of loyalty escapes them.

Clawdites are a subspecies of the native Zolanders, who harbor a vicious prejudice against their genetic cousins. The Zolanders are a deeply religious people of strong convictions, who view the Clawdites as impure and sinful. The Clawdite species branched from their ancestors hundreds of generations ago when scientists, trying to find a way to protect their people from harmful solar radiation bombarding their world, activated dormant skin-changing genes in the genetic code of some volunteers. This altered genetic trait was passed on from generation to generation, creating a whole new species who were then subjugated and reviled by their fellows. This makes the species' reluctance to have their shapeshifting abilities studied quite a rational response. After years of persecution and banishment to secured ghettos, the Clawdites decided to give themselves a name that would distinguish them from their genetic forebears.

Very select Clawdites are accepted to train with the Mabari, an ancient order of Zolan warrior knights. Learning the martial traditions of the Mabari is a strenuous undertaking, and only the most promising recruits are accepted. During the Clone Wars, however, the order limited the number of Clawdite members it accepted due to religious and societal prejudices. Furthermore, the Mabari also regulated Clawdites among their number due

DESIGNATION
Sentient

HOMEWORLD
Zolan

AVERAGE HEIGHT
1.8 meters

PRONUNCIATION
Clä'-dīt

to a genuine and well-founded concern that training Clawdites in large numbers would result in a powerful group capable of overthrowing the government. As a result, Clawdite members were closely monitored, and if Clawdites left the order, they were strongly pressured to depart the planet entirely.

During the Separatist crisis, the shapeshifting species grouped together to form a political contingent, and sought offworld assistance to aid them in resisting persecution. Their primary contact was Count Dooku, whose power was cut short during the Clone Wars when he was killed by Anakin Skywalker. As a result, the Clawdites remained in subjugation while the Empire was in power, and Imperial forces blockaded the planet Zolan to ensure that no Clawdites could leave their homeworld.

After the Empire fell, Zolan erupted into civil war, and the Clawdites finally seized control of at least 75 percent of their world. They had just settled into power and made overtures to the New Republic when the Yuuzhan Vong invasion force struck. Clawdites quickly joined forces with the Republic to infiltrate the Yuuzhan Vong with a unit comprised solely of shapeshifters. This unit, more than one hundred members strong, served valiantly, suffering an uncommonly high casualty rate as missions repeatedly took them behind enemy lines. Known as Guile Company, the unit did not lack for volunteers, however, and competition to be accepted into the unit was fierce. Only those Clawdites who demonstrated an advanced degree of control over their shapeshifting abilities were accepted. Moreover, Clawdites are not a populous species. For this reason, Clawdites with children were not accepted into the unit, as it was believed that protecting and nurturing future generations was important to the continuation of the species. It was later discovered that for this reason, many applicants and members of the Guile Company hid their offspring.

Guile Company has continued as an active unit in the Galactic Alliance military. In addition, Clawdites have moved beyond this role to become indispensable members of Alliance Intelligence infiltration units. While maintaining an aloofness from other species, Clawdites take great pride in their military service, as the few Clawdites that have made it off their homeworld typically take employment as bounty hunters and assassins. Military service provides a chance to make a contribution to the galaxy in a positive way, protecting the liberty of other species that have been persecuted as they had historically been on Zolan.

NOTABLE APPEARANCE
Episode II: Attack of the Clones

DEVARONIAN (DEVISH)

Devaronians, or Devish, are humanoids native to the world of Devaron in the Colonies region, a planet of moderate temperatures and varying landscapes, though the Devaronians tend to make their homes in the low mountain ranges. Scientists believe they evolved from a species of ancient primates that roamed the mountains, using their horns to defend themselves from predators. Although the female Devaronians lost their horns through evolution, the males did not, and it is possible that the males have maintained this characteristic because it aids the species' mating process, as the females find the horns attractive. For this reason, the males take great pride in their horns, polishing them with wax and scented oils, while females simply have spots where their horns would be.

In addition, Devaronian males possess sharp incisors that can be utilized for the rending of flesh, particularly if they are hunting, whereas the females have the blunt teeth of omnivores. The females have retained their forebears' soft coat of white, brown, or reddish fur, while the advancement of the species has resulted in the fading of hair on males, leaving them with smooth, crimson skin.

Devaronians have a unique physiology that is resilient to many toxins and poisons, though certainly not all. They have a particularly high tolerance for alcohol and other intoxicants, and it is generally known around the galaxy that to get into a drinking contest with a Devaronian is to flirt with disaster. They can indeed become intoxicated, but it takes a lot more of a given substance to bring them to that state. This is because each Devaronian has two livers, which work overtime filtering their blood. The extra organ also makes them more resistant to some of the most common diseases and allows for a Devaronian's blood to clot more quickly. However, scientists theorize that the principle reason a Devaronian has two livers is to accommodate their unique blood, which is black in color and silver-based rather than iron-based like most oxygen breathing species. Silver is an element that, unlike iron, does not efficiently carry oxygen. To compensate for this deficiency, a Devaronian's two livers work doubly hard to filter carcinogens from the blood stream and deliver much needed oxygen to all parts of their body. Strangely enough, because of this silver-based blood,

Devaronians perform with greater vigor and strength when exposed to sulfur—as silver carries sulfur throughout their body much more efficiently than oxygen. In fact, some Devaronians participate in an activity called "sulfur snuffing"—they carry small stick inhalers of sulfur, or small masks to inhale the gas. However, as sulfur is a carcinogen, overuse can cause their system to break down overtime. They can, in fact, develop an addiction to it, leading to their ultimate ruin. Sadly, as the smell of sulfur is repugnant to many species, Devaronains engaging in this activity tend to command a wider amount of personal space when interacting with other beings in public places.

Due to the Devish male's reddish pallor, sharp teeth, and horns, many other species perceive them as evil, as they resemble images of malicious beings in certain cultural tales. However, they are not generally malevolent. Still, even though they are one of the oldest spacefaring peoples in the galaxy, the Galactic Alliance has not accepted Devaron as a member world because some of its traditions violate Galactic civil law.

The two Devaronian sexes not only differ physically, but also deviate in terms of values and behavior. Devish females are extraordinarily responsible, trustworthy, and ambitious, running businesses and participating in local politics. Their attentions center on their homes and families, and on the day-to-day business that makes their world function. They rarely leave their world, unless they are being paid to do so, preferring to raise their families in the industrialized cities and villages of Devaron.

Males, on the other hand, are known to be extremely irresponsible, and have a reputation as thrill-seekers, always searching for adventure and entertainment. Their pursuits are varied and diverse, frequently making them interesting and enjoyable conversationalists, particularly since their irrepressible wanderlust has found them in a variety of story-worthy locales, serving as traveling merchants, bounty hunters, galactic traders, and explorers.

After choosing a mate and siring children, male Devaronians typically take to the roads and rivers of Devaron to find adventure, and many leave the planet entirely, rarely ever returning. Strangely, however, Devish males always send some of the money that they earn back home to their wives and offspring. The truth is, the females prefer the financial support to having the males present. So when the male Devaronians developed stardrive capabilities in order to appease their urge to travel the skies, the females soon took advantage of it by setting up trade with other systems. Their world has therefore become very wealthy, with the ever-dependable females running the economic and political systems.

Following this financial model, Devaron actually subsists mainly of its own accord, thriving on local produce with little need to import from other worlds, often not even generating enough goods to export. However, since the males are quite generous and reliable with sending home the credits they earn in their travels, the females have maintained enough capital to import items that they desire from distant systems—making their homebound lives very comfortable.

Devaron is ruled by a representative democracy of popularly elected females, who would not even consider allowing males participation, although it is unlikely that any desire it. The males are accepted as a necessary hazard of life, and are not really regarded as a functioning part of society.

Although Devaron was at one time a member planet of the Old Republic, it was denied membership in the New Republic due to the Devaronians' traditional means of capital punishment, which is considered overly severe, certainly cruel and unusual by several systems' standards. Criminals guilty of a capital crime are thrown alive into a pit of ravenous quarra beasts, which rend them to pieces in a public execution.

Seeing that joining the Galactic Alliance would be advantageous to building further business and wealth, the female rulers of Devaron are discussing whether to appeal the rejection of their former application for membership. However, deliberations on changing their cultural traditions have yet to really get off the ground, for, while most leaders can see the logic in forgoing the public executions, there are those who wish to keep this brutal practice in place, if merely for the entertainment of the masses.

Devaronians, as a people, have a noteworthy Jedi tradition and a propensity for Force sensitivity. In fitting with their dedicated sensibilities, female Devaronians tend to grow more quickly in stature and power as Jedi Knights. During the Clone Wars, Sian Jeisel was a female Devaronian Jedi Master who fought valiantly alongside Mace Windu. However, males, despite their thirst for adventure, also have produced some great Jedi warriors, the most prominent of which, Hivrekh'wao'cheklev, managed to survive capture by the Yuuzhan Vong, and played an important part in their defeat.

DESIGNATION
Sentient

HOMEWORLD
Devaron

AVERAGE HEIGHT
1.6 meters

PRONUNCIATION
Dĕv-ä-rō'-nē-ăn

NOTABLE APPEARANCE
Episode IV: A New Hope

DEWBACK

Dewbacks are large, nonsentient reptiles that inhabit the arid wilderness of the planet Tatooine. Their name was coined colloquially, derived from the dew that gathers on their bodies during their rest in the cool nighttime air of the desert wastelands. Usually employed as beasts of burden, dewbacks were domesticated long before the Empire took its place on the water-barren world.

Unlike some reptiles, dewbacks are omnivores, thriving on the sparse grasses and thorny plants of the desert landscape as well as on small animals such as baby womp rats or scurriers. For hydration, they chew the roots of local cacti that store water in their heat-resistant parts. Other than this, dewbacks require very little water to survive, and can frequently go for days without dehydration setting in.

These reptiles range between 1.3 and 2 meters in height, and 2 to 3 meters in length. Their scales are generally gray and brown, or a dull red and blue, although they have been known to change color with their environment. Dewbacks possess large, tough, flat teeth, and sharp claws for digging through sand dunes in search of brush or plants that provide moisture.

There are several varieties of dewbacks on Tatooine, the most common being the lesser dewback, which is typically the type trained as a mount and pack animal. The most vicious and untrainable kind is the cannibal dewback, so called because these animals will even eat newly hatched members of their own species, particularly if they encounter them in the wild. The cannibal dewbacks are larger than their lesser cousins, and extremely

2.0

1.5

1.0

.5

aggressive. Sadly, they are often mistaken for lesser dewbacks because their coloring is similar—an error that kills several settlers a year.

Grizzled dewbacks, meanwhile, haunt the Jundland Wastes, and are named thus for their patchy exterior. They are considered dangerous because they are usually hungry, and are actually even more immense than either the cannibal or lesser dewback. The final variety, mountain dewbacks, generally have calmer dispositions akin to their domesticated cousins, and can be found in the more mountainous regions of Tatooine. These dewbacks can also be trained as pack animals and mounts.

In the wild, Sand People commonly hunt dewbacks for their meat and their hides, using the beasts' leathery skin for boots, pouches, belts, tents, and other gear. Krayt dragons also hunt dewbacks, as they are relatively easy prey. Most dewbacks will only fight if threatened, and even then, they will typically run from any threat larger than themselves.

Dewbacks are regularly used by moisture farmers as beasts of burden, and by desert military patrols as mounts. They are also employed by Podracing teams to pull their racing vehicles to the starting line. Though sluggish during the cool of the night, the cold-blooded dewbacks can be urged to display bursts of great speed, and are faster and more agile than the bantha, the beast normally ridden by Tusken Raiders. At a full sprint, dewbacks have been able to pace landspeeders for a short distance, and local law enforcement officials have come to find them more reliable than landspeeders because of their ability to continue moving through sandstorms.

Undomesticated dewbacks are extremely solitary, exhibiting few or no parenting or herding instincts. Each year, they return to the Jundland Wastes, where they will engage in a mating ritual for several days. During the period, a male will roll on his back to exhibit his belly to the female, the color of which changes to a light sky blue when he wishes to mate. This shift in color is meant to attract her attention, which, after several attempts, it usually does. Following the mating ritual, all of the dewbacks wander back into the desert alone. A short time later, the female dewback will dig several large holes in the warm sand and deposit thousands of sand-colored eggs, each the size of a human fist. She will then bury the eggs to hide them from predators. Roughly half a standard year after being laid, the eggs hatch, and the young, without any guidance from adults, venture out into the wastelands of the Tatooine desert in the hope of survival.

Interestingly enough, dewbacks' mating season begins just as krayt dragons' mating season ends, thus timing the egg laying in such a way as to protect the dewbacks' offspring from destruction. The two lizard species have chosen a neighboring location for their mating grounds due to the fact that the sand in that area remains at an ideal temperature for incubating the species' eggs.

It is interesting to note that dewbacks will not breed in captivity. Owners of domesticated dewbacks must release them during mating season, allowing them to journey to the Jundland Wastes if they wish the beasts to reproduce. In most cases, domesticated dewbacks will return to their rightful owners. They are, therefore, very intelligent and loyal, remembering those who have fed them or shown them kindness. Because they cannot breed in captivity, they do not thrive anywhere but in their home environment, and are rarely seen outside Tatooine, unless they've been taken offworld as a solitary pet or riding mount with no expectation of having them bred.

DESIGNATION
Nonsentient

HOMEWORLD
Tatooine

AVERAGE HEIGHT
1.8 meters

PRONUNCIATION
Dēw'-băk

NOTABLE APPEARANCE
Episode IV: A New Hope

DIANOGA

The scavenger creature known as the dianoga is an amphibious cephalopod that makes its home in areas throughout the galaxy where refuse collects in moist environments. Found mostly in pools of stagnant water, dianoga have also been known to turn up in the refuse collection systems of starships, which are typically warm and full of bacterium-filled water. Dianoga prosper on industrialized worlds, commonly living in the sewer systems and river canals of urbanized areas.

Dianoga possess a single eyestalk that extends upward from their body like a periscope to observe their surroundings. Their one red eye is extremely sensitive to light, but able to see clearly in dark environments. It is encased in a single, transparent shell that protects the eye from puncturing and other potential injuries that may be encountered in the creatures' trash-filled aquatic habitats.

Seven tentacles are used by the dianoga for moving and gathering food. These tentacles have suction cups that stick to their prey and hold it tight, and can also grab on to smoother surfaces to help propel the dianoga forward. Moreover, a dianoga's tentacles quickly regenerate if damaged, making the creatures difficult to injure and kill. Once a dianoga has grasped its quarry in its tentacles, the dianoga will attempt to squeeze the life from it or suffocate it within

4.0

3.5

3.0

2.5

2.0

1.5

1.0

.5

0

minutes. Exremely large dianoga pose a substantial threat to humans and other species of similar size.

Beyond the eyestalk and tentacles, a dianoga's body consists of one sizable stomach sac and digestive system, along with a huge, toothy mouth that can swallow items far larger than the dianoga itself by stretching around them, similar to a snake. The stomach contains powerful acids for digesting items that most beings would find inedible.

It is believed that the creatures originated on the planet Vodran, crawling into the waste containment tanks of spacefaring vessels, where they then bred. At spaceports, they migrated to other ships and dispersed themselves throughout the galaxy. Now dianoga can be found in warm, watery collections of waste in nearly every known

DESIGNATION
Nonsentient

HOMEWORLD
Vodran

AVERAGE HEIGHT
3–10 meters

PRONUNCIATION
Dī-ä-nō'-gä

spaceport and many large ships. Since these creatures actually feed on and digest waste products, vessel commanders will frequently allow a dianoga to remain in their ship's refuse system once it is discovered. They rarely damage the inner workings of the system, preferring to rest along the bottom of a tank and feed, and if they grow large enough to threaten the ship's crew, maintenance teams will kill the dianoga by shooting them.

These creatures, while not necessarily possessing a significant-sized brain, have displayed their cleverness in choosing their food and in managing to migrate from one home to another. They are able to tell the difference between live creatures and those that are dead, and while they can certainly consume living beings, they will generally forgo an animate meal for one that is deceased. This, scientists believe, is actually a preference of taste. Dianoga are also intelligent enough to determine the sleep patterns of individuals who are resting, regularly attempting to migrate when there is little to no movement, and thus no one awake to notice their quiet slithering from one position to another. However, there are many reports of space crews working the late shift who have encountered a wayfaring dianoga trying to crawl its way into a new area of a ship or spaceport.

Dianogas are self-fertilizing hermaphrodites, not requiring interaction with other members of their species to reproduce. When they do produce offspring, their microscopic larvae create small colonies, and once the population number becomes too great for a certain environment, some of the dianoga will leave that colony and journey to a new, uninhabited locale. Even on the largest of vessels, dianoga can really only be tolerated in colonies of three or fewer. Once their numbers grow too great, the dianoga will either have to find a new habitat or be killed by a ship's maintenance workers.

These creatures are fairly shy and peaceful, usually only aggressive if starved or panicked—and undeniably, there are some tales of dianoga attacking humans who have inadvertently stumbled into their territories. Despite this, they are not known as man-eaters, although they are curious and tend to check each new object they encounter, testing for edibility. Some cultures have developed ways to eat dianoga, though—most popular is a dish known simply as dianoga pie.

NOTABLE APPEARANCE
Episode IV: A New Hope

DRESSELLIAN

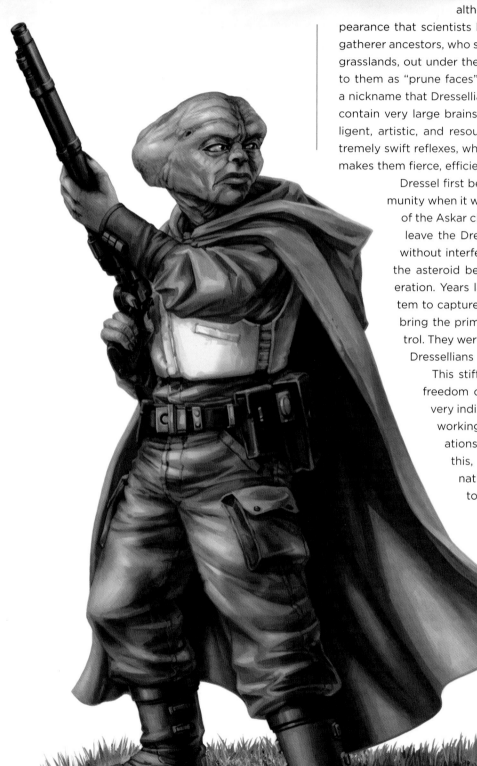

Dressellians are fiercely independent people who inhabit the Mid Rim world of Dressel. They are humanoid, although they do have a wrinkled appearance that scientists believe evolved from their hunter-gatherer ancestors, who spent most of their time in Dressel's grasslands, out under the hot sun. Some in the galaxy refer to them as "prune faces" because of their wrinkled visage, a nickname that Dressellians disdain. Their elongated heads contain very large brains, making them quick-witted, intelligent, artistic, and resourceful. They typically possess extremely swift reflexes, which, combined with their brilliance, makes them fierce, efficient, and effective fighters.

Dressel first became known to the galactic community when it was discovered by Bothan explorers of the Askar clan. The clan decided it was best to leave the Dressellians to develop on their own without interference, and instead they colonized the asteroid belt in the system for a mining operation. Years later, Imperials conquered the system to capture its natural resources, and tried to bring the primitive Dressellians under their control. They were met with hostile resistance as the Dressellians displayed their innate tenacity.

This stiff-necked species values individual freedom over all else, and its members are very individualistic. They can have difficulty working in groups, and rarely form associations containing large numbers. Despite this, when the threat of Imperial domination loomed, the Dressellians came together to form a fierce freedom-fighting force. Their motivation was the autonomy to live as they chose, on their own terms. In a like manner, they banded together to battle the Yuuzhan Vong invaders decades later, showing that when Dressellian freedom is threatened, they are unwavering in combat.

Their initial contact with humans was limited before they were attacked by the Empire, and thus the Dressellians are suspicious of outsiders on the whole, though they are highly trusting of Bothans. However, they can be very loyal to any being who assists them without desire for repayment.

The Dressellian language is simple, and until their contact with Bothan explorers it was actually written in a pictorial form. After establishing close diplomatic ties with the Bothans, they have adopted the Bothan alphabet to communicate their language in writing. Much of their literature, therefore, is gradually being translated and shared in the galaxy at large. Vastly inspirational and often deeply profound, their body of work has been hailed by critics as one of the galaxy's long-undiscovered treasures. Even so, the writers and poets of Dressel prefer to avoid the limelight, as their seclusion and privacy give them what they believe to be a more appropriate work environment.

It is believed that Dressellian society developed into significant communal city-states from their more tribal, hunter-gatherer origins. These city-states are run via direct democracy, with elected leaders who moderate group discussions. Individuals in these communities are allowed to come and go as they please; in the case of key decisions, those of dissenting opinions sometimes depart to form their own establishments.

Law enforcement in these informal groupings is accomplished through a sort of mob justice—the guilty are hunted and punished by concerned citizens. To them, a formal judiciary or court system is inefficient and ineffective. Their justice, they feel, is swift and successful in deterring antisocial behavior, and is not viewed as uncontrolled vigilantism, in contrast with how it may appear to outsiders. While their judicial techniques can be brutal, they do keep crime at a minimum.

This system of government survived underground despite the Empire's best efforts to squash it, and the state leaders became, in fact, the leadership of the Dressellian dissident movement. Although they are now part of the Galactic Federation of Free Alliances, Dressellians largely prefer to keep to themselves except when dealing in business matters. Throughout the days of the New Republic, the Dressellian Senatorial representative often failed to attend sessions except at the urging of the species' war-colleagues, the Bothans.

Economically, the Dressellians have only recently begun to grasp the concept of money, through their increased contact with other species during the war against the Empire. Theirs has long been a barter system handled on a local

rather than governmental scale. With the formation of the New Republic, however, singular Dressellians began to show interest in capitalistic ventures, seeing such undertakings as an extension of their individual quest for personal freedom. Their tenacity also encourages their entrepreneurial compunction, and following the defeat of the Empire, the Dressellians took over control of the mining in their local system, and are now making great strides in that industry. They have also created notable trade in textiles woven from the essence of their natively grown grass, as well as from their farm produce.

Despite the influx of more modern technology to Dressel, the planet still functions at a largely outdated level, with a focus on steam-driven machinery and animal transportation. However, the development of businesses such as those described above is causing technology on Dressel to evolve quickly to meet the demand for native goods.

While the Dressellians aren't industrially advanced, since the end of the Galactic Civil War, more and more offworlders have filtered new technology to them. During the war, Dressellians fought with simple black-powdered, slug-firing weapons. The Bothan underground movement supplied the Dressellians with some energy weapons, though transporting such items was dangerous, and very few actually made it to their intended recipients. Today, while they are familiar with other forms of weaponry, Dressellians still prefer to use slugthrowers, mostly as a form of cultural pride. Because of the limited numbers of shots the weapons can fire, marksmanship is highly valued.

As Dressellian society evolves, neighbors anticipate that the species will become important to the future of the GFFA. Inspirationally, they have already set an impressive example for their peers during their fight against the Empire for personal liberty.

DESIGNATION
Sentient

HOMEWORLD
Dressel

AVERAGE HEIGHT
1.8 meters

PRONUNCIATION
Drĕ-sĕl'-lē-ăn

DUG

Dugs are a vicious, bullying species that hail from the planet Malastare—one of the mainstay planets of the Old Republic. They inhabit the lush western continent of their homeworld, while another species known as the Gran dominate the eastern continent. In the early age of the Old Republic, Republic scouts set up an outpost on the eastern continent, as Malastare was directly along the Hydian Way trade route in the Mid Rim. The Gran arrived on the planet soon after, establishing their settlements and beginning trade in native natural resources and produce. The Dugs did not take this well, and began a long and brutal war against the Gran. A peace was finally negotiated by the Republic, which sided with the Gran, demilitarizing the Dugs. As a result of their greater numbers, the Gran represented Malastare on the Republic Senate instead of the world's native species, leading to a long-standing antagonism between the two groups. To this day, the Gran largely consider Dugs to be nothing more than subservient laborers.

Dugs' physiology puts them at the extreme fringes of humanoid. Their skin hangs loose over their skeleton, while their ears jut backward like fins, and decorative beads usually dangle from an extra flap of skin near the ears. The center of gravity for their skeletal structure is thrust so high on their short torsos that they literally walk on their upper limbs, with their lower limbs functioning for finer manipulation. This unusual physique may have developed because of their homeworld's high level of gravity. Outwardly, there are few differences between male and female Dugs, who can be differentiated by a large skin flap on the males' throats, which plays a role in their mating rituals.

The Dug method of choosing a mate is noteworthy, hinting that there may be a reptilian ancestry to this humanoid race. During the mating season, the extra folds of skin around the male's neck inflate, displaying an underlying vibrant color. The unpaired females of the clans gather together and inspect the males, searching for one they like. A female will poke, insult, and tease the male she prefers until he responds with a loud, screeching call that deflates his ballooned neck. The pair is then considered mated, and from that moment on they will remain together. While a couple will bully and badger each other throughout their lifetime, Dugs are extremely loyal to their chosen mates and will protect them and their children with passionate violence if they are insulted or attacked.

Despite their physical structure, Dugs

can travel very quickly across land, and they can also move swiftly through trees by leaping and swinging. Their reflexes are exceptionally quick, and many members of their species are experts at Podracing, a dangerous sport that has been illegal in most parts of the galaxy for years. The majority of the buildings on their home planet are towers, with the interiors constructed to feature open platforms. Most other species find their architecture impassable. Although the Dugs are a technologically advanced species, erecting these buildings and other complex structures, many still prefer to live in "tree thorps"—primitive villages set deep in the unsettled wilderness of Malastare.

Dugs are perhaps best known for their foul temperaments, as they are insulting and insolent, and can become violent when crossed. They have been to war with many other species, among them the Gran and the ZeHethbra, a species with colonies in the Malastare system. As previously noted, the Republic called for the Dugs to disarm as a result of their war with the Gran, leaving them extremely bitter. They consider themselves warriors, and being without armaments may have made them even more vicious and brutal. As a species, they are known to harbor grudges for years and even decades. Often, grudges will be upheld by later generations of the same family. We can hypothesize that the perceived slight in being ordered to disarm is considered by the Dug as worthy of a grudge not against an individual, but against the government as a whole. As they are resourceful, they still constructed and carried their own weapons for personal protection—the most notable of which is the b'hedda, a scooped, bladed weapon meant for use while hanging in trees. In the hands of a Dug, the b'hedda is particularly deadly.

Sociologists have theorized that the Dugs' insolent attitude is based in self-pity and insecurity, and that they mask this by trying to improve their status among their peers. Each Dug claims either a real or imagined hero or patriot in his or her ancestry, and the beads they wear in their ear fins are announcements of such heritage. Dugs also increase their own egos by insulting or degrading others.

Dug society is tribal, with various clans claiming territory as their own. These clans, however, are ruled by one Dug, a single king or queen who achieves his or her role through arranged combat. When the ruler dies, the heads of the various clans meet and fight for the empty ruling seat in a no-holds-barred (cheating allowed) battle; elimination occurs through incapacitation or death. Dug leaders who are past

DESIGNATION
Sentient

HOMEWORLD
Malastare

AVERAGE HEIGHT
1 meter

PRONUNCIATION
Dŭg

the age of fifty may not participate, but they can appoint someone to fight in their stead. This regulation hopefully allows the new leader to rule for a long time.

Once selected, the new ruler is treated with great respect and honor, and is usually the only member of the species who will not receive insults from other Dugs. Assassination and coups are surprisingly rare, most likely because while they are belligerent and grandstanding amid other species, among their own the Dugs recognize their betters.

Dugs are not remarkable galactic explorers, with many actually preferring to remain on Malastare among their own kind. Because of their experience with the Gran, they are xenophobic—or, rather, simply bigoted against other beings. If they are seen in galactic society at all, they are usually in groups of their own, and other species avoid their presence. Frequently these Dugs are criminals or risk-takers, simply out to increase their status among their own by degrading other races through thievery or swindling.

Unfortunately, Malastare has never regained the level of galactic prominence it enjoyed as a center of Podracing during the years of the Old Republic. Although the planet was conquered by the Yuuzhan Vong, it suffered little damage other than the destruction of its industrial base. Some small-scale rebuilding has taken place, such as the reestablishment of methane farms in the Malastare Wastes, which provide a small but steady income for the planet's citizens. This has allowed the Dugs to begin their recovery largely unaided by the Galactic Federation of Free Alliances while official attention has been directed toward worlds where more was lost or rendered uninhabitable. Malastare has sent representatives to the GFFA, but both the native Dugs and the resident Gran remain slightly resentful at their planet's perceived lack of attention by the Galactic Alliance.

NOTABLE APPEARANCE
Episode I: The Phantom Menace

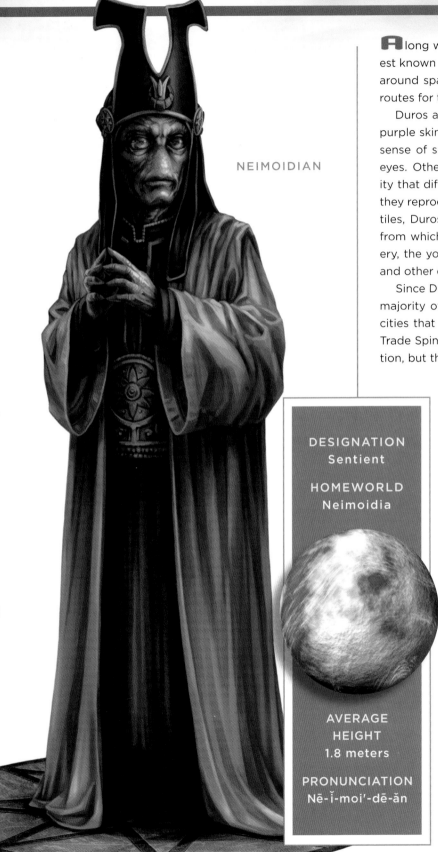

NEIMOIDIAN

Along with the Corellians, the Duros are among the oldest known spacefaring peoples. Their entire society evolved around spaceflight, and they helped blaze the hyperspace routes for trade throughout the galaxy.

Duros are tall, thin humanoids with gray-green or bluish purple skin, large red eyes, slit mouths, and no noses. Their sense of smell is conducted through glands beneath their eyes. Other than this, there is only one physical peculiarity that differentiates them from standard humanoids—how they reproduce. Since they are descended from ancient reptiles, Duros lay eggs in a specially prepared nesting room from which their young are born. In this comfortable nursery, the young are nurtured and educated by their parents and other extended-family members.

Since Duros culture centers on space travel, a significant majority of the Duros population lives in six space-station cities that orbit their planet, a Core world on the Corellian Trade Spine. On Duro, droids run farms to feed the population, but the rest of the surface is either polluted wasteland or overgrown jungle. Thousands of years ago, the world was lush and fertile, but after the Duros discovered space travel and left to dwell in orbit above Duro, they neglected the planet, leaving it to fall to ruin. The Empire finished the job, destroying the environment with contamination from its mining operations. During the later years of the New Republic era, however, the Yuuzhan Vong terraformed Duro, creating a rich and verdant ecosystem from which they could strike at Coruscant.

The Duros are incredibly technologically advanced, and build a great deal of the galaxy's spacefaring vessels in their shipyards. In fact, the shipbuilding industry dominates their economy and serves as the world's government. Those who wish to participate in politics are forced to purchase shares of stock in the corporation.

Culturally, Duros' longing for the skies drives many of their young people to become pilots or join starship crews. They constantly gravitate to different spaceports, from which they begin new journeys. To a Duros, the joy is not in where one goes, but in getting there, and they spend a lot of their time just "getting there."

Although one would characterize the Duros species as quiet, they are also very friendly, even-tempered, and love to tell stories. While

DESIGNATION
Sentient

HOMEWORLD
Neimoidia

AVERAGE HEIGHT
1.8 meters

PRONUNCIATION
Nē-ĭ-moi'-dē-ăn

they have generally pleasant dispositions, there is one way to upset them: to mistake them for Neimoidians. Although the Neimoidians are actually the same genetic species as Duros, having descended from ancient Duro colonists, the Duros are now loath to claim them as their own.

Since Neimoidians are the descendants of early Duros who settled the planet of Neimoidia in the Colonies region, they exhibit many physical attributes of their ancestors. Twenty-four thousand standard years of development in a distinct environment, however, have given them slight facial and body differences. Jawlines are lower; in addition, bodies are thinner and longer. While Duros have blue-purple skin with bright red eyes, Neimoidians have green-gray skin and dark red or pink eyes. These color differences have been attributed to specific chemicals in Neimoidia's atmosphere.

Like Duros, Neimoidians hatch from eggs and grow from a "grub" stage. But Neimoidian young are raised in communal hives from birth, and have access to limited amounts of food. Many die as a result, and those who survive learn to hoard their rations. By the time they leave the hives at age seven, they are extremely fearful of death and extraordinarily greedy.

It is for this reason that they are primarily a race of merchants, not warriors. Rather than fight in a battle where there exists a possibility of dying, Neimoidians will typically surrender, turning and running or sending others to battle for them. This was exemplified by the Trade Federation during the Clone Wars: Neimoidian leaders amassed an army of droids to serve as soldiers, pilots, and fighters.

Neimoidians are commonly seen wearing flowing robes and impressive headgear, every element of which has some special significance, indicating an individual's place in society. They are obsessed with status and influence. Extortion, bribery, and other forms of manipulation are not beyond Neimoidians in their quests for wealth, power, and prestige. They will always try to hide nefarious activities behind an altruistic façade, in order to protect themselves from embarrassment should their schemes fail. Their ability and need to handle funds contributed heavily to their rise to the top of the Trade Federation ranks, a commercial regulatory body that was particularly influential in the years leading up to the Clone Wars.

After centuries of running the Trade Federation, the Neimoidians' control of the organization subsided when the

DESIGNATION
Sentient
HOMEWORLD
Duro

AVERAGE
HEIGHT
1.7 meters
PRONUNCIATION
Dŏŏ'-rōs

DUROS

1.5

1.0

.5

0

Republic began taxing the trade routes they had established. This set them back a great deal, and their delicate financial control over the Federation began to crumble. After a particularly humiliating defeat at a trade blockade over the planet of Naboo, the Neimoidians lost whatever reputation they still possessed.

During the Imperial period, bereft of power and position, the Neimoidians turned to a desperate means for regaining their status. Seeing how respected their Duros cousins were in the galaxy, they made overtures to reunite with them as a culture—a proposition that was initially rebuffed. But with the rise of the New Republic, some Duros eventually allowed Neimoidians to work with them in corporate ventures, as they do handle money well. This contact seemed to have a reciprocal effect, influencing Neimoidian culture for the better.

NOTABLE APPEARANCE
DUROS: **Episode IV: A New Hope**
NEIMOIDIAN: **Episode I: The Phantom Menace**

ELOM/ELOMIN

Eloms are short, furry bipeds who reside in the cool desert caves of Elom, a planet located in the Outer Rim. They share the world with the Elomin, a humanoid species that lives aboveground.

With tough skin beneath thick, oily fur, and layers of fat that trap moisture in their bodies, Eloms are especially equipped for life in a harsh desert environment. Their hands and feet end in hard-tipped, hooked claws, optimal for digging; two prehensile toes on each foot can also be used to grip tools. Because they dwell in caves lit only by phosphorescent crystals, Eloms have excellent night vision, although their small, dark eyes cannot tolerate bright light.

Two sharp, rigid tusks protrude from Eloms' mouths, and they possess thick jowls for storing extra food. They are herbivores, primarily feeding on hard-shelled rockmelons and crystalweeds.

Their Elomin neighbors discovered the Eloms during a mining accident. The Elomin had been mining for lommite, an element used for shipbuilding, when the miners dug into an Elom nest, collapsing the cavern. The Elom immediately came to the rescue of the injured miners, earning the wary trust of their befuddled neighbors. After this inadvertent first meeting, the Old Republic soon recognized the Eloms as a sentient species, granting them the rights to the lands that they already inhabited.

This amused the Eloms. A peaceful, unsophisticated people with a strong sense of community, they simply continued living as they had for centuries, in townships known as cseria. Members of cseria would meet annually to resolve problems and disputes, as well as to trade goods. Although the Eloms accepted the Elomin as part of this community, their surface-dwelling neighbors felt that the Eloms did not fit within their "ordered" view of the galaxy, and so the two species remained distant until the Empire took over the mining operations on their planet, enslaving the Elomin and forcing them to mine lommite for the Imperial war machine.

During this time, the Eloms remained hidden from the Empire, but they saw the suffering of the Elomin. Horrified, groups of young Eloms decided to fight for the freedom of their world, liberating many Elomin slaves and bringing them to their safe cities hidden in the labyrinthine underground.

Since the world was liberated at the conclusion of the Galactic Civil War, the two species have become more integrated, and adolescent Eloms have frequently left to seek their fortunes among the stars. Unfortunately, many have also become criminals. Those Eloms who depart their homeworld do so because they are ambitious and intelligent, but they can often become lonely. Ignorant of the ways of the galaxy, they then fall in with the wrong crowd.

However, criminal behavior on the part of Eloms may also have other, more scientifically valid explanations. It is thought that Eloms who leave their home planet develop sociopathic tendencies as a result of physiological changes brought on by being away from fellow Eloms, and from their cave habitats. An alternative hypothesis is that Elom take on these tendencies psychologically through prolonged absence from their communities. This point of view has some evidence in the preferences of Eloms serving during the Galactic Civil War and in the New Republic military, who often sought to work directly with other members of their own species.

Meanwhile, the Eloms' neighbors, the Elomin, are tall, thin humanoids with pointed ears and four small horns topping their heads. They are believed by many anthropologists to be somehow related to the Zabrak, a spacefaring species that colonized numerous worlds in its extremely long and varied history.

When Old Republic scouts arrived on Elom about one hundred standard years before the dawn of Imperial rule, the Elomin were a relatively primitive people who employed slugthrowing weapons and combustion engines. Their lack of technology has prompted certain anthropologists to believe their inhabitation of Elom was the result of an accident—for if they are indeed descended from the Zabrak, the Elomin had long since forgotten how to build or create more modern technology. But contact with the Old Republic immediately influenced their industrial development, and they were soon constructing starships, repulsorlift vehicles, and high-end mining equipment. The Elomin allowed a shipbuilding corporation to establish itself on their world to mine lommite, an element used in making transparisteel for starships.

DESIGNATION
Sentient

HOMEWORLD
Elom

AVERAGE HEIGHT
Elom: 1.4 meters
Elomin: 1.6 meters

PRONUNCIATION
Ē'-lŏm
Ē-lō-mĭn'

Culturally, the Elomin aspire to find or create order in all things. Originally, they had no notion that another, completely different species might share their world. Even when an expedition uncovered cave formations in a distant desert region that showed evidence of being inhabited, the Elomin refused to accept the implications and omitted these findings from their reports. Only when a group of them came face-to-face with Eloms during the mining accident did they finally recognize the existence of their neighbors.

Elomin art reflects order, in that it is repetitive and mathematically structured. Their architecture is predictable and well thought out, as are the layouts of their cities; nothing they construct or create is left to chance.

As such, like the Eloms, Elomin have some difficulty dealing with other peoples, whom they often view as perpetrators of chaos or unpredictable variables. Old Republic representatives discovered that the Elomin had difficulty working in integrated space crews but excelled at navigation and piloting duties, perceiving the universe as a logical, organized puzzle and endeavoring to bring the pieces to their proper places.

After the fall of the Empire, the Elomin rewarded their neighbors with a level of unprecedented acceptance into their communities, as the Eloms had helped many of them escape Imperial slavery. Yielding some of their sense of order to accept the kindly Eloms as helpers and fellow residents was a significant but necessary step for their growth as a people. Eloms now work within the Elomin cities, helping run businesses and lommite-mining corporations. Some Eloms have actually moved from their caves completely to take up residences aboveground. As different as these two species are, they have become quite fond and protective of each other overall—an encouraging sign for the rest of the civilized galaxy as they move forward together into the future.

NOTABLE APPEARANCE
ELOM: **Episode VI: Return of the Jedi**
ELOMIN: **Heir to the Empire (novel)**

EOPIE

Eopies are quadruped pack mammals native to Tatooine. They are proboscidians, with hinged skulls supporting flexible, elongated snouts and sharp incisors in their jaws. While not as frequently employed as the faster-moving ronto, bantha, or dewback (all animals capable of carrying heavier loads), the eopie's sure-footedness and untiring steadfastness have made it a popular beast of burden on Tatooine,

3.0

2.0

1.5

1.0

.5

0

particularly in the Mos Espa region. It can be argued that overall it is Tatooine's most useful indigenous animal.

Eopies have several physical features that contribute to their excellence as work beasts in the arid wastes of Tatooine. First, their three-toed feet make them extremely sturdy, and their foot pads expand upon impact for shock absorption. Eopies rarely stumble in the sandy or rocky terrain, and are so well balanced that they are nearly impossible to topple, even when carrying heavy loads. Their knees are greatly calloused to protect their joints against the desert sand. Eopies also require little water, going for weeks without it if necessary. Herbivores, their snouts are ideal for rooting for sand lichens, their primary source of nourishment, and for eliminating potential weeds from moisture-farming lands, as such weeds will drain much-needed moisture and cut down on profits.

Eopie hides are very tough, resilient to sun and heat. Covered with thin sparse hair, the leather tanned from their hides is highly durable, and locals like to use it for making saddles or clothing to resist the twin suns' rays, as it reflects light rather than retaining it.

Although they are frequently grumpy, these creatures are fairly even-tempered. Unlike rontos, eopies rarely, if ever, startle, and will study unusual situations with a sense of interest or curiosity. They will only flee if they are personally threatened; otherwise they tend to remain calm and still, even during noisy or disruptive events. However, on the rare occasion that an eopie is surprised, it will spit its undigested stomach contents at people nearby. Fortunately, this does not happen often, and thus the creatures' reliability and stability is highly prized—for while they may be slow, one can always be sure of eopies' fortitude in fearful situations. They are completely unfazed by sandstorms, for example, keeping a steady gait in the most fierce and biting of desert winds.

Eopies are very social animals, congregating in large herds of twenty or more. They gather in herds as a means of protecting their young, which are especially vulnerable to the harsh desert environment. Although able to walk within minutes of birth, young eopies are not able to bear the heavy loads that their parents can and are therefore less valuable to their owners. In addition, eopie babies require food more often than adults, and are more at risk from predators, so they require much attention and some measure of protection. If well cared for, eopies mature to adulthood in approximately six standard years, and can live for as many

as ninety. Eopie mares have one baby a season, and are capable of bearing young for decades, although they will not conceive in consecutive seasons. The purchase of one or two quality breeding mares is sufficient for most farms to start establishing their own herds. Toward the end of their lives when they are no longer able to carry heavy loads, eopies continue to serve Tatooine farmers by eating the desert weeds that leach moisture from their crop, and are also popular as pets. Many settlers will give their children an eopie from the family's herd in order to teach them responsibility, and to prepare them for their own future lives as farmers.

Even with the requirement that an owner must have more than one eopie in order for the creatures to thrive, eopies are the least expensive of Tatooine's beasts of burden to keep. The adults eat little and require only a modest amount of attention to stay healthy, and they provide more benefits than just what they can carry. For instance, in addition to their service as pack animals, eopies are sometimes bred for their meat. Their flesh is extremely tender and tasty, and therefore is a staple for residents of Tatooine. Eopie females also provide a nourishing milk that is renowned for its nutritional benefits to humanoid infants and toddlers. The milk does spoil quickly if not kept cold, and farmers who own eopies must invest in adequate refrigeration machines.

The usefulness of eopies has led some entrepreneurs to attempt to export them to other planets. Unfortunately, these efforts have met with mixed success. Eopies are able to thrive on other desert planets and also on some overly warm worlds, but it has become apparent that they have evolved such that they biologically need heat. Temperate planets necessitate slightly more care for eopies; they must be housed in enclosed, heated holding pens at night and when temperatures fall seasonally, for instance. Eopies are not able to survive outdoors on colder planets at all, even if provided with adequate sustenance and attention. These eopies appear to starve to death, suggesting that their bodies cannot properly metabolize food in lower temperatures, although officially this has not yet been scientifically tested.

DESIGNATION
Nonsentient

HOMEWORLD
Tatooine

AVERAGE
LENGTH
2–3 meters

PRONUNCIATION
Ē-ö′-pē

NOTABLE APPEARANCE
Episode I: The Phantom Menace

EWOK

Ewoks are small, fur-covered, ursine beings who inhabit the forest moon of Endor, an Outer Rim world circling a gas giant system near the area of the galaxy known as the Unknown Regions. While Imperial propaganda depicted them as having been wiped out after the Battle of Endor, the intelligent, primitive Ewoks still live in sizable communities in their wooded home, a lush environment alive with thick vegetation and myriad forms of wildlife. The world's low axial tilt and its regular orbit around the gas giant create a temperate climate for most of the moon, and three-hundred-meter-tall trees cover many regions and are central to the landscape. For this reason, they are significant to Ewok culture and religion.

Though Ewoks suffer from limited eyesight, these small creatures have an excellent sense of smell that more than compensates. They are accomplished hunters, and, being omnivores, they also gather food from the plants that surround them. In some cases they have been known to mistakenly eat sentient beings, assuming they were simply large game to be captured. However, they can usually be convinced to put away their cooking implements after some conversation and a little bit of luck.

While they forage and hunt, Ewoks are extremely alert and easily startled. Many carnivorous creatures inhabit the forest moon, and thus Ewoks are always prepared for an attack. Some researchers have noted that they seem to possess a "sixth sense"—the ability to perceive threats to their community far in advance. It has been likened to some Jedi Force talents, although only a few Ewoks have shown the ability to truly manipulate this mysterious power.

Ewoks are curious, good-natured creatures who value community, family, and friendship. Their culture is gender-based, with the males serving as hunters, warriors, chieftains, and shamans, and the females acting as gatherers and domestics, rearing and educating their young. Music and dancing are part of everyday life; in fact, Ewoks use music to communicate with other villages via rhythmic drumbeats. As news echoes through the ancient trees, it imbues their environment with an aura of extra life.

Though their culture is rich in historic lore, art, and music, Ewoks are primitive, wearing only hoods adorned with bones and feathers for decoration and to indicate status in the community. They learn quickly, however, and when exposed to technology, they will figure it out easily—sometimes after an initial bout of jitters and mistakes. Few have yet ventured into space, and when they do it is typically by tagging along with star pilots or crews that visit their planet. Among these few are a select number who have learned modern technology enough to be useful on space crews.

Ewoks have developed no technology of their own beyond standard woodworking tools and rudimentary weapons. But they possess a flair for invention with their primitive resources—creating traps and snares that can be highly effective even against great technological threats. Their ingenuity was key to the Rebel Alliance's defeat of the Empire at the Battle of Endor, and if given leave to explore and learn the ways of technology, they will frequently become adept.

The language of this species is expressive yet simple, and can be learned and spoken by humans. Because the verbal nuances are similar, Ewoks can also learn to speak several human languages. And through their exposure to more and more offworlders since the Battle of Endor, many homebound Ewoks have taken to speaking to visitors in a pidgin form of Ewok-Basic.

Ewoks live in tribal clusters in villages built of mud, thatch, and wood, normally suspended several levels above the forest floor. Located at the center of the villages are the largest structures, including the home of the tribal chief, with the dwellings of tribe members arranged in clusters at the outskirts. Intricate walkways serve to join together residences and village squares, and stairs, rope ladders, and swinging vines help the Ewoks to get quickly from the forest floor

to their homes in the trees. Some Ewoks also reside on Endor's lakes, in floating villages constructed on stilts. Ewoks are frequently attacked by angry Phlogs, the giant Gorax, and the fearsome Duloks because of their small size, so they are often very hesitant about venturing into new territory or leaving their villages unguarded.

The Ewok people are suspicious and cautious, yet fierce fighters, brave and loyal to their tribe. This is also evidenced in their religion, which emphasizes the importance of home, family, and the trees surrounding them. A new tree is planted for each Ewok at birth, and is considered that being's "life tree." Ewoks believe that their spirits pass into these trees when they die. Moreover, Ewoks regard these trees as their guardians, and in times of crisis, the tribal leaders will commune with the oldest and wisest trees, seeking guidance. The trees, they believe, are intelligent, long-lived beings who watch over them, and in a reciprocal manner they must safeguard the trees. This belief was one of the main reasons that they aided the Rebels in their fight against the Empire, as they felt that the Empire posed a threat to every aspect of their environment.

War is not common among the Ewoks, however. Although they exist in tribes and remain fiercely loyal to them, Ewoks will greet other tribes with warmth and goodwill, as long as they act with honor and respect. They will even accept outsiders into their tribe if the visitors demonstrate a familial loyalty to them (if the strangers haven't already been mistaken for dinner). Although as skilled at building weaponry as they are at constructing their elaborate villages, arms are mainly kept handy to defend against outside threats, rather than against one another.

Because religion is so important to Ewok society, the village shaman governs a tribe side by side with the ruling chieftain. The shaman interprets signs to guide the chieftain in his decisions, and their belief system includes references to a living energy similar to the Force that feeds the trees and likewise strengthens and guides the Ewoks.

DESIGNATION
Sentient

HOMEWORLD
Moon of Endor

AVERAGE HEIGHT
1.2 meters

PRONUNCIATION
Ē'-wŏk

NOTABLE APPEARANCE
Episode VI: Return of the Jedi

FALLEEN

The Falleen are a reptilian humanoid species that occupy the Falleen star system in the Mid Rim of the galaxy. They are a handsome species, exotic in appearance, with scaled, blue-green skin and a spiny sharp ridge down the center of their backs. This ridge is indicative of their reptilian nature, as is their ability to change skin color and lung capacity, enabling them to remain underwater for long periods of time. Female Falleen look slightly different from their male counterparts in that the spinal ridge is smaller, their skin is often lighter, and the ability to change color is somewhat less active than in their male counterparts.

Unlike most reptilian species, Falleen can and will grow hair on their heads. The females like to wear their tresses long and adorned with combs and beads, while the males display their hair tied up in a single braid or topknot. In recent years, some females have taken to wearing topknots, in an effort to attain the same elevated status as the males.

Falleen are considered aesthetically pleasing to most humanoids. Although their physique is well defined and attractive, this admiration is not solely due to their appearance. Like Zeltrons, Falleen can exude pheromones at will and use them to control and manipulate the perceptions of others. Falleen pheromones are actually so powerful that they can produce an almost hypnotic effect in other humanoid species, and these manipulations have been known to take on lustful overtones. Pheromones may also be exercised between Falleen as communications tools, although they will always suspect duplicity and remain disciplined to resist the suggestions of others. A Falleen's skin color shifts with the release of these pheromones. Falleen utilize their ability to change skin color as a covert weapon, reverting from their normal shades of gray-green to red or orange, for example, in order to exude an essence of confidence or mastery. In addition to their pheromones, Falleen can exude allelochemical transmitters to produce specific emotional reactions in other species with similar body chemistry, such as fear, desire, anger, doubt, and confusion.

What also makes the Falleen species attractive is the aura of mystery in which they have wrapped themselves. They are not a talkative people, and tend to be distant, maintaining a great deal of control over their physiology. Culturally, they remain stoic, and shun outward signs of passion and anger. The Falleen are not an unemotional people; quite the contrary. They are known for intense feelings, beliefs, and emotions. Falleen simply find public displays of feelings, particulary to non-Falleen, as extremely primitive and unsophisticated. As a result, the Falleen regard beings who do express their emotions, such as humans, to be inferior.

While the Falleen have employed space travel technology for generations, they rarely venture to the stars. Because they consider the Falleen system to be a bastion of culture and sophistication, they prefer to manage their own affairs on their homeworld, rather than deal with offworlders. Their music, sculpture, art, and architecture are all a source of pride for them, although such things are very rarely shared with outsiders.

Falleen society is feudal, with noble houses ruling lower classes of artisans, technical workers, general workers, and slaves. Monarch rulers govern their kingdoms, caring more for internal political intrigues and displays of wealth than wasting resources by waging war against one another. These kings maintain commerce with each other and occasionally argue over boundaries, although such disputes are never taken to extremes. Thus, for the most part, the Falleen remain a peaceful people.

The Falleen are a long-lived species, living 250 standard years on the average, although some healthy Falleen have been known to survive for up to 400 years. Young Falleen nobles will sometimes spend part of their adolescent years on what is called a pilgrimage, which is basically a journey to tour the galaxy and experience all it has to offer. Most of them return to utilize what they have learned in order to govern their kingdoms when the time comes for them to ascend to the throne.

DESIGNATION
Sentient

HOMEWORLD
Falleen

AVERAGE HEIGHT
1.6 meters

PRONUNCIATION
Fäl-lēn'

One such Falleen was Xizor, who arrived back from his pilgrimage to find his entire family dead. The Sith Lord Darth Vader had ordered a biological weapons laboratory to be built in Xizor's home city, and a lab accident contaminated the area, allowing the release of a flesh-rotting bacterium for which there was no cure. Subsequently, in order to protect the planet's other inhabitants and to ease his own embarrassment, Vader ordered that the city and its two hundred thousand beings be burned to ashes.

From that point on, Xizor had a deep desire for revenge against the Dark Lord. Xizor hid his family history, departing his world to seek this retribution. He joined the Black Sun crime syndicate and quickly rose to power, seizing the opportunity created when most of Black Sun's upper-level personnel were killed by Darth Maul. Eventually, Xizor became what was arguably the third most powerful being in the galaxy, after the Emperor and Darth Vader—an unlikely accomplishment for a nonhuman during the Empire's rule. Xizor plotted to kill Vader, take his place, and then that of the Emperor. His ambitions, however, led to his death at the hands of the man he hated most, when he proved threatening to Vader's son, Luke Skywalker.

One more environmental disaster after the one that killed Xizor's family finally convinced the Falleen to remove themselves from galactic involvement. An orbital turbolaser strike laid waste to a small city and the surrounding countryside, and the Imperial Navy cut off system contact. For this reason, during the rule of the New Republic, the Falleen were rarely seen traveling outside their system, and displayed no desire to join the fledgling government. Following the invasion of their planet by the Yuuzhan Vong, there has been even less contact with this exotic species.

NOTABLE APPEARANCE
Shadows of the Empire (novel)

FOSH

The Fosh are a mysterious avian species that most scientists believe hail from the Corporate Sector of the galaxy. They are an extremely rare species and are believed to be nearly, if not in fact, extinct, as in recent years only one Fosh has actually been observed in person. It is possible that the species was among those exterminated during the reign of Emperor Palpatine. Much of what can be reported is reconstructed from the historical records of various other cultures and societies, and from experiences with the infamous Fosh Jedi, Vergere.

These bird-like people have thin torsos and delicate arms with four-fingered hands that appear to have evolved from wings. Considering the degree of development in the bones of their arms, it is

1.0

.5

0

unlikely that Fosh have possessed the ability to fly for tens of thousands of years. Fosh's delicate frames make them extremely vulnerable to physical blows, so they tend to remain clear of such confrontations, though they can apparently defend themselves quite well. The weakest part of their body is the neck, which they will reflexively guard during combat.

Two corkscrew antennae adorn the top of their heads, the use of which remains a mystery. Their skulls are further crowned with a feather-lined ridge that changes color depending on their mood. Green indicates inquisitiveness, thoughtfulness, or amusement; orange displays happiness; and gray is anger, disgust, irritation, or gravity. Their faces are concave, and are highlighted with slanted eyes and soft whiskers. Like many birds, their leg joints bend backward, and their flay-toed feet give them remarkable jumping abilities.

It is believed that one of the most unusual traits of the Fosh is the chemical makeup of their tears. Female Fosh, in particular, have lachrymal glands that enable them to alter their tears and produce several kinds of pheromonal substances that affect the males of their species during mating. And yet, through the Force, the Jedi Vergere had such control over her tear production that she could create a wide variety of chemical liquids, be it a substance that healed disease or a highly effective poison. As a curative, Vergere's tears were more powerful than bacta, alleviating diseases that the latter could not.

The Fosh are a very private people who prefer to remain unnoticed as they make their way in the galaxy. They speak little, preferring to focus on listening, but when they do talk it is on issues of great importance. They also choose to frequently conceal themselves, remaining hidden in large crowds or in secreted spots, and some sociologists believe part of the reason that people assume there are so few Fosh is because they are rarely seen. Instead of being limited in population, they may simply *seem* rare because they would rather stay clear of the public eye.

One characteristic that is evident from the writings of other species regarding the Fosh is their preoccupation with political intrigue. Similar to Bothans in this regard, Fosh are fascinated with creating plots within plots in order to attain complex or even very simple goals. They tend to be indirect in their requests toward others, speaking in a way that can purposely confuse or send an individual down the wrong path of thinking. They seem to find some great amusement

DESIGNATION
Sentient

HOMEWORLD
Unknown

AVERAGE
HEIGHT
1.3 meters

PRONUNCIATION
Fŏsh

in watching others chase after phantom threats, or in causing utter confusion in various species.

Theirs is a very self-serving and self-occupied people who act with only their own best interests at heart. While they may interact with others in a way that seems generous or friendly, there is nearly always an ulterior motive to their behavior. Unlike Bothans, however, Fosh are not paranoid of other species, and in fact they do not believe the victims of their double-talk capable of figuring out their plans or foiling their plots. The Fosh are, in effect, bigoted—believing themselves intellectually superior to others, and manipulating them as objects of amusement. They are wise enough, though, to respect most species for the dangers that they can present, and are vigilant in their dealings with them.

One example of Fosh manipulation is the way Vergere skillfully maneuvered her way through the brutal Yuuzhan Vong hierarchy, managing to survive for decades within their presence, until they reached the Core Worlds of the galaxy. Though some of her behavior may have called her motivations into question, much of it is believed to be cultural—or perhaps her cultural upbringing resulted in her acceptance of Yuuzhan Vong doctrine much more easily. Either way, she utilized her wiles and conversational subterfuge to simultaneously train and manipulate Jedi Knight Jacen Solo, causing him to seek out alternate Force traditions and even question the existence of the dark side of the Force, arguing that there is no dark or light, only one's intentions. Some speculate that this may have been her goal from the moment she first encountered him, and while many initially believed her death toward the end of the Yuuzhan Vong invasion to be a self-sacrifice, in light of the revelation of her influence, her sacrificial act could very well have been a self-serving one—a penultimate deed of manipulation that would further maneuver a growing uncertainty in the young Jacen Solo.

NOTABLE APPEARANCE
Traitor (novel)

GAMORREAN

Gamorreans are large, green-skinned, porcine creatures from the preindustrial Outer Rim planet Gamorr, known for their brutal strength and warrior-like nature. They are bulky beings with pig-like snouts, jowls, and tusks, and the males have horns on their heads. Members of this species communicate with one another through a series of grunts, oinks, and squeals—a complex language that suits their war-like sensibility. Although they can understand offworld languages, the formation of their voice boxes makes it impossible for them to pronounce words in any language other than their own. The exception to this is the Gamorrean Voort "Piggy" saBinring. After being genetically enhanced to have exceptionally high intelligence, saBinring joined the New Republic as a pilot and was fitted with a high-tech voice box that enabled him to speak to other pilots in his squadron.

The Gamorrean clan-based matriarchal culture centers on war and the preparation for war. In their society, males are taught the arts of combat and weaponry from early childhood, and as adolescents, they will immediately into battle. Females, on the other hand, take care of all the other necessities of life—they hunt, fish, weave, make weapons, and run businesses. They also form the clan's governing body as the Council of Matrons. These women make the decisions of when to go to war, and against whom. Generally, Gamorrean women consider Gamorrean males, and males in general, to be of lower intelligence and not to be trusted with decision making of any kind.

The campaigning season, or "war season" as it is sometimes called, begins in early spring and runs through late autumn on Gamorr. During these months, the males of the clans will wage war upon one another at the behest of their matrons—attacking tribal homes and bringing back the spoils to please their females. The males who are the most successful and valiant win the right to choose any females they desire for mates. Those males who do not succeed are often killed in battle, and this becomes the culture's own form of natural selection. Ordinarily, this practice might make for an imbalance in the ratio of males to females in a society, but reliable population estimates conclude that twenty males are born for every female Gamorrean.

Gamorreans take great pleasure in slaughter and brutality. It is for this reason, as well as for their brute strength, that they make ideal mercenaries and bounty hunters. They are so enthusiastic about violence that they are even willing to serve as slaves if it gives them more opportunities to fight.

Although many Gamorreans work as hired muscle for offworld employers, there are two stipulations that must be met before they will agree to labor for someone. First, the employer, or the employer's representative, must fight them or one of their peers; second, the contract must then be signed in blood. Evidence of a typical Gamorrean's service to an employer was the presence of Gamorreans among the guard at Jabba the Hutt's palace on Tatooine during the Imperial era. Having been sent by Jabba to secure Gamorreans to work for him, Han Solo and Chewbacca found themselves faced with the possibility of personally battling the Gamorreans. Fortunately, Solo and Chewbacca were traveling with a group of Nikto already in Jabba's employ, who were all too glad to serve as Jabba's champions. After some difficult and somewhat bloody negotiations, the contract was signed.

Once these two conditions are met, the Gamorreans serve their employer with unwavering loyalty, though they will retreat from foes who prove to be more powerful than themselves. Showing fear or running as an act of self-preservation is not considered cowardice against an indomitable foe—the species considers such reactions natural. True cowardice, to a Gamorrean, is shirking from a fight against an equal or subordinate. Gamorreans will usually kill any fellow warrior who shows such a weakness.

When Gamorreans engage in combat, they prefer traditional weapons such as swords, battle-axes, and heavy maces. The arg'garok, a traditional Gamorrean war ax, is especially prized. This weapon is engineered for wielders of extraordinary strength and low centers of gravity,

DESIGNATION
Sentient

HOMEWORLD
Gamorr

AVERAGE HEIGHT
1.8 meters

PRONUNCIATION
Gă-mŏr'-rē-ăn

and non-Gamorreans can handle one only with great difficulty. Gamorreans have learned to use blasters over the years, but high-tech ranged weapons are not implemented in the battles on Gamorr, and are considered cowardly. Still, Gamorreans employed as mercenaries often carry imported weapons and are well versed in their use, frequently spending the credits that they earn to buy more technologically advanced weaponry. However, the most advanced arms they might possess would typically amount to a high-tech vibroblade or specialty heads for their axes, such as ones containing ultrasonic generators. They do take up space travel, though, and have even colonized another world known as Pzob. They keep their ships simple, providing only the basic amenities for their crew, as well as protective shields and heavy blasters and torpedoes that serve as a means of self-defense.

While the Gamorrean people are not known for having a soft, sensitive side, they do exhibit an unusual affection when it comes to their morrts. Morrts are furry parasites that feed on blood and other biological materials. They attach themselves to a Gamorrean's body, and remain there for years at a time. Gamorreans look upon morrts lovingly as pets, and prestigious Gamorreans are often seen with twenty or more attached to their bodies at one time. They are also loving with their children and mates, and signs of affection can vacillate between a warm, tackling hug to a punch in the snout. In fact, knocking one's spouse unconscious is considered a prelude to mating, although if this is the intention, the initiator makes sure to have smelling salts on his or her person.

With Gamorrean society organized into clans, loyalty to such groups and their matrons is paramount. Even if they are contracted to a specific employer, Gamorreans will maintain their family pride and loyalty to the point of picking fights with those of other clans who serve the same employer. A wise boss will hire only from one clan to prevent such infighting in the ranks. On Gamorr, the clans have never united under a common banner of government, though they do have regular meetings to discuss trade or threaten war. Because they lack a unified political voice, their homeworld of Gamorr does not have representation in the Galactic Federation of Free Alliances.

NOTABLE APPEARANCE
Episode VI: Return of the Jedi

GAND

Gands are beings believed to be of an insect genus that inhabit a world also known as Gand, located in the Outer Rim near the Centrality. They are short humanoids identified in part by their three-fingered hands and durable exoskeleton. Because Gands refuse to be studied, their common physiological traits largely remain a mystery to xenobiologists. Nearly a dozen different physical varieties of the species have been recorded, however, through encounters with them throughout the galaxy.

The planet Gand's ecology is extremely inhospitable for other humanoid species because of giant ammonia clouds that fill the atmosphere. To account for this, all Gands have a very unique respiratory system, and most Gands do not breathe at all. They exchange gases in their body by in-

gesting food and passing waste gases through their powerful exoskeletons. There are some Gands who breathe, but they only inhale ammonia, and when off-planet they must wear a special suit with a breathing apparatus that supplies them with this ammonia in specifically regulated amounts. Nonbreathing Gands do not require such suits, but sometimes wear them anyway while traveling offworld to maintain anonymity. Scientists do not know if the ammonia-breathing Gand species is older than the nonbreathing variety and represents an evolutionary adaptation, or if it is simply another coexisting species.

For most members of the Gand species, only a minimal amount of sleep is required to function normally. As this is common throughout the Gand varieties, scientists believe this may be a result of culture rather than breeding. Some sociologists suppose that the trait is really due to the culture's values, as remaining awake and aware is a valuable skill to hunters and findsmen—one that must be honed and learned throughout a lifetime.

The planet Gand's most notable export is the skills of its findsmen. Findsmen are religious hunters who locate their prey by interpreting omens sent to them in the course of divine rituals. While many offworlders disavow the power of findsmen's rituals, their accuracy can be unsettling to the casual observer. Some findsman sects require that their pupils go through chemical baths or genetic tampering that cause knob-like growths to appear on their chitinous exoskeletons. Findsmen use these four- to five-centimeter growths as weapons during hand-to-hand combat.

Throughout the galaxy, findsmen are hired as security advisers, bodyguards, bounty hunters, investigators, and, on occasion, assassins. They can be identified by their use of the shockprod staff, which appears as a normal staff ending in a V-shaped pair of electrically charged prods. Findsmen who have achieved some level of accomplishment can sometimes earn the right to carry rare Gand dischargers, which are staffs capable of stunning or killing an opponent.

The Gand culture is complex. They are considered by most offworlders to be the humblest of people because they are usually soft-spoken and polite. This characteristic is a result of societal demands that an individual's identity be earned. They primarily refer to themselves in the third person; then, depending on what status they've gained, Gands may or may not refer to themselves by name. A Gand who has only reached the first level of status would refer to him- or herself as simply *Gand.* Once a Gand has made a major accomplishment in life, either at home or abroad, that individual may use the family name; only when Gands have become masters of some skill or achieved high praise or recognition may they finally use their first as well as their last name.

Even then, Gands very rarely refer to themselves in the first person. Only those who have become janwuine—in other words, those who have been judged to have accomplished the greatest feats of heroism or who have completed extremely difficult tasks—may use self-identifying pronouns

such as *I* or *me.* Doing so presumes that they are so prominent, everyone knows their name. Such an honor must be bestowed by the ruetsavii, a group of Gands who travel the galaxy verifying the deeds of findsmen. Dispatched by the Elders of Gand, the ruetsavii have achieved renown through their own actions and are considered able to judge the deeds of others.

If Gands believe they have acted wrongly, they feel that such an action reduces any accomplishments that they have made in their life. When this happens, they use "name reduction" to show penitence. For example, Gands who have previously earned the right to the family name might revert to the use of *Gand* in order to gain the forgiveness of someone they have offended. There have been very few Gands who have committed such unspeakable acts that they leave the society entirely. When this happens, they must discard their culture, and their culture discards them. After this, they may refer to themselves in any way they wish. For some Gands, failing to achieve the status of a findsman can cause them to abandon their culture.

While many Gands do leave their world, as findsmen or in disgrace, non-Gands are seldom, if ever, welcomed on the planet Gand itself. Outsiders usually get no closer than one of the orbiting space stations. If they are allowed on the surface, they must remain in a specified area called the Alien Quarters, centered in the spaceports. The very few who have been allowed into the culture itself have done so under the sponsorship of janwuine or the ruetsavii. A sponsored non-Gand would be accepted into society as hinwuine—a being of standing. When the New Republic Gand pilot Ooryl Qrygg was granted janwuine status, his fellow pilots were afforded a rare honor and invited to Gand to mark the occasion, although it is unclear whether they were also made hinwuine. Scientists made limited attempts to interview some of the hinwuine, but so far, no requests for such dialogues have been granted. It may be that to speak of their time on Gand would be considered a serious insult to their hosts.

DESIGNATION
Sentient

HOMEWORLD
Gand

AVERAGE HEIGHT
1.6 meters

PRONUNCIATION
Gănd

NOTABLE APPEARANCE
Episode V: The Empire Strikes Back

GEONOSIAN

Geonosians are the only advanced life-form native to the barren, rock-laden world of Geonosis, located only a parsec away from the famed desert world of Tatooine in the Outer Rim. Geonosians are a winged, flying insectoid race sporting elongated faces, multijointed limbs, and a hard, brown chitinous exoskeleton that protects them from the radiation bombardment of a nearby star that has rendered their world a red-tinted desert wasteland. One subspecies of this group is wingless, and its members serve the flying species as drone workers.

Like most insects, Geonosians begin life as eggs laid by a queen. Once a pupa hatches, it is trained and acculturated to serve in its assigned role in society. Within the warrior hives, for instance, soldier pupae grow to adult size quickly, and are ready to fight by the age of six. Adult Geonosian warriors have vestigial wings that enable them to hover for short intervals, while younger, lighter warriors can fly greater distances and are used for scouting missions.

A ring of small metal-rich asteroids encircles their planet. These asteroids are an enormous resource for raw materials used in the weapons manufacturing process, an activity that has made the Geonosians infamous. The asteroid ring is a mixed blessing, however, as it can also serve as an excellent cover for corporate spies entering the world's atmosphere, who are hidden by frequently falling asteroids and meteor showers. In addition, a dense, high-altitude fog enshrouds a large majority of the planet, creating almost night-like conditions that can last for weeks. As a result of this, and of the barrage of radiation, many of the creatures on the world are bioluminescent, and most—even the Geonosians—remain underground despite their resistance to the environmental conditions.

The Geonosian people were well known in the pre-Imperial era for their construction of battle droids, ships, and weapons technology, the use of which peaked during the Clone Wars. They first created battle droids for the Trade Federation, then expanded their enterprise to supply a growing Separatist movement led by Count Dooku. As such, except for those visiting on business, Geonosis is not a popular world for tourists.

Geonosian society is divided into a class system that evolved over thousands of years from the hive mentality of the species' insect ancestors. It is separated into two levels: the aristocrats and the warriors. Those who are flightless have no caste at all, and are considered without any value save for their use in menial labor. The workers run the manufacturing operations, and the warriors fight and defend the interests of the aristocrats. Although the warriors are fighters, they are not members of a standing army.

A subcaste of warrior pilots are trained to require no sleep. From infancy, they are paired with a specific flight computer with whom they build a unique, integrated rapport. And yet, while all of these warriors are well taught and intelligent, they lack the ingenuity found in many other sentient species, and can be easily defeated in battle by another group possessing superior creativity and wits.

The aristocrats rule and command all the operations on Geonosis. These nobles feel it is their right to govern while thousands of workers labor to serve their every whim. It was the noble class that envisioned and sparked the construction of the complex, organic architectural realm in which they all live. Based on structures built by their insect forebears in the wild, the Geonosians created refined, spire-like buildings that are highly impressive to most outsiders. Geonosians reside within these organic-looking structures in hive communities.

The worker drones, meanwhile, have almost no rights, and serve their masters without question. Workers are genetically altered to serve in three distinct subcastes in order to fill the many roles within the hive, namely those of servants, laborers, and farmers.

The Geonosian civilization is a bloodthirsty one, enthusiastically encouraging execution in gladiatorial arenas. Sociologists believe the harshness of Geonosians' environment, coupled with the rigid structure of their caste system, led to this form of barbaric cultural development. They seem to find brutality amusing, as thousands of Geonosians congregate in execution arenas to watch condemned individuals die gruesome deaths in the teeth of fearsome beasts or at the hands of other doomed prisoners.

The aristocracy thinks nothing of executing worker drones in the arena, particularly if they prove problematic to

the system. For most drones, doing their work and living in their communal environment is all they can hope for. Worker drones have no personal living space or possessions of their own, and to conserve resources, the ruling class may order drones into suspended animation or sleep stasis when their services are not required. Geonosian workers of higher intelligence use gladiatorial combat as their one means to move up in status and possibly escape their plight in the service of their masters. Considered aberrations, warrior Geonosians enter the arena willingly. There, they are often pitted in fatal games against additional Geonosians, other sentient species, or savage creatures. If the worker wins a battle, or lives to see another day, he or she is often granted life and exiled, but may find refuge at the Galard Stables. Sometime a victorious Geonosian may even move up in status, receiving acclaim and financial rewards.

Another role that workers can earn, even those who are flightless, is to serve as a picador in the gladiatorial arena, using energy pikes to control and goad vicious creatures into attacking combatants. They are also responsible for removing any bodies that are not devoured. Either way, if they earn enough prestige and wealth, they may be able to escape Geonosis entirely.

Even so, those Geonosians who can leave their world rarely do, because the hive mentality is so strong. Those who depart often show a certain amount of contempt for other species, and they cannot disconnect themselves from the hive mentality. It is a culturewide sense of xenophobia that often leads them into conflict with outsiders. Those Geonosians seen around the galaxy usually work together in groups, and send home the fruits of their labors to their hives on Geonosis.

While the Geonosians have accomplished masterful feats of engineering and managed massive construction efforts, they appear to most observers to be rather simple-minded. Many Geonosians were, in fact, easily absorbed into the Kilik hive mind during the Colony's recent expansion across the galaxy. Sociologists theorize, however, that this outcome, too, was a result of their insect ancestry: much of the Geonosians' collective intelligence is considered to be held by the leadership of the hive, a mentality that is ingrained from infancy.

DESIGNATION
Sentient

HOMEWORLD
Geonosis

AVERAGE
HEIGHT
1.75 meters

PRONUNCIATION
Gē-ō-nō'-sē-ăn

NOTABLE APPEARANCE
Episode II: Attack of the Clones

GIVIN

Givin are a humanoid species who have the appearance of animated skeletons—and their frames are indeed located on the outsides of their bodies. Their appendages are long, thin, and tubular, and they possess large, triangular eye sockets and frowning mouths that often give the impression that they are in pain. Their frames do not operate like those of standard humanoids, in that they carry their arms out from their bodies in a manner that is reminiscent of a marionette. They walk forward supporting themselves on strange, turned-out feet.

This bizarre exoskeleton setup allows Givin to survive in a vacuum. The impermeable outer bone plates of their skeleton form a type of organic vacuum suit connected by flexible membranes that seal off all orifices and openings. In order to use this evolutionary peculiarity, Givin must enter a state of hibernation, requiring them to gorge on large quantities of nutritious foods in advance. While sealed in their exoskeletons, Givin do not respire, instead producing energy from stored fats. In addition, Givin have developed a means of physiologically sensing barometric pressure, enabling them to accurately anticipate certain tidal changes that necessitate their hibernation.

All of these natural defensive traits are tailored to the unpredictable nature of the environment in which they were spawned. Sitting at the intersection of the Rimma Trade Route and the Corellian Trade Spine, the planet Yag'Dhul has three moons that orbit Yag'Dhul in fewer hours than the planet rotates, making its months well over one hundred standard hours shorter than its days. Moreover, the planet literally spins in the opposite direction of its moons, and as a result the oceans and atmosphere shift from one end of the world to the other, leaving parts of Yag'Dhul without atmosphere at seemingly unpredictable periods.

Scientists marvel that a sentient species was even able to develop on such a planet, but the Givin somehow managed to conquer these ecological challenges. Their evolutionary ancestors' first method of survival in such a habitat was to remain mobile, so that when the tides and air rushed to the other end of the world, they were carried with them. However, because the tides are so unpredictable, it was difficult to create a conventional cycle of life for reproduction, feeding, and the like. Also, temperature variations caused difficulties, as an individual may be at the frigid pole one day, the equator the next. Thus, the next step in evolution for their progenitors was a gradual sealing of their bodies in a skeletal vacuum. Through these changes, and through eventually learning to predict the alterations of their volatile world with a complex system of mathematics, the Givin grew and thrived despite the odds.

All of Givin language, culture, and religion centers upon mathematics, which is credited with their ultimate salvation. As befitting a mathematical theocracy, arithmetic is the main course of study for young people, who compete for entrance into monasteries, hoping to numerically solve the meaning and plan of life. The Givin planetary governor is selected through contests involving the calculation of multidimensional differentials. All political decisions are also made according to the guidelines of null-modal probability, by ruling bodies known as the Body Calculus and the coalition of Factors—although the respective responsibilities of these bodies have not been disclosed to outsiders. Givin religious practices are headed by extraordinarily gifted mathematicians who serve as priests and lorekeepers. The advanced study of equations is a highly devout pursuit, an attempt to reveal answers to the questions of life. With this centrality of purpose, the Givin written languages are made up of thousands of specially defined mathematical symbols. Arithmetic even extends to Givin decorative arts, and is featured in wall treatments and body adornments.

The Givin are also adept shipbuilders, and their ability to survive in a vacuum is very useful to such a business. They regard "soft" species who are not able to stay alive in a vacuum as inferior, and are only comfortable associating with Duros and Verpines—two other shipbuilding species. They cannot abide Mon Calamari, even though they are some of the finest ship makers in the galaxy, as the Mon Cal design technique is too organic and illogical to a Givin's sense of mathematical rigidity.

The ships that Givin construct are some of the most efficient and speedy in the galaxy. In their vessels, made specifically for their own physiology, only the sleeping quarters are pressurized, and the computers are used only for data storage. They do not install navigational computation software in their computers because the Givin calculate navigational vectors in their heads.

Givin reside in hermetically sealed cities that can withstand the violent and capricious weather trends of their world. Givin priests, deep in the study of the mathematical mysteries of their planet's rotation, can now predict these patterns with such accuracy so as to make their homes stable and peaceful. This enables them to also mine the world's natural resources, making them a generally wealthy species with a stable economy. Givin run one of the galaxy's largest and most efficient shipping and transport businesses with their fast and voluminous cargo vessels.

Givin traditionally greet one another with a simple quadratic equation. However, they will often greet outsiders with different problems to test their mathematical prowess. They do this because they generally do not trust strangers, but those who can meet the challenge of their greeting are elevated to the status of a peers with whom intelligent discourse can be shared. Givin are uncomfortable around beings who show a lot of exposed flesh—primarily because they cannot help but wonder why such individuals don't seal themselves from possible environmental hazards, such as a tidal deluge or the vacuum of space.

Despite their xenophobic tendencies, the Givin are members of the Galactic Alliance, seeing such membership as a statistical advantage to their people's economy and political well-being. The desire to maximize advantages has led the Givin to switch alliances as variables changed, such as when they allied themselves to the Separatists during the Clone War era, and to the New Republic after. The planet of Yag'Dhul was also the site of at least one major battle during the Yuuzhan Vong War. Presently, any ambassadors who work with the Givin must undergo extensive education in mathematics in order to negotiate with them, lest they find themselves at a considerable disadvantage.

DESIGNATION
Sentient

HOMEWORLD
Yag'Dhul

AVERAGE HEIGHT
1.8 meters

PRONUNCIATION
Gĭ'-vĭn

NOTABLE APPEARANCE
Episode IV: A New Hope

GOTAL

Gotals are a tall humanoid species native to Antar 4, one of six moons that orbit the gas giant known as Antar in the Prindaar system, located in the Inner Rim. Gray-brown, coarse skin protects their faces from extreme temperatures, and red-tinted eyes allow them to see shapes in pitch darkness. Flat noses protrude only a centimeter or so from their faces, and they possess sharp incisors for chewing meat. Shaggy gray fur also covers their bodies, but their most notable trait is the two cone-shaped horns that crown their oblong heads.

The Gotals have long been a spacefaring race. Taking advantage of Antar 4's proximity to the surrounding worlds in its system, they had already colonized four of the adjacent moons and mined a fifth before the Old Republic first encountered them. They were one of the earliest species to join the Republic around the formation of the Senate, even though they had no official government. Politically, they were and are peaceful anarchists. Since they have a special sensitivity to one another's feelings and needs, they did not require government or law, though some formal legal courts have been formed to handle antisocial or criminal behavior from offworld visitors and the occasional abnormal actions of one of their own.

Antar 4 is rich with minerals such as nickel, silicon, and iron, although the majority of the moon is comprised of magnetite. Xenobiologists believe much of Gotals' unique sensory abilities are directly related to the magnetite, which, when combined with the electromagnetic radiation from the stars Prindaar and Antar, greatly influences most of the life on Antar 4.

More than 60 percent of Antar 4 is covered by water, with extreme tidal variations caused by the moon's unusual rotation. These tides prevent ice caps from forming at the poles. Antar 4's rotational access is nearly parallel to its orbital plane, making variations in climate more severe. The night-and-day cycle of the world is also erratic because of the reflective nature of the system's star, which further complicates temperatures around the moon. At times, the entirety of the moon's surface is bathed in light; at others, it is plunged into complete darkness. For this reason, native species rely on senses other than sight to survive.

While Gotals do have noses, eyes, and ears, their sight and hearing are lacking in development, and their sense of smell is nonexistent. Because of this, Gotals have evolved an electromagnetic detection sense emitted from their cones. These cones provide the sensory perception that individuals require to locate food and perform other tasks necessary for survival. Packed with unique nerve endings and receptor cells, the cones can detect changes in magnetic fields, as well as infrared emanations, radio waves, neutrino bombardment, and practically every other form of energy emission. In addition, Gotals can detect the Force, though to them it appears as an indistinct buzzing. Electromagnetic emissions from most offworld technology can overwhelm their cone reception, however, so they will usually go out of their way to avoid standard machinery such as droids. All Gotal ship and land technology is based on chemical reactions that do not produce such emissions.

With their cones, Gotals can also sense another creature up to roughly ten meters away. Perceiving the being's electromagnetic aura, they can even determine mood, awareness, health, and level of strength.

Due to this extrasensory perception, Gotals make excellent hunters. They can sense their primary native prey, the equine species known as quivry, from great distances, counting their numbers and determining their relative health or weaknesses; at closer range Gotals can discern their mood, figuring out whether the quivry are aware that they are being hunted.

Gotals also utilize their cones to interact with one another—by sensing moods, thoughts, and desires, they avoid conflict and easily communicate their own needs. Because they read others so well, they are known to be extremely polite and sensitive, and will only speak aloud to convey abstract ideas—never to express emotion. In fact, their spoken language has no words for emotion. With the cones emanating their disposition, they do not require such linguistic forms. They also possess no vocal inflection, so other species will mistakenly perceive Gotals as nonemotional. These characteristics also cause some to mistrust them, particularly since a Gotal's involuntary communication cues remain unreadable to most beings.

DESIGNATION
Sentient

HOMEWORLD
Antar 4

AVERAGE
HEIGHT
1.8 meters

PRONUNCIATION
Gŏ'-tăl

Gotals' cone sensitivity enables them to function well as mates and parents. They do not require mating rituals or courtship, and love at first sight is extremely common for Gotals. When they mate it is usually for life, having children almost immediately and taking great delight in the raising of progeny.

Controlling their extrasensory abilities is a skill learned through maturity. Gotal children sense through their cones at birth, often causing them a great deal of pain and confusion. Until around the age of twelve standard years, Gotal children have difficulty filtering out nonessential information; the overwhelming amount of "noise" often leaves them irritable and irrational. Unfortunately, they are constantly distressed until they manage to learn to filter out unwanted transmissions.

Gotals can be found throughout the galaxy in regions where there is a strong nonhuman population. They often work as mercenaries, bounty hunters, counselors, diplomats, negotiators, and social workers. They are also successful in business and sales environments, though they have to work past their lack of vocal inflection to impress clients. As gamblers they are formidable, and most high-stakes games will not allow them at the table, although some professional gamblers take it as a challenge to try to fool a Gotal. The Empire, however, refused to employ their services because they too often sympathized with the enemy.

As mentioned, Gotal sensitivity comes with a price. Being receptive to electromagnetic emissions complicates their offworld existence. Droids, non-Gotal ships, or even a simple machine can cause them pain or disorientation. However, one inventive Gotal businessman named Alyn Rae recently developed a chemical-based "cone sock" garment that covers a Gotal's cones and filters out EM emissions, allowing other transmissions to pass through. He developed these garments with the assistance of several offworld scientists who could better use the equipment necessary to design and construct them. These preliminary cone socks are expensive, and usually only the most affluent Gotals wear them. Even so, more and more Gotals have been seen sporting them in galactic society—seeing the cost as a necessary sacrifice to make their lives abroad a little more peaceful.

NOTABLE APPEARANCE
Episode IV: A New Hope

GRAN

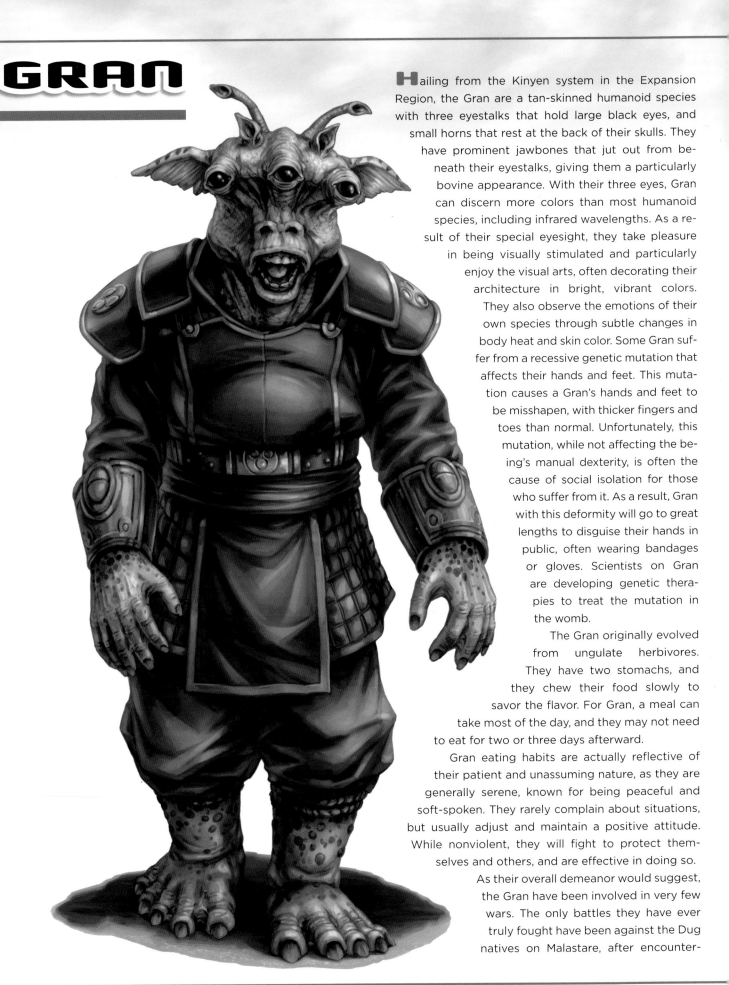

Hailing from the Kinyen system in the Expansion Region, the Gran are a tan-skinned humanoid species with three eyestalks that hold large black eyes, and small horns that rest at the back of their skulls. They have prominent jawbones that jut out from beneath their eyestalks, giving them a particularly bovine appearance. With their three eyes, Gran can discern more colors than most humanoid species, including infrared wavelengths. As a result of their special eyesight, they take pleasure in being visually stimulated and particularly enjoy the visual arts, often decorating their architecture in bright, vibrant colors. They also observe the emotions of their own species through subtle changes in body heat and skin color. Some Gran suffer from a recessive genetic mutation that affects their hands and feet. This mutation causes a Gran's hands and feet to be misshapen, with thicker fingers and toes than normal. Unfortunately, this mutation, while not affecting the being's manual dexterity, is often the cause of social isolation for those who suffer from it. As a result, Gran with this deformity will go to great lengths to disguise their hands in public, often wearing bandages or gloves. Scientists on Gran are developing genetic therapies to treat the mutation in the womb.

The Gran originally evolved from ungulate herbivores. They have two stomachs, and they chew their food slowly to savor the flavor. For Gran, a meal can take most of the day, and they may not need to eat for two or three days afterward.

Gran eating habits are actually reflective of their patient and unassuming nature, as they are generally serene, known for being peaceful and soft-spoken. They rarely complain about situations, but usually adjust and maintain a positive attitude. While nonviolent, they will fight to protect themselves and others, and are effective in doing so.

As their overall demeanor would suggest, the Gran have been involved in very few wars. The only battles they have ever truly fought have been against the Dug natives on Malastare, after encountering that species during an attempt at colonization. On their homeworld of Kinyen, there has not been such a conflict in more than ten thousand standard years, and those minor clashes that have been recorded were fought over matters of survival rather than emotional disputes.

This peaceful sensibility and levelheaded agreeability is believed by Gran scholars to be biological as well as cultural. The Gran people originated in the mountainous region of Kinyen, where they were hunted by dangerous highland predators. Their natural means of survival was to band together in herds. There was safety in numbers, and for this reason they would never leave one another alone for any period of time. The Gran learned to value their companions and rely on one another for security.

This trait has carried on through their development. Today, it is rare to see a Gran without companionship, and if left alone, a Gran will frequently go insane or die of loneliness. When two Gran mate, it is for life. If one member of a couple dies, the other generally follows within a few days. Thus, when Gran leave Kinyen for trade, they will usually travel in groups. A solitary Gran is most likely a criminal, for in their society, the most severe punishment is exile. An educated space traveler will know to stay away from a Gran who is alone, or dressed in black, as he or she is most likely criminally insane. This insanity is normally caused by loneliness, and such individuals will avoid bright colors as too reminiscent of home.

An agreeable and characteristically happy species, Gran love to chat and to meet new people. Once embroiled in conversation, it is somewhat difficult to get certain Gran to stop talking. They love to learn about other peoples, and will ask many questions, almost to the point of creating annoyance. Gran are also accused by many nonpacifistic beings as being "preachy" on the topic of pacifism.

Gran society is socialist in structure, with the needs of the individual put aside in favor of the populace as a whole. To keep Gran society on an even keel, every Gran is trained for a specific job that best suits his or her talents within the guidelines of a rigid career quota system. While many species, including humans, would be uncomfortable in such a system, the Gran see this as a fully logical way for natural-born herders to survive and thrive. There is no question as to each individual's role, with everyone from the machine worker to the farmer contributing to the greater good while politicians efficiently distribute the wealth and technology

DESIGNATION
Sentient

HOMEWORLD
Kinyen/Malastare

AVERAGE
HEIGHT
1.6 meters

PRONUNCIATION
Grăn

throughout their world using quotas and rationing. Political debate is rare, and when it occurs is painstakingly slow, with each point pondered with intense care, so that any decision made harms as few people as possible.

When the Gran first encountered the Old Republic, contact with the outside galaxy threw their society into upheaval. As many Gran left Kinyen to colonize other worlds, including Hok and Malastare, great gaps opened in the delicately balanced society. For this reason, Gran politicians then refused to allow anyone to depart the planet without permission, and forbade offworlders from visiting Kinyen's civilized centers. The Gran soon constructed quarters for outsiders in their cities, and made moving offplanet illegal, although records indicate that there were a few rare Gran Jedi during this period, and that the Gran did represent themselves in the Galactic Senate. The Old Republic accommodated this isolationist stance to enable Gran society to adapt to the extreme changes it was facing. As they adjusted, the Gran reopened contact with the Republic, just in time for it to fall under the control of the Emperor, at which time—for their own protection—they retreated to their homeworld once again. But they didn't remain safe from the Empire for long. After Imperial bombers leveled a Gran city, the population caved to their will, and around this time many Gran also began to leave Kinyen by choice.

After the Empire fell, the New Republic reinitiated contact with the Gran, and their society has opened up once more. The Gran now trade the fruits of their fertile world throughout the galaxy, primarily those of produce and livestock. As a people they have had few technological achievements that they can call their own—they import all their technology from offworld sources. Gran are commonly seen about the galaxy traveling in tour groups and as merchants, often running companies with more of their own kind for companionship.

NOTABLE APPEARANCE
Episode VI: Return of the Jedi

GUNDARK

Gundarks are large, bipedal furry primates with large ears and four arms. They have opposable digits on their hands and are extremely strong—able to rip healthy hundred-year-old trees out of the ground. All subspecies of gundarks sport either brown or gray fur, though their young are usually black, gradually changing color with age. Gundarks have keen eyesight and hearing, but their sense of smell is especially powerful. Adult gundarks can detect an intruder up to a hundred meters away, allowing them to get ready to attack while the adversary moves into range.

These creatures can be found throughout the galaxy on worlds that are generally temperate. They prefer warm climates, building their nests in hollowed-out trees or caves.

Scientists have only speculated as to how this species managed to populate so many worlds, but, as with banthas, they believe traders and other space travelers transported gundarks to different systems.

Unlike banthas, which were used for farming and pack labor, gundarks were most likely transferred from system to system for sport—game hunting or gundark fighting, the latter having been banned for years in many systems. Others were taken as slaves because they are easily trained, and still others were moved to be protected from these slavers by Old Republic agents. Even though hunting or capturing gundarks was illegal during both the Old Republic era and the current rule of the Galactic Federation of Free Alliances, gundarks are frequently sold by black-market operatives to underworld gladiatorial game promoters throughout the outer fringes of the galaxy. In such games, gundarks are the favored champions, even against such famous adversaries as the rancor, trompa, or krayt dragon, taking on their opponents with their bare hands. Gundarks often ambush their challengers, hiding until they are in range, then leaping out to grapple them and crush their windpipes. When battling larger opponents, they can crush leg and arm bones with a single squeeze. The most popular bouts are those in which gundarks are blindfolded and can take advantage of their extremely powerful sense of smell. Gundarks are costly in terms of upkeep, however, requiring special security measures, including force pikes and guards, to keep them contained. For this reason, unless significantly wealthy, a promoter will usually have only one gundark featured in his or her cast of combatants.

Gundarks are known to have very short tempers and to attack without provocation. They are omnivorous, and while it is unclear as to whether they have achieved full sentience or not, they do display enough intelligence to use items such as rocks as simple tools for cracking open nuts and hard fruits. In their natural settings, they live in family groupings of ten or more, creating homes in hollowed-out trees or caves. Several families may cluster together into a tribal-like society, working mutually for their common interests. Their lives center on the gathering of food for their community, and there are definite hierarchical roles within a gundark society. Females fulfill the role of hunter-gatherers, and take on the training of young gundarks not old enough to venture away from the tribe, while the males are the home protectors—attacking any creature coming within scent distance of the nest. This they do with great ferocity. Female gundarks normally hunt in packs, and have been known to mistake sentient beings for food.

Like most primates, Gundarks are born one at a time. At birth, they have only two arms and small ears. Parents will roughhouse with their young to teach them how to protect themselves even while they play. During puberty, youthful gundarks sprout two additional arms, their ears grow to match the width of their heads, and their strength reaches its maximum potential—thus the phrase *strong enough to pull the ears off a gundark.* These adolescent gundarks know instinctively that too many offspring can threaten a family's food supply, so sibling rivalry is often fierce. By the age of five, some young gundarks are forced out of their homes and set off to find a new one, frequently battling their way into another tribe. This tradition keeps tribe populations at a manageable number and allows for genetic diversity.

Among the subspecies of gundarks are the aquatic gundarks of Yavin 4, which possess four eyes, enabling them to see both above and below the water. This medium-sized creature exists by feeding on smaller animals, such as runyips and whisper birds. Otherwise, there is little difference between common and aquatic gundarks.

However, there is the Burskan gundark, a rather strange specimen when compared with the others. Docile creatures, Burskan gundarks have been observed to simply lie around in a lazy torpor, which is more pronounced during warmer weather. In fact, it is difficult to get Burskan gundarks to notice anything, although when sufficiently provoked they are as fierce as their more populous cousins. The odd behavior of Burskan gundarks has two other striking examples. Burskan gundarks form unusual attachments to soft items, such as cloth made of silk or fur. They will hoard such things and have been observed to fight in order to keep them. Also, Burskan gundarks are particularly sensitive to odors emitted by rotting plant matter. While this is not a problem on Burska's open tundra, it has provoked stampedes among certain gundarks in captivity. Fortunately for these creatures, their peculiar behavior makes them unprofitable for trade on the black market and useless for illegal service as gladiatorial animals.

There is another species referred to as a gundark—the "long-necked gundarks" of Kharzet III. These creatures are not true gundarks, however, as they are quadrupeds with long, prehensile necks. This species gained its name from a xenobiologist who compared the violent temperament of these creatures to that of gundarks in his notes. Sadly, he died before his notes could be adapted and a proper name given to them, and for this reason the name stuck, falling into common usage.

DESIGNATION
Nonsentient/
semi-sentient

HOMEWORLD
Vanqor

**AVERAGE
HEIGHT**
1.8 meters

PRONUNCIATION
Gŭn'-därk

NOTABLE MENTION
Episode V: The Empire Strikes Back

GUNGAN

The Gungans of Naboo, a planet in the Mid Rim, are bipedal amphibians who live primarily in cities beneath Naboo's great bodies of water. They are tall and thin, with long, expressive ears, a bill-like mouth, and webbed fingers and toes. Their skeletal frame is made of cartilage, making them more flexible for underwater movement. When swimming, their nostrils seal, nictitating membranes cover their eyes, and their eyestalks partially retract into their skulls, making underwater travel very easy for them. They also have tough skin on and around their heads, enabling them to burrow through sand and gravel with little difficulty. Compound lungs permit Gungans to breathe both air and water, and powerful legs allow them to swim very quickly. A significant number of Gungans have haillu—two long earlobes that reveal emotional states such as friendship, aggression, and fear.

This species is omnivorous, although they have large teeth for cracking open shellfish, a staple of their diet. They also consume creatures known as gumbols from the trees surrounding their homes and mollusks from nearby marshes and lakes.

In fact, Gungan culture centers on their environment and the other living things that populate it. They are particularly linked to the creatures known as kaadu, which are used as battle mounts for their Grand Army. Similar to Tusken Raiders and their banthas, Gungans believe that the kaadu are joined with them in a way that no other creatures are—they will treat them as family and mourn them in a similar fashion when they are lost. The Gungan people domesticated the kaadu thousands of years ago, and when Gungans migrated to their underwater cities, they brought the kaadu with them. They are the mainstay of the Gungan militias, or militiagung, and entire schools are devoted to teaching Gungans to ride and live in harmony with these creatures, since it is considered essential for growth.

In battle, the Gungans who ride kaadu wield the heaviest authority, and records show that they are the most effective leaders. Kaadu are given to Gungan officers with great ceremony, and officers never abandon their steeds unless they die or they are retired due to age. In a like manner, kaadu will never desert their owners, feeling a profound love and loyalty.

Gungan society and government have been built upon treaties made by the many different settlements and clans. Gungan life is governed by the rules and decisions set down by the High Council, which is led by an elected "Boss." While the members of the clans exhibit different outward biological features, they remain the same in terms of their inner physiology. The two primary tribal races within Gungan society are the Otolla, which are the most numerous, and the Ankura, a race that does not have long ears, eyestalks, or bills. Scientists believe that while these two different races share common ancestry, the Ankura have lived on land longer than the Otolla, and have therefore evolved to look more like a land-based form. The basic Gungan family unit consists of two parents and children. Children hatch in "water cradles" in tadpole forms, although they develop arms and legs within a month of birth.

Nearly one hundred standard years before the Battle of Yavin, the Gungans fought off unknown invaders on their world, assembling the first Grand Army by uniting all Gungan cities and communities. After throwing off the invaders, Gungans maintained the army as a means of defending against any foe, including their world's ever-present sea monsters. Made up of the combined might of the militiagung, the Grand Army wears leather and metal headgear and marginal body army with small circular shields; the main weapons used are plasmic energy balls. Gungan generals and officers transmit their orders via horns, wild gestures, and piercing whistles. Still, Naboo is normally a fairly peaceful world. Thus the army is more a matter of tradition than need.

Gungans are not very tolerant of those who threaten the peace of their home, and their sentencing for criminals is often severe. Minor crimes, such as vandalism, are given a sentence of exile or caning, even stoning. Once Gungans have been cast out, it may be difficult for them to return to society, and even if they do, they may find that massive peer pressure will make life quite uncomfortable until their past offenses have faded from memory.

Despite this harsh code of law, Gungans are generally a happy and gregarious people who love company and the sharing of stories. Around one another they speak their native language of Gunganese, but with outsiders they will combine their language with Basic to form a pidgin language that is usually understandable to speakers of Basic. They do welcome visitors with kindness, but are typically suspicious and quiet until the outsider earns their respect.

The Gungans are a simple but proud people who bristle at any attempt to conquer them. They are technologically advanced, although they prefer to live simply, with as little interference from machinery as possible. They use deflector shield technology to maintain bubble domes over their underwater cities, and utilize biotechnology, growing rather than building their underwater ships, force fields, and weapons. They take great care to preserve their environment and use natural resources sparingly.

Other than advances in biotechnology, Gungans live pretty much as they did thousands of years ago. They dwell in relative peace alongside the human inhabitants of Naboo, although relations between the species have not always been on the best of terms. Due to cultural differences, Gungans are suspicious of their Naboo neighbors, probably because the average Gungan has never met a human personally. However, historical records contain no references to armed conflict between the Gungans and humans, so it is believed that the estrangement stemmed from an inability to communicate rather than hostilities between the two groups. Prior to the fall of the Old Republic, Gungans had started designing space vessels, but they ceased all such development when the Empire threatened their home. It is believed that the Gungans retreated deeper into the swamps following the rise of the Empire, once again isolating themselves from the human population of Naboo. During the Old Republic era, they were represented in the Galactic Senate by Padmé Amidala, following her successful peace negotiations between the Gungans and the human peoples while Queen of Naboo. Since then, however, traffic to and from the Naboo system has grown more rare, although the sector was represented in the New Republic Senate by first a human and then a Gungan Senator.

DESIGNATION
Sentient

HOMEWORLD
Naboo

AVERAGE HEIGHT
1.9 meters

PRONUNCIATION
Gŭn'-găn

NOTABLE APPEARANCE
Episode I: The Phantom Menace

H'NEMTHE

The H'nemthe, from an Outer Rim planet of the same name, are a bipedal reptilian species with skin varying in tone from pink to blue-gray, double rows of cheekbones, gently curved noses, four small horns (or conelets) on their skulls, and three fingers on each hand. They are omnivores, feeding primarily on fruits and vegetables, with the occasional meal that includes wild game.

H'nemthe are highly efficient hunters. Their conelets can sense heat differences in their environment, and emotional variances in other creatures. For this reason, scientists have speculated that their conelets serve a similar purpose to those of the Gotal. The two species are unrelated biologically, but both come from worlds where lunar orbits cause extreme weather patterns. The planet H'nemthe has three moons, generating a collective gravitational force that creates tremendous weather fluctuations on the world's surface. As with the Gotal, these cones help H'nemthe locate food and analyze their surrounding environment not only during such inclement weather, but also in the darkness.

H'nemthe society is very structured, and is based on the fulfillment of spiritual awareness through the creation of life and the act of searching for true love. The population breakdown makes finding true love quite difficult, however. Like the Gamorreans, there are about twenty H'nemthe males for every female, although the reasons for this population anomaly among the H'nemthe is currently unknown. Xenobiologists have suggested that this may be due to a genetic defect, but because of the closed society on H'nemthe, research on this subject has not yet been thoroughly conducted. Unlike the emotionally unsophisticated and comparatively brutish Gamorreans, though, the timid H'nemthe males spend most of their adult lives seeking out a devoted mate. Although a majority do not locate their one true love, H'nemthe males take some comfort in the belief that death is the culmination of life, and that their deaths create a path for their offspring.

Along with the population disparity, the lack of love is an unfortunate result of the traditional H'nemthe mating ritual. H'nemthe males are extremely selective in choosing a mate, and after mating, the female disembowels the male with her razor-sharp tongue. Because it is fatal for the male, mating is infrequent, and is only done in cases of true love. While some may consider this calamitous, a H'nemthe male considers the ritual the culmination of spiritual fulfillment, as he goes on to the netherworld to guide his coming child. The woman is fulfilled in that she brings a new life into the world.

Due to their low numbers, females are strongly protected by H'nemthe law. Virgin females are rarely, if ever, allowed to leave the planet and do not venture out often unless given leave by their mothers to seek a mate. It is only after mating that female H'nemthe will travel offworld. Females are also not allowed to eat anything but vegetables and fruits, to ensure they do not taste flesh until they savor that of their mate. Although their limited exposure to the outside world leaves many H'nemthe females naïve about the galaxy at large, they are well educated in many subjects important to their people. Thus, most H'nemthe encountered off-planet are male, although they are almost assuredly not seeking glory or adventure. Males who are unable to find a mate or are repeatedly rejected by their chosen beloveds sometimes simply take to the stars as wanderers.

One of the more well-known H'nemthe is M'iiyoom Onith, a female virgin H'nemthe who was allowed to leave her homeworld as an experiment to see how well the females of their species would fair in finding a mate outside their native culture. Through most of her trip, M'iiyoom was accompanied by a chaperone, but she and her chaperone were accidentally separated when M'iiyoom entered the wrong ship during a layover at a transfer station. Whether she did this purposely or accidentally is unknown, but her final destination was Tatooine where she encountered a Gotal named Feltipern Trevagg, with whom she fell madly in love. Authorities later found Trevagg disemboweled from the H'nemthe mating ritual, but could find no trace of the young female H'nemthe. She later returned to her homeworld, and as she is the first of her kind to attempt mating with a non-H'nemthe, she attained some notoriety. As her mating with Trevagg resulted in no progeny (they were, after all, genetically incompatible) she is now free to travel offworld as often as she likes, though she prefers to remain home doing speaking engagements.

Befitting a culture that places a premium on true love, the

DESIGNATION
Sentient

HOMEWORLD
H'nemthe

AVERAGE HEIGHT
1.7 meters

PRONUNCIATION
Hĕ-nĕm'-thē

H'nemthe are an extremely artistic and passionate people. Their poetry and literary writings are some of the most profound in the galaxy, and are displayed in a written language that is composed of one contiguous line of flowing letters to form words. A cornerstone of H'nemthe literary tradition is the form of epic poem written by lovers to each other before they have mated. Detailing a pair's courtship and the depths of their feelings for each other, these poems are often read publicly in grand recitals after the mating ritual, as a tribute to the couple, and particularly to the late male partner. The poems are collected and reproduced in fine calligraphy.

Music is also highly valued in H'nemthe society, and skills in calligraphy and music, along with storytelling, are prized abilities. Females are expected to be personally accomplished in the arts. In addition, they study H'nemthe history and political science to prepare themselves to be the leaders of their world. The H'nemthe spoken language, however, consists of squeaks, squeals, and other noises that—unlike their written language and music—are considered displeasing by most other species.

The government of H'nemthe is also fervent and optimistic, being a direct democracy. In this society, all voices are important and must be heard. Although males are the majority of the H'nemthe population, they tend to elect females as leaders of their local governments, particularly because if a male finds a mate, he will not live long enough to fulfill his duties. All of the local governments select representatives to a world Senate, where matters of global importance are decided by a majority vote.

The H'nemthe are a self-sufficient people, rarely trading with outsiders for offworld goods save technology and ships. On occasion, H'nemthe artists accept commissions for their calligraphy and musical compositions, but these requests are seldom agreed to, as works of art are considered highly personal. Their world's ecology makes it difficult for them to trade anything except minerals, which the males take from mines beneath the planet's surface. H'nemthe gets few visitors, though the Galactic Alliance has made overtures to the female leadership in attempts to begin trade negotiations with this passionate and idealistic people.

NOTABLE APPEARANCE
Episode IV: A New Hope

HUMAN

Humans are the most populous species in the known galaxy. They are also one of the most adaptable, resilient, and diverse in physical appearance. With two legs ending in feet, and two arms featuring five-fingered hands, humans are extremely dexterous and able to perform a great range of complex tasks. Most humans have hair on their heads, which usually varies from dark brown to white or silver, and males often have facial hair, although a majority of them choose to remove it, or sculpt it through selective removal. Their pliable skin ranges in color from pasty white to deep, dark brown, and humans' eyes are also known to appear in a multitude of colors, from the lightest of blues to the darkest of browns. They inhabit all walks of life in galactic society, and have colonized thousands of worlds. Most sociologists feel that their intelligence and adaptability to new situations have allowed humans to become the most successful, and politically powerful species in the galaxy.

Being mammals, humans bear their children live from the womb, and they normally raise them in private home groupings. Multiple births are not unheard of, though it is uncommon for a female to bear more than two at a time. Among multiple births, some are genetically identical (from one ovum splitting) or fraternal (from two separate fertilized ova). Humans can typically live up to a hundred twenty standard years, though there have been isolated reports of human Jedi living as many as two hundred.

Some humans are notable due to their unique cultures. One of the most famous and numerous of human societies is that of Corellian, whose people inhabit the Corellian star system. Twenty-five millennia before the Battle of Yavin, the mysterious species known as the Rakata introduced Corellians to hyperdrive technology, and they quickly created their own more efficient and effective version of it. From that point on, they were traveling the space lanes, trading with other species, and leading the way in starship development. They are recognized for their skills as pilots and engineers—a point of pride to their people—and their talents as military strategists are renowned. Culturally, Corellians are born risk-takers and adventurers—their impulsive and sometimes unpredictable actions often setting them apart from other human civilizations in the galaxy.

Another unique group of humans are the Mandalorians, who adopted the war-like culture of the ancient Taung species. The Taung were a ruthless, near-human gray-skinned species that originated on Coruscant and ultimately relocated to Mandalore, renaming both the planet and themselves for their supreme ruler, Mandalore the First. Mandalorians obeyed the commands of their militaristic superiors without question, and this cultural tradition of combat was carried on when they united with other species, including humans, to fight their legendary battles. Over time, the original species became extinct, and although the term *Mandalorian* refers more to a culture and a mind-set than to a specific species, the majority of remaining Mandalorians were in fact humans. The genetic code of one such warrior was used to create the clone-trooper-based Grand Army of the Republic that later evolved into the army of the Empire. It is believed that, based on the reports of Captain Han Solo, the famed bounty hunter Boba Fett recently reorganized the Mandalorian warrior army in the shadow of the Yuuzhan Vong invasion, and that it was successful in liberating more than one world from the brutal aggressors.

The Lorrdian culture is also worth noting, as it is a group thought by some sociologists to be near human, though the genetic code has not been altered by environmental concerns. The Lorrdians were once slaves to a people called the Argazdans, who forbade all Lorrdians to communicate with one another. To counter this, Lorrdians devised a type of sign language consisting of subtle hand gestures, postures, and facial tics and expressions. They also taught themselves to read the body language of others. This form of interaction, known as kinetic communication, led to a new way of life, helping the Lorrdians overthrow their masters through the formation and coordination of a guerrilla force. Lorrdians today are so adept at reading body language that they can tell a person's mood and intentions within just a few seconds of observation. With more time to study a subject, Lorrdians can identify cultural background, homeworld, occupation, and class. They are also famous for being the best vocal and physical mimics, using their perceptive powers to imitate almost any beings' voice or mannerism, within the restrictions of their physical ability.

As humans are the most numerous species galaxywide, they have, perhaps unfairly, become the standard by which other species are defined. For instance, if a species is known to be "humanoid," this is not because its members are human, but because they bear specific traits that are similar to humans—namely, the number of appendages and the

practice of walking upright. Also, being a generally successful species, humans have spawned several related subspecies referred to as near humans. Near humans are individuals who are nearly genetically identical to humans, but whose inherent makeup has changed in varying degrees due to environmental influences, evolution, or other factors. Humans and near humans can interbreed with very few exceptions.

The Firrerreos, meanwhile, are one of the rarest near-human species in the known galaxy; it is believed that only a few thousand of them still exist. Firrerreos possess multicolored hair that they wear long, and their eyes have nictitating membranes that protect them against intense bursts of light as well as flying debris. This human subspecies is also able to heal quickly. Firrerreos were nearly wiped out by Hethrir, one of their own who was a pupil to Darth Vader. The surviving Firrerreo people were relocated on Belderone and Kinooine, though the former planet was subsequently conquered by the Yuuzhan Vong and the subspecies has fallen into near extinction.

Two other near-human species of import are the Mirialans of Mirial, and the Kiffar, who are native to Kiffu and Kiffex in the Azurbani system. While having notable differences, what makes these two species stand out are their tattoo markings, which hold significance in both cultures. The complex culture of the olive-skinned Mirialans includes religious beliefs based on an ancient understanding of the Force. A Mirialan's tattoos signify that individual's importance to the future of the universe. The Kiffar, meanwhile, have tattoos that signify their family heritage, specifically that of their mothers. The Kiffar believe it is the mother who gives life, and therefore the power of the Force flows through her to her children.

Humans have been traveling and colonizing the galaxy for eons. Their cultures and physical appearances are as varied and unique as all the planetary systems they inhabit. Even with all the attempts of different peoples to invade and conquer the galaxy and all the species in it, humans have managed to survive, adapt, and defend their way of life. And it seems as if humans will be in the center of galactic life for millennia to come.

DESIGNATION
Sentient

HOMEWORLD
Unknown
(believed to be
Coruscant)

**AVERAGE
HEIGHT**
1.75 meters

PRONUNCIATION
Hū'-măn

NOTABLE APPEARANCE
Episode IV: A New Hope

HUTT

Hutts are large amphibious gastropods that presently inhabit the world of Nal Hutta in the Y'Toub system, the center of an area of the galaxy known as Hutt space. They have thick bodies with a long muscular tails and small arms that protrude from their upper torsos.

Physiologically, the Hutts are an anomaly, sharing traits from a variety of species. Like sea mammals, their nostrils can close, with their large lungs enabling them to stay underwater for hours at a time. Like worms, they are hermaphrodites, possessing both male and female reproductive organs. Like marsupial mammals, they bear their young one at a time, and nourish them in a brood pouch during their earlier stages of development.

Despite all these varied qualities, scientists generally classify Hutts as gastropods because of the way they move, slithering around like giant slugs. They have no skeleton to speak of, merely an internal mantle that supports their bodies and shapes their heads. Their mouths open so wide that they can swallow just about any small creatures whole, allowing them to frequently indulge their taste for live snacks. Hutts also possess extremely tough skin that protects them against heat and chemical burns, with their mucus and sweat making their skin surface very slippery while also keeping their bodies moist.

Though hermaphroditic, the average Hutt possesses a notably healthy sexual appetite, even for members of other species. In fact, some Hutts have been known to assume male or female gender roles and pursue bi-gender relationships, a behavior that sociologists attribute to societal contamination from contact with bi-gendered species. Medical specialists disagree, deeming the alternate lifestyle a product of nature that certain Hutts simply cannot deny, given their ability to select their own genders. Whatever the reason might be, many "normal" Hutts consider this behavior a perversion, and scorn those who choose gender roles, sometimes to the point of enacting violence and murder upon them.

Hutts are among the longest-lived species in the galaxy, with a maximum life span of roughly one thousand standard years. During such a lifetime, they can grow in size to more than fifteen hundred kilograms, and because they are so long-lived, Hutts rarely reproduce. When they do, many Hutts assume female roles in order to bear young. Infant Hutts are blind and extremely small, and they will move to a parent's pouch, where they remain for around fifty years. When they finally leave the pouch, they have matured to an intellectual level comparable to that of a typical ten-year-old human. As they move toward adulthood, they gain in corpulence, a trait considered a sign of power and prestige.

Hutt culture is essentially egocentric. They consider themselves the center of the galaxy, and on the worlds they control are likened unto gods. A Hutt's success in life is comparable only to its ego, and a Hutt's ego can be tremendous. They are experts at manipulating others and getting them to do their bidding.

Before inhabiting Nal Hutta, the Hutts evolved on a planet known as Varl, a temperate forest world with two suns that the species worshipped as gods. In Hutt religious beliefs, one of the sun gods, Evona, was pulled into a black hole. When this happened, the other planets in the system collided and crushed each other into numerous asteroids that bombarded the planet Varl. The second sun god, named Ardos, collapsed itself into a white dwarf out of grief over losing its mate.

Hutts believe that they had actually become greater than the gods they once worshipped as a result of their surviving the destruction of their original system. There is no absolute scientific substantiation for the Hutts' religious tale, however, and most scientists tend to believe another version that is told by spacers and traders throughout the galaxy. This story indicates that the Hutts destroyed their own planet in a civil war, the likes of which had not been witnessed anywhere in the known galaxy.

Nal Hutta is ruled by a council containing the eldest

DESIGNATION
Sentient

HOMEWORLD
Nal Hutta
(by way of Varl)

**AVERAGE
LENGTH**
3 meters

PRONUNCIATION
Hŭt

members of the so-called Clans of the Ancients. These clans are families that can trace their ancestry back to their days on Varl. The means by which the council makes decisions is a mystery, in that the Hutts will not allow outsiders to observe the governmental proceedings. Hutts all over the galaxy—even those on the farthest outskirts—abide by the decisions of this council.

For Hutts, blood is always thicker than slime. A Hutt's clan is paramount, particularly one's kajidic, or criminal family, and most decisions are based upon how they will affect the prosperity and the position of one's clan. Vast ancestral fortunes, passed on from generation to generation, have resulted in Hutt clans controlling some of the richest holdings in the galaxy. Rivalries among kajidics are widespread and often dangerous to those involved. Assassination as a means of achieving an end is commonplace, and although it is unforgivable (but not unheard of) for a Hutt to kill another Hutt, they would think nothing of executing an underling.

The Hutts, in general, are not builders, manufacturers, or inventors. They are entrepreneurs, constantly connecting someone who needs something with someone else who can fulfill that need. More often than not, Hutts head up giant criminal empires that are secretive and vast, and a majority of the major illegal transactions made in the galactic business world likely have a Hutt connected to them in one way or another. Galaxywide, most illegal activities have a Hutt at their source, whether it be the spice trade, smuggling, gambling, or slavery.

The one area in which Hutts excel and seem to take particular pride is their aptitude for slavery. Befitting their oversized egos and substantial appetites, Hutts will trade beings as easily and with as little afterthought as they would exchange nerf hides. During the Clone Wars era, Hutts controlled all the slave trade on Tatooine and Ryloth. The Hutt penchant for subjugating other species has its roots in Hutt history, starting with their enslavement of the Klatooinians, Vodrans, and Nikto through unfair trade agreements.

At the end of the New Republic era, the Yuuzhan Vong destroyed Nal Hutta, forcing the Hutts to seek a new homeworld. Because several Hutts such as Jabba, Gardulla, and Decca had established bases on Tatooine over the years, it was chosen as their new primary home planet.

NOTABLE APPEARANCE
Episode VI: Return of the Jedi

IKTOTCHI

The Iktotchi are a humanoid species native to the Expansion Region world of Iktotchon and its neighboring moon, Iktotch. Members of this tall species possess large horns that curve downward from their hairless skulls, and rough, tanned skin that protects them from the fierce winds of their homeworld. Male Iktotchi have bigger horns than the females; these are believed to be a leftover trait from their near-complete evolution from a species of mountain-dwelling quadrupeds, as there is little other biological evidence to suggest such a genetic heritage. An Iktotchi's horns are particularly hard and durable, although it is possible that they can be broken and subsequently regrown.

Beyond their horns, the most notable feature of the Iktotchi that is not related to their appearance is their incredible gift of clairvoyance, typically manifested through dreams and visions. When the Iktotchi first encountered representatives from the Old Republic, the scouts were astounded to see, from the planet's atmosphere, the seal of the Republic carved quite clearly into a mountain plateau. The Iktotchi were, apparently, prepared for the scouts' arrival long in advance, having seen the event in dreams and precognitive visions. In fact, the Iktotchi were doubly excited to meet the representatives because, dating back generations, the horned species had legends of a time when they would join a great galactic civilization that "spanned the stars."

1.5

1.0

.5

0

Although both male and female Iktotchi share the gift of clairvoyance, most have no control over when they receive these visions, and the responsibility assumed in becoming a trained Seer is great. It is only after deep consideration and consultation with elder Seers that Iktotchi will elect to train as Seers themselves, and it is not uncommon for them to withdraw from the training once it has begun. Starting as young adults, Seers will spend years in meditative practice perfecting their control, to the point that they can enter a trance and summon insight into the future at will. Trained Seers do not do this lightly—Iktotchi feel, just as the Jedi do, that the future is always in motion and can be affected by current events and actions. Although Iktotchi will prepare for events seen in a vision, any efforts to fix a particular future, ensure a certain outcome, or, worse, personally profit from it are strongly prohibited in Iktotchi culture.

Overall, the Iktotchi are a quiet, sensitive people who hide their intense emotions behind a detached or dispassionate expression of stoicism. They are respectful of other beings and cultures, but they have difficulty forming close relationships with them, although they have been known to form deep, abiding ties with some non-Iktotchi if they are given the time. Iktotchi can sometimes show a bit of irritation with those who do not understand or take into account their precognitive powers, yet they are normally very concerned about frightening or upsetting others with their talents. Most Iktotchi will keep silent on such things unless asked, or unless the subject becomes important to the situation at hand. Unfortunately for many Iktotchi who travel about the galaxy, they can sometimes wind up viewing their clairvoyance as a curse rather than a blessing, and will avoid the topic entirely when in the company of other species.

It is no wonder, then, that the Jedi took immediate interest in this species, and even established one of the first offworld settlements on Iktotchon. Iktotchi trained as Jedi were often more powerful than other species in sensory skills, with their clairvoyant talents especially enhanced through the Force. Iktotchi Jedi were particularly adept at battlefield management and strategy, and were also gifted at creating "Force-melds," in which Jedi are linked to each other through the force during combat.

Iktotchi precognitive skills led to another great talent for which they are renowned—their piloting abilities. The Iktotchi rank among some of the best pilots in the galaxy, equal only to humans, Duros, and Mon Calamari. Among these, the Iktotchi precognition gives them the edge (especially Force-sensitives), and yet for many years after their much-anticipated entrance into galactic society, the Iktotchi were distrusted because of this power. For a time, the prejudice against the Iktotchi reached the point that many members of the species denied they had the skill in order to be accepted among others, who thought they were mind readers or doom bringers. Ironically, these Iktotchi were mostly telling the truth, in that their powers of clairvoyance seemed to diminish the farther away they were from their homeworld. Eventually, this suspicion against their species diminished, and they soon became some of the most sought-after pilots in the galaxy, with shipowners willing to pay exorbitant amounts for even the most inexperienced of Iktotchi pilots.

Iktotchi are also respected for their engineering prowess, with their skills in fixing or maintaining vessels becoming just as well known as their abilities to pilot them. They usually anticipate mechanical failures before they happen, making an Iktotchi invaluable in any crew.

During the period leading up to the Clone Wars and the rise of the Empire, many Iktotchi saw the coming bloodshed in their dreams and did their best to avert it through diplomacy. When Palpatine took control, the diplomats quickly withdrew to their world to wait out his rule, even as their Jedi brethren were slaughtered—Iktotchi Jedi being among the first to die because they posed the greatest threat to Palpatine's plans. And yet, when the Iktotchi retreated, Palpatine was content to leave them mostly alone, establishing a blockade over their world in order to keep their power under his thumb. Isolation, the Iktotchi realized, was their only way to survive as a species, and so they endured for a generation until their new visions of a crumbling Empire came to pass. Even so, some Iktotchi were reported to have slipped past the blockade to join the Rebellion.

With the rise of the New Republic, they eagerly jumped at the chance to help the fledgling government get off the ground. The Iktotchi were uncharacteristically taken by surprise by the invasion of the Yuuzhan Vong, however—the Yuuzhan Vong presence was as invisible to Iktotchi clairvoyance as it was to the powers of the Jedi.

DESIGNATION
Sentient

HOMEWORLD
Iktotchon

AVERAGE HEIGHT
1.8 meters

PRONUNCIATION
Ik-tŏt'-chē

NOTABLE APPEARANCE
Episode I: The Phantom Menace

ISHI TIB

The Ishi Tib are green, amphibious beings from the Mid Rim planet Tibrin, a world of moderate temperatures that is almost completely covered by wide oceans and coral reefs. The planet's axis is perpendicular to its orbital plane, and since the orbit is almost perfectly circular, the surface of Tibrin does not vary in temperature. The tides and currents of the planet's massive oceans circulate the warmth of the equatorial waters to the poles, creating a temperate zone over most of the world.

The Ishi Tib evolved from large, bony fish in the shallow waters of the coral reefs that form the only landmasses on their world. The ancestors of the Ishi Tib often escaped from predators by leaping onto the air-exposed portions of the coral reefs. As a result, modern Ishi Tib cities are built upon, or even grown out of, this very same coral. These cities encompass food production; Ishi Tib grow edible seaweed and breed fish and crustaceans for food in underwater corrals. Their concern for their environment is reflected in their insistence that every technological or scientific device they create be tested for its potential ecological impact before use. In addition, the seas on Tibrin are quite safe, a result of the Ishi Tib taming them through the domestication or killing off of all dangerous predators. The Ishi Tib are passionate eco-preservationists who will not sacrifice or compromise the ecological balance of their world.

The physical form of the Ishi Tib reflects their development from sea life. Their skin is rough and leathery, resistant to water evaporation. Their yellow eyes are located on two eyestalks that jut from their heads at an angle, and these eyes enable them to see in the dim light under the ocean surface. Their two pouch-like cheeks allow them to suck in and temporarily store algae and microscopic seafood, and their nostrils grant them a strong sense of smell that functions both in water and on land. They have two lungs that serve as internal gills, enabling them to breathe underwater. Ishi Tib's beaks are sharp and powerful, giving them ability to crack open tough shellfish or bite through the fingers or tails of unsuspecting attackers. Their bodies are thick and muscular, with two-fingered stubby hands and flat, fin-like feet.

Being amphibians, the Ishi Tib are still dependent on water. Their skin and gill-like lungs require frequent replenishment of moisture and sea salts, so approximately every thirty standard hours, Ishi Tib must immerse themselves in a saltwater solution comparable to that of their native oceans. If they don't, their gills and skin will eventually dry out and crack open, and if the condition worsens, the Ishi Tib will die of internal and external bleeding. This need has given rise to a lively trade in Tibrin sea salts for offworld Ishi Tib.

As in the case of their fishy progenitors, Ishi Tib society centers on "schools" or communities of no more than ten thousand people. Representatives elected to one-year terms govern these schools in accordance with ecological law. There is no marriage, and reproduction is decided based upon the needs of the school and the resources available to support an addition to the population. Fertilized eggs are laid in hatcheries in a sandbar area near the coral reef, and the school, as a community, raises the children. Because of this, no Ishi Tib is aware of who their relatives really are; inbreeding is not a concern. When the decision to reproduce is made, partners are tested to verify that no problems will arise for their offspring.

Ishi Tib communicate through a spoken language made up of honks, squeals, and beak-clacks. The Tibrinese written language utilizes a hieroglyphic system that has been in use for thousands of years, dating back to Tibrin's pretechnological era, when pictographs were still carved in soft stone-like substances.

Ishi Tib are patient, quiet, and calculating. They are rarely rash or impulsive, analyzing every choice or decision with great thought. These traits make them excellent planners, capable of maintaining organizational control over large, complex projects. Though they rarely leave home, they are highly desired around the galaxy as tacticians, executives,

DESIGNATION
Sentient

HOMEWORLD
Tibrin

AVERAGE HEIGHT
1.7 meters

PRONUNCIATION
Ĭsh'-ē Tĭb

planners, accountants, and project managers—even more so because they are a tenacious people, never satisfied with leaving a job unfinished. These qualities also made the Ishi Tib greatly valued as tacticians during the Rebellion.

In the post–Yuuzhan Vong galaxy, Ishi Tib expertise at creating balanced environments has been especially needed, and as a result, Ishi Tib have been seen offworld in increasing numbers. More and more have been lured away from their home planet with offers of exorbitant salaries. However, some unprincipled corporations, after hiring Ishi Tib, find that their environmental concerns come into conflict with certain business ventures. These unlucky souls usually end up jobless, searching the galaxy and many times hiring themselves out to anyone who can get them closer to home. While Ishi Tib are more concerned about the needs of their fellow species members and families than anyone else, when they are offworld and alone, they frequently focus this attachment on others in their association. They have no inherent fear of other beings, and will reach out to them for companionship and assistance, although this can sadly put them into relationships with some rather shady characters.

Despite their subdued and pensive nature, the Ishi Tib are truly ruthless fighters. When pressed or cornered, Ishi Tib will go berserk and even, if possible, cannibalize opponents who incite them. Some unscrupulous members of society have exploited this behavior, enslaving itinerant Ishi Tib and forcing them to be unwitting executioners. While the Ishi Tib typically try to resist their impulse to kill when compelled by cruel taskmasters, most succumb to their baser natures if pushed past their emotional limits.

NOTABLE APPEARANCE
Episode VI: Return of the Jedi

ITHORIAN

Ithorians are a mammalian species who populated the planet Ithor in the Ottega system of the Mid Rim until it was ravaged and made uninhabitable by the Yuuzhan Vong. Ithorians are often referred to as Hammerheads because their head curves forward like a common hand tool. The only other obvious traits that differentiate them from standard mammals are their two mouths, located on either side of their necks, and their four throats, similarly divided, enabling them to speak in stereo. Their native tongue is based upon this ability, and although other species find the Ithorian language beautiful, it is impossible for non-Ithorians to reproduce. Ithorian language is a mixture of notes, tones, and inflections resembling music in two-part harmony, and thus most Ithorians speak Basic in order to interact with the rest of the galaxy.

Ithor was, before its devastation, a lush, tropical world where technology and nature existed together in harmony, as designed by the environmentally focused Ithorians. Ithor was renowned as a world of uncommon beauty, drawing to it countless ecotourists and other beings seeking a place of serenity. Ithorians worship a deity referred to as Mother Jungle, and to honor her, they pledged to keep their world as unspoiled as possible. To preserve the planet's surface, they lived in floating cities called herds or herd ships, and all Ithorians contributed to support the other members of their tribes. Herd cities traveled over the planet, hovering above the semi-intelligent bafforr trees without touching down in order to do as little damage to the environment as possible. The bafforr trees grew in large groves on Ithor, and were another object of Ithorian worship. On rare occasions, select Ithorians would hear the "call" of Mother Jungle, and descend to the planet's surface to live and serve her as ecological priests, never to return to their herd cities.

These city-ships had many levels, and were the centers for commerce, culture, and industry. Every five years, the herds would gather at an event known as the Meet, where Ithorians would tell stories, celebrate, debate, and vote on planetary issues. Smaller Meets were held in space for those traveling communities not able to return to Ithor. Now these smaller events are the core of Ithorian civilization, as the species can no longer reside on their homeworld. More than ever, Meets allow Ithorians to be with others of their kind, and prevent the extinction of Ithorian culture.

Ithorians were one of the earliest spacefaring species. The interstellar ships they built for space travel are similar to their herd ships, but equipped with hyperdrives. Their vessels mimic the environment of their planet, featuring indoor jungles, artificial storms, humid atmosphere, vegetation, and wildlife. Ithorians commonly travel to other worlds in caravans in order to trade merchandise, so many were offworld when the Yuuzhan Vong attacked.

The Ithorian people are peaceful and respectful to other life-forms. They are steadfast herbivores, and for every plant the Ithorians would consume on their world, in keeping with the Ithorian Law of Life, they would plant two more to keep the environment thriving. On their ships, they continue this tradition, and when visiting another world, they are always sensitive about disturbing that planet's ecology.

Despite their peaceful nature, Ithorians did develop powerful deflector shields to protect both their own world and their herd ships, and it was this technology that gave Ithorian herds the ability to roam their planet without armaments. Sadly, their lack of weaponry made them easy prey to the ruthless Yuuzhan Vong, who ravaged Ithor and destroyed all the native herd cities.

As made apparent by their limited armaments, Ithorians are committed pacifists. The desire to achieve peace at all times is an Ithorian goal. In one known case, an Ithorian named Zorneth took this aspiration to the extreme by trying to eliminate violence completely. With the assistance of a human named Klorr Vilia, Zorneth developed an herb called savorium that immediately transformed all those who consumed it, rendering them peaceful. While Vilia managed to destroy the herb after witnessing firsthand how it drastically

and unnaturally altered a being's nature, the Ithorians were hesitant to punish Zorneth in a manner that would please the New Republic, because his intentions were good. After an involved trial he was imprisoned, with the Ithorian people declaring that peace achieved without freedom of will is a false peace at best.

With Ithorians unable to dwell on their homeworld following the Yuuzhan Vong invasion, groups of Ithorian scientists returned to seek ways to bioengineer the planet and bring life back to the poisoned soil. However, with the work showing little progress, their people began the difficult search for a new homeworld. Through the aid of Leia Organa Solo, the planet Borao was chosen as an appropriate place for the Ithorians to settle, in the hope of starting life anew. However, a small number of Ithorians do remain exiled in their starship herds, holding out optimism that the scientists on Ithor will be successful in their efforts.

Ithorians tend to pursue professions that will not draw them into conflict with others. Very seldom will Ithorians serve in military positions, and while they managed to avoid the Galactic Civil War, some joined the Rebellion and New Republic in limited numbers. In addition, Ithorian Jedi are not unheard of. It is believed that membership in the Jedi order is consistent with the Ithorian dedication to peace, as Jedi strive to serve the well-being of all. One field that Ithorians are particularly drawn to, and excel in, is diplomacy. Their drive for harmony, and their natural talents at negotiation, make them highly effective at working out difficulties and drawing up treaties among beings. Throughout the galaxy, they also often act as merchants, negotiators, ecologists, botanists, healers, and scientists of varying fields. They enjoy travel, exploration, meeting new people, and learning new things, and especially delight in finding unique items to trade and sell as their herd ships roam the galaxy. Ithorians see the sharing of information and cultures as a means to peace through understanding, and it is a credit to their strength of character that they have maintained faith in this ideal in the wake of their world's devastation. In fact, despite this tragedy, they seem even more driven to further the cause of peace throughout the known systems, while settling into a new world that they hope to one day think of as their home.

DESIGNATION
Sentient

HOMEWORLD
Ithor

AVERAGE HEIGHT
2 meters

PRONUNCIATION
Ĭ-thō'-rē-ăn

NOTABLE APPEARANCE
Episode IV: A New Hope

JAWA

Jawas are small humanoids who live on Tatooine, the harsh Outer Rim desert world that was the childhood home of both Anakin and Luke Skywalker. While Jawas layer themselves under thick robes, xenobiologists, through studying corpses and skeletal remains, have discovered that they have the appearance of gaunt, rodent-like creatures, with shrunken faces and yellow eyes.

Each Jawa is about a meter tall, with tiny, flexible hands and feet. Their evolutionary origins are a bit mysterious. Some theories contend that both Jawas and their neighbors, the Tusken Raiders, descended from an ancient species known only as the Kumumgah, while others insist that Jawas evolved from rodents. If they did evolve from rodents, most scientists believe that they gradually grew in size and learned to walk upright by reaching for lichens and fungi growing on underground cave walls—caves that once housed the rare underground springs around which their society initially developed.

These springs eventually dried up, and the Jawas adapted to their new environment with sheer ingenuity. To protect themselves from the fierce double suns of their world, they started wearing coarse, homespun cloaks with large hoods under which only their yellow, glowing eyes seem to be visible. Their eyes are magnified by polished orange gemstones embedded in their facial coverings to protect their sensitive rat-like vision from the bright sunlight. These gems, called durindfire, are found in the desert sands and are worthless to other species—but the Jawas find them invaluable.

For their own nourishment, Jawas obtain water by inserting long, thin hoses down the stems of the funnel flower, a flora native to Tatooine, and siphoning off the liquid. Their diet is primarily made up of hubba gourd, a fruit difficult for humans to digest, the name of which in the Jawas' language translates to "the staff of life."

Most humans have noted that Jawas give off a strong, distinct, and usually unpleasant odor. This is the combined result of a mysterious solution in which they dip their clothes to retain body moisture, and the fact that they do not bathe often in their water-bereft environment. It is also partly related to their communication methods, half of which are pheromonal projections.

The meaning of the Jawas' language is tied to these pheromonal emanations, which communicate their emotions and needs. It is, therefore, incomprehensible and cannot be learned by humans and other species. While Jawas can understand Basic, they have intense difficulty speaking it or any language other than their own, and thus, to trade with non-Jawas, they use a simplified form of their language that residents of Tatooine refer to as Jawa Trade Language.

To make their living, Jawas salvage, repair, and resell junk that they find in the desert. Sometimes they even "find" items that haven't been lost, especially those that haven't been locked down. Moisture farmers often discover their property disappearing, only for it to turn up in the possession of a Jawa who is selling it at a tidy profit. Because of this, they are reputed to be swindlers and thieves, but Jawas are not offended by the accusation and are instead proud of their ability to discover items that others "lose," and also proud of their proficiency at repairing equipment. For junk that is unsalvageable, Jawas utilize high-powered solar smelters that melt things down into salable ingots.

Jawa society is divided into clans or tribes. Once a year, all the clans will meet at a giant gathering in the great basin of the Dune Sea, where they share stories, trade items, and even barter sons and daughters as "marriage merchandise." The trading of family members in marriage is considered a good business deal, as it continues the diversity of their bloodlines. In fact, Jawa culture centers on family. They take immense pride in their clans and ancestry, and their language includes forty-three different terms to describe relationship, lineage, and bloodline. Clans keep track of these relations very closely, recording family lines with extreme detail. Few Jawas leave the clan lifestyle, and when they do, they can be found in disreputable Tatooine cities such as Mos Eisley and Mos Espa. Members of the clans travel together in large vehicles known as sandcrawlers—nuclear-fusion-powered ore-hauling vehicles abandoned by contractors during the reign of the Old Republic. Jawas have modified these sandcrawlers to the point that their original purpose is virtually undetectable. Each crawler carries up to three hundred Jawas and acts as a fully equipped repair

shop, allowing them to perform skilled reconstructions as they make their journey across the desert wastes.

While a portion of the Jawas are constantly on the move, searching for salvage, the remainder stay behind in clan fortresses built from large chunks of wrecked spacecraft. Master repair experts reside in these fortresses, where they perform advanced salvage procedures that exceed the capacity of the sandcrawler shops. These elaborate fortifications are often subjected to attacks by Sand People, who will kill Jawas in order to pillage their scavenged treasures and precious water. This is one of many harsh desert realities that contribute greatly to Jawas' cautious, almost paranoid, nature, and as such they have made their defense into their best offense, through the stability of the fortresses they build. Jawas are not intense fighters, and because of their size, they'll often run away when confronted. When cornered, however, Jawas have proven themselves to be very resourceful and capable users of the weapons that they scavenge from the desert sands.

The most prominent member of each clan is the shaman, a female Jawa whom the population believes possesses the ability to predict the future. While this has not been scientifically proven, recently discovered studies of the Jawas performed before the ascension of Emperor Palpatine assert that these female shamans exhibited something akin to Force abilities. Unlike any Jedi, however, they perform elaborate spells, hexes, and blessings to protect the tribe and provide wellness for its members. Each shaman takes on a student during her tenure, training this apprentice to take her place when she dies.

The clan shaman, through her influence, controls most tribal decisions relating to defenses, travel, and day-to-day life. She does not travel in the sandcrawler, but remains behind at the permanent fortress, where she can be better protected. In fact, Jawas will fight to defend the shaman even in the face of certain defeat. In his notes, anthropologist Hoole referred to an incident where he witnessed Jawas defending the shaman's home against a force of Tusken Raiders with the ferocity of beings twice their size. They did not retreat or surrender, though nearly three-quarters of the Jawas lost their lives in the process.

DESIGNATION
Sentient

HOMEWORLD
Tatooine

AVERAGE HEIGHT
1 meter

PRONUNCIATION
Jä'-wä

NOTABLE APPEARANCE
Episode IV: A New Hope

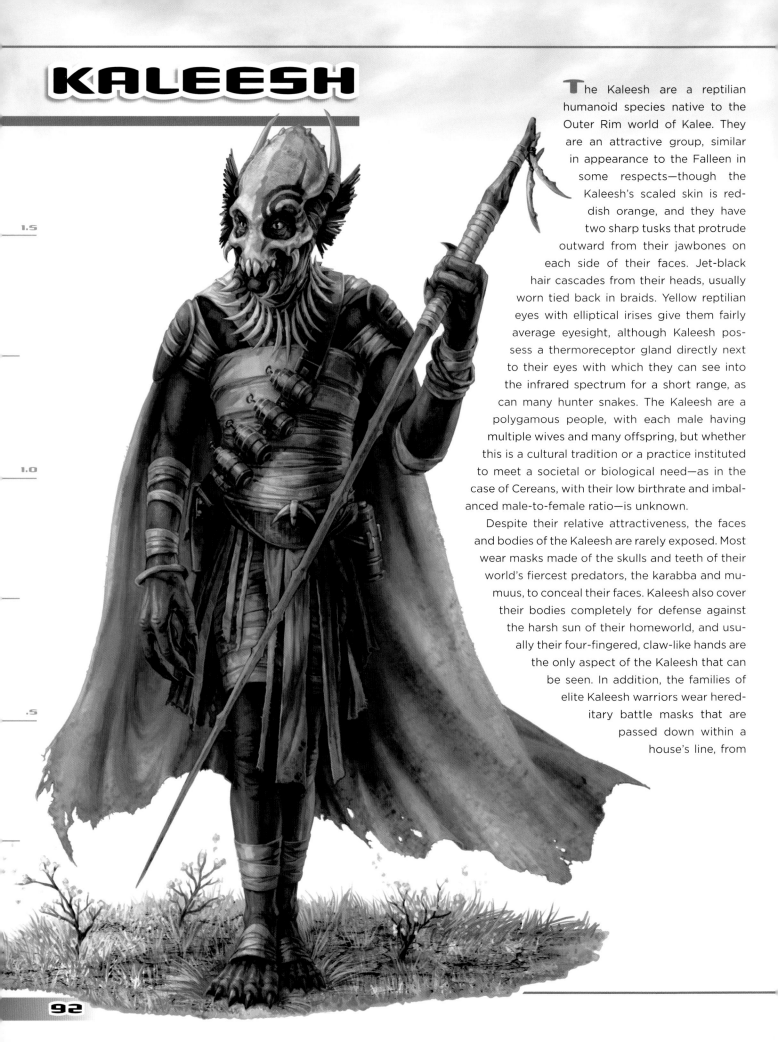

KALEESH

1.5

1.0

.5

The Kaleesh are a reptilian humanoid species native to the Outer Rim world of Kalee. They are an attractive group, similar in appearance to the Falleen in some respects—though the Kaleesh's scaled skin is reddish orange, and they have two sharp tusks that protrude outward from their jawbones on each side of their faces. Jet-black hair cascades from their heads, usually worn tied back in braids. Yellow reptilian eyes with elliptical irises give them fairly average eyesight, although Kaleesh possess a thermoreceptor gland directly next to their eyes with which they can see into the infrared spectrum for a short range, as can many hunter snakes. The Kaleesh are a polygamous people, with each male having multiple wives and many offspring, but whether this is a cultural tradition or a practice instituted to meet a societal or biological need—as in the case of Cereans, with their low birthrate and imbalanced male-to-female ratio—is unknown.

Despite their relative attractiveness, the faces and bodies of the Kaleesh are rarely exposed. Most wear masks made of the skulls and teeth of their world's fiercest predators, the karabba and mumuus, to conceal their faces. Kaleesh also cover their bodies completely for defense against the harsh sun of their homeworld, and usually their four-fingered, claw-like hands are the only aspect of the Kaleesh that can be seen. In addition, the families of elite Kaleesh warriors wear hereditary battle masks that are passed down within a house's line, from one generation to the next. These masks are painted with karabba and mumuu blood prior to a battle, in patterns that are unique to each family. After being used in combat, they are cleaned and stored until they are needed again.

The Kaleesh are a nomadic tribal people, and have become spacefaring only recently. During the waning years of the Old Republic, Kaleesh tribes united under a common leader who would later be known as Grievous, to fight off an invading insectoid race called the Huk. The Huk had already conquered and subjugated other worlds, plundering them of their natural riches. With barren Kalee, they sought to exploit the only commodity available to make a profit—people. The Huk captured Kaleesh by the hundreds and sold them as slaves.

Under Grievous's leadership, the Kaleesh banded together and drove the Huk from their planet. In the process, the Huk were completely decimated, pushed back to their own world and even beyond as Grievous, seeking revenge, co-opted Huk technology and ships for his own use, conquering their entire system and preying upon their colonies as well as the Huk homeworld.

The Huk, utterly overwhelmed by the vitriolic hatred and violence of the Kaleesh, sought help from the Old Republic, which—through the back-door manipulations of unknown forces—sympathized with the Huk and enacted economic sanctions against Kalee, enforced by the Jedi. Grievous withdrew to his homeworld angry and vengeful, to soon find it driven into the dust under the weight of economic sanctions. Witnessing his people starving and watching hundreds of thousands dying from famine, Grievous grew even more contemptuous of the Republic and the Jedi who protected it.

As if in answer to his woes, the InterGalactic Banking Clan, headed by a Muun named San Hill, offered Grievous a deal through which he could help his people financially. With his masterful military commanding skills, he would act as a collection agent against worlds that had defaulted on loans provided by the Banking Clan. Though Grievous bristled at being a paid "heavy," he took the offer. After all, the clan promised to relieve some of the terrible debts and financial stress levied upon his people, not to mention arranging to have the economic sanctions lifted.

For the most part, the Banking Clan did live up to the bargain, as did Grievous, delivering the debts of several planets to them. And yet the favorable relationship was not to last.

DESIGNATION
Sentient

HOMEWORLD
Kalee

AVERAGE HEIGHT
1.8 meters

PRONUNCIATION
Käl-ēsh'

When the Trade Federation refused to punish Grievous's old enemies for desecrating Kaleesh burial grounds on the Huk's colony worlds, Grievous abandoned his job, starting another conflict. The InterGalactic Banking Clan decided to repay him for his lack of commitment by setting off an explosive device in his ship. However, this attack was actually another ploy to keep Grievous under its sway, as the intent was never to kill him, but to make Grievous dependent and controllable. Wounded in the subsequent crash and suffering from additional injuries carefully inflicted afterward, Grievous was given a new cyborg body by Count Dooku and San Hill, who also secretly altered his mind, all with the help of the Geonosians. Without Grievous's knowledge and despite promises made to the contrary, Grievous's sense of honor as a warrior was removed, turning him into an unscrupulous conqueror. After this, the great Kaleesh military commander became little more than a lackey for the Separatists, until his eventual death at the hands of Jedi Master Obi-Wan Kenobi.

Following the fall of the Republic, and during the expansion of the Empire, the Kaleesh were generally overlooked until the New Republic rose to power. They remain a war-like people, although they are only known to be combative if provoked by outside forces. Extremely protective of what they consider sacred, the Kaleesh follow a religion that centers on ancestor worship. Their lands and burial grounds hold particular importance. Kaleesh believe that those who die in self-sacrifice and with honor are added to their pantheon of gods, and as a result, any burial ground is a holy place.

The primary area of worship for Kaleesh is an island called Abesmi, located in the middle of the warm world's single ocean, where it rises from the waves as a rectangular black formation of rock. This place is said to be the spot where Kaleesh ancestors descend from and rise to the heavens. It is customary to undertake pilgrimages to Abesmi, though most Kaleesh can make their proper worship commitments in local sculpted shrines that point in the direction of the legendary island. One of these newer shrines was built in honor of General Grievous, who is now a revered member of the religion's heavenly pantheon.

NOTABLE APPEARANCE
Star Wars Visionaries (comic)

KAMINOAN

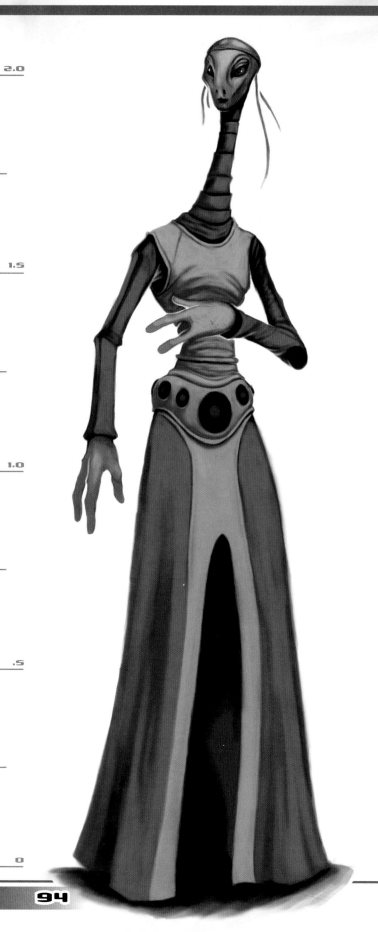

Kaminoans are thin, towering, pale-skinned humanoids who inhabit the little-known water-covered world of Kamino on the edge of Wild Space. They have long, graceful appendages, and their oblong heads sit atop slender, elongated necks. Their large, dark eyes enable them to see into the ultraviolet spectrum, and their tiny mouths are perfectly suited for the small amount of food they consume. Female Kaminoans are completely bald, while their male counterparts bear a unique headcrest.

When a severe shift in global temperatures caused the ending of a planetary ice age, flooding their world, the Kaminoans chose extreme methods to survive. They developed an exacting, detailed scientific method for cloning their own species, and enacted selective breeding to adapt their race to the changing environment through the elimination of weaknesses. As such, they are one of the most genetically homogeneous species in the known galaxy, having controlled variation from one Kaminoan to another. This is not to suggest that there is perfect genetic replication, but rather that the Kaminoans utilize a cloning process that produces children within a strict, predetermined set of genetic parameters.

Scientists are therefore greatly regarded and given high places of honor in society. Those who are most respected will literally wear a sign of their hierarchical placement on their sleeves—black cuffs are an indication of those who have earned esteem. The thicker the cuff, the higher the rank of the individual.

Kaminoans initially evolved from a species of marsh-dwelling amphibians who were focused on their communities at the suppression of individual expression. The early Kaminoans trained their young for specific tasks to serve the greater good of their people, and this communal focus has remained. While Kaminoans control their genetic codes, they also allow their children to develop their own interests and select careers of their choice within a community-approved set of parameters. The cloning process is designed to ensure sufficient numbers for each niche of society, as not all Kaminoans are employed in the cloning industry.

Because of their past struggle to survive and the Kaminoan cultural mind-set toward ending genetic weaknesses through selective breeding, the Kaminoans have developed an unspoken intolerance for physical frailty or imperfection in other species. While they are polite and gentle in their manner to outsiders, they cannot understand the tendency for most non-Kaminoans to maintain a lineage that includes any genetic imperfection. They feel all species that continue down such a pathway are inferior and deserving of eventual elimination. This attitude extends to all their cloning projects, wherein they will monitor creations for any irregularities in biochemistry, subjecting deviant clones to extensive conditioning to correct their aberrations. In keeping with their commitment to flawlessness, they have also developed methods of extreme sterilization so that clones are not spoiled with any defects. That they can keep such a large operation immaculate is considered a remarkable feat.

The Kaminoans work and dwell in huge floating cities that appear white and sparse to the naked human eye, yet all of their architectural constructions are actually decorated in the ultraviolet spectrum. They use cloned aiwhas for transportation between these floating cities. Even though Kaminoans have eliminated most of their weaknesses, they keep their living and working areas at a perpetual temperate climate, as they find the extreme temperatures of the outside world terribly uncomfortable, particularly high heat and bright sunlight. They prefer Kamino's autumn, when the skies never clear and a light rain is constantly falling. Kaminoans also have a deep respect for their origins, and the lessons learned from the catastrophe that changed their planet are continually reinforced. The cities in which Kaminoans originated now lie deep beneath Kamino's oceans, and they do not permit that environment to be disturbed, instead maintaining the ruins as sacred sites for pilgrimages.

The Kaminoans are relatively unknown throughout the galaxy at large, as they are not a species to travel beyond their home system. However, among those who are familiar with them, they are regarded as the greatest and most skilled producers of cloning technology. It was the Kaminoans who designed the cloned human soldiers who would later become the Grand Army of the Republic and eventually serve the Empire.

Despite their own prejudices, Kaminoans are forced to maintain some contact with the outside galaxy in order to trade for the raw materials and technologies that they require to sustain their highly advanced society. As a result, Kaminoans speak Basic in addition to their native language. Unlike other societies, they have not made any attempts to explore the possibility of undersea mining to obtain the materials they need, likely feeling it would only distract them from their primary focus on trade. Their products have always chiefly depended on their cloning science, which has supported them for generations, including times when they have quietly created armies of workers and soldiers for other cultures. Because Kaminoans have little compassion or feeling for beings other than themselves, they have no qualms about the questionable ethics of their cloning work. Instead, they are proud of their genetic

DESIGNATION
Sentient

HOMEWORLD
Kamino

AVERAGE HEIGHT
2.1 meters

PRONUNCIATION
Kă-mē-nŏ'-ăn

accomplishments, never taking into account the possible consequences.

While the Kaminoans were creating clones for the Grand Army of the Republic, they were also secretly designing a small clone force for their own protection. Approximately ten years before the destruction of the first Death Star, Kamino attempted to secede from the Empire. In a battle that saw clone fighting clone, with the great bounty hunter Boba Fett taking part on the Imperial side, the Kaminoans were defeated. Utilizing Boba Fett's knowledge of the facility, the Imperials destroyed the Kaminoan cloning equipment, preventing the species from ever again creating its own army. Large numbers of fleeing Kaminoans were shot down and killed as they attempted to leave the planet. However, a small contingent of cloners were forcibly relocated to Coruscant, and as a result their cloning technology survived through a good deal of the Imperial era.

After the Kaminoan insurrection, the Emperor ordered that clones would from then on be designed from multiple templates so that they would not be so easily corrupted against his New Order. However, the 501st Legion, the elite group of stormtroopers known as Vader's Fist, continued as a homogeneous entity based on the template provided by Jango Fett as they were produced in the Coruscant facility staffed by kidnapped Kaminoans. It wasn't until later years that non-Jango members were accepted into the ranks of the 501st. It is unclear whether the Kaminoans were able to reestablish their own cloning facilities on their homeworld, though there have been various reports that some Kaminoan cloning technology may have been smuggled offworld to be sold to the highest bidders.

NOTABLE APPEARANCE
Episode II: Attack of the Clones

KEL DOR

The Kel Dors are a kindly, soft-spoken people native to the planet Dorin, a world found in the Expansion Region that contains an atmosphere largely made up of helium and a second mysterious gas substance that is completely unique to the Dorin system. Kel Dors are hairless mammals who are so completely adapted to their native environment that they cannot breathe or see in other atmospheres without using special equipment. Initially, the effects of alternative atmospheres will result in eye and throat irritations, but eventually, if an environment is high enough in gases problematic for them and they are unable to hold their breath, Kel Dors will suffocate.

Members of the Kel Doran species possess greatly developed extrasensory organs located at the base of their skulls, which researchers suggests may actually be a subregion of their brains. Most Kel Dors have intense black eyes, though some are born with silver eyes, a trait that they believe marks them as strong in the Force. Their native Force-using shamans, known as the Baran Do Sages, will seek out such Kel Dors to recruit them into their ranks. The skin of a Kel Dor can range in color from peachy orange to deep red, and there are few outwardly visible differences between males and females.

As noted above, when offplanet, Kel Dors will wear an antiox breath mask and goggles. Fitted tightly against the detailed ridges of Kel Doran skulls and connecting into two breath tubes that extend downward from their faces, these masks are equipped with filters supplying Dorin atmospheric isotopes, enabling them to respire in environments that consist of oxygen, nitrogen, or carbon dioxide—substances normally deadly to Kel Dors. They will also outfit their offworld dwellings with special air locks and similar atmospheric filters and controls in order to maintain a proper habitat in which they can breathe. Kel Dors who depart Dorin must also don special eyewear to protect their eyes from burning in certain alien environments. Ironically, these goggles actually improve their eyesight, giving them superior vision when they have them on—although the masks can kill most members of other species if they tried to wear them, and the goggles can blind a non–Kel Dor. The masks also amplify the Kel Dors' voices, but even so, most need to shout in order to be heard through their filters.

1.5

1.0

.5

0

Kel Doran life is structured around the family. Couples will begin having children soon after marriage, with several generations of a family often living together in a single dwelling. This is not the result of a housing shortage or overcrowding as on other worlds, but from preference. With parents taking the lead and making major decisions, the entire family is responsible for the care of younglings, from providing for their daily care and early education to their training for professions. It is not unheard of for the majority of a single Kel Doran family to practice the same trade. However, should a Kel Doran child wish to pursue a career different than that of her or his family, they are not discouraged.

The society and economy of Dorin is technology driven. It is not surprising that they excel in the development and manufacture of environmental control devices, and this technological advancement is extended to the unique atmospheric needs of other species in addition to their own. As a result, Kel Doran environmental systems are used in homes and ships on many worlds and set the standard for the industry. Dorin enjoys a well-developed educational system in support of its industrial and scientific needs, and a free education is extended to all.

The Baran Do Sages are a long-standing Kel Doran Force tradition that predates even the Order of the Jedi Knights. For millennia, the Baran Do served as advisers and seers for Kel Doran leaders before Dorin joined the Old Republic. After they were introduced to the Old Republic, many Baran Do children entered the ranks of the Jedi Knights, though those who were too old to begin Jedi training or were passed over in the selection process carried on the Baran Do tradition as it was in the years before the Jedi came to prominence.

The Baran Do began their ascendance when adepts began exploring the Force in an attempt to expand their already powerful sensory perceptions—particularly with regard to predicting future events. Over time, their wisdom helped avert wars, natural disasters, and famines, as well as solving crimes and unraveling mysteries long left unrevealed. At the peak of their influence, they were honored as an omniscient sect that could discern the truth even in the most complex of issues. During their time in office, all Kel Doran rulers kept a sage as an adviser, as did many prominent households. Companies and government institutions used them to conduct day-to-day operations, as they could alert managers to important problems before they occurred.

Much of Baran Do training focuses on sensory deprivation—shutting down one sense to bring another to the forefront—or sensory overload—forcing oneself to concentrate amid a cacophony of sound or visual stimulation. As a result, Baran Do Jedi are usually very powerful with any skills involving their sensory perceptions, such as mental influence and telepathic communication. There have been cases recorded of Kel Dor Jedi communicating telepathically across great distances, perhaps even half the galaxy. They are rarely caught off guard, and unlike Jedi who view the future as always in motion, they can frequently pinpoint and predict immediate or even distant future events with incredible accuracy.

With the rise of the Jedi, the Baran Do fell into some obscurity, and in the mainstream of Kel Doran life, they came to be considered little more than wizards. However, the Baran Do continued to teach their ways even as the Emperor undertook his devastating Jedi Purge. As the New Republic rose to power, the Baran Do again began to make contact with the new Jedi order, in the hope that the two groups could work together toward a common goal in the galaxy.

As a species, Kel Dors are generally kindhearted and even-tempered. Besides their preponderance of Force talent, Kel Dors find great good in swift justice, and they will never refuse to help others in need. They have a strong tendency to see moral issues in very black-and-white terms, and do not always consider that there may be other issues at hand. As such, they are often encountered in policing or security roles when away from their native planet. Their sense of justice can be problematic, though, in that they have a propensity for taking the law into their own hands instead of waiting for standard methods of judgment to come into play.

DESIGNATION
Sentient

HOMEWORLD
Dorin

AVERAGE HEIGHT
1.7 meters

PRONUNCIATION
Kĕl' Dŏr

NOTABLE APPEARANCE
Episode I: The Phantom Menace

KILLIK

Killiks are an insectoid species originally native to Alderaan, a planet that had been located in the Core until it was destroyed by the Empire. While Killiks do vary in size and function depending upon their native hive, they all essentially have insect bodies covered in chitinous armor in nearly every color imaginable. Mandibles project from their faces, and four arms ending in long three-toed claws protrude from their torsos.

Killik society centers on a hive mind called the Will, with every Killik mentally connected to all the others, although the strength of the connection dissipates over distances. For this reason, a hive grouping will always act as one individual. At their core, they are peaceful—and yet they recently posed a great threat to the galaxy when their pheromonal telepathic connection to one another extended to include many other races, even non-insectoids. These "Joiners" function as one with the rest of the hive mind, losing independent will and purpose. Such an influence is actually more than simple mind control, in that it literally changes the chemical makeup of the Joiner's brain. In addition, left unchecked by environment or intervention, the Killiks will reproduce to such a degree that they will consume all natural resources in their path.

Killiks are separated into several subspecies, with each group making up a hive or "nest" of its own kind, though all of these nests are connected through a telepathic link. All Killiks begin life as larvae after hatching from eggs, but from that early point their size and function will vary, with each Killik taking on the characteristics of its particular nest. For example, the Jooj nest consists of Killiks only a few centimeters long, who create huge swarms to crawl under enemy soldiers' armor and kill them by draining their blood. The Taat are a hive of healers and warriors. Saras, meanwhile, are artists. Another nest known as the Kolosolaks consists of Killiks approximately fifty meters long and ten meters tall. With their tough exoskeletons, Kolosolaks are extremely hard to damage; they are used as armored ground vehicles.

These various Killik nests were at one time led and influenced by two others, the Unu and the Gorog. The Unu were the primary nest of all the hives, publicly directing the actions of the rest. Guided by the former human Jedi Raynar Thul (called UnuThul by the Killiks), the Unu communicated with the outside world and drew other species in as Joiners, making them part of the insect hive mind through use of membrosia, a highly addictive consumable produced by the Killiks. As the lead nest, it was the conscience of all the others, but over time, the Unu became tainted by one nest in the collective that had taken on a Dark Jedi as a leader: the Gorog, or Dark Nest.

While the nests are not Force-sensitive by nature, through the influence of their respective Force-sensitive Joiners, they took on Force-like abilities, and the Killik hive mind was sadly susceptible to corruption. During the war against the Yuuzhan Vong, the Jedi mounted an unsuccessful mission to Myrkr that, while claiming the life of Anakin Solo and resulting in the capture of Jacen Solo, was thought to have also culminated in the death of Raynar Thul. The presence of the Dark Jedi Lomi Plo and Welk complicated this tragic mission even further when Plo and Welk fled Myrkr in the Jedi's ship, not realizing that Thul was aboard. The vessel ultimately crashed in the Unknown Regions, fatally injuring the passengers, who reached out through the Force for help. They were found by the Killiks, who—despite their lack of experience with humans—healed them as best they could. As a result of these events, Thul was severely scarred from burns, and lost most of his facial features. Plo became more Killik than human, taking on several insectoid body parts, including a leg, arms, oversized eyes, and mandibles.

Prior to absorbing the minds of Thul, Plo, and Welk, the Killiks had been simple creatures. They possessed no inher-

DESIGNATION
Sentient

HOMEWORLD
Alderaan

AVERAGE HEIGHT
Varies from 3 centimeters to more than 2 meters

PRONUNCIATION
Kĭl'-lĭk

ent drive or need to live, dying and reproducing as a biological urge, not an emotional desire. It was only after these humans became Joiners that Killiks learned to value life and the individual. This new mind-set was crucial in influencing the events that followed.

The Unu under Thul's influence was mostly benign, and the Killiks simply wanted to survive. However, the hive known as the Gorog was soon corrupted to become the Dark Nest, having absorbed Lomi Plo and Welk and twisted into a secret hive bent on violence and conquest. The influence of this subverted hive spread to the others as an individual would be provoked by his or her unconscious, inducing the Killiks to dominate the galaxy by sucking in as many Joiners as they could, colonizing one populated world after another. Due to UnuThul's innocence and worsening state of madness, the Gorog was able to hide its presence and activities from him, to the extent that UnuThul denied their existence.

The Killiks began a war of conquest, seeking more and more territories into which they could expand. They started with incursions into Chiss space, and even though this soon led to the eruption of a brutal war that threatened to engulf the entire galaxy, the Killiks reached farther, eventually taking the Alliance world of Thyferra, the home of the insectoid Vratix and a base of bacta manufacturing. Ultimately, Lomi Plo was slain by Luke Skywalker, and Raynar Thul was separated from the Killik hive mind and brought to Coruscant for treatment.

The Killiks have existed for countless millennia, witnessing the creation of the famous and mysterious Centerpoint Station and the nearby Maw. Thirty millennia before the Battle of Yavin, the Celestials reportedly drove them from both Alderaan and their colony on Alsakan into the Unknown Regions, after the Killiks had consumed Alderaan's resources and were planning a move to take over a populated world. The lesson in this, and the one that was eventually heeded by the Galactic Federation of Free Alliances, is that some form of containment of the Killiks is necessary. They were finally defeated by the Galactic Alliance, but only after a great loss of life on both sides—though the Killiks did not seem emotionally affected at the individual loss of life, either their own or those of their Joiners.

NOTABLE APPEARANCE
Dark Nest I: The Joiner King (novel)

KITONAK

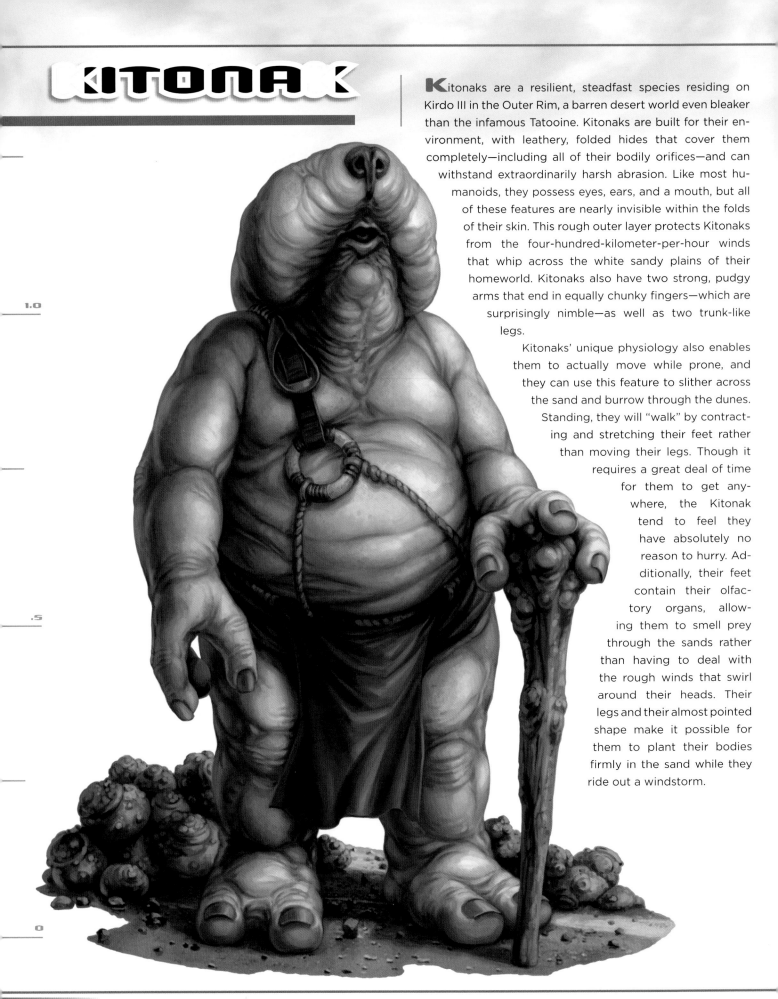

Kitonaks are a resilient, steadfast species residing on Kirdo III in the Outer Rim, a barren desert world even bleaker than the infamous Tatooine. Kitonaks are built for their environment, with leathery, folded hides that cover them completely—including all of their bodily orifices—and can withstand extraordinarily harsh abrasion. Like most humanoids, they possess eyes, ears, and a mouth, but all of these features are nearly invisible within the folds of their skin. This rough outer layer protects Kitonaks from the four-hundred-kilometer-per-hour winds that whip across the white sandy plains of their homeworld. Kitonaks also have two strong, pudgy arms that end in equally chunky fingers—which are surprisingly nimble—as well as two trunk-like legs.

Kitonaks' unique physiology also enables them to actually move while prone, and they can use this feature to slither across the sand and burrow through the dunes. Standing, they will "walk" by contracting and stretching their feet rather than moving their legs. Though it requires a great deal of time for them to get anywhere, the Kitonak tend to feel they have absolutely no reason to hurry. Additionally, their feet contain their olfactory organs, allowing them to smell prey through the sands rather than having to deal with the rough winds that swirl around their heads. Their legs and their almost pointed shape make it possible for them to plant their bodies firmly in the sand while they ride out a windstorm.

1.0

.5

0

Waiting is not new to Kitonaks. They are one of the most patient species in the galaxy—*so* patient, in fact, that they frequently irritate other species with their plodding, methodical mannerisms. They rarely do anything quickly, and this includes breathing and eating. Kitonaks possess an extra set of lungs that enables them to store oxygen for three or four standard hours, and their stored fat aids them in going without food for weeks, provided that they do not overexert themselves.

Their culture is a simple, primitive one, with no technology. Kitonaks live in small tribal groups that migrate around the desert following herds of chooba, their primary source of sustenance. Their method of hunting is most indicative of their slow-paced way of life, in that it involves standing motionless and mimicking a sulfaro plant—the chooba's favorite dish. Kitonaks will wait as the chooba climbs to the top of their head, looking for the "plant's" meaty interior, at which point they swallow the chooba whole. One of these creatures can provide a Kitonak enough nourishment to last for an entire standard month.

As the Kitonak have no natural foes, there are only two native things they fear: quicksand and caves. Should one of them fall victim to quicksand, their patient nature often permits them to simply float and breathe until help arrives. The only problem is that help isn't often very speedy.

Caves, meanwhile, are considered by Kitonaks to be gateways to the underworld. On Kirdo III, there exist many tales of Kitonaks who have entered caves and not returned, and local legends refer to such places as gateways to the Realm of the Dead. For this reason, Kitonaks will avoid going into caves at any cost, even facing the deadliest of windstorms before entering one.

Kitonaks get most of their education from tales and songs. Every evening a "telling of the story" is held, which can last for several hours. Each tribe member takes a turn adding new twists to the plot and singing lyrics to further the tale along. This tradition is meant to instruct the young on the value of patience, but it also succeeds in relaying a good deal of information about the world in which they dwell. A full story may actually last several nights, but each evening is carefully planned to end a certain episode in the tale. Many of these stories focus on the most important event for the Kitonak circle of life: the rainfall, which occurs only once a decade.

DESIGNATION
Sentient

HOMEWORLD
Kirdo III

AVERAGE
HEIGHT
1.3 meters

PRONUNCIATION
Kĭt'-ō-năk

Kitonak mating centers on the rainfall on Kirdo III, a deluge that lasts several days, creates vast lakes, and turns the dry riverbeds into flowing rivers. When the rains finally stop, Kitonaks begin their "Great Celebration of Life," in which they dive into the temporary rivers and conduct a mating ritual known as the Dance of Love. After this, they emerge downstream, and any females who conceived during the previous rainfall will surface with newborn children. This occurs because the Kitonak gestation period equals the duration of time between rainfalls, and females fertilized during one Celebration give birth at the next.

Members of the species also mature fully in nine years, just in time to take part in the next Celebration. After each rainfall, if a Kitonak tribe has grown too large, some of its younger members will depart to find another tribe that has fewer. These solitary Kitonaks will often hollow out chidinka plants to make a chidinkalu, a pipe instrument with which they play songs to attract others. Unfortunately, there have been incidents of slave traders kidnapping some of these wandering Kitonaks. As slaves, it is suspected that they did not last long, since other species have no tolerance for their slow, tenacious personalities. Sadly, there are often reports of Kitonaks being beaten or abandoned by their owners in places where they could not survive without assistance.

However, their musical traditions have become somewhat influential in the galactic music world. Kitonaks who wander the galaxy either freely or as slaves are usually engaged as musicians, as their compositions and style are original and uplifting. The most widely known Kitonak musician was Droopy McCool, who, following his release from slavery, played with Evar Orbus and his Galactic Wailers. The Galactic Wailers later became the Max Rebo Band, during an extended gig at the palace of Jabba the Hutt on Tatooine. After Jabba's death, Droopy walked off alone into the Tatooine desert, believing he heard the call of other Kitonaks. He was never heard from or seen again. While it has not been verified, there are rumors of a Kitonak colony on Tatooine, somewhere between Mos Eisley and Anchorhead. One can hope that Droopy found what he was longing for.

NOTABLE APPEARANCE
Episode VI: Return of the Jedi

KLATOOINIAN

Klatooinians, of the Outer Rim planet Klatooine, have been in the service of the Hutts for nearly twenty-five thousand standard years. They are a canine-based species that long ago evolved into sentience, with coarse brown or greenish skin and dog-like faces featuring dark eyes and heavy brows. Although the genders are rarely confused, there is little noticeable difference between male and female Klatooinians, other than the fact that males are generally slightly heavier in build. Klatooinian culture predates even the Old Republic, making them one of the oldest sentient species in the galaxy, short of only a handful of species including the Hutts and humans.

Klatooinians have proven extremely loyal foot soldiers, displaying tenacity, fierceness, and unwavering devotion. The Hutts—always the opportunists—exploited this characteristic loyalty by tricking the Klatooinians into co-signing a contract called the Treaty of Vontor that placed them and the two other species of the Si'klaata Cluster, the Nikto and the Vodrans, into Hutt servitude for an indefinite period of time. The primary Klatooinian instigator of this treaty was an individual named Barada M'Beg. M'Beg became a hero to his people because the Klatooinians saw the Hutts as near-gods, potentially the "ancients" of their legends. The treaty therefore bound them to their deities. Many Klatooinian children are named Barada or M'Beg because of M'Beg's popularity and heroic and legendary status among his people.

Of course, the Klatooinian submission to Hutt rule has proven invaluable to the Hutts, particularly since the Klatooinians were instrumental in helping the Hutts overthrow the infamous warlord Xim the Despot. It is because the Hutts still find the Klatooinians useful as foot soldiers that they remain in service today. But to the Klatooinian mentality, all things pass away in time, even treaties—a belief of which the Hutts remain wary.

This sense of impermanent servitude was evident even among the Klatooinians in Jabba's cadre, as reported by Lando Calrissian. A Klatooinian named Barada indentured under protest to Jabba the Hutt was a mechanic who maintained all of the Hutt's repulsorlift vehicles and also served as a part-time guard for the crimelord as well. Known for wearing an orange scarf to symbolize a protest against unjust servitude to others of his own people (a protest Jabba either didn't care about or didn't recognize), Barada was chafing, as many of his people eventually did, under the Hutt's control. Unfortunately, he was unable to take advantage of the freedom Jabba's death would have offered him because he was cut down by Luke Skywalker during the skirmish above the Great Pit of Carkoon. Calrissian reported one other Klatooinian named Kithaba present at the confrontation, who held the unfortunate distinction of being the first of Jabba's skiff guards to fall toward the maw of the Sarlacc. Despite his best efforts to claw his way free, Kithaba was eventually grappled by one of the Sarlacc's inflamed tentacles and devoured.

Time is pivotal to understanding Klatooinian culture. At some time before history was recorded on Klatooine, in the middle of Klatooine's Derelkoos Desert, a natural fissure to the world's crust opened, allowing a liquid known as wintrium to seep out and touch the dry desert air. This contact resulted in the formation of a large glass "sculpture," a creation that resembled a giant water spout frozen in time. The landmark is much lauded throughout the galaxy as one of the most beautiful and impressive natural formations in known space. Originally called the Fountain of the Ancients, this phenomenon is a religious symbol of patience, fortitude, and "Strength with Age." Klatooinians believe that time is the eternal truth and the most powerful of forces, because all else will pass away in its wake. Yet the fountain appears to grow stronger as it ages, and thus, as "children of the fountain," the Klatooinians feel that they, too, can strengthen with age—until they are resilient enough to perhaps become independent. Since it is such a potent symbol, they guard it protectively, and to keep the fountain as it was in the era of the ancients, no technology is permitted within a kilometer of it.

The worship of time is at the center of Klatooinian religious belief, so it is no wonder that they were in awe of the Hutts, who revealed to the Klatooinians that they can live to an age of more than one thousand standard years. In fact, many Klatooinians have come to believe that the Hutts *were* the Ancients, and so they feel it is right to serve them—for now.

Much of Klatooine life is a continuation of the species' subjugation and aims to ensure their servitude to the Hutts. As young children, Klatooinians spend their first decade being indoctrinated into history, traditions, myths, and legends in a schooling that typically drains them of all their individual-

ity. However, this instruction is done orally, as most Klatooinians are illiterate. Furthermore, in deference to their Huttese overlords and to prepare Klatooinian children for their future service, the instruction is conducted in the language of the Hutts, not Klatooinian. Usually the only difference in the children once schooling ends is their names, although even names in Klatooinian culture are drawn from a limited pool inspired by prominent Klatooinian historical figures. After ten standard years of schooling, Klatooinian children are sold into servitude in the cities or towns under Hutt rule, at which time they learn the specific trade that they will pursue for the rest of their lives. Disrespectful and rebellious youths are sold into harsher conditions of slavery, working mines, shipyards, mills, and quarries on and around Klatooine.

DESIGNATION
Sentient

HOMEWORLD
Klatooine

AVERAGE
HEIGHT
1.8 meters

PRONUNCIATION
Klă-tōō-ĭn'-ē-ăn

The collapse of the Old Republic and later descent of the Emperor's New Order into civil war inspired many young Klatooinians to escape and join the Rebellion, while others hid in the Klatooinian wilderness or even the far reaches of the galaxy. This emerging group of Klatooinian revolutionaries also began reclamation of their native language, relying on ancient and fragile texts that had somehow managed to survive undiscovered by the Hutts.

Currently, the Klatooinian government still lives in fear of their Hutt lords, although the patience of this people is becoming frayed under the weight of the contract they signed millennia ago. Klatooine is ruled by a Council of Elders that resides in a palace built around the fountain, which is now referred to as the Fountain of the Hutt Ancients. This new title has been another cause for members of the younger generations to attempt further rebellions, with uprisings becoming more and more frequent. Among the youth, it is believed that if the Old Republic and the Emperor could fall, then it might also be possible for them to free themselves from Huttese bondage, and that the members of the Council of Elders are mere cowards for their continued subservience to the Hutts. The Hutts, seeing these signs of discontent, have tried strongly pressing their will upon their servants, becoming more ruthless and cold in their treatment of the Klatooinians. But as they do, they are being met with more vigorous resistance. Societal watchers theorize that this is the beginning of the end of the master–servant relationship between the Hutts and Klatooinians, but only time will tell.

NOTABLE APPEARANCE
Episode VI: Return of the Jedi

KOORIVAR

Koorivar are tall humanoids who inhabit a tropical world of vast oceans and lush rain forests known as Kooriva, located in the Inner Rim. Koorivar vary in skin color from magenta to mauve and from dark green to black. Banding ridges crown their brows, tapering down onto their noses past sickly looking yellow or green eyes. A colorful spiraling horn rises from the tops of their heads, and this feature can be found on both males and females. Females who have borne children and preside over families wear matron's hoods, indicating a level of influence.

A Koorivar's horn grows during puberty but ceases developing upon reaching adulthood. It is a trait of great cultural and societal importance among their people, and the length or beauty of one's horn increases one's status in society. Koorivar who are genetically disposed to have larger horns tend to garner more prestige, leading to an unofficial upper class of genetically "superior" Koorivar. In general, Koorivar will decorate their horns to make them more attractive to their fellows. Loss or damage of a horn usually leads to a marked loss of status and prestige—sometimes even isolation from society.

Koorivar are a shrewd people, wary of danger and uncomfortable situations. They prefer to remain out of harm's way and will use their wits to escape a bad scene, bargaining with or fooling opponents rather than directly fighting with them. In fact, bargaining is also the way Koorivar form their families. A marriage on Kooriva is arranged by two houses who wish to join resources for a mutually beneficial financial outcome. After presenting the qualities of their offspring to their potential mate, the parents will exhibit a prospectus on the financial stability of their family and the lucrative potential of merging their business efforts with those of the other clan. Days and sometimes weeks of negotiations take place before the two families agree to business terms, and sometimes even then these "mergers" will fall through. The children who are to be married are as large a part of the process as their parents, and are traditionally involved in the bidding process. When presented with the idea of marrying for love, Koorivar often openly scoff at such an unprofitable concept, seeing the institution of marriage as a means for society to build its ultimate strength and dominance through wealth.

This cooperation and focus on mutual benefits extends to the Koorivar's business enterprises and dealings with one another as well, and many Koorivar will band together on any number of financial undertakings, pooling resources and efforts to maximize profits. Undercutting others in business, like the idea of love, is viewed as counterproductive.

Koorivarn children are groomed for this cooperative business mind-set from early childhood, as all schools on Kooriva center on the business arts. Extensive classes are reserved for developing and marketing new products, incorporating selling techniques, and practicing public speaking for the goal of negotiations.

Before they reach the age of ten standard years, most Koorivarn children have begun their first credit-earning job, with some being so ambitious as to start their own fledgling businesses.

Koorivar speak their own language, a combination of whispers, soft sibilants, and hand gestures. Although Koorivar also use Basic, they have a slight advantage over many other species as they are in tune with body language and the sensing of other beings' motives based on how they move. This skill is particularly useful because Koorivar frequently work with other species so that they may benefit from their various unique talents and contributions. Koorivarn nobles in particular will crew their ships with members of many species.

While Koorivar have adopted the name of their planet, Kooriva is not their original home. When the star of their unknown homeworld became unstable, they migrated to Kooriva, leasing the planet from the Old Republic for several centuries. After this amount of time, they adopted their new name and formally requested that the Galactic Senate allow them to finally take possession of their world of residence. When the Senate rejected their request, Koorivar set out to gain enough influence to reverse the decision. They wandered the galaxy as merchants, striking up business deals that gained them more and more sway over member worlds of the Galactic Senate. After a time, the decision was overturned.

With their remarkable talent for business, other merchants remain somewhat leery of Koorivar. They will wander from world to world, buying shares of stock or merchandise at low prices and selling them elsewhere for a considerable profit. Driven to gain power and influence, they brazenly set out to the farthest corners of the galaxy in search of profitable business deals. One of the species' more controversial ploys was to sell weaponry and war matériel such as their weather production machines to battling peoples—trading with both sides. Of course they tried to keep this tactic secret, but when it did come to light it ruined their reputation as reliable merchants. The Republic began to investigate the charges, and when the Koorivarn government tried to protect some of the more corrupt offenders, the Galactic Senate set up economic sanctions against Koorivar and blockaded their world—forcing Koorivar to pay heavy tariffs on any product shipments coming in or out of their system.

To save their economy from utter ruin, Koorivar complied with the Senate's requirements for free trade. They then learned to go to even greater lengths to keep illegal practices under wraps, or to make sure their business dealings are completely legitimate.

DESIGNATION
Sentient

HOMEWORLD
Kooriva (by way of an unknown homeworld)

AVERAGE HEIGHT
1.9 meters

PRONUNCIATION
Kōr'-ē-vär

With the rise of the New Republic, Koorivar maintained their powerful presence in the business world, sitting on the boards of most major corporations in the known galaxy. Although Koorivar sided with the Separatists during the Clone Wars, and their business interests suffered greatly from the Empire's nonhuman biases, they have, as a species, made impressive strides in regaining their wealth and influence through cunning and tenacity. However, the Galactic Alliance Committee on Corporate Oversight keeps a close eye on the commercial activities of Koorivar to ensure compliance with the law.

While Koorivar are generally business focused, they have a strong streak of militarism when it comes to guarding their interests. For this purpose they established a renowned fighting force known as the Koorivar Fusiliers during the Clone Wars. Employed by the Corporate Alliance, they performed a key roll in the Confederacy of Independent Systems' military strategy. Garbed in red head-armor (which displayed their horns), rib-armor, black metal boots, and metal gloves, they were an impressive group of fighters who employed the use of Koorivar-fabricated blasters. These soldiers were utilized by Passel Argente, leader of the Corporate Alliance, as personal guards, and General Grievous commanded divisions of Koorivar Fusiliers in his Outer Rim Sieges. They were also directed at the battles of Moorja and Bomis Koori IV by General Oro Dassyne, a Koorivar of unique status among his people.

Appointed a general of the Fusiliers by Passel Argente, Dassyne was greatly enamored of glory and often requested frontline action. As a result, he was wounded and suffered skull trauma that damaged his horn. To compensate for his physical loss, he wore a miter that was even larger than his horn had been. Even though loss of a horn usually incurs a loss of status, Dassyne maintained his status through sheer force of will. But this overcompensation ultimately led to his downfall. His clever leadership of troops in the past was replaced with a reliance on greater firepower for defense. Sent to protect Bomis Koori IV, a stronghold of the Corporate Alliance defenses, he fortified the world with highly powerful artillery and shields anticipating an attack from a Jedi army. Instead, he was outwitted by only two Jedi, Obi Wan Kenobi and Anakin Skywalker and soundly defeated. Had he survived this battle, his loss of status would have left him in utter ruin, exiled from his people.

NOTABLE APPEARANCE
Episode II: Attack of the Clones

KOWAKIAN MONKEY-LIZARD

Kowakian monkey-lizards are a playful reptilian species hailing from the Outer Rim world of Kowak. These small, quick, and agile creatures have long floppy ears, beak-like noses, tufts of brown or black hair on their heads and backs, and wild, yellow eyes. Monkey-lizards have twiggy extremities, but their bellies are distended from overeating—particularly when they are domesticated—and some subspecies have prehensile tails. While these reptiles may give the appearance of easy prey to any larger predator, their nimble bodies, acute hearing, and sharp eyesight make them extremely difficult to catch. Their brown skin will actually shift its tint in different environments, often making them virtually invisible to pursuing predators.

Monkey-lizards live primarily in tree nests, and enjoy swinging through the verdant rain forests of their homeworld. They feed on insects, worms, and small rodents, eating frequently, as their tiny, energetic bodies require a great deal of nourishment. Monkey-lizards are traditionally scavengers, preferring carrion to fresh meat or vegetation. As carrion is not particularly healthy to eat in most circumstances, some have speculated why monkey-lizards have this odd preference. They may prefer to have others do their work for them in acquiring food, or it may be the result of an innate avoidance of predatory dangers.

While they do display a fair amount of intelligence, monkey-lizards still appear to be on the brink of further evolution. They have no structured society to speak of, although they do exhibit hierarchical boundaries within a group of nests. Leadership appears to fall to the oldest female, and each monkey-lizard in a nesting group is assigned a specific role: one will be a food gatherer, another will maintain the nest, while yet another will scout for predators. Little is known about their reproductive habits in the wild, and the monkey-lizards managed to drive off the last group that attempted to study them. In captivity, they are usually not kept with others of their species, as the noise they make is simply too great. However, it is believed that monkey-lizards lay eggs once a year, with a few of the eggs surviving to hatch.

1.0

.5

0

Being curious and prone to exploration, these creatures can be quite destructive. Monkey-lizards acquired as pets often end up sold off when private owners are unable to control them. Primary complaints from owners concern their disruptiveness, their tendency to break valuables and deface artwork and furniture, as well as their habit of rummaging through garbage compactors.

In the wild, these creatures are rarely alone, preferring to move in packs for protection. One of the most notable features of monkey-lizards—their incessant, annoying laughter—is a noise they will often make to frighten away predators. Moving in groups, they can create a great clamor so as to intimidate would-be opponents. Once they discover a source of food, they will scuffle with one another over the meal rather than sharing it, a trait that betrays a certain temperament. Monkey-lizards have the capacity to be mean-spirited and cruel (to use a term typically applied to known sentients) to other beings, whether they are members of their own species or not. They will take easy opportunities to mock others with direct laughter or through minor attacks such as throwing things at them, simply because it amuses them. In addition, as mentioned above, University of Coruscant researchers reported that while camped on Kowak to observe the monkey-lizards, the creatures put snakes in their sleeping gear, and even placed buckets of water in trees, only to drop them on the researchers when they passed by unawares.

There has been a great debate in the scientific community as to whether monkey-lizards are sentient or not, and the issue has not been officially decided, though some declare that they must be sentient, for no simple-minded beast could be so clever. While monkey-lizards do not have any art or culture to speak of, they clearly possess a distinct, if questionable, sense of mischief and humor. They can learn to mimic most languages, and according to some observers, actually communicate in those languages if they feel like it. They will even laugh, strangely enough, at appropriate—or sometimes inappropriate—moments during conversations. It is common knowledge in certain circles that monkey-lizards can repeat back what they hear with some accuracy, and for this reason many underworld kingpins keep them as pets who double as excellent spies. However, it is widely believed that, sentient or not, monkey-lizards are obnoxious creatures, and to call someone a "Kowakian monkey-lizard" is an insult.

One piece of evidence that supports their sentience is that some have been found to be Force-sensitive. Records from the Empire refer to Picaroon C. Boodle, a monkey-lizard captured by the Imperials as a research subject because of his latent Force abilities. He was mutated, pressed into service to the Dark Jedi Jerec, and sent to the fabled Valley of the Jedi, where he died in battle with the Jedi Kyle Katarn. It is possible that additional monkey-lizards are Force-sensitive, but none have been identified to date due to their capricious and troublesome natures.

Meanwhile, a large number of monkey-lizards have been encountered in the galactic underworld, tied to criminal organizations. One of the best-known monkey-lizards to serve a criminal figure was Salacious Crumb. While it is not known how this monkey-lizard came by his name, Crumb was employed by Jabba primarily as a court jester, but vague and perhaps unreliable reports assert that Crumb was also tasked with eavesdropping on Jabba's visiting competitors and members of his court, listening for any signs of intrigue that could harm Jabba's business dealings or, worse, his health. First captured by Jabba when he was trying to steal food from him—and almost becoming a meal himself in the process—Crumb parlayed his value as a spy and a source of amusement into the comfortable position he held until perishing on Jabba's sail barge in the Dune Sea.

At one time, these creatures were rarely seen off their native world. However, they have consistently managed to sneak onto visiting ships, and often wind up in the strangest of places. They have also become a fad among some of the wealthy upper class, who, like their underworld counterparts, keep them as pets for entertainment. However, they are clearly not always well looked upon as household creatures in proper or polite society because they are quite untrainable, no matter how much time or effort is devoted to it or what method is used.

DESIGNATION
Semi-sentient
(or sentient)

HOMEWORLD
Kowak

**AVERAGE
HEIGHT**
70 centimeters

PRONUNCIATION
Kō-wä′-kē-ăn
Mŏn-kē-Lĭ′-zărd

NOTABLE APPEARANCE
Episode VI: Return of the Jedi

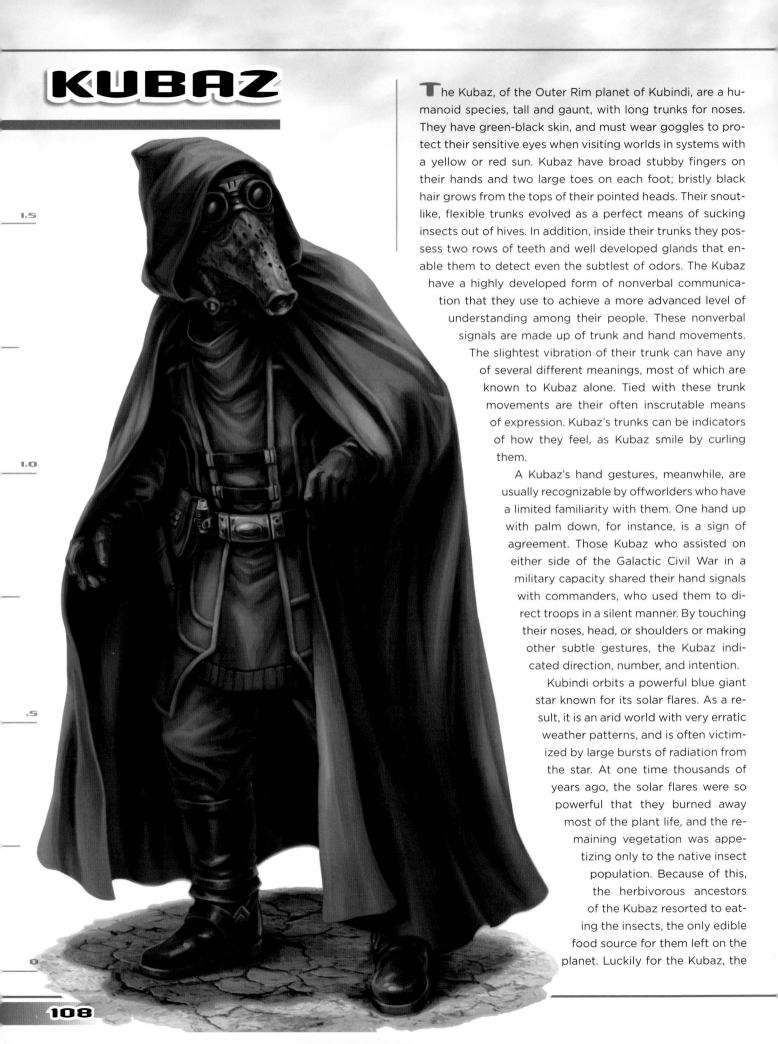

KUBAZ

The Kubaz, of the Outer Rim planet of Kubindi, are a humanoid species, tall and gaunt, with long trunks for noses. They have green-black skin, and must wear goggles to protect their sensitive eyes when visiting worlds in systems with a yellow or red sun. Kubaz have broad stubby fingers on their hands and two large toes on each foot; bristly black hair grows from the tops of their pointed heads. Their snout-like, flexible trunks evolved as a perfect means of sucking insects out of hives. In addition, inside their trunks they possess two rows of teeth and well developed glands that enable them to detect even the subtlest of odors. The Kubaz have a highly developed form of nonverbal communication that they use to achieve a more advanced level of understanding among their people. These nonverbal signals are made up of trunk and hand movements. The slightest vibration of their trunk can have any of several different meanings, most of which are known to Kubaz alone. Tied with these trunk movements are their often inscrutable means of expression. Kubaz's trunks can be indicators of how they feel, as Kubaz smile by curling them.

A Kubaz's hand gestures, meanwhile, are usually recognizable by offworlders who have a limited familiarity with them. One hand up with palm down, for instance, is a sign of agreement. Those Kubaz who assisted on either side of the Galactic Civil War in a military capacity shared their hand signals with commanders, who used them to direct troops in a silent manner. By touching their noses, head, or shoulders or making other subtle gestures, the Kubaz indicated direction, number, and intention.

Kubindi orbits a powerful blue giant star known for its solar flares. As a result, it is an arid world with very erratic weather patterns, and is often victimized by large bursts of radiation from the star. At one time thousands of years ago, the solar flares were so powerful that they burned away most of the plant life, and the remaining vegetation was appetizing only to the native insect population. Because of this, the herbivorous ancestors of the Kubaz resorted to eating the insects, the only edible food source for them left on the planet. Luckily for the Kubaz, the plant life eventually grew back and adapted to the solar flare activity that is still common on Kubindi, and new variations of insects began appearing after each incident of solar flaring—most likely the product of the mutative radiation, as some of these insects grow as large as Tatooine banthas. Over time, Kubaz's physiology adjusted to their new diet.

Eventually, Kubaz stopped hunting for insect hives and instead began farming them in greater numbers, although individual hives could be stolen and difficult to claim if recovered. Thus, Kubaz developed designer strains of insects, declaring distinctive results for specific clans on Kubindi. Then, to increase variety in their meals, the clans began trading individual hives, and capitalistic commerce on Kubindi was soon under way. Kubaz society became dominated by certain clans, which each control millions of insect hives. Today, Kubaz culture, business, finance, and space and computer technology have developed entirely out of the production and sale of insects, along with a very special high-class insect cuisine. Kubaz insect banquets are a highlight of their culture, and the food is considered a delicacy. While Kubaz will not be insulted if a guest does not wish to partake in an insect meal, they would probably conclude that the visitor simply lacks both refinement and good taste.

This singular diet has caused them difficulties interacting in galactic society, as they do not recognize sentient insectoid species as anything other than food. The Old Republic discouraged the Kubaz from developing starship or hyperdrive technology until they acknowledged the rights of intelligent insectoids. The Empire later maintained this policy for no other reason than its overarching attempt to keep other species separated from humans. Kubaz were still eager to explore the galaxy, though, and threw all their scientific efforts into developing hyperdrive technology, but through subterfuge and sabotage, the Empire disrupted their plans. Furthermore, the Empire blamed the destruction of their earlier hyperdrive designs and other scientific developments on the defunct Republic, which encouraged the Kubaz to aid the Empire in various ways—most frequently as spies.

Kubaz are particularly skilled at establishing networks of business associates and information suppliers, often knowing someone who knows someone and using this to their advantage. They are also extremely talented reading intentions through observation, another natural trait that made them very valuable to the Empire. However, not long into the

Galactic Civil War, Kubaz discovered the Empire's treachery through their observational prowess, and many left Kubindi to join the Rebellion.

Outside of the spy business, Kubaz are a highly educated people who enjoy the arts, music, literature, and other sophisticated entertainments included with the gentrified ways of society. Espionage cannot be taken as the defining characteristic of Kubaz life or sense of morality. Highly social beings, they are extremely focused on manners and refinement, as well as traditions and history. Decorum and tact are also highly valued.

Kubaz love to dote on their families—raising their children at home until the age of five standard years, then sending them off to the clan crèche, where they are raised by single females. After transferring their offspring to the crèche, the parents maintain a strong presence in the children's lives through daily visitations and shared mealtimes. Academies are maintained on Kubindi for the advanced study of science and the arts, and entry is competitive and highly prestigious. Graduates of these academies either undertake apprenticeships to further their skills or assume positions of societal influence upon completion of their training.

Kubaz are extremely interested in all that occurs around them. They have a love of learning and will ask many questions, almost to the point of creating annoyance. With outsiders they are extremely honorable, forthright, and morally rigid, although they do not view maltreatment of insectoids or the act of spying as morally questionable.

Following the fall of the Empire and rise of the New Republic, the Kubaz had no choice but to join the inestimable ranks of refugees forced to flee their homeworlds when their planet was taken over by the Yuuzhan Vong. Following the Yuuzhan Vong's defeat, the remaining Kubaz, greatly diminished in number, have begun the process of returning to their world to pick up the pieces of their fractured society.

DESIGNATION
Sentient

HOMEWORLD
Kubindi

AVERAGE HEIGHT
1.8 meters

PRONUNCIATION
Kōō'-bǎz

NOTABLE APPEARANCE
Episode IV: A New Hope

MON CALAMARI

The Mon Calamari are an idealistic, noble people from the Outer Rim planet that commonly bears their name in Basic, although in the Mon Calamari and Quarren languages, the planet and its home star system are properly known as Dac. The Mon Calamari were once considered the soul of the Rebel Alliance, as well as a cornerstone of the New Republic. A positive, forward-thinking species with cultural goals of justice and fairness, they have established themselves as leaders and instigators of galactic harmony.

The Mon Calamari, often called Mon Cals, are an amphibious species with salmon-colored skin, webbed hands, high, domed heads, and huge, fish-like eyes. Similar to other amphibians, they are born in a "tadpole" stage, complete with gills; as they grow into adulthood, they develop lungs. These lungs are quite powerful, and enable them to remain underwater for long periods of time.

Within their water-

1.5

1.0

.5

0

based society, Mon Cal science grew out of simple fish farming and kelp cultivation on their ocean-covered world. Initially, their scientific and technological advancement progressed at a slow pace because it was difficult to get necessary materials from the planet's core. This problem was later solved with the assistance of their neighbor species, the Quarren, who live at the greatest depths of Mon Calamari's oceans. Thus began their symbiotic relationship with the Quarren, who had the ability to mine minerals found only at those depths.

Soft-spoken and gentle, the Mon Calamari are a peaceful people. They are even-tempered, slow to anger, and possess a remarkable capacity for intense concentration. Mon Cals are also legendary for their determination and for a dedication that can sometimes border on obstinacy. They are naturally heroic and idealistic, taking on causes that would seem hopeless to others simply because they feel it is right to do so, and once they have made a decision, they are not easily swayed from it. One such resolution was their quest to reach "the islands in the galactic ocean"—the stars, a goal they ultimately achieved due to their tenacity.

The Mon Calamari and Quarren live in multileveled cities that float upon the surface of their vast oceans. The Mon Cals dwell on the upper levels of the immense structures, as they prefer more sunlight, while the Quarren reside in the lower levels where there is more comforting darkness. These cities are the centers for civilized culture on their world, and their repertoire of art, music, and literature is impressive.

Mon Calamari technological talents are renowned throughout the galaxy. They can engineer starships or structures for almost any environment. The Mon Cals believe technological or architectural design must be organic, growing and changing with the users.

Mon Cal spaceships are highly complex, and are frequently the vessels of choice for the Gallactic Alliance. Each of these ships is unique in design, and they are constructed specifically for Mon Calamari physiology unless they are built under contract for an offworld client.

When the Mon Cals made their first foray into space, they established contact with peoples from other worlds with great enthusiasm and excitement. Along with the Quarren, they eventually gained representation in the Galactic Senate. But in the days before creation of the Empire, Mon Calamari Senator Meena Tils joined a growing number of Senators who spoke against Palpatine's increasing powers. By the time Palpatine declared himself Emperor, the Mon Cals began to realize their

DESIGNATION
Sentient

HOMEWORLD
Mon Calamari

AVERAGE HEIGHT
1.7 meters

PRONUNCIATION
Mŏn Căl-ä-mär'-ē

fatal mistake. The Emperor viewed the Mon Cals as easy slave labor, and the Empire conquered their world with the assistance of some disgruntled Quarren, who deactivated the planet's protective shield. Both the Quarren and the Mon Cals were put to work as slaves, although the Mon Cals began a movement of passive resistance. In order to squash this opposition, the Empire destroyed three of their floating cities.

It was then that this peaceful species put aside their pacifistic ways and fought back against their taskmasters. Using simple kitchen implements, hand tools, and any other weapons they could find, they and their Quarren counterparts—with the aid of the Rebellion—drove the Empire from their world. Mon Calamari then became the first world to officially throw its full support behind the Alliance.

To this day, there is friction between the Quarren and the Mon Calamari, stemming from both the incident involving the deactivation of the shield, as well as previous tensions over many Quarren siding with the Separatists during the Clone Wars.

Despite this friction, Mon Calamari society continues to function. They have a highly efficient government, organized much like the Republic Senate. Quarren and Mon Cals are equally represented in this body, and because of the Mon Cals' peace-loving nature, they continue to work toward consistent harmony with their Quarren fellows.

The Mon Cals were also largely responsible for freeing the galaxy from the oppression of the Empire. Nowhere was this better represented than by the great Mon Calamari naval commander Admiral Ackbar. A brilliant tactician, Ackbar quickly rose through the ranks to become admiral of the combined Rebel fleet. In addition, through his steady guidance, Ackbar brought Mon Calamari into the Alliance, which aided tremendously in turning the tide of the war. He served as long as he was able, eventually retiring to a quiet life on Mon Calamari. Ackbar passed away from old age toward the conclusion of the war against the Yuuzhan Vong, after briefly coming out of retirement to contribute to the military strategies that defeated the invaders.

NOTABLE APPEARANCE
Episode VI: Return of the Jedi

MUSTAFARIAN

The title *Mustafarian* applies to two subspecies of the same genus native to the planet Mustafar in the Outer Rim, a world of molten lava rivers, active volcanoes, and jagged, rocky landmasses. Both subspecies are hard-shelled arthropods with large, insectoid eyes and long snouts, and evolved in the cooled underground tunnels of their world. Their chitinous exoskeletons lie in plates over their leathery skin, protecting them from the intense heat that they encounter day by day on Mustafar. Unlike most life-forms, Mustafarians have little water in their bodies.

Mustafar's volcanic environment is caused by the gravitational pull of two nearby gas giants, Jestefad and Lefrani. While Mustafar could serve as a moon for either star, it stays in its own orbit, traveling closer to Jestefad while at the same time being pulled on by Lefrani—with all three planetary bodies navigating the star system at a similar rate.

Flourishing in this tumultuous environment, the taller northern Mustafarians are the physically weaker of the two subspecies. Because their bodies are more prone to frailty, the northern Mustafarians who serve as sentries or security forces often have their limbs enhanced with mechanical prosthetics to increase their strength, speed, and endurance. Northern Mustafarians ride insects called Mustafar lava fleas, which they domesticated as mounts in order to move quickly from one cooled lava landmass to another. The lava fleas are large, six-legged insects capable of walking across the cooler surfaces of hardened lava, and they can leap over the flowing lava rivers with ease.

2.0

1.5

1.0

.5

The smaller southern Mustafarians, meanwhile, are more sturdy and hardy. Working in cooperation with their genetic cousins, they handle most of the "heavy lifting," or physically demanding jobs, in Mustafar's expansive lava-mining operations. This shorter subspecies can withstand higher temperatures than the northern Mustafarians, and since they spend more time on the surface than their compatriots do, they wear armor and breath masks to protect themselves from the intense heat. The southerners handle the harvesting platforms, skimming the surface of the lava rivers for metals with large pole-mounted cauldrons.

Mustafarians are a self-involved, egocentric people always bent on improving the limited life on their world. They are technologically savvy, and somewhat creative in that they have managed to find many unique ways to market the products they mine from Mustafar. Even so, their only reason for interacting with outsiders is to trade for new life-improving materials. They care little for any other people besides their own.

While Mustafarians are not naturally aggressive, like most species they have developed weaponry to protect themselves. Since their skin and exoskeletons defend them from heat-producing weapons such as blasters, the weapons that they use fire bolts of kinetic energy. Both vessels and people who are armored to guard themselves against blaster-fire would find themselves vulnerable to such unique armaments.

Mustafarians live and work in saucer-shaped buildings near their mine entrances. The structures are constructed to extend several levels belowground, often utilizing empty mines that no longer produce ore. They also dwell in the cooler hollows of dormant volcanic mountains. The atmosphere on Mustafar is not very hospitable to living beings, and it is a testament to the creatures and animals native to the planet that they have managed to survive. Filled with smoke, ash, and bits of volcanic rock and glass, the air on Mustafar makes drawing every breath a chore for most humanoids.

As mentioned, the Mustafarians had no initial interest in life off their world. But when the Techno Union became fixated on the idea of mining their lava for precious metals, the Mustafarians agreed to help build and manage the operations on Mustafar. This gave them membership in the Confederation of Independent Systems, though their planet was relatively untouched by the Clone Wars.

DESIGNATION
Sentient

HOMEWORLD
Mustafar

AVERAGE HEIGHT
2 meters (northern)
1.5 meters (southern)

PRONUNCIATION
Mōōs-tä-fä'-rē-ăn

Techno Union technology offered the Mustafarians extra protection from the heat, and improved their standard of living drastically. One such item used by workers is a Kubazian skirt equipped with a cooling backpack turbine. And yet, despite some of these helpful devices created by other species, the Mustafarians remain fairly uninterested in larger galactic affairs and are perfectly happy to work on their own world in peace.

The Separatist movement under Count Dooku used Mustafar as one of its main headquarters for operations. As the Clone Wars raged, the Separatist Council enlisted the Mustafarians to build a stronghold on their planet to be used as a protective retreat in the event that the Republic prevailed. The fortress was near impenetrable, bearing the combined protection of Mustafar's dangerous environment with a powerful tractor beam and ray shielding.

The Mustafarians were indifferent to the Separatists' politicking, and helped construct the climate-controlled fortress in the hope that it would someday fall under their control. Their work paid off when Darth Vader slaughtered the Separatists along with the Techno Union leaders on Mustafar, leaving the planet and its people to manage their own affairs.

As the Empire rose to power, however, the Mustafarians had to deal with a new problem. The renegade Geonosian Separatist Gizor Dellso holed himself up in the fortress, refusing to surrender to the Empire. Dellso managed to get a hidden droid factory on Mustafar up and running again, and began generating a series of fresh battle droids that he intended to use as his own army. The 501st Legion of stormtroopers was dispatched to Mustafar, and both Dellso and his battle droids were eradicated. It is believed that both fortress and factory were decimated by Star Destroyers in a subsequent orbital strike.

NOTABLE APPEARANCE
Episode III: Revenge of the Sith

MYNOCK

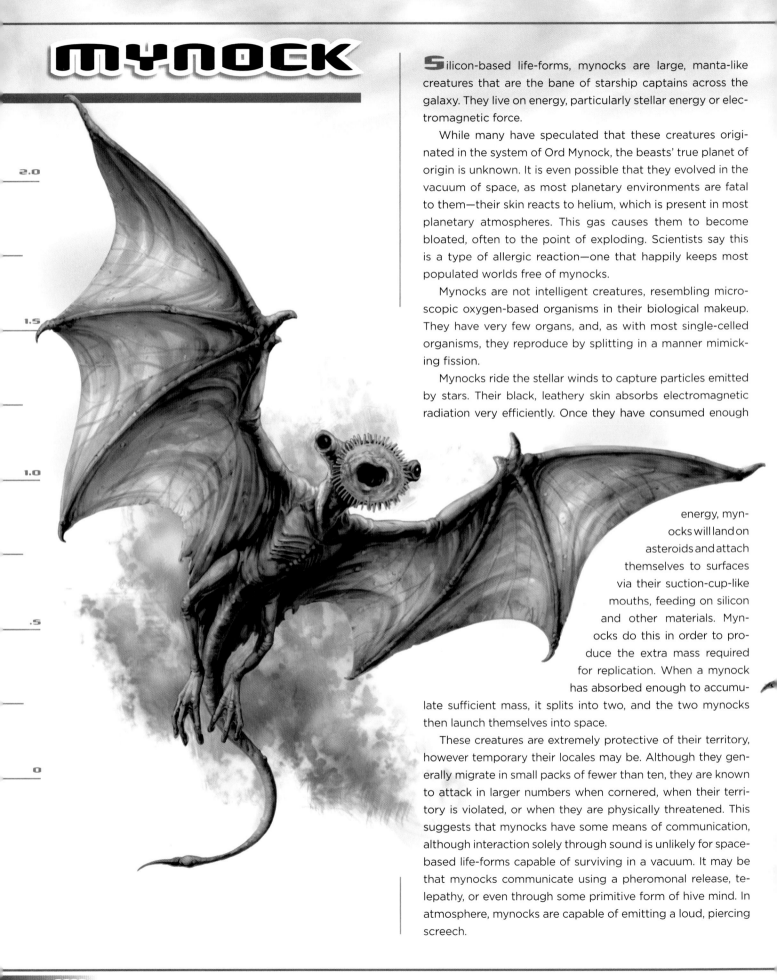

Silicon-based life-forms, mynocks are large, manta-like creatures that are the bane of starship captains across the galaxy. They live on energy, particularly stellar energy or electromagnetic force.

While many have speculated that these creatures originated in the system of Ord Mynock, the beasts' true planet of origin is unknown. It is even possible that they evolved in the vacuum of space, as most planetary environments are fatal to them—their skin reacts to helium, which is present in most planetary atmospheres. This gas causes them to become bloated, often to the point of exploding. Scientists say this is a type of allergic reaction—one that happily keeps most populated worlds free of mynocks.

Mynocks are not intelligent creatures, resembling microscopic oxygen-based organisms in their biological makeup. They have very few organs, and, as with most single-celled organisms, they reproduce by splitting in a manner mimicking fission.

Mynocks ride the stellar winds to capture particles emitted by stars. Their black, leathery skin absorbs electromagnetic radiation very efficiently. Once they have consumed enough energy, mynocks will land on asteroids and attach themselves to surfaces via their suction-cup-like mouths, feeding on silicon and other materials. Mynocks do this in order to produce the extra mass required for replication. When a mynock has absorbed enough to accumulate sufficient mass, it splits into two, and the two mynocks then launch themselves into space.

These creatures are extremely protective of their territory, however temporary their locales may be. Although they generally migrate in small packs of fewer than ten, they are known to attack in larger numbers when cornered, when their territory is violated, or when they are physically threatened. This suggests that mynocks have some means of communication, although interaction solely through sound is unlikely for space-based life-forms capable of surviving in a vacuum. It may be that mynocks communicate using a pheromonal release, telepathy, or even through some primitive form of hive mind. In atmosphere, mynocks are capable of emitting a loud, piercing screech.

This parasite is the main food staple for the giant space slugs that often inhabit asteroid fields. In turn, before being completely digested, mynocks will feed for a time on the space slug's veins and intestinal linings. Due to their sheer size, giant space slugs have been known to be found with large numbers of living mynocks within their bodies. For this reason, some orbital spaceports will try to keep at least one space slug in the vicinity to cut down on the local mynock population.

Constantly thirsting for energy, mynocks often attach themselves to passing starships, chewing on power cables or sucking on ion ports. Mynocks can also absorb matter from a vessel's hull, causing it to slowly dissolve. This is a particular problem that could result in a significant amounts of damage if not discovered and repaired in time, and through the years, there are tales of many ships and lives that have been lost due to hull breaches in open space. The space lanes abound with reports, both anecdotal and verified, of ships launching, only to later discover that a mynock or two had damaged the ship's exterior or, worse, had stowed away and were causing harm while the ship was already in flight. Often, vessels' sensors will detect breaches and the loss of hull integrity, but if sensors are faulty, catastrophic events have sometimes occurred. In addition, if a pack of mynocks infests an orbital shipyard, the economic consequences can be severe and drive a company to near bankruptcy.

In recent years, a new version of sport hunting has emerged called Mynock Puffing, wherein hunters will spacewalk to shoot and kill mynocks with helium-based grenades that attach to the creatures' hides, causing their bodies to balloon into round balls. The creatures quickly die and immediately float away. Bets are placed on which sharpshooter can "puff out" the most mynocks. Legislation to monitor this activity is being met with resistance from the gambling establishment and the Free Spacers Guild lobby.

Several reports have documented subspecies variants of the mynock. Vynocks, an air-breathing, planetbound subspecies, have been found in the Kalarba system in the Mid Rim and on Corellia in the Core Worlds; apparently, this subspecies does not suffer from the theorized helium allergy. These creatures pose a particular problem for inhabited systems, as not just ships but also buildings, structures, livestock, and even humanoids sleeping outdoors are at risk. Additionally, the pirate Chorssk bred a domesticated version of the mynock, noted for its blue-mottled skin and reproduction methods. Unlike common mynocks, the Chorsskian, or blue, mynock gives birth to live offspring, with the mother sacrificing herself for her child. Chorssk learned to breed mynocks so that he could use them as a weapon; he sought to develop a group of creatures that could attack a ship on command, making his strikes on vessels in the space lanes that much easier. Another variant known as a salt mynock has also been spotted on Lok, but little is presently known about this subspecies due to a lack of corroborating evidence.

In sum, regardless of the variety, mynocks can pose a hazard regardless of their environment. It is a common experience to walk through even the most lightly populated of spaceports and hear cries of "Mynocks on a power cable!"

DESIGNATION
Nonsentient

HOMEWORLD
Unknown
(popularly
attributed to
Ord Mynock)

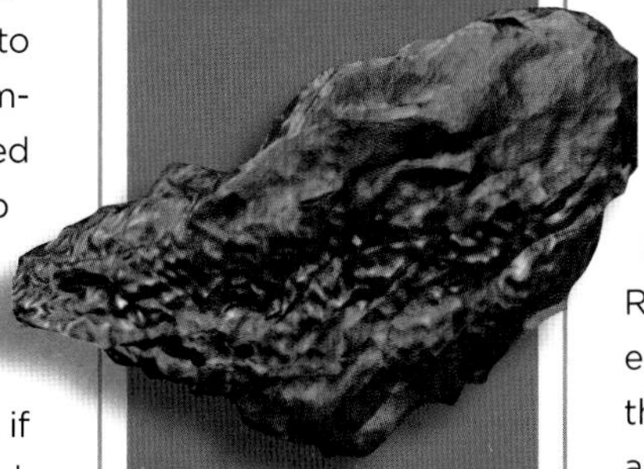

**AVERAGE
LENGTH**
1.6 meters

PRONUNCIATION
Mī'-nŏk

NOTABLE APPEARANCE
Episode V: The Empire Strikes Back

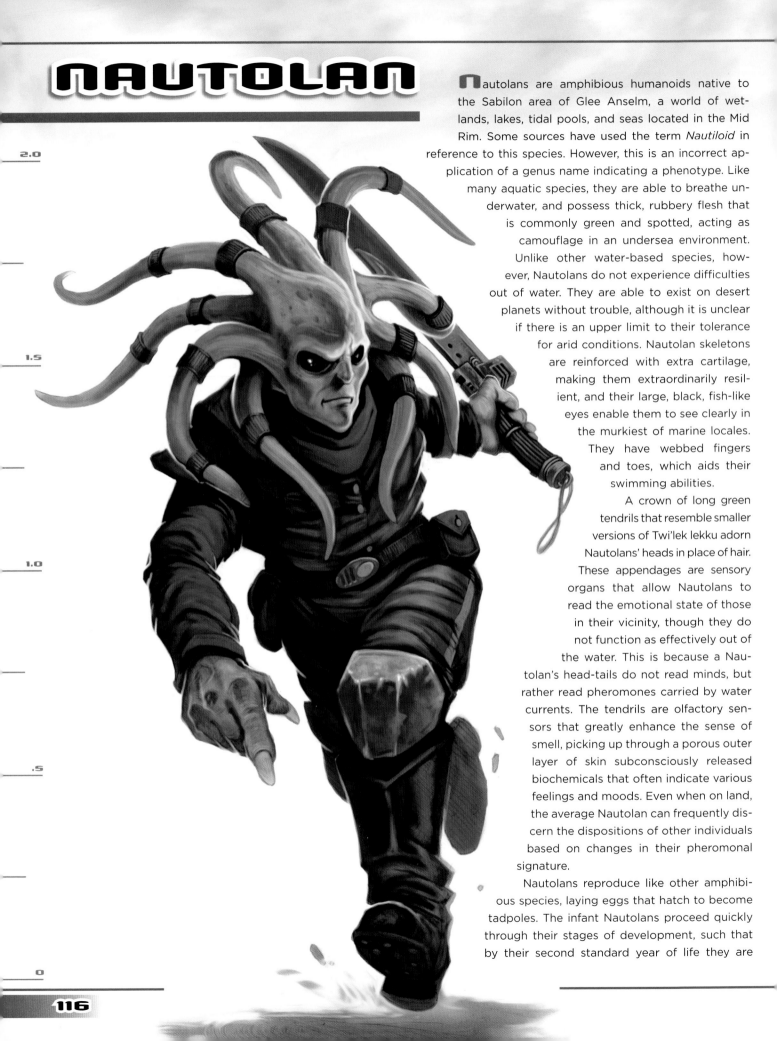

NAUTOLAN

Nautolans are amphibious humanoids native to the Sabilon area of Glee Anselm, a world of wetlands, lakes, tidal pools, and seas located in the Mid Rim. Some sources have used the term *Nautiloid* in reference to this species. However, this is an incorrect application of a genus name indicating a phenotype. Like many aquatic species, they are able to breathe underwater, and possess thick, rubbery flesh that is commonly green and spotted, acting as camouflage in an undersea environment. Unlike other water-based species, however, Nautolans do not experience difficulties out of water. They are able to exist on desert planets without trouble, although it is unclear if there is an upper limit to their tolerance for arid conditions. Nautolan skeletons are reinforced with extra cartilage, making them extraordinarily resilient, and their large, black, fish-like eyes enable them to see clearly in the murkiest of marine locales. They have webbed fingers and toes, which aids their swimming abilities.

A crown of long green tendrils that resemble smaller versions of Twi'lek lekku adorn Nautolans' heads in place of hair. These appendages are sensory organs that allow Nautolans to read the emotional state of those in their vicinity, though they do not function as effectively out of the water. This is because a Nautolan's head-tails do not read minds, but rather read pheromones carried by water currents. The tendrils are olfactory sensors that greatly enhance the sense of smell, picking up through a porous outer layer of skin subconsciously released biochemicals that often indicate various feelings and moods. Even when on land, the average Nautolan can frequently discern the dispositions of other individuals based on changes in their pheromonal signature.

Nautolans reproduce like other amphibious species, laying eggs that hatch to become tadpoles. The infant Nautolans proceed quickly through their stages of development, such that by their second standard year of life they are roughly the same size as a human infant and already possess arms and legs, though their legs are not yet strong enough to support their weight when learning to walk. An infant Nautolan's head-tails begin to develop their extrasensory abilities between their second and third years. This may be a programmed result of evolution, as this is also the time when many Nautolan children begin to speak, and thus their tendrils are able to start aiding in interpreting the potentially confusing input that they are receiving from the world around them.

Because of their empathic abilities, Nautolans' moods often reflect those of nearby individuals. If those around them are feeling joyous, then they are as well, but if others are upset, Nautolans will generally feel the same sadness. If they are attacked in anger, they will respond in kind. As a species, however, Nautolans are a fairly happy people who express joy with abandon, particularly when they are free to use their talents without restraint. For instance, Nautolans have been known to flash a wide, brilliant smile when in the midst of physical combat. While the delight behind the smile is quite genuine, this flash of passion can also be intended to emotionally disarm their opponents, who may perceive it as a sign of the Nautolans' combat superiority.

Other than the fact that their tendrils do not function quite as well out of water, Nautolans prefer aquatic life for another reason—one directly related to their language. Spoken on land, their native tongue, Nautila, is unpronounceable, and loses a good deal of its meaning because much of it is tied to pheromone projections that are released in conjunction with spoken words. As a result, Nautolans will speak Basic with those who use the standard tongue of the galaxy, or Anselmian, the language spoken by the Anselmi, their land-dwelling neighbors on Glee Anselm. The ability to speak Basic has encouraged many Nautolans to take to the stars, chasing a spirit of adventure.

Nautolans are an extremely loyal people, and as such, they will mate for life. Most Nautolans see a happy mating as a necessary requirement of existence, and families are raised with equal input from both parents. Marriage choices are in most cases made through courtship, as is typical in many humanoid societies. Although arranged marriages have declined among the Nautolans in the last few centuries, they do still occur. Those taking part in sociological studies report that they do not feel as if they have surrendered their

choice in mates by participating in such an arrangement, as the parties have the right of refusal upon reaching adulthood. They simply respect the well-considered effort made on their behalf. When an arranged marriage is declined, both parties will go their own way, with no ill will involved.

Nautolan settlements are governed by an elected Council of Elders—although in this case *elders* is a title of respect rather than a sign of age—and the centralized government takes the form of a body of representatives from each settlement. A subcommittee of this body works cooperatively with the overall leadership of Glee Anselm.

One of the best-known Nautolans in history was the Jedi Master Kit Fisto, renowned for his skills with a lightsaber. Fisto's lightsaber, it is said, could operate underwater because of two unique crystals that he used to power it. Also famous for his strength of spirit and his wisdom, Fisto was instrumental in the defeat of the Quarren forces that sympathized with the Confederacy of Independent Systems during a conflict on Mon Calamari. In addition, Master Fisto was unique in that he was one of the few non-Twi'leks able to read Lekku, the Twi'leks' elaborate language of head-tail movements.

Nautolans have coexisted in peace with the Anselmi for thousands of years. Any wars that they have had with each other have been short, though quite passionate and bloody. Some of these conflicts were instigated over underwater developments, as well as fishing rights and the dumping of waste products. The Anselmi, being land dwellers, will often infringe on Nautolan territories to construct new developments when housing is required, sparking the majority of such disagreements. However, the Nautolans are stronger and better fighters, giving them the advantage over their neighbors in such struggles. Many of these conflicts were mediated by representatives of the Old Republic government, though no disagreements between the species are known to have arisen in recent years.

DESIGNATION
Sentient

HOMEWORLD
Glee Anselm

AVERAGE
HEIGHT
1.8 meters

PRONUNCIATION
Nă'-tō-lăn

NOTABLE APPEARANCE
Episode II: Attack of the Clones

NELVAANIAN

Nelvaanians (also referred to as Nelvaans) are the native inhabitants of the frigid planet Nelvaan in the Koobi system of the Outer Rim. A primitive people, they were easily victimized by the Techno Union and the Separatists during the Clone Wars. Nelvaanians are a canine humanoid species with blue-green fur tipped with a black headcrest, long snouts, black eyes, and sharp teeth. As they age, their hair whitens and their upright, pointed ears begin to fold down and back. During the Clone Wars, many of the species' males were genetically altered by the Techno Union as part of a secret mutant warrior development project, becoming large hulking versions of their former selves. Newer generations of males carry the genetic patterns of their altered forebears, and as a result are much larger than their female counterparts. For whatever reason, the genetic manipulation did not result in mutated females in subsequent generations.

Nelvaanian religious beliefs are central to their simple tribal culture. Life in the tribe is organized around the extended family and other closely related individuals. The strongest male Nelvaanians become warrior scouts, and are responsible for hunting game and providing protection for the tribe from natural predators. Female Nelvaanians, however, have the most important role of all in their society. Not only are females the builders and gatherers among the Nelvaanians, managing the day-to-day life of the tribe, but they also must raise the clan's young. Motherhood is sacred to Nelvaanians, so much so that it forms the basis of their religious beliefs and is revered in all its forms. Regardless of gender, children are a treasured source of joy to all Nelvaanians.

Great respect is paid to the elderly members of the tribe for their experience and wisdom, and typically the tribal chief is one of the eldest members of the group, assuming this role following a long and productive life. The chief leads with the help of his or her bond-mate, and is advised by a tribal shaman. All members of the tribe share communal duties and take part in ceremonies equally, so beyond experience and astuteness, no other special training is required for the role of chief. The responsibility is granted through a show of respect and deference rather than through a trial or other selection process. There is no competition for the position of tribal chief; an individual's ascension to the role is decided by the grace of the "Great Mother," and accepted without question by all members of the tribe.

The responsibility of motherhood in Nelvaanian religious beliefs takes the form of worship of the Great Mother—the planet itself. The Great Mother is the mother of all things, who guides and nurtures the Nelvaanians. Her shaman passes down traditions through stories and tales that are repeated from one generation to the next, and are often recorded in cave paintings. Nelvaanian tribal tales contain one particularly interesting story—one that if studied closely may have helped to predict Anakin Skywalker's eventual transformation into Darth Vader.

While on Nelvaan in pursuit of General Grievous during the last year of the Clone Wars, Obi-Wan Kenobi and Anakin Skywalker encountered the Nelvaanians, who, although initially distrustful of the Jedi—as Skywalker interrupted an important rite of passage for one of the tribe's younger males—did bring them back to their village. The shaman told the Jedi that the Great Mother's inner fires had seemed to go out, as her tears—her rivers—had frozen, and her cries were carried on the wind. Warriors had been dispatched to

discover the cause of the Great Mother's ills, but one by one they disappeared, leaving the women, children, and elderly of the tribe alone. Moreover, their shaman had predicted the dawn of an ice age, but this event came on much too suddenly to be natural.

Old Nelvaanian lore tells the tale of a one-handed warrior known as the holt kazet, or "Ghost Hand," who would fight for the Nelvaanians in their time of greatest need. A fierce warrior, the Ghost Hand would lose his hand in battle but, after taking on a new one, would overcome his limitations and grow to newfound strength. The Ghost Hand is ultimately consumed by his own power, influence that blocks all light and strangles the life from his loved ones. The Nelvaanians believed Anakin Skywalker had the gift of the Ghost Hand.

Given this belief, Skywalker was charged by the Nelvaanian tribal shaman with finding the source of the sickness that was plaguing the Great Mother. He discovered that the disappearances of the warriors and the frozen nature of the land were both due to the work of the Techno Union. Inspired by the cyborg technology used to create General Grievous, the Separatists had created a laboratory in the caverns near the Nelvaanian village. In this facility, they implanted captured male Nelvaanians with cyborg control harnesses, replacing one of each of their arms with a blaster to study how the technology could be applied on a larger scale, in an effort to create advanced fighters that would ultimately replace battle droids. During Skywalker's eventual assault on the facility, the Techno Union released these mutated warriors to attack the Jedi, but one of them, still in the mutation process, retained some of his sensibilities and was able to reach through to his tribesmen by reminding them of who they were. Skywalker was sickened by what the Techno Union's Skakoan scientists had done, as the proud Nelvaanian warriors were now monstrosities, and in a fit of rage, Anakin killed the scientists using the Force. The mutated Nelvaanians helped Anakin Skywalker defeat the remainder of the Techno Union forces and destroy the laboratory. The warriors then returned to their village, and after some initial hesitation were accepted back into their tribe.

DESIGNATION
Sentient

HOMEWORLD
Nelvaan

AVERAGE HEIGHT
1.5 meters (females)
2 meters (males)

PRONUNCIATION
Něl-vā'-nē-ăn

NOTABLE APPEARANCE
Clone Wars, volume 2 (animated series)

NERF

Nerfs, once native to the peaceful world of Alderaan, are four-legged, herbivorous ungulates. Since these creatures were and are raised on planets outside Alderaan, the species has survived their homeworld's destruction. Nerf meat is some of the most delicious and expensive in the known galaxy, and nerf steak restaurants are ubiquitous in any medium- or larger-sized Core World city. Nerf meat can also be served in other forms, such as nerfburgers—a favorite of many young people, often served with hubba chips—and nerfspread. In addition, nerfs' fur and hides can be utilized to create excellent wool and leather goods. Although their fur must be treated with strong chemicals to mask its smell before being spun into wool, it is used galaxywide by couturiers and hobbyists alike. Nerf-hide coats are an expensive but common luxury. Given the creatures' utility, nerfs can usually be spotted near most established settlements in the Core and innermost Mid Rim of the galaxy. However, nerfs are not commonly found in great numbers beyond the Mid Rim, as ranchers there tend to raise local favorites such as banthas, which do not pose some of the unique challenges that nerfs do.

Changes in environment and selective breeding have led to the development of several subspecies of nerfs, in addition to the naturally occurring varieties located on several worlds. For example, a particularly rare subspecies has been reported on Grizmallt—a group that appears very dissimilar to common nerfs in that they bear more of a resemblance to eopies with antlers. This change in body shape and neck length could be the result of thousands of years of reaching into trees to eat leaves or berries on high limbs. In addition, before it was destroyed, Alderaan was home to two nerf subspecies: the common, or plains, nerf and the rangier, thinner forest nerf. Another subspecies, the mountain nerf of Fennesa, has adapted to the mountainous terrain of that world and tends to be nimbler than both the plains and flatlands varieties.

In general, these are all herd creatures with dull, curving horns and coarse, curly fur that covers their muscular bodies. They have hard, round hooves and long, furry tails. Nerfs will chew their cuds, and because of this trait, they tend to build up a great deal of saliva in their mouths, making them expectorate a great deal. Nerf spit is black in color, sticky,

and foul smelling; it is impossible to remove from clothing without harsh detergents. In addition, mountain nerf spittle is slightly acidic, and can sting and leave welts if a herder is unlucky enough to be struck on exposed skin. Sadly, all varieties of these creatures are known to spit with great accuracy.

Nerfs are recognized as being some of the smelliest beasts in the galaxy, and those who deal with them regularly tend to reek of the species' aroma. Most nerf herders lose their sense of smell after years of working with the animals. These simple people are eternally patient, living outdoors and traveling with their creatures as they migrate about the grassy plains to feed. They are usually battered, bitten, and bruised by their wards, and their clothes are often covered in black, sticky spittle, giving them a haggard and scruffy appearance. In fact, *scruffy-looking nerf herder* is a common insult throughout the galaxy. Although it is a difficult life, nerf herders are proud, hardworking people, and third- or fourth-generation herders are quite common.

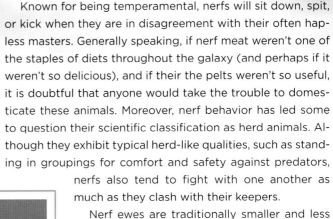

DESIGNATION
Nonsentient

HOMEWORLD
Alderaan

AVERAGE HEIGHT
1.3 meters

PRONUNCIATION
Nŭrf

Known for being temperamental, nerfs will sit down, spit, or kick when they are in disagreement with their often hapless masters. Generally speaking, if nerf meat weren't one of the staples of diets throughout the galaxy (and perhaps if they weren't so delicious), and if their the pelts weren't so useful, it is doubtful that anyone would take the trouble to domesticate these animals. Moreover, nerf behavior has led some to question their scientific classification as herd animals. Although they exhibit typical herd-like qualities, such as standing in groupings for comfort and safety against predators, nerfs also tend to fight with one another as much as they clash with their keepers.

Nerf ewes are traditionally smaller and less powerful than the domineering rams. With horns that spiral more elaborately, the rams have a tendency to charge, harass, or batter the females and trample over the young. For this reason, they are isolated from the herd during certain times in order to keep the others safe.

On most worlds, nerfs are held in traditional ranch-like settings with enclosed pens and pastures. Fennesa natives differ from this practice by allowing their nerfs to roam free on the mountains, where the creatures often hide in caves or among rocky outcroppings. During mating season, females are allowed to mix with the males, but otherwise males are mostly prevented from grazing within the herd. Young nerfs are born one at a time, and remain with the ewes regardless of gender until they have aged roughly one standard year, at which point the male young are placed with their gender counterparts in order to replace an older ram who is taken to market. Female offspring will go to the field to replace ewe, although sometimes they are taken to market themselves.

Typically, herders take the females and young out into the field for weeks while the males are fed harvested grasses on the ranch. While they are grazing, nerfs can be at risk of attack from predators or rustlers. Herders are therefore frequently armed with slugthrowers—or blasters if they can afford them—to protect their livelihood. Unfortunately, because of the rough nature of their work, these hardworking people are looked down upon by more genteel society.

NOTABLE MENTION
Episode V: The Empire Strikes Back

NEXU

Nexus are fierce, agile feline carnivores native to the planet Cholganna, located near the Perlemian Trade Route in the Outer Rim, specifically the Indona continent. They are quadrupeds, and members of the forest subspecies have four eyes, the second set of which enables them to see in the infrared spectrum of light. Nexus' large mouths, which span the length of their spade-shaped heads, are full of sharp teeth. Tan-brown fur covers their bodies, giving them warmth in cold environments and camouflaging them in their native grassland and forest habitats. Taut, strong muscles can be seen beneath their hides, and sharp, spiny quills adorn nexus' backs to protect them from overhead attacks. These quills will stand erect when a nexu is engaged in a fight. A nexu's forked semi-prehensile tail gives it extra stability, as it can grip inanimate objects for balance. The nexu

employs a squat, sprawling stance for even surer footing, and usually strikes with its primary claw, although it can easily attack with either of its front claws. Its shorter secondary claws are often used for gripping tree trunks in the nexu's native habitat.

Several breeds of nexus exist on their native world in different regions, adapting to local conditions, primarily the cool forests of the north and the balmy jungles and rain forests of the south. All nexu breeds will bear litters of ten cubs at a time, which they then protect with the same ferocity that has made them renowned throughout the galaxy. Cubs are pure white at birth, although their fur changes color at about three months. At approximately six months, the mother will abandon her young, as she will soon forget to recognize them as her progeny and be tempted to eat them. As a result, nexus are very solitary, marking their hunting territories with a musky smell they excrete from scent glands in their tails, or by rubbing scent glands located on their heads on trees, rocks, or bushes.

1.0

.5

0

In its home environment, the nexu tends to remain in the forests, using its infrared vision to hunt in the dim light of dusk and evening for the heat signatures of warm-blooded prey, particularly the arboreal octopi and bark rats that make up its primary diet. To kill its prey, the nexu will clamp down on the victim's neck and shake the creature until it dies, often breaking the neck bones in the process.

Most nexus trained as guard animals or arena beasts are taken from their mothers as young cubs. Nexu cubs are not harmless, though: they are born with sharp claws, teeth, and quills. It is crucial that nexus intended for use in patrol or guard duty are taken before they are taught to hunt by their mothers, preferably within an extremely narrow window of three standard months. Otherwise, they will be uncontrollable and unable to be domesticated. During this time, it is also possible to train nexus to not prey on specific creatures, such as their humanoid trainers. In these first three months, the goal is predatorial play, which a trainer will hone so that the nexu respond to specific attack commands. Only after the animal has been thoroughly taught to only strike

DESIGNATION
Nonsentient

HOMEWORLD
Cholganna

AVERAGE
HEIGHT
1 meter
LENGTH
WITH TAIL
4.5 meters

PRONUNCIATION
Nĕ'-xōō

on command will it be trained to attack live targets. As can be expected, training nexus is done only by dangerous-animal experts.

Nexus destined for gladiatorial combat are raised differently from domesticated nexus. Gladiatorial animals are allowed to stay with their mothers for longer periods of time—up to six months—before their removal. This is to ensure that the animals know how to hunt and chase prey instinctively. (A longer period of time is not possible, because the young are frequently preyed upon by their mothers, as mentioned above.) These animals are harder to control, of course, but receive no less training once they are brought into captivity. Gladiatorial nexus must be trained to attack without fear, as they may face beasts larger than themselves in the arena.

Known for their speed and agility, nexus are often used to guard the strongholds of major underworld figures, and they can make a quick meal of trespassers. Since they are not easy to train or domesticate, nexus are more often used as executioners, or as gladiatorial foes on Outer Rim worlds such as Geonosis. Nexus have been featured in staged animal-fighting matches on some of the galaxy's more violent worlds, where the grisly blood sport is the subject of intense and high-stakes wagering. On Malastare, nexus are utilized as guard animals on patrol shifts. However, escaped nexus are a menace to the local populace, killing farm animals, destroying crops, and making away with settlers' children. They are rarely kept in zoos or animal preserves because they do not inhabit spaces with other animals well—often killing additional species, as well as members of their own kind.

As some of the most dangerous creatures in the known galaxy, nexus are frequently the targets of big-game hunters. Nexu pelts, and their teeth or bone ivory, are exorbitantly expensive and prized by the upper class of galactic society.

NOTABLE APPEARANCE
Episode II: Attack of the Clones

NIKTO

Of all the beings in service to the Hutts, the Nikto are the species most closely identified with their masters. They are fierce people, and probably the most dangerous species to work as the Hutts' enforcers and warriors. They are a fearless and humorless group native to Kintan in the Outer Rim.

The Nikto are a reptilian species consisting of five different subspecies, each displaying unique cosmetic and biological features. These subspecies evolved due to an intense amount of stellar radiation bombarding their planet from a dying star known as M'dweshuu. Although each subspecies exhibits superficial differences, they are genetically compatible and can interbreed. Ninety-three percent of Nikto children born of mixed parentage maintain the characteristics of one of the parents, and carry on those characteristics through their own offspring. The remaining 7 percent—those who show signs of mixed breeding—are

maltreated and abused by the rest of society. They are outcasts, unable to thrive and succeed among their own people. Mixed-breed Nikto usually head offplanet as soon as they reach their adult years, to find work as guards, soldiers, or bounty hunters.

All Nikto have obsidian-black eyes, which are protected by transparent membranes when they are underwater, and also during Kintan's windstorms. They all possess leathery, reptilian skin, and sport various horns or spikes.

The Kajain'sa'Nikto, or Red Nikto, come from the Wannschok, or Endless Wastes—the desert region of Kintan. They have a series of ridges on their foreheads, with eight horns ringing their eyes, and two horns on their chins. Their noses are concealed beneath moving flaps of skin that hang above their mouths. To breathe, they expand this permeable membrane, preventing them from inhaling blowing sand, grit, and other contaminants from their desert environment. They also have a pair of breathing membranes on either side of their necks that are protected by thin breathing pipes. These pipes filter out contaminants and capture exhaled water vapor in order to keep it recycling through their systems, enabling them to go for longer periods of time without water.

The Kajain'sa'Nikto have a particular history of producing some of the strongest fighters in the galaxy, an ancient secret society known as the Morgukai. By the time of the Geonosian crisis, the Morgukai were on the verge of extinction. It is rumored that Morgukai warriors were so fierce with their cortosis ore weapons that they were even a match for the Jedi Knights, and that, through training, they were highly resistant to mind manipulation. Although little is known about the Morgukai, recovered records from that time period indicate that the Morgukai tradition was passed down in the male line only from father to son, in a training system similar to that of the Jedi–Padawan relationship. Of utmost importance to the Morgukai was personal honor, to the degree that they would overlook issues of good and evil as long as honor was maintained.

The Kadas'sa'Nikto, or Green Nikto, originated in the forested and coastal regions of Kintan. This race has green-gray skin with visible scales and small horns surrounding the eyes. Green Nikto have discernible noses that are sensitive enough to allow them to pick up the scent of other creatures in a forest or jungle environment. They also sport long claws that enable them to climb trees.

Mountain Nikto, usually referred to as the Esral'sa'Nikto, are blue-gray in color and have pronounced facial fins that expand from their cheeks. Like the Kajain'sa'Nikto, they have flaps of skin that cover their noses, with permeable membranes above the mouths. Their long fins are lined with small vibrating hairs that enhance their hearing. By fully expanding these fins, they can disperse excess heat, and by flattening them against their skulls, they can insulate themselves against the cold. They also have expanding and contracting neck cavities that diffuse or trap heat and recycle moisture in their systems. Their claws are small and recessed.

The Pale Nikto, or Gluss'sa'Nikto, are white or gray and populate the Gluss'elta Islands, a chain of a dozen islands on Kintan. These Nikto have ridges of small horns surrounding

DESIGNATION
Sentient

HOMEWORLD
Kintan

AVERAGE HEIGHT
1.8 meters

PRONUNCIATION
Nĭk'-tō

their eyes, like Kadas'sa'Nikto, but they also possess small fins similar to the larger fins of the Esral'sa'Nikto.

Finally, the M'shento'su'Nikto, or Southern Nikto, have white, yellow, or orange skin. They do not have horns or fins at all, but possess a multitude of breather tubes on the backs of their skulls that tend to be much longer than their cousins' standard breather tubes. These act as primitive ultrasonic sensory tubes, and scientists believe the extermination of natural predators on Kintan slowed the full development of these organs in other Nikto races.

Because the Nikto subspecies frequently banded together to protect themselves from predators, they eventually became a unified people. Stellar radiation over Kintan had caused horrific monsters to evolve on their world, and that constant threat drove the Nikto to develop tools of defense, as well as cities with high protective walls and other military strategies. They literally fought themselves to the top of the food chain, burning down forests and swamps to force the most dangerous creatures into extinction. But by doing so, they turned their planet into a barren wasteland.

Twenty-five thousand standard years before the Battle of Yavin, Nikto astronomers discovered the star M'dweshuu. Inspired by this star, a strange cult arose that initiated blood sacrifices to appease the spirit of the celestial body. The cult spread quickly across the world, killing thousands of Nikto who did not bow to the cult's control.

After this group ruled Kintan for thirty years, Churabba the Hutt and her clan visited and witnessed the cult in action. They were interested in taking the star system for themselves, and had already enlisted the Nikto's neighbors, the Klatooinians and the Vodrans, as servants. Churabba quickly realized that the cult was suppressing a very disgruntled people. To turn the Nikto to her side, she bombarded the cult's stronghold from space, wiping it out completely. The grateful Nikto people, regarding her as a savior, joined the Treaty of Vontor, which required them to serve the Hutts indefinitely.

This cult rose again, about a thousand years before the Battle of Yavin, and temporarily pushed the Hutts off Kintan, but the Hutts in turn sent armies of mercenaries to squash the rebellion. Since then, the Nikto have remained in the service of the Hutts, although not without the occasional incidents of unrest.

NOTABLE APPEARANCE
Episode VI: Return of the Jedi

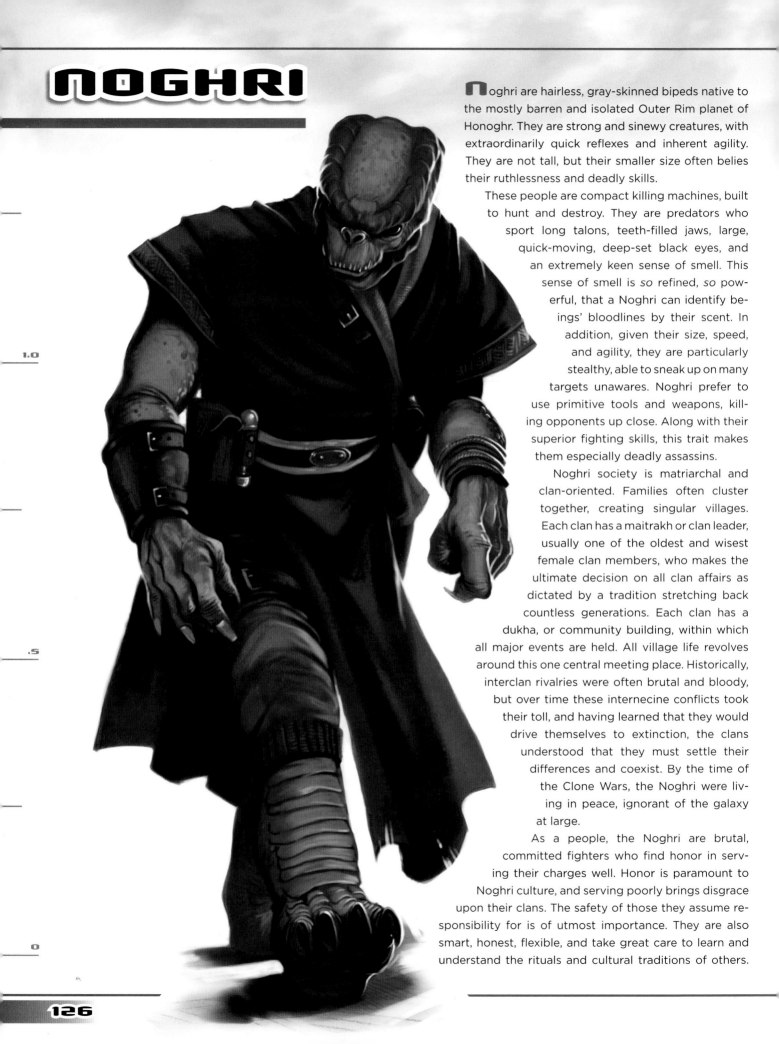

NOGHRI

Noghri are hairless, gray-skinned bipeds native to the mostly barren and isolated Outer Rim planet of Honoghr. They are strong and sinewy creatures, with extraordinarily quick reflexes and inherent agility. They are not tall, but their smaller size often belies their ruthlessness and deadly skills.

These people are compact killing machines, built to hunt and destroy. They are predators who sport long talons, teeth-filled jaws, large, quick-moving, deep-set black eyes, and an extremely keen sense of smell. This sense of smell is so refined, so powerful, that a Noghri can identify beings' bloodlines by their scent. In addition, given their size, speed, and agility, they are particularly stealthy, able to sneak up on many targets unawares. Noghri prefer to use primitive tools and weapons, killing opponents up close. Along with their superior fighting skills, this trait makes them especially deadly assassins.

Noghri society is matriarchal and clan-oriented. Families often cluster together, creating singular villages. Each clan has a maitrakh or clan leader, usually one of the oldest and wisest female clan members, who makes the ultimate decision on all clan affairs as dictated by a tradition stretching back countless generations. Each clan has a dukha, or community building, within which all major events are held. All village life revolves around this one central meeting place. Historically, interclan rivalries were often brutal and bloody, but over time these internecine conflicts took their toll, and having learned that they would drive themselves to extinction, the clans understood that they must settle their differences and coexist. By the time of the Clone Wars, the Noghri were living in peace, ignorant of the galaxy at large.

As a people, the Noghri are brutal, committed fighters who find honor in serving their charges well. Honor is paramount to Noghri culture, and serving poorly brings disgrace upon their clans. The safety of those they assume responsibility for is of utmost importance. They are also smart, honest, flexible, and take great care to learn and understand the rituals and cultural traditions of others.

Noghri speak Basic in addition to their own language, albeit in gravelly, chilling voices. They are not a fun-loving or sociable people, and in fact have very little in the way of a sense of humor.

Honoghr was originally a lush planet teeming with a wide variety of animals and plant life, with a yearly rotation that is only half a standard year. Now it is a barren world barely capable of supporting its inhabitants. Honoghr's environmental problems began with a space battle about twenty years before the Battle of Yavin—a clash between a Republic cruiser and a Separatist science vessel carrying a poisonous defoliant. Unfortunately, the Separatist ship crashed into Honoghr's surface, spilling its toxic chemicals and resulting in an ecological disaster. This incident poisoned Honoghr's soil and atmosphere, destroying much of the planet's life. Shortly after the end of the Clone Wars, the Sith Lord Darth Vader came to Honoghr, prepared to make servants of the Noghri. Vader convinced the Noghri that the Republic was to blame for the damage to their planet, and that only he and the Empire could repair their environment. In return, seeing that they were gifted, effective warriors, he requested they serve him personally as assassins and bodyguards.

The Noghri, who were at the time of Vader's intervention an agrarian people and facing famine, felt they had no choice but to agree to Lord Vader's solution. Bound by their word of honor as given to the Empire, they served Vader and later Admiral Thrawn, who enlisted the Noghri to be his servants when he announced to them that he was Vader's successor.

It was not long after, as the New Republic was struggling to combat Admiral Thrawn's brilliant battle plans, that Thrawn ordered the Noghri to kidnap Princess Leia Organa Solo, who at the time was pregnant with twins Jaina and Jacen. The Noghri tracked Leia to Kashyyyk, where she was under the protection of the Wookiees. Because of her scent, they recognized her immediately as the Mal'ary'ush, or daughter of Vader.

After stopping the Noghri team and turning them to her side, Leia traveled to Honoghr and asked the Noghri to work with her in overthrowing Thrawn. Leia was initially refused by the clan leaders because of their word of honor to Thrawn, but the Noghri finally agreed to betray the Chiss admiral when Leia showed them that the "help" the Empire was giving them was not curing their destroyed world. The kholm-grass planted by the Imperials was not a restorative but a

DESIGNATION
Sentient

HOMEWORLD
Honoghr

AVERAGE HEIGHT
1.4 meters

PRONUNCIATION
Nō′-grē

poison that infected the soil even more by preventing other plants from growing. Every effort expanded by the Empire on Honoghr was aimed at keeping the Noghri enslaved.

The Noghri were enraged and vowed revenge on Thrawn and the Empire that had maintained the deception for so long. Because Thrawn still trusted the Noghri, his own Noghri bodyguards were able to get close enough to slay him. Then, having transferred their unwavering dedication to Leia, to their "Lady Vader," for her attempts to truly repair the Honoghr environment, they undertook self-appointed service as her personal bodyguards, and as bodyguards for her children as they grew up. The Noghri's loyalty to Leia and her family is not unlike that of a Wookiee life debt. The Noghri would sooner die than see Leia come to harm. In fact, several have given their lives to protect her.

Before destroying Thrawn, however, some Noghri decided to take their world's environmental woes into their own hands, in an attempt to begin the rebuilding that the Empire had at one time promised. They discovered and cultivated what they named "The Future of the Noghri," a valley under a series of cliff walls near a river visible only from directly above. This place is a small agricultural oasis on a nearly dead world. Unfortunately, the planet may never fully recover. Despite the best efforts of Princess Leia and New Republic scientists, the devastation was simply too severe and too widespread. Meanwhile, with Leia's assistance, the Noghri have established the thriving colony of New Nystao on Wayland. Although the Noghri rarely venture out of their settlements alone, they have continued to increase their presence in the larger galaxy, going so far as to participate in missions against the Yuuzhan Vong during the height of their invasion.

NOTABLE APPEARANCE
Heir to the Empire (novel)

ORTOLAN

The Ortolans, from the ice planet of Orto, located in the Sluis sector of the Outer Rim, are short, pudgy bipeds with trunk-like noses and beady black eyes. They have floppy ears, and their large hands feature four chubby fingers with not-quite-opposable thumbs. To make up for Ortolans' lack of manual dexterity, their fingers possess suction capabilities for manipulating tools. Their mouths are tiny, but can easily accommodate the large quantity of food they like to consume. An Ortolan's body is covered with a thick, baggy hide, over which resides a soft thin layer of white or light gray fur that resembles soft velvet. While one would see older Ortolans on Orto in their natural color, Ortolan youth have a tendency to dye their fur strange hues using food coloring. Young Ortolans cannot understand why one would take the time to use dye in one's food, but using it on one's person apparently seems great fun. And so, one could very well happen upon Ortolans of all sorts of interesting colors throughout the galaxy.

1.5

1.0

.5

0

Ortolans were originally nocturnal, hence much of their physiology is adapted to night living. Their eyes are almost completely pupil, making them more comfortable in dim lighting while bright illumination hurts their eyes. Ortolans' trunk possesses an incredible smelling ability, allowing them to detect food up to two kilometers away. It also has extremely sensitive tympanic organs that channel low-wavelength sounds up to flexible eustachian tubes in their ears. When this input is added to the sounds registered by the ears, which are also extremely sensitive, Ortolans can pick up the entire range from subsonic to ultrasonic sound waves. Their trunks are also used to generate sound, particularly at the subsonic range. In fact, much of their language is carried out at these extreme frequencies, so that to observers from other species, they seem to be almost mute, save for the rare times they decide to communicate at normal levels.

As would be expected of a species with such highly developed hearing, the Ortolans' favorite form of entertainment is music. Concerts on Orto feature all levels of sound, from subsonic to ultrasonic. Every new performance, live or recorded, of even the most familiar music, is a unique experience for Ortolans, as they can detect nuances in music that other species cannot. These performances are usually held in food bars, and are extremely loud to drown out the sounds of food venders and eating. Furthermore, Ortolans are considered to be some of the finest musicians in the galaxy. When they are found offworld, they are most likely traveling musicians.

Food is the most important thing to an Ortolan because it is so scarce on their world. Ortolans are known to be sociable and pleasant, especially with those who offer them food. Their food fixation has caused other species to think of them as unintelligent—they will often work for food. And yet they are wily enough to use this mistaken perception to sneak food (or other valuables) from their detractors.

The Ortolans' home planet, Orto, is a frozen wasteland. Due to its extreme elliptical orbit around a red sun, its axial tilt, and its thin atmosphere, Orto's growing season is a scant 161 standard days long. This is barely long enough for crops, and most must be grown near the equator for appropriate temperature and water. For this reason, a heavy layer of blubber serves as insulation and provides an auxiliary energy supply for Ortolans in case food becomes scarce, and they eat at every possible opportunity, as periodic famines are not uncommon.

DESIGNATION
Sentient

HOMEWORLD
Orto

AVERAGE
HEIGHT
1.4 meters

PRONUNCIATION
Ôr-tō'-lăn

Ortolans have few children. When a child is born, muscles and teeth are fully developed. Parents educate their own children, and when a child shows a gift that the parents are not equipped to address, they participate in a "teaching swap": another Ortolan family teaches their child in exchange for a special service or supplies. At the age of seven, to help conserve the family's supplies, most children are simply thrown out of the house to fend for themselves—unless one exhibits a talent particularly valuable to the family's well-being.

While Ortolan society is industrialized, it is not on a par with much of the galaxy technologically. Their chief trade with other species is in the raw materials and fossil fuels that are plentiful beneath their frozen planet's surface. This trade has introduced the concept of money to Ortolans, but their economy still remains largely barter-based. Ortolans will primarily barter for what they need and save the money they receive to buy foodstuffs they normally cannot obtain at home.

During the Clone Wars, Orto was invaded by the Confederacy of Independent Systems, despite the efforts of Ortolan Jedi Nem Bees. Later, under Imperial rule, Orto was taken over by the Empire as a source for raw materials. The Empire forbade Ortolans to travel offplanet—for their own protection, presumably, although the true reason was to control the Ortolan mining trade, allowing only preselected companies with strong Imperial ties to trade there. As long as this appeared to be the case, the Ortolans were left alone to a large degree. In truth, the Ortolans were trading with the Empire, the Rebellion, and whoever else might provide the best food at the time. However, smugglers managed to kidnap Ortolans to sell into slavery. Many of these ended up serving in the underworld, even if they escaped—they knew of nowhere else to go. After the Battle of Endor, Ortolans were quick to make a break for the stars, drawn by the lure of new and interesting cuisines to savor. They can be found in most active port systems where there is known to be an active nightlife that includes music and all-night buffets.

NOTABLE APPEARANCE
Episode VI: Return of the Jedi

PA'LOWICK

The Pa'lowick are shy, slender-limbed amphibians from the planet Lowick, located in the Outer Rim. They have plump, rounded bodies and long frog-like arms and legs. Their skin is very smooth, and speckled in a pattern of greens, browns, and yellows, causing them to easily blend in with their natural, equatorial rain forest environment. Males tend to have more angular patterns running along their backs and arms than females. The most distinguishing Pa'lowick attribute are their thin, tube-like trunks, which sprout from the center of the face, ending in almost incongruous human-like lips.

Some Pa'lowick possess a second mouth, with tusks resting just beneath the trunk. Youthful Pa'lowick retain this extra mouth through young adulthood, at which time it disappears, absorbed into their facial skin. The second mouth helps the youthful Pa'lowick gain more nutrition during their growing years, as the trunks take in only a limited amount of food at a time. Adults require a smaller amount of food and energy, and so the extra mouth disappears. The tusks, which fall off at the same time the mouth is absorbed, provide young Pa'lowicks with an extra means of defending themselves.

There is a subspecies of Pa'lowick, however, that retains its tusks through adulthood. This subspecies is believed to be older than the species that loses its tusks, though scientists have not been able to determine genetically which species is the progenitor of the other. The tusken variety, however, are localized in a specific area of Lowick where there are more forms of predatory wildlife. This seems to verify the belief that they are the older variety of Pa'lowick, as those subspecies who do not require the extra protection live in other less-hazardous regions. Tusked Pa'lowick tend to be a bit more aggressive than their fellows, but this is only a protective measure. Among their own and outsiders they come to know, they are as gentle as their untusked cousins.

Lowick is a watery world of vast oceans, seas, and mountainous regions. The Pa'lowick developed near the planet's equator, a region of marshes and deep green rain forests. Pa'lowick bodies are therefore made for their marshy home. Their long legs allow them to move easily through the still murky waters of salt marshes searching for fish, reptiles, and waterfowl for nourishment. Their snouts are perfect for eating giant marello duck eggs, which they puncture with their tongues to suck the yolk through their tube-like mouths.

Their eyes, which rest at the end of two stalks sprouting from their foreheads, allow them to hide underwater while keeping a lookout for predators. Fortunately, Pa'lowick's lungs are well developed, and they are able to hold their breath long enough for most dangerous creatures to pass them by. Pa'lowicks have large air bladders that allow their lungs to expand down into their bellies. These air bladders aid them in swimming as well as singing. In addition, these air bladders make their bodies extremely light and aid their thin legs in supporting their torsos.

Pa'lowick reproduce by laying eggs, and the female will guard the eggs in her home until they hatch. Pa'lowick homes are roofed, hut-like nests made of dried mud, reeds, and grass. Children are raised and educated within their agrarian communities, which are run by noble families in a feudal system. Pa'lowick are omnivorous, eating what they can gather from the salt marshes and also growing a wide variety of foodstuffs. The veejy fruit is a particular delicacy, growing in great quantities all year long in Lowickian rain forests. Characterized by its prickly skin and oblong shape, the yellow flesh of this fruit is sweet tasting, making it a popular export. The veejy fruit is largely responsible for the Pa'lowick's success in the post–Yuuzhan Vong era. When invading Pa'lowick, the Yuuzhan Vong destroyed the planet's mechanical harvesting machines, not the veejy crops themselves. As the Pa'lowickian agricultural base remains intact, their economy is already well on its way to recovery.

Miners looking for valuable Lowickan firegems in the Lowick asteroid belt discovered the species before the Clone Wars. Lowickian firegems are rare but useful, although they are often used for nefarious purposes. Extremely volatile, Lowickan firegems explode when placed near most forms of radiation. For this reason, they are often used as incendiary devices, both in legitimate mining and to cause injury and bring down starships.

Pa'lowick are therefore quite new to galactic society. They are enthusiastic about offworld contact, and enjoy trading food and native items for technology. Pa'lowick are very primitive, and prefer to live a simple life farming and fishing, but they are fascinated by technological items that make their lives easier. Even so, such items have done little to change Pa'lowick culture and life on the whole. While the ruling nobility at times considered joining the New Republic, the New Republic didn't seek them out for membership. Being so new, and offering so little in terms of trade, they tended to be ignored in the shuffle. However, this didn't seem to offend the Pa'lowicks, who really don't pay attention to galactic events anyway.

The Pa'lowicks are a generally patient people, who like to cling to rituals and traditions, rarely changing their ways of doing things. And yet they'll embrace technology that helps them do things the traditional way, only better. Because their heritage is so important, singing and storytelling are valued pursuits. In addition, vocal music is often a religious experi-

ence; a great many songs are written with sacred themes. This should not, however, suggest that all Pa'lowick music is religious. Many Pa'lowick sing for the pure enjoyment of it. Written language is a relatively new development in Pa'lowick society, so the need for an oral tradition to pass down history is not surprising. Much Pa'lowick lore is handed down through songs, including family lineages, historical events, and morality tales. Pa'lowick children grow up surrounded by music, and many vie for the few openings as apprentices to community storytellers. Technology is also slowly having an effect on Pa'lowick music.

With the discovery of the planet, some Pa'lowick have begun to learn Basic and adapt the Basic alphabet to spoken Lowickese (to the uneducated, however, it looks like nonsense written in Basic). This, along with the technology to record their songs and music, is allowing Pa'lowick to share their music beyond their own world.

Some ambitious Pa'lowick have taken this long treasured talent of singing to the stars, introducing a whole new, critically acclaimed sound to the galactic music scene. Pa'lowick music has become extremely popular and can be heard in cantinas thoughout the known worlds. Moreover, groups featuring Pa'lowick singers are among the most requested acts on the HoloNet.

While still new to the galaxy, this species was brought to greater public awareness when one female Pa'lowick named Larisselle Chatrunis won the Miss Coruscant beauty contest in the years leading up to the Clone Wars. Lariselle overwhelmed the judges with her singing ability during the talent portion of the contest, then truly impressed them with her knowledge of and sensitivity to the state of the galaxy—unusual for a people who'd only recently learned of the galactic society. Her fame was cut short when the Emperor initiated his anti-alien policies, but Lariselle, being more savvy than many of her fellow Pa'lowick, joined the Rebel Alliance. Using her talent as a singer, she toured the galaxy with a band of musicians, gathering information to pass along to the Alliance. Thought to be in competition with the often-lauded Sy Snootles, a perception she encouraged to deflect attention from her true work, Larisselle's only goal was to make music in order to win freedom from oppression for alien peoples. She survived the civil war and returned home to Lowick where she retired to a quiet life with family and friends.

DESIGNATION
Sentient

HOMEWORLD
Lowick

AVERAGE HEIGHT
1.6 meters

PRONUNCIATION
Păl'-ō-wĭk

NOTABLE APPEARANCE
Episode VI: Return of the Jedi

Polis Massans are a humanoid species inhabiting the small asteroid mining colony of Polis Massa in the isolated reaches of the Outer Rim. These short, thin, mute beings originally evolved on a world in the Subterrel sector. No records exist containing details of the species' previous life. After a natural cataclysm broke apart the world known as Polis Massa several centuries ago, they moved their entire society to that world to mine for artifacts from its lost Eellayin civilization, hoping to preserve the memory of these ill-fated people—or to resurrect them through cloning. These alien researchers believe they are descendants of the Eellayin, and because they have been working on this archaeological project for so long, they have become known as Polis Massans themselves, a name they accept with a sense of honor and humility.

These ardent archaeologists and exobiologists are delicate in appearance, with pale faces and gray skin. A Polis Massan's skin is thick and smooth, with some insulating qualities. This suggests that Polis Massans may have evolved from aquatic creatures, possibly within the cetacean genus. Their heads are practically featureless because an osmotic membrane covers the front of their faces. Polis Massans' thin arms end in four long, nimble fingers. They use a form of sign language and technological devices to communicate with others because they do not have vocal cords. In addition, they use a mild form of telepathy to share simple thoughts and feelings. Polis Massans have intensely focused eyes, which help them in their underground and medical research work. Growth rings circle their wiry bodies, although the specific biological reason for this is currently unknown. Most Polis Massans work in a mining capacity, or as medics or exobiologists, and they wear formfitting bodysuits with built-in signaling technology, medical instruments, and utility belts to do their work.

The Polis Massans are an industrious species. Most are seasoned spelunkers, working every day in the deep core of the Polis Massan asteroid field to find artifacts. Other peoples have speculated on the relationship of the present Polis Massans to the original inhabitants—other than their belief that they are their descendants—but the Polis Massans keep such information in solemn secrecy. They are generally known to have an insatiable desire for data on other species, so it might be argued that they have no ulterior motives for their archaeological research other than discovering their own background.

DESIGNATION
Sentient

HOMEWORLD
Polis Massa
(by way of the
Subterrel sector)

**AVERAGE
HEIGHT**
1.4 meters

PRONUNCIATION
Pō'-lĕs Mă'-sän

While they interact little with offworlders, Polis Massans are known for their remarkable medical skills and to be compassionate beings who value life and freedom in all forms. If the Polis Massans oppose outside contact, it is to discourage treasure hunters from invading the archaeological dig sites they are uncovering. Piracy is rampant in the Outer Rim, so the Polis Massans are desperate to avoid bringing attention to themselves. Polis Massan medical technicians are trained in cloning techniques, although their cloning technology is not as advanced as that of the Kaminoans who originally taught them. To carry out their cloning research, the Polis Massans built a high-end medical facility in one of their sealed habitats, although it is equipped mainly for the physiology of the Polis Massans.

Luke and Leia Skywalker were born in this very medical center on Polis Massa when Obi-Wan Kenobi and Bail Organa brought in their mother, in critical condition. While the Polis Massans did their best to save Padmé Amidala, she died in childbirth. Known for their honor and secrecy, the Polis Massans revealed nothing of the happenings there, and kept the knowledge of the Skywalker children a close-guarded secret. The Polis Massa asteroid field would play another important role, serving as a Rebel base in the early days of the fight against the Emperor's New Order. Many sorties were launched from Polis Massa during the Rebellion, and in turn the Empire raided Polis Massa. One such raid sought the stolen Death Star plans—which were not found, although the Imperial 501st did find evidence that Leia had them. This discovery led directly to the raid on her ship *Tantive IV,* and to her capture by Darth Vader.

Still, the planet's precious dig sites remained untouched, and the Polis Massans were able to resume their archaeological work. Nor did the site suffer damage during the war against the Yuuzhan Vong; its remote location held little strategic or resource value to the invaders.

NOTABLE APPEARANCE
Episode III: Revenge of the Sith

QUARREN

The amphibious Quarren share the Outer Rim world of Mon Calamari (Dac in their native tongue) with the forward-thinking Mon Calamari species. Quarren have leathery orange skin, turquoise eyes, and suction-cupped fingers. Quarren have the ability to alter their skin color, but this is done only during mating rituals. Since four tentacles sprout from the lower half of their faces, they have earned the not-so-flattering nickname of Squid Heads by which they are known to outsiders. While the Mon Calamari are dreamers and idealists, the Quarren are more practical and conservative. They've made a place for themselves in the galaxy acting as accountants and business managers. Despite this, not many leave home, as they prefer their peaceful ocean life to the vastness of the star-studded void.

The two species share a common native tongue, but, because the Mon Calamari have stopped using the language almost completely in favor of Basic, the Quarren continue to speak their own language regularly, unless dealing with outsiders.

Relations between the Quarren and the Mon Calamari have not always been peaceful. Quarren lived at greater depths than the Mon Calamari, and for many generations, they lived in completely separate and isolated communities. When the Quarren started traveling to higher levels of the oceans, they encountered the Mon Calamari and attacked their more technologically advanced neighbors. These battles proved disastrous for the Quarren, who were nearly driven to extinction. As a means of preventing unending wars between their species, the Mon Calamari attempted a daring social experiment aimed at civilizing the Quarren.

During these wars, the Mon Calamari captured nearly one million Quarren. The Mon Calamari were reluctant to release the Quarren, fearing that they would take up arms once more, forcing the Mon Calamari to kill them in battle. Desperate for another solution, the Mon Cals removed a generation of Quarren children from their captured parents and raised them in Mon Calamari cities, educating them in philosophy, mathematics, and science. Otherwise, they made no effort to force their beliefs on the Quarren children or change their hatred of Mon Calamari. After a decade, the children were returned to their families, and the results of the experiment was readily apparent: the children exhibited new respect for the Mon Calamari. Quarren elders felt the children had been brainwashed; the children in turn perceived the elders as primitive savages. The generations no longer had anything in common. Fifteen years later, the children had grown to adulthood and assumed control of Quarren society, and several years after that opened diplomatic relations with their world-mates. While this was a controversial approach on the part of the Mon Calamari, it perhaps saved the Quarren and, in turn, themselves.

After building something of a political friendship, the Mon Calamari encouraged the Quarren to work with them in pursuing dreams of space and advanced science. The Mon Cals provided the ideas, and the Quarren provided the raw materials. Together they built impressive ships for deep space, as well as impressive floating cities that dominate the oceans.

These giant cities extend far below the surface of the water, and serve as centers of learning, culture, and government. In contrast with the Mon Calamari, who prefer more daylight and live in the upper levels of the cities, the Quarren live in the lowest levels of the metropolis in the cool security of the deep. This fits with their cultural identity as a pragmatic people, unwilling to trust or embrace the new idea or lofty concept. Their literature reveals a people who do not dream of brighter tomorrows, but hold fast to remembered yesterdays. Thus, they feel they belong in the sea, not in space.

And yet, many Quarren have followed their neighbors offplanet. Quarren are able to live on land as long as they are able to keep their skin moist. As they benefited from the discoveries and achievements of the Mon Calamari, they have grown dependent upon them. This dependency has caused friction between the two peoples, and may have prompted the Quarren to join Count Dooku and the Confederacy during the Clone Wars. Though an armistice was reached before the end of the wars and the creation of the Empire, it is believed that the Quarren betrayed their ocean compatriots the day that the Imperial fleet arrived. On that day, Mon Calamari's planetary defense systems failed to protect them from invasion. Rumors persist that the Quarren aided the Imperials by sabotaging this protective network.

DESIGNATION
Sentient

HOMEWORLD
Mon Calamari

AVERAGE
HEIGHT
1.7 meters

PRONUNCIATION
Kwä'-rĕn

The Empire enslaved both the Quarren and the Mon Calamari, forcing them to work in labor camps. There, the two species found a unifying cause, and cooperated in a plan of passive resistance. The Empire retaliated by destroying whole cities on Mon Calamari, filling the ocean with the blood of both species. This incited these peaceful peoples to rise up in rage. Using only primitive utensils, hand tools, and sheer will, they forced their Imperial taskmasters to leave their world.

Today Quarren and Mon Calamari live in peace with each other, although there still is some lingering resentment. Persistent elements of Quarren society recall the wars against the Mon Calamari and the Mon Calamari's deceptive "theft" of their children. Some Quarren believe that Mon Cals brought havoc to their world by exploring space in the first place. Similarly, some Quarren believe the adoption of *Mon Calamari* as a name for their planet is one more example of the Mon Calamari species seeking its own glorification at the Quarren's expense. These Quarren do their best to enact revenge against the New Republic and the Mon Cal without bringing harm upon their own. There has been an effort by some Quarren to find another homeworld—one they would not have to share—following the Battle of Mon Calamari during the New Republic era. And yet one sign that healing is occurring between the two peoples is that more interspecies romances are being recorded, one of the better known being the relationship involving two Rogue Squadron pilots: the late Ibtisam, a Mon Calamari, and Nrin Vakil, a Quarren. When Ibtisam was killed in action, their relationship became public knowledge, leading to more openness about the two species interrelating. For many residents of Mon Calamari, this is evidence of hope for their people and their world.

NOTABLE APPEARANCE
Episode VI: Return of the Jedi

RANCOR

Rancors are huge, mostly vicious reptilian creatures found on several worlds throughout the galaxy. There are several different varieties, but all have nearly the same physiology and temperament. How they managed to spread to so many different systems is still a mystery, but most scientists believe that they were taken to some worlds by sentient species who used these massive creatures as battle mounts or beasts of burden.

Standing on two trunk-like legs, more than five meters tall, rancors provide an intimidating sight to those who face

7.0

6.0

5.0

4.0

3.0

2.0

1.0

0

them. Rancor hides are often a combination of gray, green, and brown in color; they have glistening black eyes. Their arms are very long, somewhat slender, and out of proportion when compared with the rest of their muscular bodies. Rancors have huge saliva-dripping fangs, and long, sharp claws on their fingers and toes. These creatures are repto-mammals (part reptile, part mammal), and as such, they lay clutches of two eggs at a time. Rancors care for their young, although they do not suckle. When the creatures are hatched, the parents are gentle with their three-meter-tall offspring—showing a gentle, loving nature that is often incongruous with their fearsome appearance. The mother shares her food with her young, which ride on her back until they are three years of age. At maturity, a rancor leaves its family for the rest of its life.

Carnivorous, rancors prefer fresh, raw meat, particularly large herbivorous creatures. They will eat vegetable matter if nothing else is available, but it is by necessity only. In the wild, rancors have few natural predators, instead being the predators themselves. In addition, some creatures are thought to be subspecies of rancors, such as the terentatek of Korriban, which has larger spines and a more armored head. Another such subspecies is the pygmy rancor, thought to be the result of bioengineering. Although this theory is still in dispute in scientific circles, the pygmy rancor is smaller in stature than the common rancor, but distinctly a rancor according to genetic analysis. Latest theories hypothesize that the pygmy rancor was engineered and released into the wild either by accident or on purpose, to breed. Similar theories have been put forth regarding Dathomiran rancors, which are larger than average.

Rancors are fearsome fighters. Their fists can smash prey flat, while their massive jaws enable them to swallow human-sized morsels whole. Their thick powerful hides make them highly resistant to blasters and other handheld energy weapons. Even melee weapons cannot puncture their tough layers of skin. Rancors' eyes are able to see clearly in dim light, and their sense of smell allows them to track prey over great distances.

The influence of rancors goes beyond their own environments. For example, Rancor Rising is a sequence of movements in the teräs käsi martial arts tradition, based on rancors' hunting characteristics. Also, rancor hide is used in leather consumer goods such as boots. There is also a valuable trade in items carved from rancor teeth. In her days as a Jedi Knight, the Hapan Queen Mother Tenel Ka used a light-saber with a hilt carved of a rancor tooth from her mother's homeworld of Dathomir.

Despite their fierce fighting abilities, rancors are actually inherently benign creatures when they are well fed and allowed to live alongside their own kind. They can be successfully domesticated and trained for riding or to haul goods. In the case of the Witches of Dathomir, rancors have been trained to perform construction labor and serve as transportation. However, training a rancor is not an easy task and should not be attempted without extensive training in zoological behavioral techniques and prior experience with dangerous creatures. Because the Witches of Dathomir are themselves raised with rancors, they come by this training naturally.

Rancors have shown a capacity to bond with other species if given the chance—particularly with those who feed and care for them. This is the case with the breed on Dathomir, whose intelligence makes them extremely useful as battle mounts and protectors. Dathomiri rancors are also very loyal to their owners.

If abused or maltreated, however, these beasts can be driven into an almost perpetual rage that is only temporarily abated by regular feedings. If they are driven to this state, they'll eat anyone or anything that comes within reach out of utter despair and fury. Luke Skywalker reported that he encountered a rancor in this very state on Tatooine. Jabba the Hutt employed a dangerous creature specialist named Malakili from the Circus Horrificus as his rancor keeper. Malakili bonded with the creature, but Jabba would not let him feed the rancor regularly, preferring instead to feed the rancor his enemies and others who displeased him. While this happened frequently, the meat was from beings rather than sustenance animals, and thus did not meet the rancor's basic needs. When Skywalker was tossed into the rancor's pit beneath Jabba's throne room, he had to lure the creature to its death in order to put it out of its misery. Sadly, when a rancor reaches this point, there is little else to do but euthanize it. Even if removed from that environment and placed in one where it can be cared for properly, an abused rancor never seems to forget. It will not get over the distrust, or learn that food and care can be counted on. Zoologists commonly believe that there can be no rehabilitation of a rancor that has been mistreated for a long period of time.

DESIGNATION
Nonsentient

HOMEWORLD
Dathomir/
Ottethan

AVERAGE HEIGHT
5+ meters

PRONUNCIATION
Răn'-kŏr

NOTABLE APPEARANCE
Episode VI: Return of the Jedi

REEK

The reek is a large quadrupedal mammal native to the plains of Ylesia in Hutt space, and often bred on ranches on that world's Codian Moon. Large tusks protrude from their cheeks, which they use for headlocks in contests for dominance among their own kind. One central horn is used to attack an opponent head-on. While they are herbivores by nature, they are often used for exhibition sport as execution animals. When used this way, reeks are fed meat and then starved so they develop the instincts to attack arena gladiators or other animals. Reeks cannot continue to thrive on a meat diet, so arena animals are fed just enough plant matter to keep up their strength and incite their hunger. Heavy and muscular, the reek is a fierce combatant. Its powerful jaw muscles, which usually slice through tough wood-moss chunks with ease, can take off a human limb without much effort. All reeks, even the subspecies, are normally some sort of brown in color with leathery skin, but if fed a diet of meat their skin turns a mottled red.

Reeks tend to reside in small herds in the mossy grasslands and are very protective over their chosen area of wood-moss turf. They use their front claws for digging up wood-moss, which is their primary source of nourishment. Because their cheek horns grow continuously, reeks will rub their horns on trees and rocks to shorten and sharpen them. The horns of male reeks are usually larger than those of females, and they display them to attract a mate. During mating season, male reeks battle each other in ramming contests for the choice females among their herds.

Reeks have been transported to other worlds for various purposes, causing them to adapt to new environments. One subspecies of reek, principally adapted to the world of Ithor, was wiped out in the Yuuzhan Vong invasion. While the Ithorians are very technologically developed, they preferred to use a more natural means of planting and growing. They used reeks as plow animals because they were strong, slow, and naturally gentle. This reek subspecies was, therefore, larger than those found on Ylesia, and stronger for pulling large plows. The animals' horns were also smaller, as they were not as motivated to fight among one another. The Ithorians wisely placed males and females in separate pens and isolated planned pairs for mating, to reduce competition. These reeks were yellow in color because of their consumption of Ithorian flora, with a special affinity for the leaves of bafforr trees.

DESIGNATION
Nonsentient

HOMEWORLD
Ylesia

AVERAGE HEIGHT
2.24 meters
LENGTH
4 meters

PRONUNCIATION
Rēk

One other subspecies was developed on the Zabrak world of Iridonia. When the Zabrak first took to the stars, they saw reeks as excellent animals to use for war mounts in that they were naturally armored. Riding reeks into battle, they charge at their opponents, using the animal's horns as an added weapon. Iridonian reeks have tougher skin for resisting blunt or sharp weapon attacks and the harsh Iridonian winds. Zabrak do not feed their mounts meat, preferring them to be strong and fierce with natural vigor. These reeks are more compact in size than the original reek, and gray in color from consuming the native vegetation. Their primary horns are longer and sharper, and they are often decorated with markings mimicking the tattoos the Zabrak adorn themselves with. These tattoos may speak of a reek's personality, its given name, or the family to whom it belongs. Iridonian reeks are encouraged to fight for dominance and for mates as this desensitizes them to violence, making them less likely to bolt or buck in battle. The Zabrak skill of reek riding declined in use as the Zabrak became more technologically advanced, but the skill of riding a war mount is still taught at most schools focusing on the military arts.

While reeks are not terribly fast, they are intelligent. If given patient, gentle training, they can make excellent pack animals. The Codian Moon harbors several reek ranches for this purpose, though diminishing resources and plummeting profits have caused several ranchers to start breeding their reeks for the gladiatorial arenas, feeding them meat and starving them to bring out their wild anger.

In such a situation, reeks are fearsome foes. Snapping their strong jaws, they can bite a humanoid in half, slicing through flesh and crushing bones without effort. Their usual tactic is to gore their opponents with their horns and trample them under their giant, heavy feet.

NOTABLE APPEARANCE
Episode II: Attack of the Clones

RODIAN

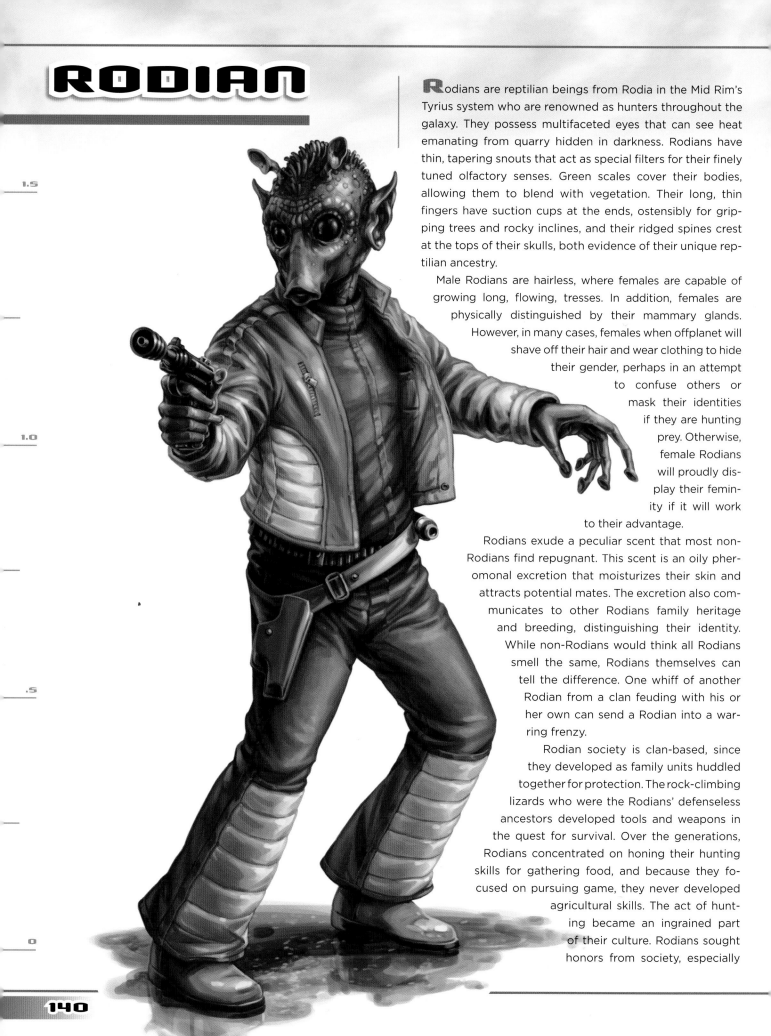

Rodians are reptilian beings from Rodia in the Mid Rim's Tyrius system who are renowned as hunters throughout the galaxy. They possess multifaceted eyes that can see heat emanating from quarry hidden in darkness. Rodians have thin, tapering snouts that act as special filters for their finely tuned olfactory senses. Green scales cover their bodies, allowing them to blend with vegetation. Their long, thin fingers have suction cups at the ends, ostensibly for gripping trees and rocky inclines, and their ridged spines crest at the tops of their skulls, both evidence of their unique reptilian ancestry.

Male Rodians are hairless, where females are capable of growing long, flowing, tresses. In addition, females are physically distinguished by their mammary glands. However, in many cases, females when offplanet will shave off their hair and wear clothing to hide their gender, perhaps in an attempt to confuse others or mask their identities if they are hunting prey. Otherwise, female Rodians will proudly display their feminity if it will work to their advantage.

Rodians exude a peculiar scent that most non-Rodians find repugnant. This scent is an oily pheromonal excretion that moisturizes their skin and attracts potential mates. The excretion also communicates to other Rodians family heritage and breeding, distinguishing their identity. While non-Rodians would think all Rodians smell the same, Rodians themselves can tell the difference. One whiff of another Rodian from a clan feuding with his or her own can send a Rodian into a warring frenzy.

Rodian society is clan-based, since they developed as family units huddled together for protection. The rock-climbing lizards who were the Rodians' defenseless ancestors developed tools and weapons in the quest for survival. Over the generations, Rodians concentrated on honing their hunting skills for gathering food, and because they focused on pursuing game, they never developed agricultural skills. The act of hunting became an ingrained part of their culture. Rodians sought honors from society, especially the Grand Protector, the leader of their civilization, for their hunting skills.

After a time, all the predators Rodians hunted on their homeworld became extinct. When this happened, the Rodians began to hunt one another. Manufacturing excuses for wars, they nearly brought themselves to extinction and laid waste to their entire environment. To this day, the Rodian people are obsessed with violence.

Though extinction at one time seemed inevitable, before this could happen, a very wise Grand Protector named Harido Kavila developed one of the Rodians' greatest cultural gifts to the galaxy. He founded Rodian Theater and, with it, helped stop his race from destroying itself.

Since Rodians romanticize violence, drama offers them a catharsis for their violent tendencies without them having to actually bring harm upon one another. Their dramatic efforts developed gradually; the early works were little more than staged fights. But Rodian dramatists quickly realized that the effect of drama was magnified if the fights were presented as elements of an even greater story. Soon the complexity of Rodian stories grew, and they came to be as good as the choreographed violence.

Rodian drama is today highly regarded throughout the galaxy, because although it is violent, it deals with motivations and situations that provoke strong emotional responses in audiences of most species. In addition, these dramas show the realistic effects of violence, so non-Rodians—and even Rodians, if the drama is well written—are struck by the moral impact of each play.

Rodians now import much of their food and many other resources from offplanet, as their own proclivity for hunting and industrial expansion has destroyed Rodia's once lush ecosystem. Meanwhile, they export the weapons they create. Rodians are renowned as brilliant weaponsmiths, and most work in the vast factories that manufacture their famous products. Their main export fits well with their legendary talents as hunters—talents that they also offer for profit. Those who sell their talents often make a great deal of money and gain widespread fame on their homeworld and beyond. Bounty hunting has become an honored profession for Rodians. Prizes are awarded annually for "Best Shot" (for deceased catches), "Longest Trail" (awarded for persistence), "Most Notorious Capture," "Quickest Catch," and "Most Difficult Hunt."

DESIGNATION
Sentient

HOMEWORLD
Rodia

AVERAGE HEIGHT
1.6 meters

PRONUNCIATION
Rō'-dē-ăn

Because hunting is treated as a challenge and a contest on Rodia, when Rodians leave home to participate in bounty hunting, they find it irrelevant that they are participating in law enforcement, not sport. Rodian bounty hunters often "pad" catches, following their quarry and allowing them to commit additional crimes or do more damage, substantially raising the value of the final bounty. While this infuriates their underworld clients, it certainly makes for greater recognition from their own—which they crave.

Despite their hunting prowess, however, Rodians are often viewed as cowards by other species. They are mostly distrusted and reviled. Rodians are generally unwilling to take risks, or put themselves in danger to bring in quarry. For this reason, they often use the biggest and most destructive weaponry available to complete a task. In addition, since Rodians usually receive prizes when returning home with a kill, they will charge less to their employers, especially if they can keep the remains. Rodians demand exorbitant fees for bringing in live prey because it often increases risk, and usually the Rodian will conveniently "forget" that part of a bounty agreement during the hunt.

Rodians are rarely seen in groups on any other world besides Rodia unless they are touring in a dramatic troupe. They hunt alone, believing that life is dangerous enough without getting in the way of or upsetting another of their own kind.

Despite their vicious tendencies, Rodia has participated in galactic events. At the time of the Clone Wars, Rodians were members of the Jedi Order and also represented themselves in the Galactic Senate. However, at the end of the New Republic, Rodia was taken over by the Yuuzhan Vong, who used the Rodians to create a genetically altered slave race called the Vagh Rodiek. In a planetwide project, the Yuuzhan Vong shapers merged Rodian biological material with pieces of other creatures to create a beast with four crab-like legs and arms of half-meter-long bone hooks. In a case of re-creating the Rodians in their own awful image, Yuuzhan Vong transmuted Rodians' headspines to puncturing quills.

NOTABLE APPEARANCE
Episode IV: A New Hope

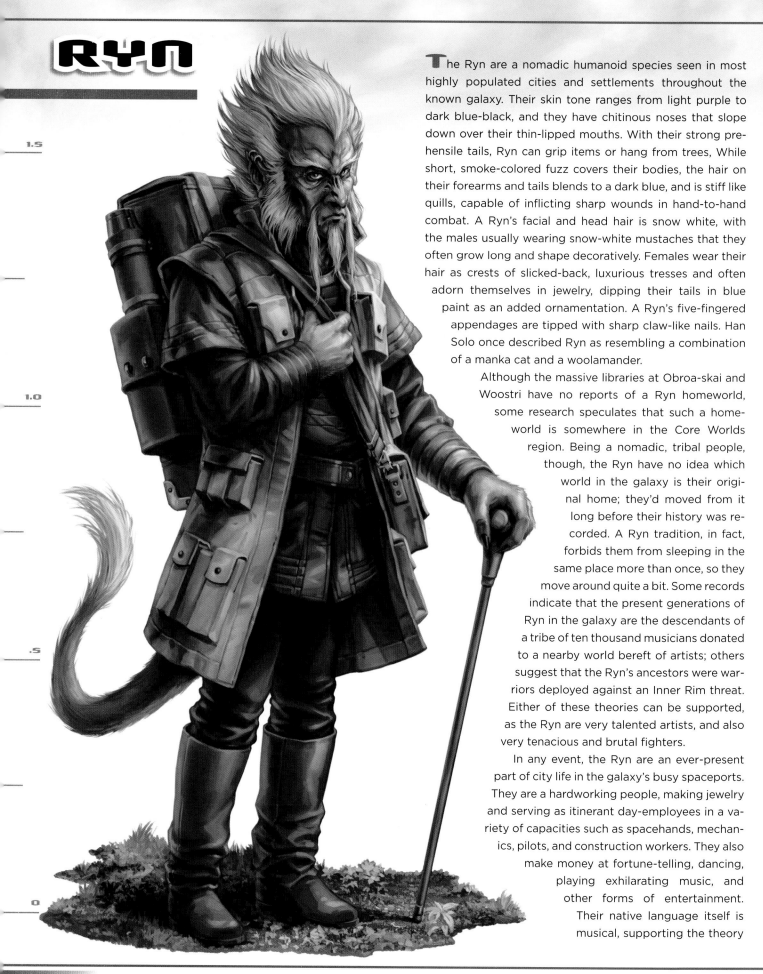

RYN

The Ryn are a nomadic humanoid species seen in most highly populated cities and settlements throughout the known galaxy. Their skin tone ranges from light purple to dark blue-black, and they have chitinous noses that slope down over their thin-lipped mouths. With their strong prehensile tails, Ryn can grip items or hang from trees, While short, smoke-colored fuzz covers their bodies, the hair on their forearms and tails blends to a dark blue, and is stiff like quills, capable of inflicting sharp wounds in hand-to-hand combat. A Ryn's facial and head hair is snow white, with the males usually wearing snow-white mustaches that they often grow long and shape decoratively. Females wear their hair as crests of slicked-back, luxurious tresses and often adorn themselves in jewelry, dipping their tails in blue paint as an added ornamentation. A Ryn's five-fingered appendages are tipped with sharp claw-like nails. Han Solo once described Ryn as resembling a combination of a manka cat and a woolamander.

Although the massive libraries at Obroa-skai and Woostri have no reports of a Ryn homeworld, some research speculates that such a homeworld is somewhere in the Core Worlds region. Being a nomadic, tribal people, though, the Ryn have no idea which world in the galaxy is their original home; they'd moved from it long before their history was recorded. A Ryn tradition, in fact, forbids them from sleeping in the same place more than once, so they move around quite a bit. Some records indicate that the present generations of Ryn in the galaxy are the descendants of a tribe of ten thousand musicians donated to a nearby world bereft of artists; others suggest that the Ryn's ancestors were warriors deployed against an Inner Rim threat. Either of these theories can be supported, as the Ryn are very talented artists, and also very tenacious and brutal fighters.

In any event, the Ryn are an ever-present part of city life in the galaxy's busy spaceports. They are a hardworking people, making jewelry and serving as itinerant day-employees in a variety of capacities such as spacehands, mechanics, pilots, and construction workers. They also make money at fortune-telling, dancing, playing exhilarating music, and other forms of entertainment. Their native language itself is musical, supporting the theory that the musical arts are at the very root of their culture (though young Ryn also learn to speak Basic, to aid them in navigating galactic society). By blowing air and covering and uncovering the holes in their beak-like noses, Ryn mimic sounds or make music like a wind instrument.

The Ryn are a flamboyant, fun-loving species, and are believed to be the inventors of the gambling game sa-bacc—they often use sabacc cards for fortune-telling. They wear colorful attire and jewelry and travel in large extended-family or tribal communities, sometimes making their living through con games and theft. These activities have spawned a general galaxywide distrust of the Ryn, who are ostracized and mistreated by society, almost as a rule. Most beings will not even notice Ryn, looking past them as in-significant. While such maltreatment is mostly due to their criminal tendencies and their *do-anything-to-survive* outlook, they are also rejected because of their views on personal hygiene. Their superstitions preclude them from bathing regularly, giving them a rather ripe odor.

Interestingly, although their moving about the galaxy prevents them from training as Jedi, Ryn have demonstrated talents in the Force as spirit adepts. Generally speaking, spirit adepts develop their skills removed from knowledge of Force traditions and often on worlds with-out a Jedi presence, following local beliefs and superstitions. As Ryn often move from world to world, this path to the Force seems uniquely suited to them. Spirit adepts learn to hear the Force speaking to them as the voices of their ancestors, and the wise listen to their counsel, some never realizing it is the Force at all. Ryn spirit adepts often become clan elders, drawing on the Force to lead their people. It is possible that Ryn fortunetellers could be spirit adepts channeling their skills in this manner, using sabacc cards as a convenient prop.

During the Yuuzhan Vong invasion, Ryn were relegated to the worst part of refugee camps near the latrines because their scent offended the other refugees. In the camps, Ryn were outcasts not worthy of a name, often finding that their species was listed as "other" in camp rosters. However, the Ryn's status as refugees also allowed them to effect some small measure of change in how they were viewed by the galaxy at large. In fact, a Ryn named Droma was responsible for saving the life of Captain Han Solo on the *Jubilee Wheel* when it was attacked by the Yuuzhan Vong. Droma became Solo's companion for a period of time; it is said that, for the

Solos, his company eased the pain of Chewbacca's death earlier in the war.

Throughout their history, the Ryn have been victimized by galactic society. Slavers, in particular, have found them a lucrative commodity, particularly with the Hutts, who place a great deal of value on the species' card-based fortune-telling. On the few worlds where they attempted to establish permanent settlements, Ryn often saw their lands (and often their meager possessions) taken from them in "ethnic relo-cation" programs, which were no more than rich landowners trying to seize the property of those without the power to refuse. On most of these Ryn settle-ment worlds, young male Ryn were frequently arrested for theft in community sweeps, at the mere suggestion that thefts had occurred.

As a result of their persecution, the Ryn have grown more secretive, self-sufficient, and sus-picious, with an almost defiant will to survive. They do not trust help from outsiders, but have an avid interest in observing them. Information is a moneymaker for them, but also a means to keep them and their people far from danger. They place a tremendous value on secrets, and are very good at keeping them. It was these skills, along with the Ryn's near-total social in-visibility, that allowed the Ryn to create what is perhaps their species' greatest achievement— the development and operation of a diverse, pervasive, and very effective spy network that greatly aided later New Republic war efforts against the Yuuzhan Vong.

Although unconfirmed, some Galactic Alli-ance intelligence sources suggest that the Ryn network may have been in fact sponsored by the known information broker Talon Karrde, to aid the war effort against the Yuuzhan Vong. It has been suggested that by keeping his role and input a secret, Karrde expanded his existing network to include the Ryn. Through these machinations, the Ryn do not suspect they were not independent or that they did not come up with the idea of a spy network themselves. This hypothesis may have merit, as Karrde has countless con-tacts throughout the galaxy and the Ryn would be only too easy to manipulate, given their prideful and boastful natures. Whatever the source, the Ryn spy network and the coura-geous efforts of its members contributed greatly to the war effort, often providing conduits for information that could not have been passed along otherwise.

DESIGNATION
Sentient

HOMEWORLD
Unknown

AVERAGE HEIGHT
1.6 meters

PRONUNCIATION
Rĭn

NOTABLE APPEARANCE
Agents of Chaos I: Hero's Trial (novel)

SARLACC

The creature known as the Sarlacc is a mystery to modern zoology, as very few scientists have been able to get close enough to a specimen to study it. One of the largest recorded examples of the species rests in the Great Pit of Carkoon in Tatooine's Dune Sea, although others have been reported on various worlds, including Dathomir and Aargonar. The personal experiences of Luke Skywalker and his fellows on their mission to rescue Han Solo from Jabba the Hutt have been well documented.

What scientists do know is that the Sarlacc is a massive, omnivorous arthropod with plant-like tendencies. While very rare, Sarlaccs are extremely long-lived; estimates place its life span at 20,000 to 50,000 standard years. It has been discovered that the creature reproduces via spores called sarlacci, which travel through space until they find a suitable world. Just how the sarlacci manage this is a matter of speculation. As is the case with the dianoga, it may be that sarlacci find their way into outbound starships. Due to their estimated age, however, it seems unlikely that this is the only means of transport—Sarlaccs predate space travel on many worlds. Yet biological studies do not seem to indicate whether or not sarlacci can survive in vacuum, as mynocks do. The Sarlacc's initial planet of origin is unknown, but research suggests that it could be Tatooine. The spores are discharged from an oviduct below the Sarlacc's epidermal layer. The sarlacci form male–female pairs, crawl to the surface, and migrate from there. Sarlacci are extremely vulnerable during their immature phase, at risk for either starving to death or being eaten by other creatures. Fortunately very, very few sarlacci take root. When a sarlacci spore implants itself in the ground, it grows downward into the soil or sand like a plant, forming a pit.

From the edge of its sandy pit, the Sarlacc looks like a great hooked beak with a snake-like head coiling from its center, and an enormous, mucus-dripping mouth descending to a trunk-like body surrounded by dozens of writhing,

grasping tentacles. This is only the uppermost part of the creature—the enormous body of the Sarlacc is buried deep beneath the surface, extending out to one hundred meters or more. By burying most of its massive body underground, the Sarlacc protects itself. All its vital organs are inaccessible, rendering the creature nearly impervious to serious or life-threatening damage.

The female Sarlacc is the true danger. Growing to enormous sizes, it is the dominant of the two sexes. Male Sarlaccs are much smaller, and parasitic, attaching themselves to their mates to feed off them. Males do not differ from females other than in size. However, a report from a University of Coruscant anthropological survey team detailed finding the remains of a mutated male Sarlacc that had over the course of many thousands of years grown large enough to consume its mate. No such other remains have been found.

Much of the Sarlacc's anatomy aids it in capturing prey. By hiding the majority of its body underground, it does not betray its inherent danger to its victims. A Sarlacc's teeth are helpful in keeping captured food imprisoned

DESIGNATION
Semi-sentient

HOMEWORLD
Tatooine (not confirmed)

AVERAGE DIAMETER
3 meters (mouth only)
LENGTH
100 meters

PRONUNCIATION
Sär'-lăk

because they slant inward to prevent a meal from escaping. The Sarlacc uses its tentacles to snag prey and drag it down to its cavernous mouth. These tentacles have been known to reach a full four meters beyond the pit to grab unsuspecting victims. However, the Sarlacc's main means of capturing prey is through scent. The Sarlacc gives off odors that attract herbivores and scavengers, bringing them within reach.

Sarlaccs are completely immobile. Because the Sarlacc cannot hunt for prey and lives in the middle of the desert, it does not feed often; it must wait for prey to come to it. Still, with its extremely slow but highly efficient digestive system, the Sarlacc doesn't need to eat with great frequency. When necessary, the Sarlacc will immediately digest a meal in a primary stomach. During times when sustenance is not critical, the Sarlacc's body can preserve food for incredibly long periods of time, digesting it slowly and storing it in a series of secondary stomachs until nourishment is demanded again. Victims are held in the secondary stomachs by rope-like, meters-long cilia. The Sarlacc's gastric juices in these secondary stomachs are weaker than those in the primary stomach, consisting of specific acids that do not kill victims but slowly decompose them, ensuring fresh meat for the duration of the digestive cycle. Sarlaccs have been rumored to digest their victims over the course of a thousand years.

One of the most prevalent rumors about the Sarlacc is that the creature is mildly telepathic, and over millennia actually gains sentience from victims as it consumes them. Although Sarlaccs do not have advanced neural systems, it is believed that they gain consciousness by assimilating the thoughts of the beings and creatures they consume.

Data that anthropologist Hoole secured from the bounty hunter Boba Fett appears to confirm this. According to Fett's experience in the belly of the beast, not only was the Sarlacc sentient, but it enjoyed torturing those it was digesting. It manipulated the thoughts of its victims, and even kept their intelligence stored in its memories so it could savor their pain at another time. Footage from Fett's helmet recorder revealed a more plant-like physical structure than most scientists had believed, and the secretion of some plant enzyme that might be the cause of the beasts' hallucinogenic power over their victims.

NOTABLE APPEARANCE
Episode VI: Return of the Jedi

Shistavanens, often called Shistavanen Wolfmen, are hairy, canine bipeds from Uvena Prime and their colonized worlds in the Uvena system of the Outer Rim Territories. Like most canine-based species, they have high-set dog-like ears and long muzzles, large, sharp teeth, and sharp claws on their hands and feet. Shistavanens' bodies are covered in thick brown or black fur, and they can walk on four legs as well as upright on two. A particularly notable feature of the species is a Shistavanen's eyes, which glow red. Physically, male Shistavanens tend to be taller and more muscular than their female counterparts.

Because of their canine ancestry, Shistavanens are innately excellent hunters and trackers. They can follow prey with ease, using heightened senses to navigate crowded urban streets and open plains alike. Their sense of sight is so highly developed that they can see in near-absolute darkness with no loss of visual acuity, still able to detect color and detail. They move with great speed and possess remarkable endurance.

Shistavanen society is based on an isolationist ideal. They do not like outsiders visiting Uvena or meddling in their affairs. While they haven't outlawed outsiders from coming to their world, their open prejudice toward non-Shistavanens is made clear by their restrictive laws and trade. Uvena Prime is a self-sufficient world, and the Shistavanens have even colonized all the unpopulated worlds in the Uvena system to prevent strangers from doing so. Most of the population is at hyperspace-level technology, though some pockets of civilization remain at a lower level because of their isolationist ideology.

As a result of their xenophobic societal rules, most Shistavanens are not talkative with beings of other species. While on other worlds, they remain most often by themselves or with others of their own kind. Shistavanens communicate using a language consisting of loud barks and growls, but many also learned Basic after the rise of the Empire. A small minority, however, are actually outgoing. These few are frequently hired as scouts, pilots, bounty hunters, or security guards. While Shistavanens are suspicious of other species, other species are openly afraid of Shistavanens.

At home, Shistavanens are family-focused, raising their offspring (called pups) in family dens. A den, which is a home hewn from natural rock or formed in hard-baked clay, usually houses immediate family and sometimes in-laws, depending on the amount of space available. Pups are homeschooled using a government-approved system of education that utilizes comlinks for grading. After school lessons, all the pups of an area come together to cooperatively learn and practice "outdoor skills"—hunting, tracking, survival, and martial arts. Adults from the various dens trade off responsibilities in training the youngsters to master these skills. Pups graduate to adulthood once they make their first "kill" hunting alone in the forests of Uvena Prime.

As a largely xenophobic people, Shistavanens do not often travel from home; those who do are usually young and adventurous. Following the rise of the New Republic, more and more Shistavanens took to the stars, hoping to learn new things. This caused some conflict with the older generation, who prefer to remain focused on the affairs of their world. If seen at large, Shistavanens generally serve those who can afford to pay them. Shistavanens take great pride in their work, and they charge high fees.

A primary trait that lends itself to success in pursuits such as bounty hunting is Shistavanens' tendency to be loners. Coupled with their tracking skills, they are very dangerous to those they stalk—and very valuable to those desirous of their abilities. During the height of the Empire, Shistavanens were often employed by Imperial Intelligence, providing a service that was more important to the Imperials than politically oppressing their remote, nonhuman world. As a trade-off, the Empire simply restricted Shistavanens' ability to pursue trade openly. Prior to Palpatine's New Order, Shistavanens also served the Old Republic, including a rare Shistavanen Jedi who took part in the Battle of Geonosis. As fighting troops, Shistavanens are specialists as snipers and at flanking opposing forces, a skill useful to the Rebellion on many occasions. When two Shistavanen hunters work together in this capacity, they are especially deadly and can turn the tide of a battle. Even the New Republic's fabled Rogue Squadron has had a Shistavanen member.

Personality-wise, Shistavanens tend to be belligerent, proud, boastful, and arrogant. Some are able to temper these qualities with a good sense of humor, making them tolerable to others. In addition, while they are very intelligent, they are also very violent and aggressive. But even Shistavanens who are able to negotiate social situations have difficulty working past their cultural prejudices, and few are able to completely rid themselves of them. Usually, Shistavanens are more likely to go out of their way to insult and offend others, simply because they don't like any species but their own.

DESIGNATION
Sentient

HOMEWORLD
Uvena Prime

AVERAGE
HEIGHT
1.8 meters

PRONUNCIATION
Shĭst'-ŭ-văn-ĕn

NOTABLE APPEARANCE
Episode IV: A New Hope

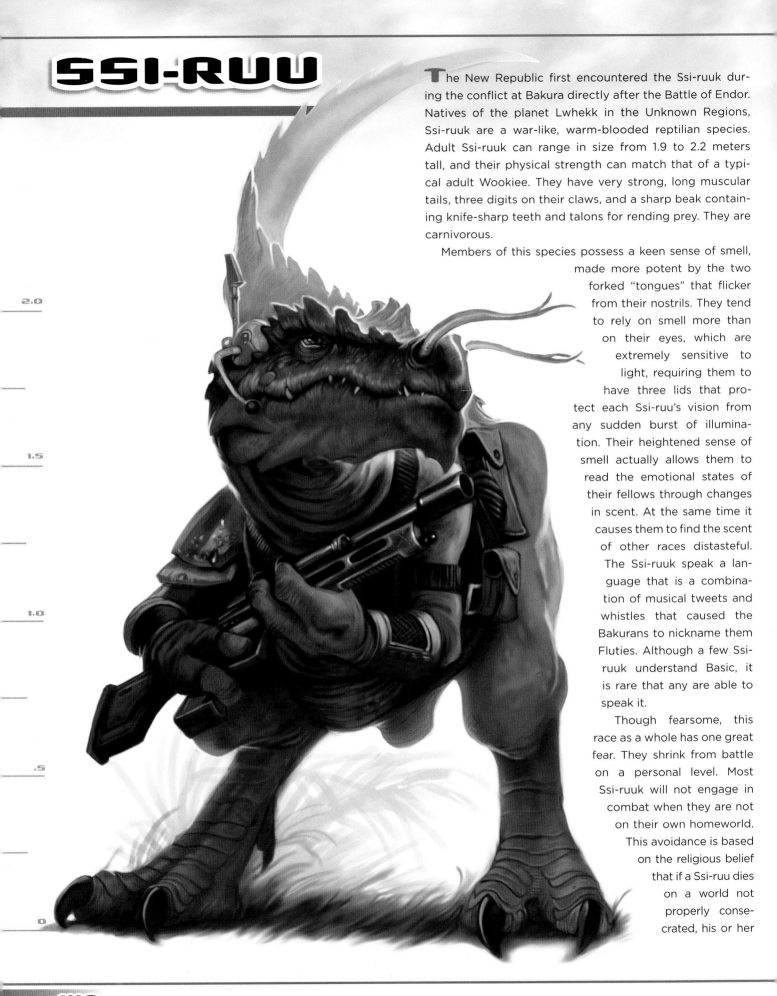

SSI-RUU

The New Republic first encountered the Ssi-ruuk during the conflict at Bakura directly after the Battle of Endor. Natives of the planet Lwhekk in the Unknown Regions, Ssi-ruuk are a war-like, warm-blooded reptilian species. Adult Ssi-ruuk can range in size from 1.9 to 2.2 meters tall, and their physical strength can match that of a typical adult Wookiee. They have very strong, long muscular tails, three digits on their claws, and a sharp beak containing knife-sharp teeth and talons for rending prey. They are carnivorous.

Members of this species possess a keen sense of smell, made more potent by the two forked "tongues" that flicker from their nostrils. They tend to rely on smell more than on their eyes, which are extremely sensitive to light, requiring them to have three lids that protect each Ssi-ruu's vision from any sudden burst of illumination. Their heightened sense of smell actually allows them to read the emotional states of their fellows through changes in scent. At the same time it causes them to find the scent of other races distasteful. The Ssi-ruuk speak a language that is a combination of musical tweets and whistles that caused the Bakurans to nickname them Fluties. Although a few Ssi-ruuk understand Basic, it is rare that any are able to speak it.

Though fearsome, this race as a whole has one great fear. They shrink from battle on a personal level. Most Ssi-ruuk will not engage in combat when they are not on their own homeworld. This avoidance is based on the religious belief that if a Ssi-ruu dies on a world not properly consecrated, his or her spirit will wander aimlessly throughout the galaxy for all eternity.

Ssi-ruuvi society is dictated by a rigid honor code. Ssi-ruu believe that they are superior to all of ther species, due to an ancient pictograph called the G'nnoch. According to Ssi-ruuk, other races are inferior and are no more than sustenance creatures.

Ssi-ruuvi society is a clan-based hierarchy, and each clan is designated by the color of their scales. The highest-ranking group is the blue-scaled clan. Other clan colors are the gold scales (primarily religious), red-brown scales (military), and the green scales (workers). Most Ssi-ruuk are of the latter caste, which is the lowest caste to still receive esteem and honor. The clans strictly avoid interbreeding with one another, as the products of such unions, determined by their brown scales, are the lowest caste of all. Rare black-scaled Ssi-ruuk are trained as assassins and bodyguards for Ssi-ruuvi leaders. Ssi-ruuk's coloring is obvious as they do not wear clothing, instead carrying belts with pouches for any needed items. They find other species' need to cover themselves humorous.

On their homeworld of Lwhekk, an absolute ruler—called the Shreeftut—controls the Ssi-ruuvi government. Two councils advise this monarch: the Elders' Council and the Conclave. The Elders' Council is made up of the most respected citizens of Lwhekk. Words from an elder are considered as important as those of the monarch himself. The Conclave is a group of spiritual leaders who guide the Shreeftut in setting and enforcing laws that adhere to and complement their religion.

The Ssi-ruuk initially left their home system to search for new energy resources. Since they have not developed fusion technology used by most spacefaring races in this galaxy, they developed instead a process called "entenchment," wherein a living creature's life energy is drawn from the body and transferred into a droid, ship, or other piece of technology to give it power. When offworld, Ssi-ruuk use droid ships in battle to protect themselves, powered by the entenched life forces of captured prisoners. At first, they entenched and enslaved a race called the P'w'eck from their own homeworld. The Ssi-ruuk also use other sentients besides the P'w'eck as slaves, and all of their slaves are brainwashed through a type of mind control that completely subverts their will. This mind control can be broken, but the entenchment process leads to unavoidable death. Entenchment nevertheless is an imperfect process that leaves its victims in perpetual agony;

DESIGNATION
Sentient

HOMEWORLD
Lwhekk

AVERAGE HEIGHT
2 meters

PRONUNCIATION
Sē'-rŏŏ

they do not last long in a ship or other system before needing replacement.

Before the Battle of Endor, the Ssi-ruuk began expanding toward Imperial Space in an attempt to gain captives in sufficient numbers to power their military ships for an escalating war with the Chiss. During this time, Emperor Palpatine made contact with them. Wanting the entenchment technology for himself, Palpatine secretly ceded them a number of Outer Rim systems and allowed Ssi-ruuvi slave raids to go unchecked, blaming the attacks on the Rebels. One of these incursions brought the Ssi-ruuk to the Imperial-controlled world of Bakura. Although the Rebels had destroyed the second Death Star just the day before, they intercepted a drone ship bearing an urgent distress call from Bakura and dispatched a small battle group to assist. Working with the Imperials stationed on Bakura, the nascent Alliance of Free Planets forces turned back the Ssi-ruuk toward their own region of space. It would be years before the Imperial Remnant and the New Republic would sign an armistice, but this joint effort marked the first time the two groups would work together to repel a common enemy.

During this conflict, the Ssi-ruuk discovered that Force-using humans could exceed their expectations as a power source—and could also draw life energy from other creatures to themselves, thereby expanding an entenchment to have a broader area effect. Luke Skywalker foiled a plot to capitalize on this, and afterward set out to find other Force-sensitives to protect them from being exploited in such a way again.

For decades the Ssi-ruuk made no forays into Republic space, but this changed during the war against the Yuuzhan Vong. After the birth and ascension of the mutant, multicolored P'w'eck leader known as the Keeramak, the P'w'ecks approached Bakura with a peace treaty, claiming to have thrown off Ssi-ruuvi domination. Of course, the treaty was a Ssi-ruuvi ruse to take over the planet and gain more slaves, as they had further perfected the entenchment process, allowing for a life force to power a mechanical system indefinitely. With the help of the New Republic, the Ssi-ruuk were defeated again and driven back to Lwhekk, where they came face-to-face with a Yuuzhan Vong armada. The genuine P'w'eck Emancipation Movement did sign a treaty with Bakura, allying themselves for the common good.

NOTABLE APPEARANCE
Truce at Bakura (novel)

SULLUSTAN

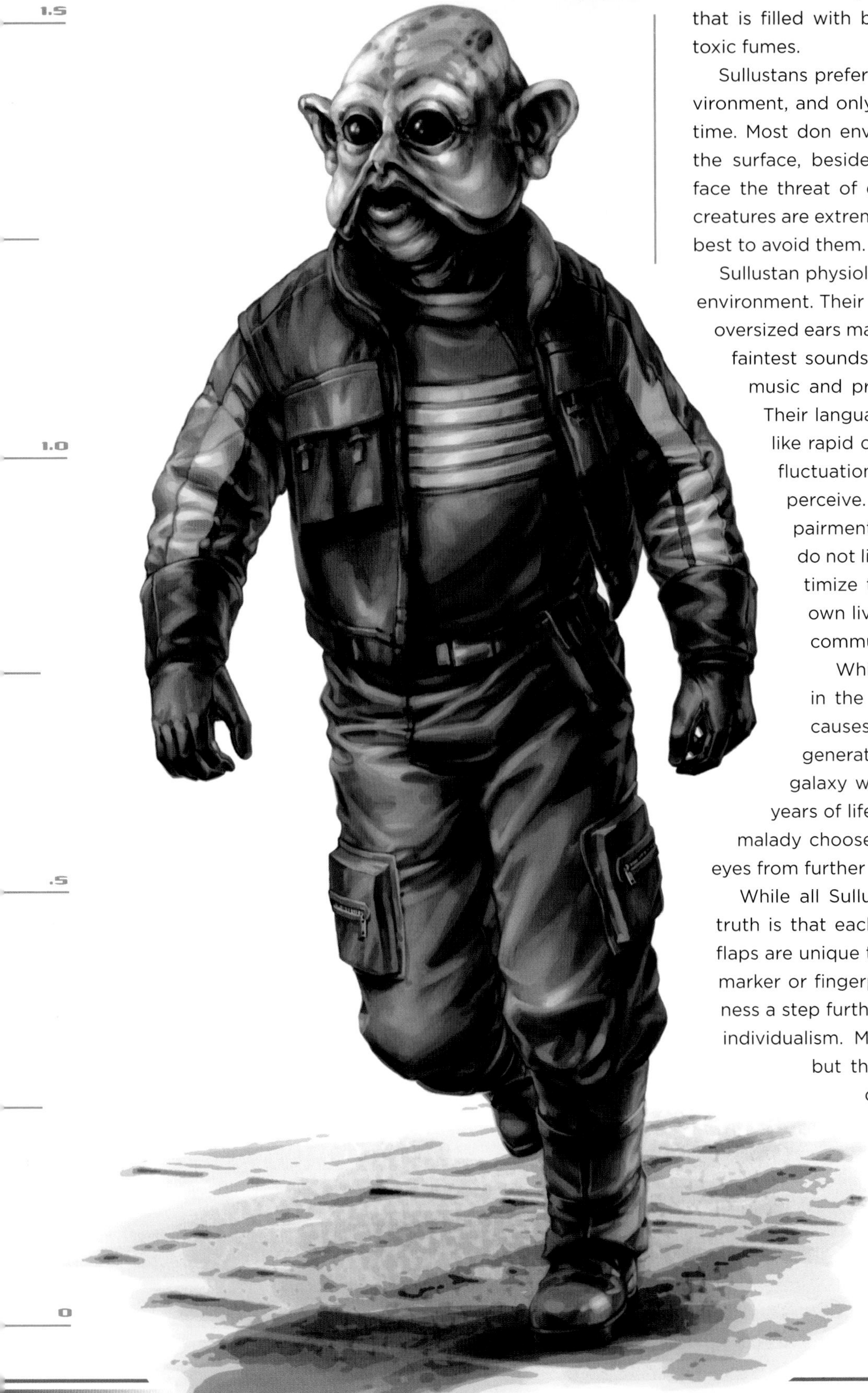

Sullustans are jowled, round-eared humanoids with large, round, black eyes. They inhabit subterranean caverns beneath the surface of Sullust, a volcanic planet with an inhospitable atmosphere that is filled with black clouds of volcanic ash, dust, and toxic fumes.

Sullustans prefer to remain in their cool, humid cave environment, and only go to the surface for short periods of time. Most don environment suits for long excursions. On the surface, besides facing the heavily polluted air, they face the threat of dangerous predators. Many of Sullust's creatures are extremely tough to kill, and Sullustans do their best to avoid them.

Sullustan physiology is well adapted to the underground environment. Their eyes see very well in dim light, and their oversized ears make them extremely sensitive to even the faintest sounds. Due to their skilled hearing, they love music and produce very fine musical compositions. Their language, although it sounds to most species like rapid chatter, includes extremely subtle sound fluctuations that only Sullustans can reproduce and perceive. Any Sullustan born with a hearing impairment has extreme difficulty. Deaf Sullustans do not live long, partially because predators victimize them, but also because they take their own lives out of despair that they cannot truly communicate with their own.

While their unique vision allows them to see in the dark, regular exposure to natural light causes Sullustans to suffer from corneal degeneration. Those who are regularly out in the galaxy will start to see these effects after thirty years of life. Those who start to be affected by this malady choose to wear special visors to protect their eyes from further damage.

While all Sullustans look similar to one another, the truth is that each Sullustan's cranial markings and dew flaps are unique to that individual—as unique as a retinal marker or fingerprint. Some Sullustans take this uniqueness a step further to add ritual tattoos, reinforcing their individualism. Most Sullustans are completely hairless, but those who can grow hair (on their faces only) do so to further announce their uniqueness. Sociologists theorize this emphasis on the individual is prompted by their unique economic system. Most Sullustans work for one corporation, so while variety in what one does is not always possible, diversity in how one looks makes all the difference. In fact, how one looks is so important that Sullustans developed an art of hairstyling and cosmetology. The barbers of Sullust are renowned for their skill, even though most Sullustans have no hair.

All Sullustans also have an enhanced sense of direction, which allows them to find their way through the labyrinthine passages of their cities. Moreover, this ability makes them some of the best navigators and pilots. It has been said that once Sullustans have traveled a path, they never forget it, even when traveling through hyperspace.

The Sullustan people have turned their underground environment into a near paradise. Their passageways lead to beautiful underground cities, where visitors walk cobblestone streets, eat at cafés, and shop for unique items available only in the subterranean markets.

Sullust is home to the SoroSuub Corporation, a leading mineral-processing company that maintains space mining, food-packaging, and technology-producing divisions throughout the galaxy. Important, almost 50 percent of the Sullustan population works for Soro-Suub. During the rule of the Empire, SoroSuub proclaimed its loyalty to the New Order. With the Empire's support, the SoroSuub Corporation dissolved the legal government of Sullust and took control of the entire world. Many Sullustans supported the Rebel Alliance because it was actively fighting the Empire. Inspired by the Alliance's just cause, many left Sullust quickly to help in the fight, distinguishing themselves with honor. At the decisive Battle of Endor, Sullustans flew many of the Rebel B-wings; Sullustan hero Nien Nunb flew as Lando Calrissian's copilot in *Millennium Falcon*. Before joining the Rebel Alliance, Nunb had gained renown among his people by raiding SoroSuub Corporation sites and stealing its starships. When the Empire fell, the leadership of Soro-Suub tried to escape the wrath of the populace. SoroSuub executives were captured, put on trial, and imprisoned. A new board of directors took control of SoroSuub, and the people returned to their original, democratic form of government. In the ensuing years, Sullustans continued to serve important roles within the New Republic.

A Sullustan core family grouping is called a Warren-clan. Each of these clans is headed by one female, who bears children by several husbands, all of whom live together or in nearby quarters. Females without husbands, called "Fems," are active as leaders and employees of SoroSuub until they are "Ready"—or ready to begin breeding. At this point a Fem seeks out mates to establish a Warren-clan. After establishing a Warren-clan, she will no longer work outside the home, considering maintaining her Warren-clan to be her primary job. The husbands, however, work outside the home and some travel offplanet as pilots to supplement their clan's income.

As a people, Sullustans are happy, practical, and fond of playing pranks on their friends. And yet they can be very formal in their social expectations and traditions. All of the elements of their ceremonial traditions bear in mind social status and have specific meaning, as exemplified by their funeral services. Sullustan mourners wear bright-colored tabards to signify their status in society or relation to the deceased. The body is placed in wall crypt and closed in with blocks of transparisteel. All mourners place a block in the wall in order of their social status and relationship to the deceased. The deceased's immediate family goes first, followed by the married males of his clan, other blood relatives, close friends, and representatives of SoroSuub; finally, the one who is considered closest to the deceased (be it friend or spouse) places the last block. Before placing this block, the last person must give a brief statement of as many words as the deceased's age in standard years. The speaker must not eulogize the dead, which would insinuate that others present did not know the deceased as well as the speaker. This comment is to be forward-looking and from the heart. Any deviance from this protocol causes great insult and can lead to some nasty confrontations. Sullustans have similar protocols for all special occasions, be they birthdays, weddings, or holidays.

They enjoy meeting new species and getting to know them. Perpetually curious, they enjoy learning new things, not just about science and technology but also about cultures, traditions, art, and music. Sullustans especially like to learn things through personal experience, making them somewhat reckless. As pilots, they tend to take a lot more chances than the average humanoid, as if testing how much their ships can take. Despite this, they are favorite members of any crew because of knowledge, talents, and wholehearted love of flying.

DESIGNATION
Sentient

HOMEWORLD
Sullust

AVERAGE
HEIGHT
1.5 meters

PRONUNCIATION
Sŭl'-lŭs-tăn

NOTABLE APPEARANCE
Episode VI: Return of the Jedi

TALZ

The Talz are a tall, physically powerful species from Alzoc III, a frigid world blanketed with fields of snow and ice. They are covered head-to-foot with thick white fur, and their extremely large hands end in sharp-clawed talons that are used for digging through frozen layers of ice and snow. Their fur protects them from the cold, as does an extra layer of blubber beneath their hair. The Talz possess four eyes—two large and two small—and each set can be utilized to accommodate varying degrees of brightness. During the day, their larger eyes are often shut, as the glaring sunlight reflecting off the snow can be almost blinding. At night or in dimly lit environments, Talz will rely on their bigger eyes, which allow them to see better in darker surroundings. In addition, a small, tube-like snout enables them to breathe in sufficient oxygen, something that would normally be a difficult task in exceptionally cold temperatures.

A generally quiet, gentle species, the Talz are also tireless in their work, which is done with simple handmade tools. They are peaceful and curious—perceiving their surroundings with an almost scientific interest. Although the Talz are fairly ignorant of most other species, they will not speak up to ask questions of strangers, instead preferring to learn through observation. Their society is clan-based, keeping supplies plentiful through a sophisticated system that distributes resources for the benefit of all Talz communities.

Because of this largely distributive society, one of their common cultural traits is the Talz's lack of a sense of posses-

2.0

1.5

1.0

.5

0

sion. For instance, while all Talz may have tools to do their work, as well as household implements and the like, they do not feel these items actually belong to them specifically. If Talz possess something that goes unused, they will find someone who does need it and give it away. If they need an item that they do not have, they will often go to a neighbor's living area and simply borrow it without asking, although out of courtesy they will usually let others know in case they need the item themselves. In the midst of other cultures, this can cause some confusion in that the Talz normally do not employ such terms as *hers, his, mine,* or *yours.* Sometimes they give things away that are not currently being used (often items of sentimental value to their non-Talz friends). Species familiar with Talz, particularly those who share company with them on a regular basis, know to keep any materials they value under lock and key, as explaining ownership to a Talz can frequently be a wasted effort. Unfortunately, those ignorant of Talz traditions will sometimes view them as thieves, and as a result they often end up being prosecuted for theft on certain worlds they visit, or, even worse, being hunted by crimelords for unwittingly giving away something of great value.

Although they carry many characteristics of humanoids, the Talz reproduce like insects. A female will lay her eggs, which eventually hatch and produce larvae that are carefully guarded and kept warm by the parents. After a standard year, the larvae cocoon themselves, remaining in a chrysalis state for another year and growing while they slumber, until they crack out of their cocoons as full-sized Talz. However, when the Talz leave their cocoons, they possess little knowledge beyond the language they learned as larvae, and must be educated for several years before becoming full adults. The Talz have no formal schools, and most Talz "children" are home-taught via cooperative family tutelage. Parents who stand out in certain subjects will partner with those who excel in others, so that their offspring will receive as well-rounded an education as possible.

Outside of the Talz Jedi Foul Moudama, who served during the Clone Wars and fell at the hands of General Grievous, the species had little to no interaction with the rest of the galaxy before the Empire rose to power. The Empire essentially discovered the Talz just as the Imperials had crushed the last remnants of the Old Republic, and immediately took advantage of the benign species, seeing them as an easy slave labor force to mine the mineral wealth of

DESIGNATION
Sentient

HOMEWORLD
Alzoc III

AVERAGE HEIGHT
2.1 meters

PRONUNCIATION
Tălz

Alzoc III. To this day, some primitive Talz continue to tell tales of when "rocks fell from the sky," bringing with them the brutal strangers who forced them to create caves. The Talz suffered through the Rebellion period hoping that the strangers would leave and let them live in peace.

While the Empire greatly benefited from the slave work of the Talz, they never actually recorded the "discovery" of the species, keeping them a secret from the majority of the galaxy. Only a few Talz left their homeworld during this time, and then usually in the presence of Imperials as servants or slaves. If they wandered too far from their masters, they were summarily captured and sent home to the mines. The fall of the Empire spelled freedom for the Talz, and under the New Republic they began to trade and interact more with the galaxy at large, having assumed ownership of their mines. Despite this, they are still wary of their trading partners, and rarely journey off their world to explore the galaxy. They remain rather primitive, preferring to live in obscurity in the cold, uninviting environment of Alzoc III.

Sadly, the suffering of the Talz people did not necessarily end with the fall of the Empire. While they were freed from slavery and allowed to take over their mining operations and trade with other species, Warlord Zsinj captured many Talz for scientific experimentation for his Project Chubar and Dr. Edda Gast's Operation Minefield—the intentions of which were to alter alien races to make them more "human." After these operations were dismantled by Wraith Squadron, the victimized Talz were returned to their homeworld and welcomed with open arms despite their mutations, a sure example of the peaceful acceptance that is at the core of their culture.

NOTABLE APPEARANCE
Episode IV: A New Hope

TAUNTAUN

The frigid planet of Hoth has very few indigenous life-forms, but one of its most numerous is the tauntaun, a bipedal, reptomammal also referred to as a snow lizard. Used as beasts of burden by Rebel Alliance personnel during their stay on Hoth, tauntauns are tall, sturdy ungulates with inherently ornery dispositions. Several different types of tauntauns have been identified in various regions of Hoth, from the glacier tauntaun to the small climbing tauntaun, which uses its muscularity and claws to scale canyons and cliffs. The appearance of these subspecies can also differ from the common fur-covered tauntaun, as they possess a more reptilian appearance with longer forelimbs and thinner frames.

As a result of their native environment, tauntauns have remarkably cold-resistant bodies. Their warm blood is extremely heavy, and their inner organs are close inside their skeletons to keep them safe from cold. A thick layer of fat also acts as insulation under the tauntauns' oily pelts. They have four nostrils: a large pair on the upper portion of their muzzle that helps conduct oxygen to the bloodstream during times of physical exertion, and a smaller pair directly beneath them. When blizzard winds blow, or when tauntauns lie down for the night, their larger nostrils will seal to keep snow out, and the second pair will take over the responsibility of keeping minimal amounts of oxygen flowing to their lungs.

Tauntauns are quick-moving creatures, running on their two rear legs at speeds nearing fifty kilometers per hour. They use their smaller

1.5

1.0

.5

0

forelegs for balance, and also to forage for food, utilizing their dexterous claws to grapple stones or chunks of ice and move them out of their way.

Tauntauns are herbivores, feeding on unique varieties of lichen and fungus that grow beneath the frosty surface of Hoth. They exude waste products and oils through special ducts on their skin, giving them a foul odor. To match their smell, they are irritable creatures, spitting and gurgling in protest when forced to do something they really don't want to do. Their ill temperament may be enhanced by their inhospitable environment, which could be enough to give members of any species a bad temper.

Female tauntauns are more cantankerous, as they outnumber males and are always in competition for mates. They sport curved horns on the sides of their heads with which they battle other females. However, their most effective weapon is their spitting ability, which they can use to disable their opponents, spitting with surprising accuracy and often aiming for the eyes. The gooey saliva is not deadly, but the liquid can freeze instantly in such a frigid environment, and the effect can be lethal, temporarily blinding adversaries and further exposing them to the many hazards of the icy planet Hoth.

While on Hoth, the Rebel Alliance had some initial difficulty training tauntauns as mounts because of their foul tempers. In addition, it was discovered that tauntauns are particularly sensitive to the ultrasonic frequencies emitted by certain droids. When they grew agitated by the droids, the tauntauns were known to sometimes smash them with their tails. General Carlist Rieekan, however, suggested working with the beasts' instincts rather than against them, and to eliminate competition for males, he made sure the only animals trained to be mounts were female. The Alliance then kept the mounts warm, and fed and rewarded them with mook fruit when they performed to standard. Using this method, these intelligent creatures were effectively trained, and served the Alliance well as they adapted various other transport machinery to operate in the cold.

While tauntauns are resilient in extremely bitter temperatures, they are not impervious to them. Like any other warm-blooded creature, they can only take so much cold before they freeze to death. While they can last longer than most species, they often cannot survive for more than three to four standard hours in intense subzero temperatures without finding shelter. In such conditions, they are smart and

DESIGNATION
Nonsentient

HOMEWORLD
Hoth

AVERAGE HEIGHT
1.8 meters

PRONUNCIATION
Tän'-tän

dexterous enough to find shelter, or to burrow into a snowdrift in order to create warmth and conserve energy.

Scientists have also identified a subspecies living among the ice caves of Hoth. The animals known as scaly tauntauns are covered with smooth scaly skin over a thick layer of insulating fat and a thin layer of hair. Scaly tauntauns may get their name from their reptilian appearance, but they are indeed reptomammals. For scaly tauntauns, the lack of thick fur mitigates much of the smell associated with common tauntauns, and the males possess smaller horns than their distant cousins, whereas the females lack horns completely. It is thought that the males do not use their horns, which are thus gradually fading with evolution. Otherwise, scaly tauntauns resemble their cousins in size and configuration.

For scaly tauntauns, survival in the frigid environment of Hoth largely means reliance upon hot springs and geothermal vents that heat tunnels below the planet's surface. These caves are several kilometers below ground level, and herds ranging in size from five to ten animals spend most of their lives in these areas. Scaly tauntauns are omnivorous, unlike common tauntauns, and although they eat lichen, they also dine on insects and small vermin found near the hot springs. Herds migrate to follow the availability of a food source. A herd will protect its young, although all varieties of tauntauns would rather run than engage a dangerous predator. Wampas have been known to venture deeper into the Hoth cave systems at night and during blizzards, and even though wampas are exceedingly uncomfortable near the heat of the hot springs, they will ignore their discomfort if hungry enough. When threatened with such an attack, one of the scaly tauntaun herd will frequently sacrifice its life to protect its herd-mates.

As in the case of wampas, tauntaun herds have suffered from hunting. The occasional hunting party, or even a criminal seeking escape, will come to Hoth and often kill indiscriminately. As a result, some scientists have begun a campaign to have tauntauns listed as a protected species.

NOTABLE APPEARANCE
Episode V: The Empire Strikes Back

THISSPIASIAN

Thisspiasians are a reptilian species from Thisspias, a world located in the Expansion Region of the galaxy. They can be clearly distinguished from other reptiles because their upper body appears to be humanoid, typically covered in long flowing hair that emanates from their head and face. Their lower half, however, is serpentine, wrapped in scales similar in color to their hair. Their two sets of hands contain five fingers that end in sturdy, elongated claws.

It is believed that Thisspiassians have four hands as a result of their evolution from quadruped reptiles. However, for many Thisspiassians, the smaller, lower set of vestigial arms and hands do not have the strength or dexterity of their larger, upper set. In fact, most upperclass Thisspiassians have taken to wearing voluminous robed garments that hide their second set of limbs completely by omitting a second set of sleeves and incorporating a wide, belt-like sash. In addition, many Thisspiassians go as far as to use hidden apparatuses to bind their lower arms to their bodies. Among this group of Thisspiassians, it is considered unseemly or unsophisticated to publicly show the lower limbs. Physiological studies suggest that over the generations, this may be the cause of the lower limbs' weakness due to continued biological adaptation. It has been demonstrated that among the working classes, lower limbs do not show a similar muscle weakness.

Their prehensile tails give Thisspiasians the capability to carry heavy objects, freeing up their hands to perform other functions. This makes the species even more effective when they are in combat, as well-trained Thisspiasian warriors may strike out with their tails as well as their hands.

There is one particular Thisspiasian trait that other species frequently find a little unnerving, and that is their preference for eating their food live. Like their snake-like ancestors, Thisspiasians principally dine on small, live animals such as rodents, birds, and bugs. While they are omnivorous, consuming their fair share of vegetables, a Thisspiasian feast would not be complete without several cages of tiny species from around the galaxy being placed in the center of the table. After dipping a treat in several sauces containing various seasonings, a Thisspiasian's jaw unhinges at the joint, allowing the mouth to widen and take in the animals whole. As they've come to be in the presence of more and more offworld species who do not share their enthusiasm for squirming meals, many Thisspiasians have taken to eating cooked food for the benefit of companions and guests of other traditions, though they have been known to state with certainty that such food is lacking in zesty flavor.

One other prominent reptilian trait is carried on through the Thisspiasian genes: the tendency to shed their skin every few years. Unlike snakes, however, Thisspiasians will not slip out of their outer layer of skin in one piece. To ease the process of shedding, and to make the progression less noticeable when in the presence of outsiders, they will lubricate their skin with sweet-smelling oils and salves, peeling off the dead membrane in portions during their daily private grooming sessions.

A race of ancient warriors, Thisspiasians have perfected a culture bent on taming their most savage emotions. When the Old Republic was forming, they eagerly joined the fledgling government, aiding it in overcoming threats both internal and external. They are perceived as being calm, wise, and dispassionate, and yet they commonly manage this through several hours a day of intense meditation. Average Thisspiasians meditate for five to six standard hours per day; otherwise, they can become moody and irrational. Because they spend so much time in meditation, they only require about two actual hours of sleep per standard day.

One of the best examples of Thisspiassian mental discipline was displayed by the Old Republic Jedi Master Oppo Rancisis. Combining the natural mental abilities of his species with his Jedi training, Rancisis specialized in Jedi battle meditation. He was able to formulate complex and near-unbeatable battle plans and direct his forces over great distances. His murder at the hands of the fallen Jedi Sora Bulq was a blow to the Republican forces that they were hard pressed to overcome.

The Thisspiasian homeworld is ruled by an absolute leader known as the Blood Monarch. This position is carried on through the bloodline, and it has remained unchanged for

DESIGNATION
Sentient

HOMEWORLD
Thisspias

AVERAGE HEIGHT
1.5 meters (coiled)

PRONUNCIATION
Thĭs-pĭ-ăs'-ē-ăn

thousands of years, although a democratically elected parliament handles much of the legislation on the planet. As with most monarchies, a portion of the populace is of the opinion that the leadership is corrupt, degenerate, and tied to archaic customs that no longer apply to their modern way of life.

During the waning years of the Old Republic, Master Rancisis inherited the role of Blood Monarch over his homeworld, which he rejected in favor of remaining with the Jedi Order. When Count Dooku threatened the Republic with his Separatist movement, Rancisis asked the standing monarch to help in the struggle against the Separatists. Per species tradition, Rancisis had to best the monarch in unarmed combat to have his boon granted. When the Blood Monarch lost to Rancisis, he agreed to lend warriors to several battles.

When the Empire ultimately came to power, Thisspias was bombarded by Imperial warships, and its people were conquered and enslaved. Eager to please the Emperor, an overzealous Imperial governor assassinated the Blood Monarch and imprisoned the crown prince. The outraged Thisspiasians rebelled, but their insurrection was quickly subdued by the Imperials' superior firepower. Not long afterward, Rebel spies infiltrated the Imperial troops' headquarters on Thisspias and freed the prince. Humiliated, the governor threatened the Thisspiasians with annihilation, but he was eliminated by the Emperor's Hand before he could enact his threats. The Hand had been sent to punish the governor for his failure to hold the Thisspiasian heir. The world was then placed under military quarantine, though several Thisspiasians slipped out to join the ranks of the Rebel Alliance.

Following the Battle of Endor, the crown prince of Thisspias returned to reclaim his throne. When he did, he found himself rebuffed, as a vocal portion of his people were declaring their desire for a more democratic government. This confrontation incited a brief yet extremely bloody civil war, wherein the Blood Monarch was returned to power. During the years of the New Republic and the subsequent Galactic Alliance, the people of Thisspias have become convinced that the monarchy has evolved very little, remaining tied to its decadent lifestyle and largely antiquated ancient political traditions.

NOTABLE APPEARANCE
Episode I: The Phantom Menace

TOGRUTA

Togrutas are a humanoid species native to the temperate planet Shili, positioned in the Expansion Region of the galaxy. All Togrutas have colorful markings on their skin, a genetic trait left over from their predatorial ancestors. Long, striped, curved, hollow horns spiral upward from the top of their skull, and three darker striped head-tails (similar to a Twi'lek's lekku) drape downward, two to the front, falling over their chest, and one thicker tail that is centered at the rear base of their skull. Togrutas' skin is deep red, and their dark eyes and gray lips are embellished by the white markings that adorn their face. Vertical red and white stripes cover the skin of their chest, back, arms, and legs. As Shili is covered in thigh-high turu-grass that is typically a blending of red and white colors, the Togrutas' ancestors (and the Togrutas themselves) blended in with the natural environment, confusing both prey and other predators. When hunting, their head-tails aid them by providing echolocation abilities and a finely tuned spatial sense, which they use to encircle herbivorous prey.

Togrutas are a peaceful, quiet people who are fierce in combat. Loyal to a cause and happy in larger groups, they work well with others and easily fit into teams of mixed cultures. Most do not like to be alone, however, and will tend to follow other members of their group around simply for companionship.

Many outsiders have the misconception that Togrutas are venomous, as they possess prominent incisors that give the impression of a snake's venom-projecting teeth. Togrutas frequently have no idea how this perception originated, but sociologists believe it is because Togrutas prefer to eat their smaller prey while it's still alive, much like Thisspiasians. One of their favorite meals is thimiars, small rodents that hide in the grasslands of Shili. Togrutas will take a living thimiar and bite into it with their incisors, killing the creatures quickly and painlessly, and so observers have been known to mistake the thimiar's death throes for the jolts of an animal dying of poisoning. But even though these convulsions are merely postmortem muscle spasms, most Togrutas will not correct the misconception that they are venomous.

The Togrutas' evolutionary ancestors were predators that lived and hunted in packs, and thus modern Togrutas are also effective hunters who prefer to dwell in dense communal villages camouflaged by the forest canopies and sheltered in hidden valleys. Some vestiges of the Togrutas' beginnings as pack animals remain in their social customs. First, as a habit, Togrutas do not wear shoes whenever possible, feeling that by covering their feet they are cutting themselves off from the land in a spiritual way. Also, every available able-bodied person is expected to take part in the village hunts, and the spoils are shared equally. This is expected even of young children as soon as they are able to effectively hold a weapon, and typically occurs without any specialized training. Togrutas believe that those who are unable to keep pace with the pack should be left to die, and on Shili, those who are unable to fend for themselves often do. Togrutas will not shed any tears over such as loss, a characteristic that can give the impression to outsiders that they are unfeeling beings. This is not the case, though, and the lack of remorse is instead a belief that the death of those unable to defend themselves is simply the course of nature.

In addition, Togrutas wear the results of their hunts proudly, and as a sign of adulthood. It is common to see Togrutas wearing the skins of the animals they've killed, or other trophies of the hunt. For example, the akul is a large, carnivorous animal often hunted on Shili because it is the only native animal that poses a serious threat to the Togrutas. Fierce creatures that emit frightening growls, these orange-furred quadrupeds predominate on the open plains of Shili, attacking settlements and villages. By tradition, akul teeth adornments can only be worn by a Togruta who has slain one without assistance—not an easy task, as akul seem strangely gifted at sensing the presence of other predators, and will begin howling as soon as one is near. The animal's teeth are the common trophy mostly because akul are known for the strength of their jaws, and breaking the hold of an akul is nearly impossible for a normal humanoid. Like a nexu, an akul will use their hold to shake their prey until the victim's neck breaks. The standard jewelry crafted from akul teeth for both males and females is a headdress worn across the forehead and down around the Togruta's eye patches, a combination of indigenous metals, stones, and pearls. Recovered images of the Old Republic Jedi Master Shaak Ti dating back to the time of the Clone Wars have shown her wearing such an akul-tooth headdress, signifying that this is a particularly strong tradition, as she even combined the adornment with her standard Jedi wardrobe.

Akul are not normally native to worlds other than Shili, but they have been exported. When released into the wild on other worlds, they reproduce without the normal ecological safeguards of their native environment and can quickly overwhelm a planet's ecosystem. Inbreeding both on Shili and on other worlds can raise the frequency of naturally occurring mutations, the most common of which is albinism. Akul are often caught for zoos, where they thrive in captivity. However, at great risk to their handlers, both normal and albino akul are trained to perform in lavish stage shows and holonet productions, despite their ferocious natures.

As Togrutas prefer company and normally shun individual in-

DESIGNATION
Sentient

HOMEWORLD
Shili

AVERAGE
HEIGHT
1.7 meters

PRONUNCIATION
Tō-grōō'-tä

dependence, those who live solitary lives away from their people can suffer from acute bouts of depression, putting great pressure on themselves to make up for the life they left behind. Jedi Master Shaak Ti recorded some of her own troubles with this problem even as she proudly espoused the Jedi lifestyle. Some attempt to cling to their non-Togruta friends in order to make up for what they miss in their pack-based life back home. In their culture, individuality is considered somewhat deviant, and yet those who take leadership positions among their people are sometimes forced to achieve their goals through calculated individualism. Sociologists claim this is a sign of the further social evolution of the Togruta people.

With very few exceptions, Togrutas who venture offworld are members of the Jedi Order, and, notably, they tend to be female. Although there is no independent Force tradition on Shili, recovered historical records indicate Togrutas have joined the Jedi as far back as the very beginning of the order, often serving with distinction. As already noted, Shaak Ti was a Jedi Master, one of several Togrutas to earn the rank. In addition, a Togruta female youngling named Ashla was a Padawan at the Jedi Temple on Coruscant during the Clone Wars, and perhaps not coincidentally, her name is an ancient word associated with the light side of the Force. Although reasons for the Togrutas playing such a considerable role in Jedi history are at best speculative due to Emperor Palpatine's destruction of records specifically related to the Jedi and the achievements of non-human species, it appears this species has a special affinity for the Force. How they achieve this heightened Force sense is also a point of speculation, as they have, at best, average midi-chlorian counts in comparison to other species. However, given that Togruta feel a bond with the land (or the planet they happen to be on), as demonstrated by their preference for being barefoot, they may have a unique ability to tap into the life essence of the universe in ways that defy description in terms of the Force or simple midi-chlorian counts. Furthermore, Togrutas are a herding and hunting people, which heightens the detailed spacial sense imparted from their montrails, even for non-Force sensitives. With such an instinctual response to their environment, Togrutas would find feeling the Living Force easier than other species. Unfortunately, there are no current known Togruta members serving the Jedi order, so the source of their affinity for the Force will remain an unknown for the time being.

NOTABLE APPEARANCE
Episode II: Attack of the Clones

TOYDARIAN

Native to the planet Toydaria in the Hutt sector of space, Toydarians are a short species with small wings and vaguely avian features. Ranging in color from blue to green to pink, they sport stubby trunks on their faces that rest above short tusks, and their thin legs end in webbed feet. The males of the species usually show sparse whiskers.

Despite their undersized wings, Toydarians can fly quite rapidly. Their wings beat nearly ten times every second, and while their bodies appear pudgy and heavy, Toydarians are actually very light because their tissues are spongy and filled with gas. Their pot-bellied stomachs are also gas-filled, making them function much like small balloons. Nonetheless, their flying requires a great deal of energy, and as a result they must eat constantly to maintain their strength.

Another unique trait of this species is its brain structure. While this is seemingly no more complex than that of an average human or other sentient species, Toydarians are able to resist attempts at mind control and Force domination.

Like most mammals, Toydarians are born live and fully developed—resembling smaller versions of their parents. Unlike most avian species, they can fly immediately at birth, with little help. They prefer to fly everywhere, rather than walk, hence the sky over Toydaria is constantly filled with buzzing Toydarians. Spaceship traffic on the planet is restricted, with vessels only permitted to land and take off at certain times and in specified areas to prevent midair collisions. There is little solid ground on the planet, and Toydarians have survived over the centuries by flying virtually everywhere, only landing on the relative safety of algal mats.

Using speeders is prohibited on Toydaria because of all the "air traffic." Consequently, Toydarians have constructed a light-rail system to take offworlders from city to city. Beyond this, they do not have a technologically advanced society, although they have incorporated some offworld technology into their day-to-day lives.

Toydaria is mostly covered with nutrient-rich muck lakes that support a number of predators, including a dangerous species known as grabworms. Toydarians evolved by at first living on the nutrients found in these lakes, and ultimately developed high-end farming techniques to provide food for the populace. But because the amount of sustenance they require is so great, war will often break out between Toydarian confederacies when food supplies are low. During hard times, they feel the simplest way to cope is by stealing provisions from their neighbors, and Toydarians will form armies and fight bitterly, sometimes to the extent of poisoning another group's food supply in the belief that if they can't have it, then no one should. However, when these types of situations eventually improve, the war will immediately end and life will return to normal. This pattern usually recurs roughly every thirty standard years, depending on weather cycles.

Toydarians are talented hagglers. Their economic structure requires constant bartering, and as a result they are very skilled at negotiating prices and striking deals. By nature, they love to gamble and will take a chance on a business deal that looks lucrative, sometimes even despite the odds. Toydarians can be, at their best, professional and business-savvy, but at their worst they are greedy and petty, and will cheat when it serves their purposes. Either way, they are a shrewd and intelligent species—and usually well educated. Toydarians generally speak Basic and Huttese as well as their native language, Toydarian.

Toydaria operates like a sovereign feudal system. There is one ruling king, who is typically good about taking care of his people and is therefore well respected. However, Toydaria is no stranger to violence, as there is always a group of feudal vassals who govern most of the huge system beneath the king—competing and jockeying for positions of power, along with land and natural resources. These vassals are often very rich, and the king will grant favors and orchestrate shifts of power in order to make certain that he always has the allegiance of his vassals by keeping them happy. In turn, the vassals take care of the people and pay their taxes to the system. Oftentimes the king will allow a certain amount of infighting among his vassals, as it weeds out treachery and reveals character and weaknesses among them. In this way, the king is always aware of who is plotting against who, and his vast knowledge of those beneath him keeps the vassals from ever daring to challenge him. By ruling through these methods, the king also promotes the ideas of honesty, loyalty, power, and displays of strength, which, along with wealth, are all important in Toydarian culture.

Members of their species have been found living on worlds beyond Toydaria, but they seem to prefer locales where they can make a profit with little government interference, such as Tatooine. An enterprising species, they will pour all their efforts into a business venture and frequently turn it into a modest success where others could not. One example is the junk shop owned by the Toydarian trader Watto in the city of Mos Espa on Tatooine. Although Watto never made exorbitant numbers of credits on his business, he lived comfortably, if modestly.

Watto's greater role in galactic history was as the onetime slave owner of Shmi and Anakin Skywalker, the young boy who would ultimately become Darth Vader. Although Watto controlled every aspect of their lives, he did at times exhibit a genuine affection for them, going as far as selling Shmi into freedom when the opportunity for her to have some happiness arose, and she became the wife of a moisture farmer. For Watto, slavery was a convenient means to keep Shmi and Anakin around, while also possibly making a profit from the young Anakin's Podracing abilities.

DESIGNATION
Sentient

HOMEWORLD
Toydaria

AVERAGE HEIGHT
1.4 meters

PRONUNCIATION
Toi-dăr'-ē-ăn

TRANDOSHAN

Trandoshans, who refer to themselves as T'doshok, are large bipedal reptilians known for their ruthless, warrior culture. Like most reptiles, Trandoshans are cold-blooded and possess scaly skin, which they shed roughly every standard year. Their super-sensitive orange eyes can see into the infrared range, and they are able to regenerate lost limbs, at least until they reach Trandoshan middle age. Each of their appendages ends in three digits with sharp claws that are excellent for fighting, although they lack in manual dexterity, causing their finger movements to be rather clumsy. Their oversized, oddly shaped feet also prevent them from wearing any sort of footgear, which is sometimes an impediment when on the hunt or in combat.

As members of a saurian species, female Trandoshans lay clutches of four eggs at a time, and nest them in a warm place in their home. When young Trandoshans hatch, they are already able to walk, and possess a natural instinct

2.0

1.5

1.0

.5

0

for the hunt—usually chasing their clutch brothers or sisters around the home in a type of hiding game. When they reach two standard years of age, the parents take their children out on their first hunt, instructing them on how to track beasts in the wild, and by the age of ten most Trandoshans are proficient in unarmed combat, firearms, and the use of melee weaponry.

This species is extremely violent by nature. Trandoshans' culture is based on the hunting and tracking of beings less powerful than themselves. They worship a female deity known as the Scorekeeper, who awards jagannath points to Trandoshans based on their success or failure in the hunt and mortal combat. Those hunters who earn the most have the highest status in society, and are considered valuable mates by females.

When Trandoshan males have proven themselves successful in the hunt, they return to their homeworld to mate with a convenient clutch mother. These relationships are arranged, and are not considered binding. Once a couple have mated, the female lays her eggs and watches over them until they hatch. As soon as they are old enough, the male children will go out into the galaxy to begin scoring points for their goddess.

The Trandoshans have a particularly adversarial relationship with their insystem neighbors, the Wookiees. Before the birth of the Empire, they attempted to colonize the Wookiee homeworld of Kashyyyk, but were soundly defeated after several bloody battles. When the Wookiees enacted numerous laws to discourage big-game hunting in the system, as well as regulations to protect local ecosystems, the Trandoshans were incensed. They had come to rely on the capital influx from tourism, and they resented the Wookiees' discouragement of the industry in their system. In retribution, they conducted another series of raids on Kashyyyk, this time in an attempt to plunder the natural resources the Wookiees had sought to protect. While bloody conflicts raged on both worlds, the Wookiees appealed to the Senate of the Old Republic, and the governing body intervened, enacting strict trade sanctions against the Trandoshans unless they withdrew from Kashyyyk. They did, once again vowing revenge.

When the Emperor took control of the galaxy, the Trandoshans saw another opportunity to have their vengeance. They aided in the Imperial strikes on Kashyyyk, helping to capture Wookiees in large groups and turning them over

DESIGNATION
Sentient

HOMEWORLD
Trandosha
(referred to as
Dosha or Hsskor
by Trandoshans)

**AVERAGE
HEIGHT**
2 meters

PRONUNCIATION
Trăn-dō'-shăn

to become slaves for the Empire. When the Empire fell, the New Republic demanded that the Trandoshans once more cease their raids on Kashyyyk, under the threat of economic sanctions and military action. They did so with much grumbling, though their previous deeds in support of the Empire have caused them to remain one of the least trusted species in the galaxy.

Making no attempt to disguise their dispositions, Trandoshans continue to enforce the stereotype that they are a violent, egocentric, and malicious people. Aggressive and vindictive, they love competition for its own sake, although it is especially appealing to them as a means of dealing out vengeance. Interclan rivalries have been known to claim numerous lives, and turn son against father. In certain cases, however, they can still show compassion and mercy—particularly if it is a matter of honor. Trandoshans will, like their Wookiee nemeses, pledge their lives to protect another being who has saved them from death—although they would have a difficult time making that pledge to a Wookiee. To this day they despise their Wookiee neighbors, and will never be caught in their company, except in the rarest of circumstances.

And yet, despite their highly aggressive culture, some Trandoshans have been known to show a streak of independence, preferring to keep alternative elements of their society running effectively. These Trandoshans are still considered hunters, although not in a traditional sense. Scientists, for instance, will "hunt" for answers in the study of science, while xenobiologists "hunt" for details on other worlds and their various cultures. Engineers "hunt" for superior weapons or ship designs. Most day-to-day professions can be considered honorable in the sense of the hunt, as long as they produce something that improves or enriches society—though admittedly, Trandoshans would most likely find little value in being an actor or comedian.

NOTABLE APPEARANCE
Episode V: The Empire Strikes Back

TUSKEN RAIDER (SAND PERSON)

Tusken Raiders, also referred to as Sand People, are tall, strong, aggressive, nomadic humanoid warriors who reside in the desert wastelands of Tatooine. From head to toe, every Raider is always covered in strips of cloth-tattered robes that are belted together with dewback-hide leather. They see by using tube-like shields that protect their eyes, and breathe through simple filters that keep them from inhaling the sand particles that constantly swirl through the Tatooine air. Every piece of their attire serves to keep moisture trapped near their bodies, and hygiene is only attended to in complete privacy, for seeing another individual's face, even accidentally, is cause for a blood duel. Only a Tusken's mate is allowed to glimpse his or her face without the bandaging.

Tusken Raiders are ruthless fighters, hardened by their harsh environment to show no mercy to other species. They fear little, although they can be driven away by a substantial display of force. Traveling in bands of up to twenty or thirty, they nearly always ride their bantha mounts in a straight line, journeying one behind the other to hide their numbers from enemies. Their weapon of choice is the gaderffii, or gaffi stick, which is basically a double-edged ax made of cannibalized metal scavenged from abandoned or wrecked vehicles. Some carry blaster rifles, but Tusken blasters are not the most powerful or technologically advanced weapons.

This nomadic people was the dominant sentient species on Tatooine before settlers began to colonize the world during the days of the Old Republic. The Jawas, the only other sentients on the planet, while more intelligent, were not as large or fierce as their brutal neighbors, although there is some scientific evidence that suggests the two groups may both be descended from the same species, an ancient race known as the Kumumgah. The Tusken Raiders received their galaxy-recognized name from an attack they launched on a human settlement called Fort Tusken. While their attempt to force out the offworld settlers failed, this assault became renowned for its brutality. In response, the settlers set about to attempt the utter destruction of the Sand People, eliminating entire tribes at a time—leading to their near extinction before the few remaining tribes retreated to hide in the desert wastes.

As a result of these incidents, Sand People are inherently angered by the presence in their territories of offworld settlers, whom they feel encroach upon their ration of water and food. They will often attack moisture farmers and settlers without provocation—simply for the sake of intimidating those they perceive as enemies.

Despite their bullying natures, Tusken Raiders will typically shy away from massive Jawa sandcrawler fortresses, heavily protected farmsteads, large cities, and even settlements, as well as from the vicious krayt dragons. It is evident that they favor situations where they have the upper hand, and will only take calculated risks.

Since they are a nomadic people, they maintain no permanent shelters and keep few possessions, viewing such belongings as liabilities. Regardless of their willingness to move regularly, they allow no other changes in their society or culture. Tusken Raiders fear machinery, the power of which has decimated their people in the past, and are thus thoroughly resistant to technology, stealing very little of it from hapless patrols, caravans, and moisture farmers. They feel that killing with more primitive weapons brings them the bravest of victories.

To most outsiders, the language of Tusken Raiders is an unintelligible, angry combination of consonants and growls. They have no written language, so they rely on a long and complex oral tradition to keep track of their lineage and legends. Each tribe has a storyteller, whose duty is to preserve and retell the group's history. The storyteller chronicles the coming-of-age tales for each member of the clan, and once he or she gives an account for the first time, not one word is permitted to change from that time forward. At some point, each storyteller will take on an apprentice and begin teaching the clan history, although the learner is not allowed to practice the history aloud, as the words must never be spoken incorrectly. If the apprentice makes a mistake, he or she is killed outright, as it is consid-

ered blasphemy. Once an apprentice has learned every tale of each lineage perfectly, he or she becomes the next storyteller, and the teacher will wander into the desert to die.

Because they live such a cruel, war-like existence, the process of coming of age is very important to Tusken Raiders. Children are cared for by adult Tuskens, but they are not considered people until they have endured the actual ceremonies that bring them into maturity. Babies often perish because of the difficult desert life, and Sand People take great pride in knowing that only the strongest survive. To earn the distinction of adulthood, each youth must perform a great feat of skill or prowess, the magnitude of which determines his or her station in the tribe. A solemn ritual is held to prepare Tusken youths for their journey into the wilderness, during which they are given totems, armaments, and some water to carry with them. Saying no words, and showing no fear, they mount their banthas and head off into the desert. If they return with trophies showing that they have been victorious, they are greeted with grand rejoicing. A bonfire is lit, food prepared, and amid great ceremony the storyteller adds the young Tusken's tale of bravery to the tribal history. If they do not return, no word is mentioned of them again.

Sand People make no social distinction between males or females. Only clan leaders keep records on sexes, so that they can arrange marriages, and as soon as a youth becomes a recognized adult, he or she is assigned a mate. Through a ritual that mixes the blood of husband and wife with that of their bantha mounts, they are joined for life.

In extremely rare instances, Tuskens have been known to accept outsiders into their tribes. The Jedi Sharad Hett lived for some time among the Tuskens, and the Jedi Tahiri Veila was raised among the Sand People after her parents died in a Tusken raid.

During the time of the New Republic, fewer Tusken Raiders were reported encroaching on human settlements. A cyclic pattern of harsh sandstorms threatened and destroyed many human settlements, and sociologists believe several of the tribes were affected as well. It is unclear how many Tusken Raider tribes currently reside on Tatooine, as they continue to remain resistant to outsider study.

DESIGNATION
Sentient

HOMEWORLD
Tatooine

AVERAGE
HEIGHT
1.8 meters

PRONUNCIATION
Tŭs'-kĕn Rā'-dĕr
(Sănd Pēr'-sŭn)

NOTABLE APPEARANCE
Episode IV: A New Hope

TWI' LEK

Twi'leks are tall, generally thin humanoids indigenous to the Ryloth star system in the Outer Rim. Their most notable features are their tentacle head-tails—called both lekku and tchin-tchun—that protrude from the back of their skull, distinguishing them from the multitude of other species found across the known galaxy. These fatty, tapered, prehensile growths serve both sensual and cognitive functions, including the storing of memories. In fact, some of the records located from the Old Republic era indicate that this storage capacity allowed the Jedi Aayla Secura to recall her Jedi training after her memories were stolen from her. In conversation, Twi'leks will often refer to their lekku individually: *tchin* meaning "right lekku" and *tchun* meaning "left lekku."

Twi'leks' smooth skin comes in many variations of blue, red, yellow, orange, deep green, and even striped. Sharp, claw-like nails punctuate their long, flexible fingers, and their orange or yellow eyes are especially good for seeing in the dark.

Ryloth is a dry, rocky world with a peculiar orbit that has resulted in half of the planet becoming a barren, unlivable desert where the sun's rays constantly scorch the surface. The other side is always trapped in frigid darkness. Most of Ryloth's indigenous species inhabit the cold, dark portion of the planet, while the Twi'leks live in cities carved out of the mountains in the "twilight" section of the world—where the temperature is somewhat comfortable.

Theirs is a primitive industrial civilization, based on windmills and air-spun turbines that provide power for heat, light, air circulation, and minor industry within their city complexes. Frequently, hot air blows from the sun-based regions; referred to as heat storms, these winds drive the turbines and windmills. The dry twisters can reach temperatures in excess of three hundred degrees Celsius, with gusts hitting five hundred kilometers per hour. While very dangerous, they provide the warmth necessary to sustain life.

Twi'leks are omnivorous, cultivating edible molds and fungi, and raising bovine rycrits for food and clothing. While their ancestors might have been hunters who struck out upon the frosty plains to find game for sustenance, present-day Twi'leks have developed a more agrarian society.

The Twi'lek people are highly intelligent, capable of learning and speaking most galactic languages. Their own dialect combines verbal sounds and subtle movements of their lekku to communicate complete concepts.

Even the most advanced linguists have difficulty interpreting all the head-tail movements inherent to the Twi'leki language. For this reason, when two Twi'leks converse in public, their discussion often remains completely private, unless it is observed by another Twi'lek or a quality protocol droid.

This linguistic feature has been the cause of much suspicion on the part of many outsiders throughout history, particularly Imperials, who believed that since Twi'leks sent secret signals with their head-tails, they were duplicitous spies. In truth, Twi'leks see their lekku as "spiritual appendages," and in jostling them, they express the movement of inner divinity. While this may indeed be considered extra communication, it is actually contact at a metaphysical level. While the meaning is mostly private between speakers, it is usually not two-faced or deceitful to those outside the communication, unless absolutely necessary. Normally it is merely truthful and real, and cannot go against their verbal expression—not, at least, without extreme concentration. Recent studies done by the Jedi of the New Republic found that Twi'leks are in fact a generally Force-sensitive people, and that their lekku interaction is tied to their inherent Force sensitivity. This may also explain some of their suspect treatment at the hands of the Empire.

Contrary to the paranoia expressed by the Empire, the people of Ryloth are not at all warlike, and remained clear of the Imperial conflict during the Galactic Civil War, although if they had been called upon to spy for either side, they would have been quite good at it. They prefer cunning and slyness over physical confrontation.

Hidden beneath the surface of their world, their city complexes are massive interconnecting networks of catacombs and chambers. Built into rocky outcroppings, they blend right in with the environment of the planet—vivid evidence of this people's subtle nature.

Each of their cities is autonomous and governed by a head clan consisting of five Twi'lek males who collectively direct industry and trade. These leaders are born to their positions, and exercise absolute power. When one member of the head clan dies, the remaining four are driven out to follow their colleague to the "Bright Lands," making room for the next generation. If there is no immediate generation to follow, a set of regents takes over until a new head clan can be selected. Given that a seat within the head clan is handed down within families, intra- and interclan rivalries

abound. Subterfuge within one's own clan is almost to be expected, although Twi'leks who are caught and disgraced among their people are also driven into the Bright Lands.

Because Twi'leks possess no spacefaring capabilities of their own, they have grown dependent on neighboring systems, as well as on pirates, smugglers, and merchants, for much of their galactic interaction. One of their greatest exports is the mineral ryll, which is used in many medicines, but also as an expensive and addictive recreational drug. Ryloth has become very vulnerable to the underbelly of galaxy life: slaving vessels have often combed the planet to stock their thriving ryll stores, while smugglers often raid ryll storehouses. Some head clans have actually given their own people into slavery as a protection payment, feeling threatened by the possibility of widespread pillaging.

Slavery has historically been a serious problem among the Twi'lek clans, particularly for their female members. In traditional Twi'lek society, women are expected to be subservient to men, and are often treated as afterthoughts or accessories. They are not considered particularly intelligent or capable, having value only to the degree that they please others. Twi'lek women were commonly sold into slavery, even by their own clans, to become dancers or companions, as their beauty and grace is favored galaxywide by many different species. Lethan, or red-skinned Twi'lek women, fetch a startlingly high price on the open market.

With the dawn of the New Republic, some head clans on Ryloth banded together to stop the slave trade and protect one another from the retribution of angry smugglers and traders. This has created a much safer environment, and more and more legitimate trading organizations have started to bring business to the world. Following this, Twi'leks began to take on a visible and influential role in the New Republic, often serving as pilots, as advocates, and in other positions. This new prominence was almost jeopardized when the rogue Imperial Warlord Zsinj brainwashed Twi'leks into attempting to assassinate Admiral Ackbar and Republic hero Wedge Antilles. Following this, all Twi'leks were temporarily removed from active military duty until the plot was discovered—thankfully, before it could reach its conclusion. The Twi'lek species was vindicated, and returned to its former level of influence in galactic affairs.

DESIGNATION
Sentient

HOMEWORLD
Ryloth

AVERAGE
HEIGHT
1.7 meters

PRONUNCIATION
Twē'-lĕk

NOTABLE APPEARANCE
Episode VI: Return of the Jedi

UGNAUGHT

Ugnaughts are small, porcine humanoids known for their tireless work ethic. They are especially good mine workers, whether this be gas or mineral mining. Their short, stocky, muscular bodies are able to withstand long periods of work under harsh conditions.

This species is native to the planet Gentes, located in the Anoat system, although very few—if any—remain on that world. Unfortunately, the Ugnaughts suffered the fate of many other primitive species throughout the galaxy, in that entire tribes of the pig-like aliens were gathered by human merchants, smugglers, and traders and taken to new worlds to live and work as indentured servants and slaves.

One of the largest populations of these creatures can be found at Cloud City on Bespin. When the Corellian eccentric Lord Figg decided to build this floating Tibanna gas mine colony high in Bespin's atmosphere, he knew the project would require cheap manual labor. Figg rounded up by force three Ugnaught tribes—the Irden, Botrut, and Isced—and took them to a space station near Bespin to offer them a deal. If they would build his floating city, he would then grant them their freedom. Further, they and their descendants would be allowed to live and work in the colony and share in the company's profits. The Ugnaughts accepted, and went right to work on Figg's project. After the city was finished, they began to reap the profits of their labor.

When Lando Calrissian became the legal administrator of Bespin, he honored the agreement with the Ugnaughts until he lost control of the facility to the Empire. With the onset of Imperial occupation, the Ugnaughts were enslaved once more, and forced to work longer hours under harsh conditions. Many were removed from the facility altogether. Lando eventually returned to Bespin and, with the help of Luke Skywalker, Lando's friend Lobot, and the Ugnaughts, he regained control of the city. He later turned control over to the Ugnaughts' chosen leader of all the tribes, King Ozz. Today they own the city that they helped build.

Although now modernized, the Ugnaught people retain the rich oral tradition they have long maintained. Even after being transplanted to countless new worlds, they have held on to many of the customs and laws they established in the time before their enslavement. Immediately upon their acceptance of Figg's offer, tribes reestablished their ruling councils called Terend, elected officers called ufflor, and chose traditional "blood professions."

Blood professions are vocations passed down from gen-

DESIGNATION
Sentient

HOMEWORLD
Gentes

AVERAGE HEIGHT
1.2 meters

PRONUNCIATION
Ŭg'-nŏt

eration to generation within each family. A miner will teach his children to mine, and a mechanic teaches his children to repair and construct machinery. When Ugnaughts reach the age of twenty, they become candidates for their inherited profession. If the number of new candidates for any given profession exceeds the community's needs, the candidates call a blood duel. Through a series of fights to the death, young Ugnaughts battle for the right to inherit their blood profession.

A similar ritual takes place when a young male Ugnaught wishes to take a bride. All males who wish to be considered for marriage will come together once a year to meet the females who are considered eligible for marriage. If a conflict ensues over one female, the contesting males must compete against each other, with the female choosing the means of competition. Sometimes this is a contest of physical strength, but other times it is a match of wits. Either way, the ruler acts as judge in the single bout to determine who will take the bride home with him.

Despite these arcane traditions, Ugnaughts are a predominantly nonviolent, peaceful species. They tend to shy away from contact with other races, and usually do not learn to speak Basic—though they do understand it—except for the ufflor and members of the Terend. Ugnaughts feel more comfortable when dealing with members of their own tribes.

Ugnaughts are robust, meticulous, skillful, and unpretentious. They are thoroughly committed to their family and their occupations. Ugnaughts who are idle are usually restless and irritable. The best way to keep them happy is to keep them busy.

Of the three tribes on Bespin, the Isced has encountered the most difficulty with outsiders and with the other tribes. This is because they have a vicious sense of humor, and are prone to playing potentially dangerous practical jokes.

During their indentured servant years, a majority of the Ugnaughts lived in the Bespin mining quarters. Once the city was liberated, the Ugnaughts inhabited all portions of the facility. However, council meetings, folk-story telling, dances, and blood duels still take place in various arenas located, by tradition, in the mining quarters area. And while the King of the Tribes meets with the Terends of the tribes in the administrative levels of Cloud City, his coronation and all other special government events are held in this same area, as a reminder of the Ugnaughts' proud tradition as menial laborers.

NOTABLE APPEARANCE
Episode V: The Empire Strikes Back

UTAPAUN
(UTAI AND PAU'AN)

Utapauns is really a name for two species that inhabit the world of Utapau, a barren world of rocks and deep sinkholes located in the remote Tarabba sector of the Outer Rim. The Pau'ans are the upper class of Utapaun society, making up nearly a third of the world's native inhabitants. This species is the taller of the two, with slim builds, gaunt, gray, lined faces, and dark eyes. Dressed in tightly bound, thick clothing, usually only their hands and faces are visible. They serve as governmental administrators, officials, and bureaucrats. Their neighbor species, the Utai, meanwhile, are short and stocky, with round faces and long eyestalks. The Utai serve as the menial laborers, technicians, and ground crew for docking areas. On each foot they have only two toes, and on each hand three fingers and a thumb—but nevertheless they are nimble and dexterous, completing complex manual tasks with ease. Their large, dark eyes allow them to see in the dimmest of light underground.

The Pau'ans are a very long-lived species, and are often called the Ancients because of their longevity. While they originally made their home on the surface of Utapau, climatic changes caused stronger and stronger hyperwind storms, so they were forced to build a new home in the sinkholes, where they first met their native neighbors.

The Utai, in contrast, are often called the Shorts because of their stature—but also because comparatively their lives aren't very long. Utai colonized the walls and crevices of Utapau long before the Pau'ans ever thought of doing so, and while they are not as long-lived, they are the older of the two species. Between the efforts of the two species, entire cities were built beneath the surface of the planet in the tunnels, crevasses, and walls of massive sinkholes. Because of their environment, both species prefer darkness, and Pau'ans in particular prefer to eat meat raw, rather than cooked.

The Pau'ans govern Utapau in a way that allows for a great deal of autonomy among the local cities. Local administrators, called Masters of Port Administration, act as a type of mayor of their city, and they are assisted by an advisory committee. Each of these individual port administrators is a member of the Utapaun Committee, which is managed by the chairman of Utapau, the planetary head of state. As only Pau'ans have these leadership roles, they often serve in them for many

2.0

1.5

1.0

.5

PAU'AN

0

years because of their long life span. They receive their positions because of their heritage, with family lines holding on to leadership roles through generations. For example, Tion Medon was an administrator for Pau City, and he was descended from Timon Medon, who first unified the Utapaun peoples.

When the Pau'ans first met their fellow residents, they taught their diminutive cousins how to generate wind power. Over time, the Pau'ans found themselves falling naturally into the leadership role, a role the

UTAI

DESIGNATION
Sentient

HOMEWORLD
Utapau

AVERAGE HEIGHT
1.4 meters (Utai)
1.9 meters (Pau'an)

PRONUNCIATION
Ōō-tä-pŏn
(Ōō'-tai / Pä'-wăn)

Utai easily, and readily, relinquished. Although the balance of power is tipped in favor of the Pau'ans, there is no ill will on the part of the Utai. Even though they are relegated to menial or lower-level labor positions, they are not maltreated or underappreciated by their compatriots.

But while there is no conflict between the species, there is some conflict among cities as a whole. Each city on Utapau has its own Pau'an dialect and culture, and rivalry has often been fierce among them. Arguments and competitions have erupted in the politics of the Utapaun Committee on many occasions, though the competing cities always band together to face a worldwide threat.

Such cooperation occurred when the Confederacy of Independent Systems laid siege to the Utapaun homeworld during the Clone Wars. The Utapaun Committee was not at all happy with its plight, and did not like harboring General Grievous, the commander of the Separatists' massive droid army. Committee members quickly and quietly agreed that they would turn him over as soon as the opportunity arose, and when Obi-Wan Kenobi came to Utapau to investigate the situation there, they immediately told him of their situation despite being watched by their overseers. Obi-Wan told them they would be liberated by Republic forces, but sadly Palpatine took control as Emperor and put into play the programming he'd installed in his clone warriors to wipe out the droid army—but take control of Utapau at the same time.

While the Emperor reigned, Utapau remained a dominated world, held in bondage to Imperial forces. When the New Republic came to power, the planet eagerly joined the new government, hoping to take a more active role in galactic society in order to prevent such a political travesty from ever again happening to their world.

NOTABLE APPEARANCE
Episode III: Revenge of the Sith

VARACTYL

Varactyls are saurian, four-legged herbivores native to the plant Utapau. While they are reptiles, they possess many features of the bird family, such as feathers dotting their scaled skin and long, bird-like tails. A giant, sharp beak of a nose protrudes from the center of varactyls' faces, and two small, dark eyes rest on the sides of their elongated heads. A ring of feathers surrounds the varactyl's neck.

This reptile has an armor-plated skull that protects its brain from blunt injury. Its neck is extremely flexible, and both males and females have crests and a ridge of midbody spines. Some of these defensive quills have developed into feathers, which are used for mating and threat displays. A female varactyl's plumage and overall coloration tend to be more vibrant.

Their large feet have strong claws with five digits, giving them the ability to climb the rocky walls of Utapau's sinkholes at incredible speeds.

Varactyls are cold-blooded lizards, and as such they like to sun themselves on the walls of Utapau's sinkholes. They are most active during daylight hours, crawling up the rocky cliffsides to remain in the sun as it shifts across the sky, avoiding the darkness as it fills the cavernous canyons of the planet surface. They eat the most during the day, feeding on green lichens in the lower, wetter portion of the sinkholes and punching through the dried sandstone in the upper levels to consume arterial roots that weave their way through the soft rock.

Varactyl nests are primarily located in the warmest outcroppings of the sinkhole wall, where during the day they are warmed with the most sunlight. A female varactyl will lay a clutch of about a dozen eggs at a time, and these eggs take nearly two months to hatch. These nests, while they lay where the sun can reach them, are also placed where there is a crag or crevice into which varactyls can hide themselves and the nest to protect their young from predators.

During the night varactyls are more lethargic, and therefore vulnerable to the native predators. One is the dactillion, a distant genetic cousin of varactyls. Dactillions often fly in and attack varactyl nests to eat their eggs or hatched young. For extra security, varactyls will group together for warmth near their nests in the sinkhole walls. While dactillions and varactyls are natural enemies, when domesticated they can be corralled in the same pens.

Varactyls' scaled skin is waterproof, and they are excel-

DESIGNATION
Nonsentient

HOMEWORLD
Utapau

**AVERAGE
LENGTH**
15.24 meters
HEIGHT
3.9 meters

PRONUNCIATION
Vŭ-răk'-tĭl

lent swimmers. They only swim during the middle of the day, however, when sunlight is striking the bottom of the caverns where the water gathers in grottoes. The vicious nos monster is active in the hours of darkness, so they will not attempt the water at night.

While usually calm, imperturbable creatures, varactyls will defend themselves and their young with great ferocity from attack. Females, especially, are more tenacious in this regard. The fan of erect spines along a female's tail would seriously injure an opponent attacking her from the rear. Varactyls are also extremely strong, and their heads, made of strong bone impervious to most blunt attacks, cause a good deal of damage when used in a head-butting maneuver.

The Pau'ans and Utai of Utapau have bred varactyls for centuries as pack animals and mounts because of their pleasant demeanor, strength, and speed. It was the diminutive Utai, though, who learned how to domesticate and train them for their present use. The Utai serve today as the varactyl wranglers for mounts. Dactillions are excellent steed and pack animals. Because of their high-boned backs, both creatures must be fitted with high-backed saddles to give riders appropriate balance.

This is a very intelligent species, loyal to their masters and clever with regard to combat. They are also credited with having long memories. A varactyl will remember all of its riders, and will respond favorably or negatively to them based on past treatment. When they have been treated well by a rider, varactyls respond with loyalty and great affection. If a rider abuses a varactyl mount, the creature will not allow that being to ride them and, in extreme cases, may attack the person. There are reports of many beings having been killed when this happened.

One abusive rider reportedly had a varactyl remember him after he had been offplanet for several years.

NOTABLE APPEARANCE
Episode III: Revenge of the Sith

WAMPA

Wampas are burly, vicious primates that inhabit the ice-covered world of Hoth. They stand up to three meters tall, and possess razor-sharp claws and fangs. Wampas that have passed puberty usually have jagged, curving horns on their heads that continue to grow larger and more imposing with age.

Because of their acute sense of smell and the coat of thick white fur that blends perfectly with the landscape of their native planet, wampas make excellent hunters, and are very rarely themselves the victims of predators. They wander the icy wastelands of Hoth preying on tauntauns, antlered mammals called rayboo, and other unwary creatures. After disabling their prey, they drag it to their cavernous, frozen lairs beneath Hoth's surface. Using their saliva, wampas moisten portions of their victims' bodies, then place them against the ceilings of their caves so that the victims will freeze in place, suspended from the ice. Because wampas prefer fresh meat, they often keep their prey alive until they choose to consume it.

Wampas typically hunt alone, but occasionally band together to lash out against a threat to the local wampa population, such as a human settlement. In this, they show a rudimentary form of intelligence and cunning, particularly since they will often scout their enemies' location and strength before formulating an attack.

Luke Skywalker, the renowned Jedi Master, has claimed that these creatures even have long memories. During a routine patrol when the Rebel Alliance had its base established on Hoth, Skywalker was attacked by a wampa, and barely escaped its lair by slicing off its arm with his lightsaber. When he returned on a later visit to Hoth, the same one-armed wampa discovered him, and attacked Luke and his cohort Callista. This time, Luke managed to slay the creature with his lightsaber, allowing them to escape.

During the Alliance encampment on Hoth, wampas repeatedly attacked the Hoth base and its personnel. It was soon discovered that wampas are strangely attracted to the sounds made by astromech droids. After some research, it was revealed that the tweets and whistles emitted by the droids were similar to those made by a female wampa in search of a mate. No doubt some male wampas were disappointed to find a mere piece of machinery waiting for them instead of a new companion, thus further justifying their regular vicious rampages once they had discovered the source of the sounds.

Wampas mate during the warmer months of the Hoth yearly cycle, during which they will gather in regions where game is plentiful, to search for companionship. The males go on the hunt while the females stay together and wait. Once the male succeeds in a kill, he will smear the blood of his victim on his chest and return with the game to show it to the females—demonstrating his ability to effectively care for a mate. Sometimes the males will fight each other for a female's attention, and the victors in these various melees are those who win their preferred female; they are thus treated as the alpha males of the region until the next mating season occurs.

While they are primates, wampas could also be considered marsupials in terms of their reproduction methods. Their cubs are born live, but very underdeveloped—almost resembling a miniature worm that could fit upon a caf spoon. These tiny infants crawl to their mother's pouch, where they nurse, grow, and develop over a period of roughly three months—after which time they leave the pouch with a full set of teeth, small needle-sharp claws, and an innate attitude of invincibility. The mother and father will then teach the children to hunt, to survive in the cold, and to care for game.

Galactic scientists have further discovered that wampas mourn their dead with great intensity. They are protective of their own, and when one is slain, they will fly into a rage directed at the killer. If the death was natural, the grieving wampas will simply take out their anger on their surroundings, smashing walls and ripping apart anything or anyone in their way. Some wampas have been reported to accidentally cause avalanches and underground cave-ins during these fits of hysteria, leading to even more deaths. After expending all their energy, grieving wampas will bury the body in the snow, and keep guard over it for several days—ensuring that the remains are not eaten by other predators.

These intimidating creatures have become popular prey for big-game hunters, and have also been spotted in some of the illegal gladiatorial games that pop up on a number of

the Outer Rim worlds. Hunters and poachers are more and more willing to brave the severe cold of Hoth for sport or to make a profit from wampas. While they are not the friendliest of creatures, wampas were included in Galactic Alliance legislation to protect endangered species from extinction.

Some wampa subspecies are found on other worlds, and while it is clear they were transplanted, scientists have been unable to trace how the creatures found their way there from Hoth. One of the more notable subspecies is the swamp wampas of Dromund Kaas. Dark brown in color to blend in with their marshy environment, swamp wampas form cave-like huts of bog moss in which to hide their kill. They are identical to the wampas of Hoth in nearly every other way, prompting scientists to believe that they are indeed descended from their icy cousins. How and when they came to be on Dromund Kaas and developed their present appearance is unknown, but it does speak volumes of the species' adaptability.

The Empire, meanwhile, bioengineered another subspecies of wampa known as the "cliff wampa," after they received reports of how wampas wreaked havoc upon the Rebel base of Hoth. This rock-climbing variety was used to guard Imperial interests on the Outer Rim planet Gall. Gray or light brown in color to blend in with their rocky habitat, the sharp, iron-strong claws of these creatures allows them to dig into solid rock walls to form caves, just as the Hoth variety would dig into ice.

One species that is often mistaken as a wampa relative is the Tatooine Howler, which is sometimes called a "desert wampa." While they do bear a resemblance to the wampa being covered in hair and adorned with tusks, genetic testing has proven that the mysterious, howling desert hunter is no relation at all to the wampa but a separate species altogether.

DESIGNATION
Semi-sentient

HOMEWORLD
Hoth

AVERAGE HEIGHT
2.5 meters

PRONUNCIATION
Wäm'-pä

WEEQUAY

Weequays are a humanoid species from the desert world of Sriluur, located in the system of the same name. They are a strong, rugged people, with countenances weathered by the harsh desert winds. Their skin is coarse and gnarled, and typically black, gray, brown, or tan in color. The males wear topknots drawn to the peak of their otherwise bald heads, while the females usually shave their skulls completely. Male Weequays who are offplanet wear individual topknot braids for each Sriluur year that they are not at home. When they return to Sriluur, they shave off the topknot braids in celebration.

In keeping with their rough appearance, Weequay have a unique resilience to injury from blunt trauma and burns. Their skeletal frames are more dense than those of most humanoid races, and their skin is more like a tough hide. A Weequay's skin can withstand blaster fire and attacks from blunt weapons with little injury—though at close range a blaster will cause their skin to smolder. Average knife attacks are also ineffective, though a vibro-blade can puncture their skin. It is not resistant to lightsabers, however. This natural body armor makes them extremely durable fighters in close quarters and renders them very desirable as personal guards to organized crime figures and the like.

Often seen as threatening, Weequays will not usually speak in the presence of a non-Weequay, instead often hiring a trustworthy non-Weequay to speak for them. In fact, they do not talk much at all, even in the presence of their own people. This is largely because they possess a type of pheromone-based communication that enables members of the same clan to communicate in complete silence. This type of interaction is as clear to the species as the spoken word, but it works only with other clan members.

These people are, indeed, dangerous. Theirs is a complex, impersonal, brutal culture centered on the worship of a multitude of gods that symbolize both natural forces and animals. Their primary deity is Quay, the god of the moon, from whom their people's name is derived. (*Weequay* means, literally, "follower of Quay.") To contact their gods, Weequays use totems that symbolize the sphere of control of each given deity. Their main totem is a spherical object that they utilize for obtaining advice from Quay himself. They address the totem as Quay in an effort to please the god. This totem actually behaves much like a child's toy, and on other worlds it has found use as an amusement device. All Weequays carry one on their person, and will shake it and wait for advice or inspiration to appear, directing them in every important decision they must make. They have a great devotion for the totem, and will grow violently angry if anyone questions the validity of an answer derived from it.

The Quay totem produces its own problems, however, as Weequays may shake the object for hours seeking the answers they wish to receive. But in doing this, they will remain patient, assuming that because all Weequays have totems, the god was probably busy answering the questions posed by others.

The totem also controls Weequay mating. When a male Weequay wishes to take a female as a mate, he questions the totem first as to whether it is a wise idea. If the totem answers in the affirmative, he seeks out the prospective female, who in turn consults her own totem. This process may go around several times until the two have matching answers. In a like manner, Weequays can also end a marriage by consulting the totem. The only part of Weequay life not truly determined by the totem is the producing of children, which the species leaves up to chance, accepting offspring as a special secret present from the gods—though many Weequays still, out of eagerness, ask Quay to tell them the gender and number of children to be born.

While they do take great pride in their offspring, life in a Weequay clan is completely impersonal, and clan members do not even have names, since individuality is not a concept they understand; they will only take a name when they leave their homeworld. Weequays employ limited technology, though they are known as skilled makers of melee weapons such as force pikes.

Weequays were originally a nomadic, desert-dwelling people, but eventually they established large clan cities in coastal areas of Sriluur. At the center of these cities are religious shrines called thal, made of black polished stone, where followers known as sant can leave anonymous offerings. Building thal offplanet is not allowed, although Weequays who are not on Sriluur may sacrifice a strong animal or adversary to the gods. Such traditional religious

DESIGNATION
Sentient

HOMEWORLD
Sriluur

AVERAGE HEIGHT
1.8 meters

PRONUNCIATION
Wē'-kwā

sacrifices can often attract unwanted attention from local peoples, as occurred on at least one occasion on Tatooine. Weequay guards and mercenaries in the employ of the crimelord Jabba the Hutt had taken to slaughtering considerable numbers of banthas in their rituals. However, some of these banthas were the bonded mounts of Tusken Raiders, who were angered at the deaths of their beloved animals. Although the Tusken Raiders could not prove the Weequays were to blame, Jabba kept the peace by making it appear as if local humans were behind the deaths.

While it might seem incongruous, there have been Weequay Jedi. Sora Bulq was a well-known Jedi at the time of the Clone Wars, even though his own people would not have been able to identify him by name. While the rest of his species relied on their Quay totems to guide their lives, Sora, raised in the tradition of the Jedi from infancy, saw them as little more than gambling baubles in comparison to the Force. Private notes recorded by Bulq were discovered in Jedi Holocrons in the years following the rise of the new Jedi order. In these, Bulq stated a firm belief that a good number of his people held the potential for Jedi training, but were hopelessly inhibited by their cultural mores. While Bulq might have worked to bring his species to a higher level of development, during the Clone Wars he unfortunately fell under the influence of the dark side before he was ultimately slain by the Jedi Quinlan Vos.

Other Weequay Jedi played an important part during the Clone Wars. Que-Mars Redath-Gom served faithfully during the final years of the Galactic Republic. He was killed in the Battle of Geonosis in the Petranaki Arena. Kossex, a female Weequay, was a Jedi Master who served at the Battle of Kamino as a starpilot. Because they were raised apart from their people, all of these Jedi demonstrated independence from the traditional reliance on the Quay totem that has so engaged their people. Sadly, this has made their memory largely unaccepted by the Weequay populace.

NOTABLE APPEARANCE
Episode VI: Return of the Jedi

2.0

1.5

1.0

.5

0

Whiphids are tall, bulky bipeds with long yellow-white or golden fur. They live on the icy planet known as Toola, and are characterized by their prominent, hairless faces, which boast exaggerated cheekbones and forehead. Two tusks protrude from their lower jaw, and their two massive arms end in three-fingered hands with razor-sharp claws.

The bodies of Whiphids maintain a thick layer of blubber that traps heat in their system, providing protection from their cold environment. Their fur, which is covered with a natural oil, repels water so that they can swim in the frigid seas of their homeworld. In warmer settings, they will shed several centimeters of fur and burn off much of their fat, while their hollow cheeks widen, creating a broader face that serves to dissipate heat.

Whiphids are ferocious, carnivorous predators who have no greater joy than tracking something down to kill it. They have few principles and are motivated by their appetite for wealth and exotic cuisine. However, they exhibit pleasant, easygoing personalities, and when dealing with offworlders, they will take great care to determine who is proper prey and who is not. When encountered offplanet, Whiphids are usually involved in some sort of shady business dealings or are managing underworld operations. Nevertheless, there have been rare Whiphids able to overcome their natural instincts, as demonstrated by those few who traveled offplanet to become Jedi, such as Master K'Kruhk, who served the Republic during the Clone Wars.

On Toola, Whiphids live in nomadic tribes consisting of three to ten families. During the warmer months, these clans build permanent shelters of rocks, skins, and animal bones, to which they return each summer. In winter, the tribes migrate across the snowy steppes, following food and constructing temporary dwellings. They track the native grazing animals known as motmots by sniffing the air, and they are strong enough to slay the large creatures using only their bare hands and tusks. Most Whiphids, however, use spears, crude sabers, and clubs for hunting, carrying their kill on sledges. The most successful hunters, called Spearmasters, become the leaders of these Whiphid tribes, and thus determine where each tribe camps and what quarry it will hunt.

Toola's temperatures are rarely above freezing because of the planet's distance from its sun, as well as its thin atmosphere. The world does, however, have a brief summer when snow melts and plants can grow. If they haven't begun one

DESIGNATION
Sentient

HOMEWORLD
Toola

AVERAGE HEIGHT
2 meters

PRONUNCIATION
Hwĭ'-pĭd

already, Whiphids will start their families based on these seasonal changes. Most Whiphid children are born to their parents in the summer period, as they are frequently conceived during the cold winter months when more time is spent with loved ones in the protection of their interim shelters. The Whiphid gestation period typically equals the length of their winters, and there is a great celebration when all of the new children are formally introduced to others in the tribe. A grand hunt is conducted; the eating and celebrating can frequently go on for several days at a time.

Whiphid infants have no tusks for their first two years, though they do possess teeth enough to consume meat from the hunts. These children learn quickly to survive under harsh conditions, and require little instruction in order to grasp new concepts. They are shrewd and astute, much like their parents.

Whiphids entered galactic society when advanced species from dry, desert worlds arrived on Toola to harvest its ice in order to fulfill their water needs. Impressed by the technology and other conveniences the strangers brought with them, many Whiphids departed with the water harvesters to find work across the galaxy as mercenaries and bounty hunters. Others established businesses of their own after having learned the ways of offworlders.

One such entrepreneur is Lady Valarian, who made her mark as the owner of the Lucky Despot Hotel and Casino on Tatooine. Crafty and ambitious, not to mention intelligent, Valarian was able to avoid having her name associated with many of her more nefarious endeavors. According to the scant criminal records available, Valarian, the daughter of two gangsters, arrived on Tatooine planning to build her own empire. She ran into competition with Jabba the Hutt, and although the two negotiated a truce, each wanted the other out of the way, not caring much about how that happened. Valarian renovated a grounded ship and turned it into a thriving business, imbuing it with culinary and decorative themes unique to her native culture. Lady Valarian's luck proved better than Jabba's, however, when Luke Skywalker and his comrades disposed of Jabba during their rescue of Han Solo, further opening Tatooine for the Whiphid's exploitation. It is believed that after Jabba's demise, Lady Valarian assumed control of many of his criminal enterprises on Tatooine.

NOTABLE APPEARANCE
Episode VI: Return of the Jedi

WOOKIEE

Wookiees are intelligent, arboreal sentients from the jungle world of Kashyyyk. Possessing many natural strengths and abilities from the day they are born, Wookiees are known to be one of the most physically strong sentient species in the galaxy. They are also incredibly bright, with an extraordinary talent for repairing and adapting machines and technology.

Tall, hairy primates, Wookiees possess varying eye colors and fur that ranges in shades from white to light brown and black. Their fur is often a blend of different tones. They have retractable claws on their feet and hands, which they use almost exclusively for climbing. In their culture, employing their claws in hand-to-hand combat is forbidden, and is considered dishonorable or even insane behavior.

Wookiees are especially known for their loyalty and dedication to honor, as well as their capacity for great kindness, sharp wit, and friendship. They are devoted to friends and family, and particularly to those whom they owe a life debt. In the life-debt tradition—which is ironically similar to a tradition of their hated nemeses the reptilian Trandoshans— Wookiees pledge their existence and servitude to an individual who has saved their life, or who has given them another, similarly intense cause for loyalty.

Perhaps the best example in recorded history of the depth of a life debt is that of the one owed to Han Solo by the Wookiee warrior and Clone Wars veteran Chewbacca. While serving in the Imperial Navy, a young Han Solo aided in Chewbacca's escape from slavery, leading to his discharge from the navy. Chewbacca pledged him a life debt. The two became best friends, and over the decades, one was rarely seen without the other, with Chewbacca coming to Solo's rescue more than once. In an act of ultimate sacrifice, Chewbacca gave his life during an early strike by the Yuuzhan Vong, to save Han and Leia Organa Solo's son Anakin.

Wookiees are also known for having short tempers, especially when honor is at stake, and can fly into berserker rages if they, their families, or their "honor families"—those with whom they share a life debt—are threatened. They have a reputation for hostility, and have been known to smash objects and beings when angered.

Theirs is a cultured society, though, and they exist in harmony with the environment of their world, living in well-developed cities on the seventh level of vegetation on Kashyyyk, high in the wroshyr trees. Wookiee cities and homes demonstrate a deep appreciation for their environment. Constructed of native woods with sweeping, gentle lines, the Wookiees' structures seek to bring the outside, inside. Liftcars, held by unbreakable kshyy vines, carry Wookiees from one level to the next, although they can also climb up or down if they are so inclined. Though Wookiees wander the many upper levels of their planet, they rarely ever venture any lower than the fourth, given the many dangers the lower levels hold. Wookiees believe there are nightcrawlers that feast on the blood and spirits of their victims in the darkness of the bottomworld, and that the spirits of those who did not honor their life debts reside there, waiting to trap and kill the unsuspecting. Indeed, no Wookiee who has gone to the lowest level has ever returned. This region of Kashyyyk has yet to be a subject of scientific exploration. Kashyyyk does have several oceans, the beaches of which are the only areas on the planet where the soil is visible and accessible.

When Wookiees reach adulthood, they leave their families to explore the lower levels of the forests, particularly to hunt the dangerous quillarats that live just under the fifth level. These small, brownish-green creatures, standing only half a meter tall, have long needle-sharp quills covering their bodies, and can hurl these quills with deadly accuracy. Hunting on the lower levels represents a rite of passage for Wookiee adolescents known as the hrrtayyk, and is a long-standing and important tradition in Kashyyyk society. The hrrtayyk may be attempted alone, with an older relative, or with friends. For a successful passage, the adolescent seeking adult standing must return with physical proof of bravery: a trophy that may be displayed or worn. Following a successful return from the lower levels, a newly recognized adult Wookiee will often take on a new, more mature name. Under certain circumstances, hrrtayyk may also take place in other forms, sometimes even offplanet, as long as sufficient courage is demonstrated.

Feats of courage extend to Wookiee courtship rituals as well. Male Wookiees will hunt quillarats as an offering that they present when they propose marriage to a female. They must, however, catch the quillarat bare-handed, and kill it without using a weapon. If the female Wookiee accepts the proposal, she will show her approval by biting into the creature's soft underbelly. When they marry, Wookiees become mates for life.

Though Wookiees reside in a very natural environment, they are a mechanically advanced species, and a few thousand standard years before the Battle of Yavin they developed much of their own technology, constructing huge cities in the trees of their homeworld. They also developed high-tech weapons and tools unique to their own culture, the most famous of which is the bowcaster, or laser crossbow. Even the design of Wookiee weaponry captures their love of nature. Often curved and with housings made of

DESIGNATION
Sentient

HOMEWORLD
Kashyyyk

AVERAGE
HEIGHT
2.3 meters

PRONUNCIATION
Wŏŏ'-kē

wood, weapons such as Wookiee bowcasters can sometimes be mistaken for musical instruments by the uninitiated. They prefer, however, to use simple, homemade implements for accomplishing everyday tasks.

Because Wookiees are very protective of their natural home, they discouraged tourism to their world even as they themselves took to the stars. This greatly upset their Trandoshan neighbors, who had come to depend on tourism as a means of boosting their economy. This, combined with the Trandoshans' historical desire to colonize, soon drove the two peoples into a war that was eventually resolved by the Old Republic Senate.

Their Trandoshan enemies, however, were not impressed and bided their time to enact vengeance. With the emergence of Imperial rule, the Trandoshans suggested that the Empire use the powerful primate people as slave labor. The Clone Wars had barely ended before the Empire quickly overwhelmed the Wookiees, taking them to work in camps located throughout the galaxy. The prisoners helped—under duress—to build the Death Stars. But the Wookiees did not give in easily, and even those remaining on their home planet maintained an undercurrent of rebellion. The Empire made it virtually impossible for those Wookiees to leave their world, and enlisted Trandoshan hunters to capture any Wookiees who did manage to escape. For this reason, there remains quite a bit of animosity between the Wookiees and their Trandoshan neighbors.

Wookiees communicate via a system of grunts, growls, snuffles, barks, and roars, as the structure of their vocal chords and voice boxes won't allow them to speak Basic. For this same reason, humans find their language difficult to reproduce. Their primary dialect, used for trading and dealing with outsiders, is known as Shyriiwook, or "tongue of the tree people." There are various dialects, such as Xaczik, spoken by Wookiees indigenous to the Wartaki Islands. Because the Imperials thought all Wookiees were alike, they did not discover these other dialects, and when the Wookiees were enslaved, they often used Xaczik for delivering secret information to members of their resistance movement.

Today, Wookiees are an active member species of the Galactic Alliance. Now free of Trandoshan and Imperial oppression, they are open to share their innovative talents with the rest of the galactic community.

NOTABLE APPEARANCE
Episode IV: A New Hope

XEXTO/QUERMIAN

Hexto are an arboreal species native to the Outer Rim planet Troiken, where they live in tree-based villages. They are the genetic progenitors of the long-necked Quermians, a resultant subspecies from the Arkanians' genetic experimentation in an illegal research project seventeen thousand standard years before the Battle of Yavin. Fearing legal repercussions for their work, the Arkanians abandoned their new creations to evolve on their own.

Both of these species grew to be technologically advanced by the time the New Republic discovered them. They each joined the Old Republic, rediscovering each other in the process. At first, the Xexto refused to acknowledge their genetic cousins, but when scientific proof of their evolutionary link was produced, they begrudgingly accepted it, though they chafed at the titles the Old Republic gave their races initially: Troiken Xexto and Quermian Xexto. While by and large the Xexto see the Quermians as a shadow of their own greatness, with the dawn of the New Republic, and subsequently working with them in various capacities in the fledgling government, they began to find a sense of common ground with their genetic cousins.

The Xexto have four arms, each with six fingers, and two legs with ten toes. Their skin ranges in color from pasty white to pale yellow. Similar in color, Quermians also have four arms but with fewer fingers. The Xexto and the Quermians have almond-shaped blue eyes and two brains, with one in their chest cavity. The upper brain controls their base emotions and body functions, while the lower controls creative thinking and logic. In their genetic alteration, the Arkanians gave the Quermian creations extra-long necks and moved their olfactory organs to one set of their fingers—the reason why remains a mystery. Quermians' facial expression is much more peaceful; they wear a pleasant smile all the time. Quermians also like to appear more human, keeping their extra set of arms hidden, while their Xexto cousins use their multiple appendages without reservation.

Like most arboreal mammals, the Xexto and their Quermian cousins bear their children live, one at a time. At birth, the children are born with all their limbs, but their necks are only slightly longer than that of a standard human child. As children grow, their necks increase in length, and their spinal columns and bone structure thicken to support the necks. While Xexto and Quermian adults can use their limbs independently, children usually use their hands in tandem for three to four years, unable to move them independently of one another. By the age of five, they fully develop the dexterity and mental capacity to grasp and use objects in their separate limbs. Prior to this, they tend to cling to others or stable objects with all their arms, a trait that xenobiologists believe comes from their arboreal beginnings. Many tree-climbing species cling to tree branches to feed on leaves, and their young hug their parents' necks or tree trunks until they are able to climb and make their way through the trees on their own. While this species left the trees long ago, children still hang on for support while their bodies and minds mature.

Personality-wise, the two species are similar in their calm demeanor, though the Xexto are more enamored of adventure and risk taking because of the harshness and danger of their home environment. The Xexto's lightning-fast reflexes, born of their arboreal ancestors' quickness in pursuing prey and avoiding predators, inspires them to compete in Podraces and games that feed their desire for exhilaration. It has been speculated that this interest in new thrills made them more likely to welcome the Arkanians. One Xexto historian records that mysterious visitors offered members of one community the chance to see a "whole new world," and they jumped at the chance. They vanished not long after and were thought lost. When the Xexto encountered the Quermians in the Old Republic, their conclusion was that their ancestors could not have known that they were to be genetic experiments—while they are adventurous, they are not willing victims. The best way to anger Xexto is to question their bravery.

Even so, both species are levelheaded and cool-tempered. The Quermians are more peaceful and contemplative, influenced, sociologists believe, by the beauty of their garden-like terraformed homeworld, Quermia. Unlike the Xexto, the Quermians did not need to fight to pursue their dinner. Quermians are therefore not as quick as their Xexto cousins and do not seek adventure. They prefer instead to solve problems through reason and logic.

In the Quermian physiology, however, there is a flaw that is not seen in their Xexto cousins. Because their mental abilities have been genetically altered, some Quermians are known to develop sudden psychoses, such as obsessive compulsive disorder, dissociative identity disorder, and the like. The development of the dissociative identity disorder often happens when one of their brains takes on one personality while their second takes on another—causing an internal battle in the individual. Because a Quermian's mental pathways are so complex, it can be a difficult condition to treat, and many of these unfortunate disorder victims commit suicide. Obsessive compulsive disorders, mean-

while, develop when both of a Quermian's brains process input in tandem rather than sequentially. While a Quermian's brain can perform most functions in tandem, input must be processed in order between the two brains. A system of retraining the brains has been useful in treating this genetic condition. In cases where a Quermian suffers from a malady of this sort, the onset of the disorder is usually triggered by a traumatic experience. One example of a Quermian suffering from this latter condition is Dr. Murk Lundi, whose overwhelming obsession with finding a Sith Holocron led to his death. His mental illness was triggered by incarceration.

While most Quermians do not develop such disabling disorders as those mentioned, they will usually have at least one mild phobia or minor compulsion, which will not be debilitating. These sorts of mental conditions seem to be well contained among Quermians who follow the Jedi path, as the training coaches them to deal with fears and habitual behaviors.

Quermians are also telepathic, and communicate by locking eyes with their fellows. Geneticists claim this is a result of their genetic manipulation, though it was a latent trait—one the Xexto could develop in time. When they joined the Old Republic, many Quermians became Jedi, which of course made their world a target during the rise of the Empire. Even non-Jedi Quermians were the victims of violence when Imperials incited mobs by spreading the misinformation that all Quermians were Jedi who could read minds and spread evil thoughts via telepathy. Those who could escape withdrew to their world, remaining in seclusion during Palpatine's reign. With the rise of the New Republic and the subsequent Yuuzhan Vong invasion, Quermians left their solitude to rejoin the galactic community.

Some of the greatest Jedi to come from the Quermian people are Yareal Poof, a member of the Jedi Council at the time of the Battle of Naboo who was greatly skilled in the art of battle meditation. This skill allowed him to give courage to his forces while weakening the resolve of the opposing army. Along with Poof, three other renowned Jedi served the Republic at that time—Loo Raelo, Kindee Ya, and Vinian Ska. All three were known to have great skill in telepathically based Force abilities like Yareal Poof, though little more is known about them. It is obvious to most scientists that Quermian mental abilities make for stronger Jedi—a trait their Xexto forbears have not achieved.

DESIGNATION
Sentient

HOMEWORLD
Troiken/Quermia

AVERAGE HEIGHT
Xexto: 1.4 meters
Quermian: 2.4 meters

PRONUNCIATION
Zĕx'-tō
Kwer'-mē-ăn

NOTABLE APPEARANCE
Episode I: The Phantom Menace

YARKORA

The Yarkora are rarely seen, appearing in the company of the lowest levels of galactic society, particularly in the Outer Rim Territories. They are tall, bipedal creatures whose huge faces are characterized by two wide-set eyes, a large nose with a pair of unusually large nostrils, and furry whiskers that protrude from each cheek. They have the appearance of an ungulate species, though they do not chew their cud like unintelligent ungulates. They bear thick, heavy black claws on their three-fingered hands, and these indicate an ancestry that can be traced back to hoofed creatures.

Only one Yarkora has ever been examined by scientists (post-mortem) and much was learned of their physiology from that research. As mentioned above, they are an ungulate species, and while they do not chew their cud they have two stomachs. One stomach is always digesting food, while the other stores food to be digested. Yarkora, therefore, like to snack all day to maintain full capacity in both their stomachs. However, because they always have a food store, they can go a good amount of time without eating when necessary.

The Yarkora also have two pancreases, four kidneys, and three livers, and this system redundancy contributes to their longevity. All these organs keep their bloodstream free of corrupting toxins and carcinogens, producing very strong white blood cells. They very rarely die of natural causes, save extreme old age. And even after suffering violence, internal injuries are unlikely to kill them outright, as additional organs take over for any damaged organ. Yarkora also have a remarkably high tolerance for alcohol and other addictive substances. They do not tend to become addicted—as their bodies filter out the chemical that causes the addiction. The only thing that can decrease their long lives is regular smoking, as they do not have additional lungs. But they do not tend to smoke to excess because the addictive qualities of tobacco have no effect on them.

The Yarkora's eyesight is also very unique in that they are able to focus on the tiniest of objects over a distance of 1,600 meters. The inner lenses of the eye are able to focus in and out, almost like a camera zoom. It is believed the Yarkora's keen eyesight is pivotal to discovering some of the information they use for sale, bribery, and manipulation. They also use this ability to cheat at cards and other games of chance.

Their hearing works in a similar manner as they are able to isolate and pinpoint sounds within a morass of noise. Their aural talents allow them to overhear singular conversations within a 10-15 meter radius.

Their powerful senses, of course, tie into the focus of their entire culture. What little scientists have been able to glean about this people indicates that they seem to be obsessed with the gathering and controlling of information for their own gain. They are masterful at extracting information from others without revealing anything about their species, their history, or even their present agenda.

Most of the Yarkora seen in the galaxy are known to be con artists or criminals who prey on the gullibility of others. While members of the species tend to be rather unassuming, sentients who have encountered them have consistently noted that they seem to project an aura that makes others uncomfortable. They exhibit the ability to intimidate others, via either size or demeanor. Some scientists theorize that the Yarkora simply use their ability to observe and exploit a victim's own weaknesses, while recent discoveries of important Yarkoran documents indicate they may actually possess some sort of projected empathy.

While much remains unknown about the Yarkora, an archaeological dig on an as-yet-unnamed world in the Outer Rim yielded a buried settlement that belonged to a Yarkoran community. In this small settlement, collections of written and digital recordings were found, the most useful being the creations of one Yarkora named Saelt-Marae, who filled several journals with information spanning several hundred standard years—proving that these people are long-lived.

Saelt-Marae's journals contained many of his personal observations of the galaxy at large, information he used for bribery and intrigue. They also contained page after page dealing with his traditional courtship with his chosen mate—a courtship that took nearly two hundred years to come to fruition.

According to the journals, all Yarkora woo their intended through extended conversations that can be written or verbal, the topics of which must be examined from every possible angle. Through these conversations, the two come to know each other in a way that they feel is more intimate than simple physical gratification. A conversation on a single topic can take several years, and they are not allowed to start a new topic until the previous one has been exhausted. Saelt-Marae and his beloved continued their discussion as they traveled to different places in the galaxy, sending their discourse in information packets through the HoloNet. In face-to-face conversations, Saelt-Marae wrote of the ability he and his intended had to "read" and "speak" their feelings, not just through glances and body language but also through psychic means—though whether this is a unique latent Force ability or a trait of the species is unclear.

DESIGNATION
Sentient

HOMEWORLD
Unknown

AVERAGE
HEIGHT
2 meters

PRONUNCIATION
Yär-kōr'-ä

This cultural form of discussion and discovery explains why any Yarkora who have been encountered in the galaxy at large tend to be extremely tenacious about specific subjects, preferring to argue a subject to death over simply winning. It is just one more trait that observers feel make the Yarkora's presence unsettling at best—at worst, positively irritating.

Another characteristic revealed by Saelt-Marae's writings is that Yarkora bear their children live, one at a time. A female Yarkora can only bear children every fifteen standard years, and usually only one at a time, making their race very sparse indeed. Every female, therefore, must become a mother at some time in her lengthy life, to keep the species from going extinct. Because they come so few and far between, all Yarkoran children are treated as firstborns—they are doted upon and acculturated to be rather solitary. As a result, married couples usually do not share the same abode, but build dwellings next to or near the other's so they can have appropriate privacy. Families share meals together at one dwelling or the other, and children usually remain with their mothers—especially during the formative years—but overall, Yarkora prefer to live alone.

Several Yarkora helped the Rebel Alliance in gathering intelligence, but they were given a sizable salary for doing so. A few served the Empire, with some being discovered as double agents, selling information to both sides and making an admirable profit in the meantime. It is clear from his journals that Saelt-Marae is one of the latter. More Yarkora have been seen in the galaxy at large since the rise of the New Republic, the Yuuzhan Vong invasion, and later incursion by the Killiks, but their political interests remain a mystery.

NOTABLE APPEARANCE
Episode VI: Return of the Jedi

YEVETHA

The Yevetha were a highly xenophobic, reptilian species from the planet N'zoth in the Koornacht Cluster, an isolated collection of about two thousand stars that has yielded very little intelligent life in its system. This species was wiped out by the Yuuzhan Vong, who saw them as a threat to their planned dominion.

The Yevetha were thin, tall, bony humanoids. Males of the species had scarlet facial crests along their cheeks, jaws, and the tops of their heads. These crests swelled up when a male was spurred to violence, and their primary headcrest engorged when a male was prepared to mate. The females of the species exhibited no such features.

Yevetha had wide-set black eyes and retractable dewclaws, one on the inside of each wrist above six-fingered hands. Yevethan skin incorporated vestigial armor on the back of the neck and down the spine. Their brains were located in their thoraxes behind thick bone brain cages and a line of indentations along their temples contained fine hair cells that controlled auditory sensing.

Yevetha reproduced by laying eggs in "birth casks" or external wombs called mara-nas, often kept in special climate-controlled rooms. If the children remained in these birth casks past birth, the casks were then referred to as nestings. Unborn children were fed blood, which they absorbed through the eggshell. The mother's donated blood was preferable, though the blood of any Yevetha would do. Yevethan leaders often killed underlings and fed their blood to their unborn or nesting children in the casks. The victims considered this a great honor, and would often volunteer for such a death. Most male Yevetha lived day to day with the knowledge that, at any moment, a superior might kill them simply for their blood.

This biological need for blood was the central focus of the Yevethan culture and religious belief system, therefore they were constantly bent on violence to harvest blood. They were a dutiful, attentive, cautious, but fatalistic species shaped by a strictly hierarchical culture. A viceroy—called *darama,* or "the chosen one," because of his dual role as religious and political leader—headed the Yevethan governing body called the Duskhan League. He was at the top of a complex hierarchy, served by military leaders called primates and administrators called proctors. All of these obeyed him without question, and would eagerly have died for him. They were ruthless fighters, unwilling to surrender even in the face of certain defeat.

DESIGNATION
Sentient

HOMEWORLD
N'zoth

AVERAGE HEIGHT
1.9 meters

PRONUNCIATION
Yĕ-vē'-thä

The Yevetha did not fear death. In their legal system, a killing was only considered murder if an inferior killed his or her superior. As mentioned above, dying to feed a superior's children was considered honorable. When Yevetha of lower standing failed in a mission or caused dishonor upon their superiors, they were called *nitakka*—a word meaning "dishonored." The *nitakka* would kneel before their superiors and offer their necks to the superiors' dewclaws, hoping to die as sacrifices to the superiors' children—reestablishing honor upon their own families as well.

Until their contact with the Empire, the Yevetha believed they were the only intelligent creatures in the universe. Initially they submitted to Imperial rule. Then, around the time of the Battle of Endor, the Empire became lax in its control. Without warning, the Yevetha rebelled violently, slaughtering every human stationed on N'zoth, both military and civilian. They spent the next decade mastering Imperial technology, then struck out at neighboring systems to eliminate all non-Yevethan peoples in their sector. Twelve years after the Battle of Endor, the Yevetha began a "cleansing" known as the Great Purge, wiping out all non-Yevetha within the borders of the Koornacht Cluster. The New Republic sought to intervene diplomatically when Yevethan expansion threatened Republic-allied worlds, but the Yevetha attacked instead. The New Republic eventually fought them back, but it cost many thousands of lives and nearly toppled the fledgling government.

As a result of their experience with the Empire, Yevethan ethnocentrism became xenophobia, causing them to consider all other intelligent life morally and physically inferior. They abhorred contact with other species and would go to extreme measures to avoid alien contamination, engaging in intense purification, bathing, and disinfecting procedures if they spent time in close quarters with outsider "vermin." They found the smell of other species distasteful, and claimed that without bathing or purifying themselves, they could still smell the stink of other beings on their own persons.

Yevethan xenophobia was so extreme that even in the shadow of the Yuuzhan Vong, they refused aid from any other galactic species. As a New Republic squadron commander, Jaina Solo reported in her logs that the very last of the Yevetha committed suicide by crashing his starship rather than be aided by her squadron.

NOTABLE APPEARANCE
Shield of Lies (novel)

YUUZHAN VONG

The Yuuzhan Vong are bipedal humanoids native to Yuuzhan'tar, the parent of the sentient, wandering world Zonama Sekot. Around fifteen thousand standard years before the Battle of Yavin, they were cut off from the Force by their world because of their violence and their manipulation of biotechnology. Angered at their world's actions, they increased their production of biotechnology, causing the death of their world. Evacuating in living vessels known as worldships, they set out to wander the stars looking for a place to call home.

The Yuuzhan Vong resemble humans in many ways, but are usually taller, heavier, and have less hair on their heads. Their faces look like lumps of pulsating flesh with droopy eyes underscored by bluish eyesacks. Their foreheads are sloped, giving them a barbaric appearance magnified by the ritual tattooing and self-scarring resulting in grotesque mutilation and reshaping of the features.

This type of disfiguration exemplifies a ritualized system symbolic of a path or a journey each Yuuzhan Vong must experience. In order to accomplish a rise in rank, individuals must make one more physical change to re-create themselves in the shape of one of their gods: they sacrifice a body part, an organ or a limb, to bring themselves closer to perfection, and thereby closer to their gods. They then graft other parts onto themselves—limbs from another creature, or bioengineered body parts. The Yuuzhan Vong never seem to maim themselves in any way that might hinder their ability to function, but only in ways that change their appearance or improve their abilities. Warriors, especially, are given the opportunity to replace sacrificed limbs with limbs from the bodies of their defeated foes or with parts from particularly vicious predators, perhaps a sharp-taloned claw. Those whose changing ceremony has failed, and who are functionally maimed, are demoted to the lowest ranks of the lowest caste—mere workers, or Shamed Ones.

Everything these people do is for the greater glory of their gods, as they follow their path of conquering and dominating the galaxy, re-creating it—like their own bodies—in the image of their gods.

Yuuzhan Vong warriors will not surrender to an enemy under any circumstances, for fear of insulting their gods. They use bioengineered weapons, tools, and ships to further their cause, and they find the use of actual machinery extraordinarily offensive. They refer to those not of the Yuuzhan Vong as infidels, and take perverse pleasure in their own pain and in the pain of others. An attack on their pride is cause for a death duel, which also can be considered a sacrifice to their gods. To die in battle is among the highest honors they can achieve.

Yuuzhan Vong society is divided into regimented levels or castes, ruled by a supreme overlord. The Yuuzhan Vong people look upon the supreme overlord as a god, for if his victories become legend he will, in their belief, become a god. It is a common belief that the supreme overlord speaks to the gods directly, so his orders are never to be questioned—only obeyed. The other castes include priests, shapers, warriors, intendants, and workers. While a person's caste is usually determined by birth, some have risen out of their assigned caste through marriage. More often, however, priests and warriors fall out of favor and end up a part of the intendant caste, or even as low as the Shamed Ones.

Members of the priest caste are responsible for communicating the will of the gods to the people and act as advisers to the supreme overlord and the warriors. The shapers, meanwhile, create all the weapons and tools the Yuuzhan Vong use in their conquest based upon a very stringent set of religious guidelines. Ignoring even one of these guidelines is heresy, and will engender a swift and brutal penalty. Warriors comprise the caste most frequently encountered in the galaxy. They are vicious fighters who will fight to the death with religious zeal. The highest-ranked warrior is the warmaster, followed by the supreme commander, commander, subcommander, subaltern, and warrior.

Intendants, meanwhile, care for the shapers' creations and maintain supply lines during an invasion. Intendants also work as spies, excelling in subterfuge and deception—tasks below the honor of a warrior.

The lowest caste, the workers, perform the least desirable tasks in a military culture. They also care for the shaped creatures, and harvest the equipment. Workers are made up of those born to that caste, those who have fallen from other castes, enslaved peoples, and Shamed Ones—Yuuzhan Vong whose bodies reject the grafting on of new limbs or organs, or who are deformed.

The Yuuzhan Vong consider all other sentient life-forms to be inferior to themselves, therefore their modus operandi is to enslave or eliminate lesser beings. They consider most species unworthy of slavery, but those who fight back courageously are given a swift, merciful death. In their goal of conquest, the Yuuzhan Vong are inspired by their worship of Yun-Yammka, the Slayer. It was in deference to his commandments that they extended their armies across the galaxy, led by their vanguard force the Praetorite Vong, in the hope of bringing all other beings under their rule or destroying them.

All Yuuzhan Vong weapons, equipment, tools, and clothing are bioengineered organic life-forms. Their ships, for instance, are propelled by dovin basals, living gravity-well projectors, which create warps in space–time to move their ships through hyperspace. Using many dovin basals in concert, the Yuuzhan Vong are able to even move a whole planetary body from its nestled gravitational orbit, as evidenced by the crash of the moon Dobido into its planet, Sernpidal.

The Yuuzhan Vong are unique in that the Jedi cannot sense them through the Force. Luke Skywalker, the Yuuzhan Vong heretic shaper Nen Yim, and a Yuuzhan Vong priest named Harrar discovered that because their homeworld, Yuuzhan'tar, cut the Yuuzhan Vong off from the Force, they are completely devoid of it. As a result, they do not believe it exists, mocking those who do. In fact, Yuuzhan Vong hate Jedi more than any other galactic residents. They receive great honor for killing one.

As the New Republic was beginning to take hold, scout ships reached the known galaxy and set plans in place for invasion. Twenty-five standard years later, the Yuuzhan Vong swept into the galaxy, destroying and conquering everything in their path, eventually claiming Coruscant at the galactic center. With their strange weaponry, brutal tactics, and religious zeal, they took the New Republic completely by surprise, murdering countless thousands of people and demolishing system upon system in the name of their gods. Their conquest ended at Coruscant when Zonama Sekot finally took them as her own, realizing this was the only way to end the bloodshed and teach the Yuuzhan Vong a new way to live—one that transcended pain and violence.

DESIGNATION
Sentient

HOMEWORLD
Yuuzhan'tar

AVERAGE HEIGHT
1.8 meters

PRONUNCIATION
Yōō'-zän Vŏng

NOTABLE APPEARANCE
Vector Prime (novel)

ZABRAK

The Zabrak, also known as Iridonians, are a humanoid species native to the inhospitable world of Iridonia in the Mid Rim—a world of dangerous stalking predators, deep canyons, fierce winds, and acidic seas. Zabrak resemble humans, though their heads are crowned with varying patterns of vestigial horns. For both males and females, horns begin to grow at puberty, and signal the time that their rite of passage is near. Like humans, Zabrak have different skin colors, but these hues are the result of genetic dominance. The variety of colors include a peachy white, tan, brown, and black, with many tonal shadings. Zabrak can also grow hair or be completely bald, depending on subspecies. Horn patterns are often linked with hair growth (or lack thereof). Hair colors are similar to those of humans, although Zabrak do not have eyelashes, eyebrows, or any other facial hair. Zabrak eye colors are also analogous to human, though yellow, purple, red, and orange are also seen on occasion.

Zabrak wear facial tattoos made up of thin lines that they receive during their rite of passage. These tattoos can be symbolic of many things, such as family lineage or where they came from, or a personal design of their own. The Zabrak Sith Lord Darth Maul had black tattoos placed upon his red skin that had special Sith significance.

Zabrak are a self-assured people, confident that they can attain any goal they set out to achieve. To some they seem single-minded, being usually focused on one given idea, concept, or task at a time—with the conviction to accomplish their goal successfully. While with others such confidence might lead to prideful superiority, it isn't within a Zabrak's nature to denigrate other species. All Zabrak demonstrate great pride in their home colony, and while there is some competition among these colonies, intra- or extracultural insults or fights are not common occurrences without extreme provocation. On the contrary, most Zabrak are proud of their species' diaspora, believing that their varied colonies and experiences add to their species' overall value to the galaxy as a whole. The motivation to make a contribution to the greater good is a driving force for many Zabrak.

With instincts developed by tolerating their homeworld's environment, they are renowned

ASKAJIAN

Askajians are a portly humanoid species that seem to be misunderstood by the galactic populace at large. Only recently brought into the galactic arena, they are peaceful and unsophisticated, preferring a life spent at home with their children.

Due to their bulk, they are often dismissed as corpulent, unattractive humans. However, their appearance is due to the ecology of their homeworld, which is an arid desert planet where water is scarce. The Askajian biology, therefore, is specially adapted to hoard water in epidermal sacs that help them survive long periods of time without moisture. When they are in less hostile environments, Askajians can be far slimmer. They can expend up to 60 percent of their stored water without detriment to their health.

The planet Askaj is a desolate world on the Outer Rim, far off the path of the Rimma Trade Route. By and large, Askajians are a primitive people with almost no technology. They live in tribal societies with no central form of political government. Each tribe consists of an extended family community of hunters and gatherers, and is headed by a chieftain whose role is imparted by bloodline. A male typically holds this position, but sometimes a female will rise to this rank in the absence of a male heir. At times, tribes will band together in alliances to war with other tribal groupings, usually over water or hunting rights.

Askajian females give birth to sets of up to six children at a time. They refer to their children as cubs, and each female possesses six breasts with which to nurse her multiple offspring. According to long-standing Askajian tradition, cubs are not given names until their first birthday. When names are conferred, they are chosen with great care, as they are believed to be a harbinger of the cub's future. Names are selected by the parents in consultation with the tribe's shaman or shamaness to reflect the parents' and tribe's hopes for the cub, and to please their primary deity, the Moon Lady.

Dancers maintain a religious role as the keepers of a tribe's history and lore, serving as shaman or shamaness. While all members of the tribe hunt and gather food and handle day-to-day living chores, dancers are considered the spiritual leaders. Their primary functions are to advise the chieftain and to perform and pass on the history of their tribe. As spiritual leaders, they lead the group in worship of the Moon Lady.

Life in these tribal groupings centers on the migration of the tomuon, large woolly herbivores that populate the more habitable regions of Askaj. Askajians use tomuon for everything to benefit their lives—wool for clothing and other fabric essentials, meat, milk, fat for soap, hooves and bones for tools and adhesive, and so forth.

Askaj's main trade and the basis of its economy is the sumptuous and elegant fabric woven by Askajian artisans. This elevates the weaver to a role of prominence within the tribe. Created from wool shorn from namesake animals, tomuon cloth is soft, warm, and wrinkle-resistant, making it highly desirable in the Core Worlds of the galaxy. The weavers' technique is shrouded in secrecy, as master weavers take few apprentices and train them in closely guarded quarters. Weaving skill is so valued that wars have been fought to capture skilled weavers from other tribes. It is even rumored that Emperor Palpatine favored tomuon wool for his personal wardrobe.

DESIGNATION: SENTIENT
HOMEWORLD: ASKAJ
AVERAGE HEIGHT: 1.6 METERS
PRONUNCIATION: ĂS-KĀ'-JĔ-ĂN

NOTABLE APPEARANCE: EPISODE VI: RETURN OF THE JEDI

BARAGWIN

Baragwin are a hunchbacked, saurian humanoid species. They are bipedal, with thick, three-fingered hands, stocky bodies, and heads nearly as wide as their shoulders. There are no obvious differences between males and females. They have thick wrinkled hides in various muted medium to dark green shades. Baragwin are among the species with highly developed senses of smell, able to detect emotions simply from a being's odor. Baragwin are typically treated as less intelligent than other species due to their lumbering gait and ponderous mannerisms, but they are in fact highly intelligent. They generally do not correct these misperceptions, which they use to their own advantage.

Although not particularly numerous, Baragwin are found on many worlds throughout the galaxy. However, their planet of origin has long since been forgotten, even by the Baragwin themselves. Possibly one of the first species to achieve spaceflight, the Baragwin have been travelers so long that no one remembers from where they came. However, the Baragwin have been noted throughout recorded history for their talent as weaponsmiths and armorers. They are particularly renowned for their weapons customizations, creating weaponry for species that may not have the limbs or appendages to use such devices without modification. The Baragwin maintained ties to the Empire and then the Imperial Remnant for many years, even after the Battle of Endor. This relationship continued until Imperial Intelligence Director Ysanne Isard developed and released the Krytos virus on Coruscant, targeting nonhumans. The Baragwin community suffered significant casualties, and the Baragwin switched their allegiance to the New Republic.

DESIGNATION: SENTIENT
HOMEWORLD: UNKNOWN
AVERAGE HEIGHT: 2 METERS
PRONUNCIATION: BĂR'-Ă-GWĬN

NOTABLE APPEARANCE: EPISODE VI: RETURN OF THE JEDI

COLO CLAW FISH

One of the more ferocious predators on Naboo, the colo claw fish is an extremely long sea serpent, with a powerful hinged snout that contains sharp, pointed teeth. Four-legged, the colo claw fish's front set end in claws capable of rending flesh. From its tail, jagged protrusions jut out as potential weapons against prey. Colo claw fish are aquatic carnivores, hiding in underwater tunnels and caves near Naboo's core to hunt. These fish stalk potential prey with great patience, waiting hours for a meal to pass by a hiding spot. Their mottled greenish brown skin helps them blend in with their surroundings, making them invisible to unsuspecting prey.

When it spots its quarry, a colo claw fish will spring from its lair with astonishing speed, capturing its victim in its huge pectoral claws. It then disorients its prey with a hydrosonic shriek produced by structures in its head and throat. Prior to consuming its meal, the claw fish incapacitates its victim with poison emitted through its fangs. Claw fish can dine on creatures of surprisingly large sizes, swallowing them whole—their jaws are hinged, and their luminescent skin expands to allow for large meals. Unfortunately for the victim, a claw fish's stomach acids are not very strong and food is digested very slowly, in a fashion similar to the Sarlacc (although not as long as the Sarlacc's estimated thousand-year digestive cycle).

Colo claw fish have been cloned successfully on Kamino. The saberjowl is a more vicious and adaptable hunter than its progenitor. Otherwise, saberjowl are physically the same as their Naboo cousins, except that the saberjowl's skin tends to be green or greenish blue.

DESIGNATION: NONSENTIENT
HOMEWORLD: NABOO
AVERAGE LENGTH: 40 METERS
PRONUNCIATION: CŌ'-LŌ CLÄW FĬSH

NOTABLE APPEARANCE: EPISODE I: THE PHANTOM MENACE

DACTILLION

Utapau is home to the carnivorous reptavians called dactillions. Domesticated as mounts by native Utapauns, these four-winged creatures are capable of flight. As old a species as the Utapauns (if not older), dactillions are natural predators that in fact once preyed on the Utapauns themselves, during the Utapauns' prehistoric evolutionary period. Dactillions are by nature solitary and nomadic. The Utai first domesticated the genetically related varactyl, but the dactillion was tamed not long after when the Utai discovered that they could gain loyal mounts to take them beyond their sinkholes by providing dactillions with fresh meat.

Dactillions use their limbs to climb the cliff faces of sinkholes to get high enough to soar on rising thermal drafts. They hunt within the sinkhole, diving for grotto fish and other small prey and carrion. If the amount of food within a sinkhole dwindles or dactillions are seeking a mate, they fly to the surface, where they are able to ride the strong winds that buffet the barren Utapaun landscape.

Utapauns gained an understanding of their world's complex weather patterns by observing the flight and migration patterns of dactillions. The Utapauns realized that dactillions fly out of the sinkholes when the prevailing winds are at their weakest. This enabled Utapauns to predict the best times for their people to leave the sinkholes and work on their planet's surface, where they built windmills and other structures, harnessing the limitless wind power available to them.

DESIGNATION: NONSENTIENT
HOMEWORLD: UTAPAU
AVERAGE HEIGHT: 6 METERS
WINGSPAN: 24 METERS
PRONUNCIATION: DÄK-TĬL'-ÉL-ŎN

NOTABLE APPEARANCE: EPISODE III: REVENGE OF THE SITH

DRALL

The Drall are small, furry, bipedal creatures native to the planet Drall in the Corellian system. They have large, black eyes and a gentle countenance, leading many people to perceive them as cuddly pets. In actuality, the Drall are members of an intelligent and highly dignified species who bristle at that perception. They do love learning about others, however, and gossiping about their families—talking to anyone who will listen and asking many questions of their friends both Drall and non-Drall.

Drall society is a combination of matriarchy and meritocracy, in a clan-based organization. There are no elected or hereditary leaders on Drall; instead, each clan follows the dictates of its Duchess, a female appointed for life to lead due to her intelligence, wisdom, and experience. The clan Duchess is the owner of all a family's property, which she keeps until she steps down or appoints an heir. The closest the Drall have to a planetary leader is the most powerful and prosperous Duchess, whose example is followed as a matter of tradition.

Methodical and levelheaded, Drall are perhaps best known as excellent scholars and scientists. They are, by nature, abstract thinkers—preferring to develop new scientific theories rather than put them into practice. Therefore, despite their advanced status in scholarly pursuits, they often trail behind the galaxy in technological achievement. They usually implement technologies developed elsewhere.

Most Drall have positions that involve processing medicinal agriculture—Drall's primary industry. Although they are rarely seen elsewhere in the galaxy, offplanet corporations have hired Drall to serve as scientific researchers.

DESIGNATION: SENTIENT
HOMEWORLD: DRALL
AVERAGE HEIGHT: 1 METER
PRONUNCIATION: DRÄLL

NOTABLE APPEARANCE: AMBUSH AT CORELLIA (NOVEL)

FALUMPASET

Natives of Naboo, falumpasets are large mammalian omnivores that inhabit swamps in small herds of one bull and four to seven cows and their nurslings. They have long, stilt-like legs for wading and are superior swimmers, although they are not able to breathe underwater. Falumpasets eat plants and crustaceans found at the midlevel of Naboo swamplands. Individual falumpasets have unique bellows that allow them to be identified at great distances, and they tend to bellow most at twilight and dawn. The strongest beasts of burden on Naboo, falumpasets are intelligent and trainable, but sometimes ill tempered. Two specially trained handlers are required to properly control a falumpaset.

In addition to their use on many Naboo farms and as personal transports by important Gungan leaders, falumpasets are vital to the Gungan army. They are used in battle to pull war wagons filled with ordnance and to move war machines such as catapults into position.

DESIGNATION: NONSENTIENT
HOMEWORLD: NABOO
AVERAGE HEIGHT: 3 METERS
PRONUNCIATION: FĂL-LŬM'-PŬ-SĔT

NOTABLE APPEARANCE: EPISODE I: THE PHANTOM MENACE

FAMBAA

Like the falumpaset, the fambaa is a domesticated native of the Naboo swamps, and is also used by the Gungan army. Fambaa are the largest herbivores found in the Naboo swamps, and they are slow, clumsy, and not too intelligent, albeit even-tempered. However, they are extraordinarily strong and hardy creatures. Although amphibians, they have thick, scaly hides reminiscent of reptiles; these hides are soft upon hatching, hardening as they mature. Similarly, fambaa are born with gills that are absorbed as they age.

Fambaa are known to knock down trees to get at leaves, fruit, and berries, but they also are able to eat deep thick-stemmed underwater plants without difficulty. In the wild, fambaa will travel in herds of up to twelve creatures, although in captivity, they are corraled in groups of three. Main Gungan breeding herds are often so large that they are pastured in sacred areas of the swamps. The Gungan army uses fambaa to transport particularly heavy or cumbersome war matériel, such as the powerful shield generators and massive projectile weapons used on the battlefield. In addition, a fambaa's hide is used to produce the saddles used on kaadu mounts.

DESIGNATION: NONSENTIENT
HOMEWORLD: NABOO
AVERAGE HEIGHT: 5 METERS
PRONUNCIATION: FÄM'-BÄ

NOTABLE APPEARANCE: EPISODE I: THE PHANTOM MENACE

FLORN LAMPROID

Among the galaxy's most dangerous predators, Florn Lamproids are a warm-blooded snake-like species now known to be native to the planet Florn in the region of the galaxy referred to as Wild Space, although it was once thought they were native to many worlds. Evolved from intestinal parasites, their bodies are masses of gray-skinned, thick, heavily muscled coils with a loosely hinged jaw full of venomous fangs. Like the snakes they resemble, Lamproids' bodies are natural offensive and defensive weapons. Their tongues carry saliva poisonous to most other species, and they are able to use these tongues to smell. In addition, they have a barbed stinger that can be used to attack with astonishing speed. A hunter species, they use their coils to hold and kill captured prey. Lamproids are able to see using light sensors on the ends of eyestalks, often allowing them to escape other predators.

Thought to be animals by much of the galaxy, Lamproids are in fact sentient and quite intelligent. Additionally, there have been Force-sensitive Lamproids, and some do communicate feelings telepathically, although this is not known to be a specieswide trait. Florn Lamproids were Rebel sympathizers during the Galactic Civil War and often worked behind the scenes to recruit new troops.

DESIGNATION: SENTIENT
HOMEWORLD: FLORN
AVERAGE HEIGHT: 1.3 METERS
PRONUNCIATION: FLŌRN LĂM'-PROID

NOTABLE APPEARANCE: EPISODE IV: A NEW HOPE

GEN'DAI

The Gen'Dai are a mysterious and rare species with an extraordinarily long life span; some have reportedly lived for more than four thousand standard years. Their long lives may be attributed in part to unique nervous and circulatory systems that make them highly impervious to injury. The Gen'Dai nervous system consists of millions of nerve clusters spread throughout the body, which gives them extraordinary reflexes. In addition, Gen'Dai do not have a central heart; instead, an extensive vascular system distributes blood. Due to their lack of centralized vital organs, Gen'Dai can withstand multiple injuries that would kill most humanoids. Although it has never been verified, it is rumored that Gen'Dai are able to survive complete dismemberment. They are able to enter into a state of hibernation for long periods of time in which they heal wounds, cure diseases, and slow their aging process.

The Gen'Dai are a nomadic species who have wandered so long, their homeworld is no longer remembered. They are not prolific in terms of numbers, as they have a particularly low birthrate, perhaps a result of their long lives and regenerative abilities. However, this long life also causes their minds to weaken with age, and the Gen'Dai are susceptible to mental disorders such as depression, hysteria, and even forms of psychosis. It is most fortunate for the galaxy that by nature the Gen'Dai are not an aggressive species.

DESIGNATION: SENTIENT
HOMEWORLD: UNKNOWN
AVERAGE HEIGHT: 2.5 METERS
PRONUNCIATION: GĔN'-DĀ

NOTABLE APPEARANCE: STAR WARS REPUBLIC #51 (DARK HORSE COMICS)

GOSSAM

Gossams are a small saurian species native to the planet Castell in the Colonies region of space, not far from the Core Worlds. Known for their intelligence and cunning, Gossams have green scaly skin, wide yellow eyes, and heads that slope back on an incline. Balancing their thin bodies on three-toed feet like dancers on toe point, Gossams also possess three-fingered hands that are long and graceful, and like to wear elaborate clothing with platform shoes in order to appear more impressive when encountering other sentients. Female Gossams take great pride in their hair, molding it with oil-based creams to form sweeping sculptures. The traditional female hairstyle is a wave sweeping up from the back of their heads.

Like most reptiles, Gossams are hatched from eggs, which the female Gossams guard and preen over as status symbols. Being a species that is very appearance-driven, when eggs are about to be laid, Gossam families will construct elaborate nests of fancy warm fabrics and pillows to show off their progeny even before they hatch. They will also throw elaborate parties for "egg viewing"—wherein the eager parents receive gifts from their friends and relatives. Of course, the higher the status of the parents, the more exotic and expensive the gifts. These parties are usually thrown late in the eggs' incubation period in the hope that the eggs will hatch during the event.

Most Gossams are independent-minded, and yet many served as indentured servants to the Commerce Guild on Castell for a portion of their lives. This tradition came about when Castell was embroiled in a devastating economic depression. The depression became so severe, and life so harsh, that Gossams were slaughtering one another for necessities such as food, jobs, and passage offworld. In return for their servitude, the Commerce Guild rescued the world and the Gossams by buying vast tracts of Castell real estate and infusing their economy with large monetary investments. The world soon became a center point to the Commerce Guild's manufacturing operations, and the guild appointed a Gossam whom it had saved, Shu Mai, as chief of property resources after she rose through the corporate ladder. Shu Mai had thus managed to bring this world out of its financial slump through keen business acumen and shrewd negotiation tactics. She later repurchased Castell, but raised rents and demanded tribute from her people, leading to her further advanced standing within the Commerce Guild. Shu Mai was ultimately chosen as the guild's president.

Part of Shu Mai's solution to keep her people employed and fed was to offer contracts for them to serve the guild exclusively for a minimum of ten standard years, in return for food, housing, and a modest income. Once Castell grew out of its depression, the tradition continued, with most young Gossams taking indentured contracts to gain business experience before venturing out into the corporate world on their own. Gossams who were able to amass any amount of wealth largely invested those credits in offplanet banks, not trusting their own. Many Gossams established offworld estates for recreational purposes, with a large contingent choosing to settle on Felucia, and investing in local business ventures as a means of acquiring influence.

Gossams are therefore some of the shrewdest businesspeople in the known galaxy. Their products are often inexpensive to fabricate in mass, and overpriced. Gossams are excellent at bartering and working an angle that benefits them in the end. Their self-centeredness and greed know no limits—scheming to beat others out of every credit they can, and often lying and cheating to obtain what they want. Their word of honor means little, and anyone who does business on a verbal agreement with them is asking for trouble, as the Gossams put no value in it.

Members of this species who are seen throughout the galaxy can be legitimate merchants, or quite the opposite. Due to their industrial relationships with many offworld compa-

nies, most Gossams speak Basic, in addition to their own language. Many are involved in smuggling operations and piracy. Because of their size and calm demeanor, they are frequently underestimated—a perception they will always use to their advantage. However, Gossams generally do not rise to positions of power, with Shu Mai being one well-known exception. Their innate independence and greed seem to prohibit the long-range planning necessary to achieve true influence.

Although the Gossams raised military forces to support the Confederacy of Independent Systems in the Clone Wars, they do not have much of a presence in the galaxy in the post-Imperial era. Having allied themselves with the Commerce Guild and the CIS, the Gossams and their planet were a primary target of Palpatine's reign of terror against nonhuman species. The population was largely enslaved, and Castell's industrial base was repurposed to produce military goods for the Imperial Navy. This total societal takeover left the Gossams mostly unable to join the Rebellion in any substantive numbers. Although the Gossams later gained their freedom through the Rebel victory, their planet has yet to fully recover.

DESIGNATION: SENTIENT
HOMEWORLD: CASTELL
AVERAGE HEIGHT: 1.65 METERS
PRONUNCIATION: GŎSS'-ŬM

NOTABLE APPEARANCE: EPISODE II: ATTACK OF THE CLONES

KAADU

Kaadu are large flightless omnivorous reptavians native to Naboo, where they are the primary mounts used by the Gungans. Two-legged, kaadu have sharp hearing and a well-developed sense of smell. They also have bills containing short, sharp teeth (although they lack incisors) that can inflict a nasty bite if a kaadu is annoyed. Their stubbed tails counterbalance their heads.

Kaadu come in a variety of colors. The majority display a pattern of green shades, but they are also seen in blue, red, or a rusty yellow. Agile creatures, kaadu are extremely fast in even the thickest of Naboo's swamps and possess a great deal of endurance. They are also superior swimmers, and benefit from large compound lungs that allow them to breathe both on land and in water. Being surprisingly intelligent, courageous, and loyal, they make excellent mounts for their riders, whom they seldom abandon.

Their breeding grounds are protected because while adult kaadu are not in danger from natural predators, their eggs are. Kaadu eggs are a favorite of such predators as the peko peko, a flying creature that lives in the Naboo swamps. Kaadu eggs can be easy prey, as female kaadu lay them in elevated nests made of mud on the open ground. Not found on any world other than Naboo, Gungans raise kaadu from hatchlings, forming a lifelong bond with them. A well-trained kaadu is a prized animal, awarded to Gungan soldiers upon their elevation to officer.

DESIGNATION: NONSENTIENT
HOMEWORLD: NABOO
AVERAGE HEIGHT: 2.24 METERS
PRONUNCIATION: KÄ'-DŌŌ

NOTABLE APPEARANCE: EPISODE I: THE PHANTOM MENACE

KOUHUN

Kouhuns are small, silent arthropods from Indoumodo in the part of the galaxy known as Wild Space. They are deadly to almost all mammalian beings and creatures. Kouhuns are commonly seen in two varieties, one with a larger segmented body than the other, which in turn has a less pronounced stinger. Kouhuns have two means of carrying their venom to their prey, by either their tail stinger—which delivers a painful but nonfatal wound—or a fast-acting nerve toxin injected by pincers in their mouths, which kills.

Kouhuns are favored by many assassins and bounty hunters (at least those who don't mind a dead target) because they can by passed through even tight security and are nearly impossible to trace back to the person using them. Assassins often starve their kouhuns before they use them to attack a victim, which causes the kouhuns to head for the nearest warm-blooded life-form when released.

DESIGNATION: NONSENTIENT
HOMEWORLD: INDOUMODO
AVERAGE LENGTH: 30 CENTIMETERS
PRONUNCIATION: KŌ-HŌŌN'

NOTABLE APPEARANCE: EPISODE II: ATTACK OF THE CLONES

KRAYT DRAGON

Krayt dragons, are large, vicious, carnivorous reptiles that inhabit the mountainous regions of Tatooine's Jundland Wastes. They walk on four squat legs, at the ends of which are four-toed claws with sharp nails that can shred steel. Their sense of smell is activated by the flickering of their forked tongues, which, as in most snakes and reptiles, collect the smell for their nostrils. Like most reptiles, they are cold-blooded, and they shed their yellow-brown skin on a yearly basis. Unlike their lizard relatives, however, they continue to grow throughout their lifetimes, and do not weaken with age. An average krayt dragon can grow to be nearly five meters in length and weigh about two thousand kilograms. They can live to be a hundred standard years old.

Despite their ferocity, krayt dragons are often hunted by big-game hunters. Although hunting such creatures may not seem wise, the average krayt dragon's gizzard holds an incredibly valuable and beautiful dragon pearl. One pearl would easily make a person a millionaire; hence many foolhardy hunters try to obtain it. Not many have lived to talk about their experience.

High summer in the Jundland Wastes is the krayt dragon mating season. During this time, the mountains ring with their bellowed cries. Most intelligent beings refuse to venture into the wastes at this time, but those who do are very mindful of the sound, because a dragon in a mating frenzy will kill everything it can reach.

DESIGNATION: NONSENTIENT
HOMEWORLD: TATOOINE
AVERAGE LENGTH: 4.5 METERS
PRONUNCIATION: KRĂT DRĂ'-GŎN

NOTABLE APPEARANCE: EPISODE IV: A NEW HOPE

LANNIK

The Lannik are a small humanoid species native to the violent Mid Rim world with which they share their name. They have long ears that protrude from their skulls and are capable of rotating to register the faintest of sounds. Lannik's skin ranges in color from orange and reddish tones to purple and blue, and while they appear to be hairless, most of their hair normally blends in with the color of their flesh. Hair that is allowed to grow long is often worn in a topknot. Lannik's eyes are also commonly the same color as their skin, although variations have been observed. They are not very expressive, and are usually seen wearing what appears to be a grim scowl on their faces.

A dour expression fits the Lannik culture, for theirs is a long history of combat, with warrior skills honed both by hunting the ferocious predators of their world as well as by engaging in heated battles with one another. Their thin bodies give them a delicate appearance, but Lannik are more strong and agile than they appear. The females are usually thinner than the males, but this makes them no less hardy. Lannik are known to live hundreds of years if they are not killed in a physical confrontation, though early death is an unfortunate possibility for all Lannik. A period of military service is compulsory, and given the factions on their world, combat is an all-too-familiar presence in most Lannik's lives.

The Lannik are a fierce people—quick-minded, clear thinking, and prone to abrupt anger. They have little patience for outsiders who waste their time. Because of their forbidding expressions, non-Lanniks tend to view them as perpetually angry, a misconception that typically affords them a wide berth despite their diminutive presence. Lannik place great value on personal honor, bravery, and defiance in the face of incredible odds. While these traits would make them seem somewhat socially akin to human Corellians, the Lannik's focus on these attributes is the result not of a strictly cultural mind-set or bravado, but of their history as warriors experienced in strenuous and dangerous combat. Wounds suffered in battle are treated so that health may be maintained, but they are not hidden. It is not uncommon to see Lannik fighters with scars crisscrossing their bodies and faces, or perhaps missing a digit or an eye. To the Lannik, the remnants of wounds are a badge signifying personal accomplishment and survival, as opposed to something to be ashamed of.

When the Lannik were discovered by human and Duros explorers from the Old Republic, the arrival of products, technology, and forms of business sent their world into political and economic upheaval. Political factions arose, sharply divided and arguing bitterly regarding how the new technologies would be traded on their planet, creating a social instability that Lannik has never truly recovered from. Underworld organizations, seeing an opportunity to capitalize on the chaos, did just that, establishing contacts that would give them safe haven and encourage their burgeoning black-market businesses. The Core World governments, realizing how the sale of technology in particular had affected the world, tried to limit the sales of certain products on Lannik, but this action only served to make the underworld element more powerful.

Corellian diplomats soon endeavored to broker agreements with the Lannik in order to bolster a legitimate trade in technology with the Core Worlds, but the most powerful of the underworld organizations, terrorists known as the Red Iaro, tangled the process in bureaucratic wrangling within the courts. In the years after the Battle of Naboo, Red Iaro agreed to hold peace negotiations on Malastare with the legal Lannik government. In their most daring move, Red Iaro members actually plotted a complicated ruse to further their cause by killing the Lannik head of state, Prince R'cardo Sooflie IX, along with the Jedi sent to assist in treaty negotiations. Fortunately, the Lannik Jedi Master Even Piell managed to uncover and halt the scheme before it could succeed.

When the Empire rose to power, the flow of trade to Lannik stopped almost completely, throwing the world and its people into near obscurity. In the age of the Galactic Federation of Free Alliances, they are rarely, if ever, seen off their world, and the possibility of the Lannik ever entering into galactic trade or politics again remains remote. Their monarchical government is ruled by a prince whose only interests are to keep his world functioning and to continue the constant rebuilding of the species' economic structure.

DESIGNATION: SENTIENT
HOMEWORLD: LANNIK
AVERAGE HEIGHT: 1.2 METERS
PRONUNCIATION: LĂN'-NĬK

NOTABLE APPEARANCE: EPISODE I: THE PHANTOM MENACE

MASSIFF

Fanged reptiles commonly found in the Outer Rim (particularly on Geonosis and neighboring Tatooine), massiffs are domesticated as pets by Geonosian aristocrats and Tusken Raiders alike. To the Geonosians, massiffs are symbolic of their authority. They give them shelter in return for the massiffs' hunting of sand snakes and other vermin outside their homes. Like most reptiles, massiffs lay eggs in the soft, warm sand of the worlds they inhabit, and females guard their nests with an uncommon ferocity. Males hunt for prey as meals for their young and their mother, and they mate for life. Massiffs howl to other massifs as a form of instinctive communication. With thick hides in shades of brown, massiffs blend in with their environments. When attacking larger creatures, they will attack in packs and will stand on strong hind legs to reach a creature's more sensitive areas.

DESIGNATION: NONSENTIENT
HOMEWORLD: TATOOINE OR GEONOSIS
    (UNKNOWN)
AVERAGE HEIGHT: 76 CENTIMETERS
    AT THE SHOULDER
PRONUNCIATION: MÄ'-SĬFF

NOTABLE APPEARANCE: EPISODE II: ATTACK OF THE CLONES

MIDI-CHLORIAN

Midi-chlorians are microscopic symbiotic life-forms present in all living beings. When present in sufficient numbers, midi-chlorians allow a being to feel the Force. Furthermore, if that being is able to quiet his or her own mind, a greater level of communion with the Force is possible, in which the individual may know the will of the Force. Jedi have particularly high midi-chlorian counts; it is said that Anakin Skywalker's count was the highest ever recorded. Recovered Jedi journals from the time of the Emperor's rise reveal a suspicion that Anakin Skywalker may have even been conceived by midi-chlorians, and the name of his father was never recorded at the Jedi Temple.

In the years after the end of the Clone Wars, those Jedi who survived, along with the families of children whose parents feared they might have high midi-chlorian counts, took drastic measures to hide this information from Imperial forces. In the Imperials' hunt for the Jedi, mandatory blood tests for midi-chlorians were common on Inner and most Mid Rim worlds. This gave rise to a black-market trade in mostly ineffective blood products and drugs used to fool Imperial examiners, in addition to trade in forged identity documents. Although faulty blood scans and corrupt, bribe-taking examiners allowed many beings to slip through the Empire's grasp, many were also caught, taken into Imperial custody, and never heard from again.

> DESIGNATION: SENTIENT
> HOMEWORLD: NOT APPLICABLE
> AVERAGE HEIGHT: NOT APPLICABLE—MICROSCOPIC
> PRONUNCIATION: MǏ'-DĒ-KLŌ'-RĒ-ĂN

NOTABLE APPEARANCE: EPISODE I: THE PHANTOM MENACE

MUSTAFAR LAVA FLEA

Used by Mustafarians as a mount, lava fleas are giant, hard-shelled arthropods found in the northern areas of the volcanic world of Mustafar in the Outer Rim (the term *lava flea* is being used, as the Mustafarian name for this species is unpronounceable). Six-legged, these agile creatures can walk on crusted, cooled lava flows or jump over thirty meters of moving lava in a single bound.

Lava fleas evolved underground, like the Mustafarians themselves. They begin life as half-meter larvae with crystalline exoskeletons. Using acidic enzymes in their digestive tracts, the larvae draw nutrients from mineral-rich rock dust located in inner caverns of the planet. By the end of their first year of life, the larvae have grown to almost a full meter and have encased themselves in pupae for a monthlong period, from which they will emerge with their six legs. Young lava fleas are able to consume soft rocks directly from the cooling lava through an armored feeding tube. To protect their eyespots from the fiery environment, lava fleas have a nictitating eye membrane that closes involuntarily. Older lava fleas shed their protective shells, which were used by early Mustafarians as armor that allowed them to move beyond their caves to the planet surface in safety.

Lava fleas were so entwined in Mustafarian culture that when the Techno Union brought repulsorlift technology to the planet, the natives would not give up the mounts they had learned were worthy of trust. The lava flea is reliable and, unlike technology, does not break down. Attempts to import the lava flea to other worlds have largely been a failure, as the rock dust and lava on Mustafar contain unique nutrients necessary for the lava flea's diet, and these foodstuffs are too costly to ship offplanet or replicate using local materials. Furthermore, the materials cannot be recycled, as the metabolic process renders them useless. However, there are disturbing reports that lava fleas have been used in their acid-filled larval form as a means of torture and corpse disposal by crimelords and in less-than-reputable sectors of the galaxy.

> DESIGNATION: NONSENTIENT
> HOMEWORLD: MUSTAFAR
> AVERAGE HEIGHT: 4.3 METERS
> PRONUNCIATION: MŌŌ'-STÄ-FÄR LÄ-VÄ' FLĒ

NOTABLE APPEARANCE: EPISODE III: REVENGE OF THE SITH

MUUN

Tall, thin bipedal humanoids, Muuns are natives of the planet Muunilinst in the Outer Rim. They have elongated, featureless heads without visible nostrils; their skin is grayish. Muuns' circulatory system is unique in that they have three hearts. Extremely intelligent, Muuns tend to be greedy yet cautious when it comes to money. They will favor a calculated risk before a rash action. Muuns are extraordinarily talented at mathematics and statistics; in fact, mathematics is the basis of their written language. Spoken Muun is a series of *eh* and *um* sounds combined in varying pitch patterns similar to Binary Flash Code, a droid language. Muuns will rarely venture off their world, and when they do, it is usually to conduct business. While away, they experience a great deal of homesickness and think only of their return.

During the Old Republic, Muunilinst was the home of the InterGalactic Banking Clan. The Muuns poured their wealth into their largest cities, which were notable for their detailed and opulent architecture. Muuns were later one of the few nonhuman species to escape the oppression of the Emperor's human-centric New Order. This was due to their impressive financial skills, in that no others were deemed better managers of the galactic economy, and the Imperial government did not wish to draw upon itself financial reprisals. Muuns were given Imperial overseers to ensure that they were not directing funds into Rebellion coffers, but there was in fact little need for this—although Muuns are a greedy species, they approach financial matters with great integrity. Muuns served in this capacity well into the era of the New Republic. In recent years, the surface of Muunilinst was unfortunately destroyed in a Yuuzhan Vong planetary bombardment.

DESIGNATION: SENTIENT
HOMEWORLD: MUUNILINST
AVERAGE HEIGHT: 1.9 METERS
PRONUNCIATION: MÖÖN

NOTABLE APPEARANCE: EPISODE II: ATTACK OF THE CLONES

NAGAI

The Nagai are a bipedal, humanoid, warrior people, whose weapons of choice are daggers and knives. Tall, beautiful, and exceedingly thin, with straight black hair and pale, almost white skin, Nagai might fool an unaware observer into thinking they are delicate or weak. This is not the case at all,

as Nagai warriors can be formidable. They are intense, focused, and very disciplined. Nagai are known to kill without hesitation if it suits them, particularly if honor demands it, but if there is no honor in killing, or if a foe is weak, they will take no pleasure from the victory.

The Nagai came upon the galactic scene following the truce of Bakura while fleeing their cruel oppressors, the Tofs. After centuries of brutality and oppression at the hands of the Tofs, Nagai are temperamentally ruled by two things: a deep sense of honor and fear of the Tofs. They fear little else. The Nagai have few loyalties other than their immediate families, but will let concern for others override their need for personal freedom. The Nagai once claimed to be from another galaxy, but Nagi, their homeworld, is actually in an uncharted star cluster on the fringe of the Unknown Regions. Many believed the Nagai were on a mission of conquest, when they were actually fleeing. This is because they spread this misinformation to other species to keep their homeworld a secret.

DESIGNATION: SENTIENT
HOMEWORLD: NAGI
AVERAGE HEIGHT: 1.8 METERS
PRONUNCIATION: NÄ-GÄ'-Ē

NOTABLE APPEARANCE: STAR WARS #91 (MARVEL COMICS)

NOSAURIAN

Bipedal reptiles from New Plympto in the Core Worlds, Nosaurians have four-fingered hands and three-toed, bird-like feet. Their heads are crowned by a row of horns, and they have long beaks. They have amazing reflexes, a trait that allowed them to participate in (and live through) many Podraces.

Nosaurians are color-blind, seeing only in black and white. However, they do not find this particularly bothersome and have adapted to it. Nosaurians are able to make the inside linings of their mouths phosphoresce at will. It is believed this is an artifact of evolution, as one theory asserts that Nosaurians descended from insect-eating reptiles who used the ability to lure prey. Nosaurians now use the ability as a signaling device to contact others in the dark forests of New Plympto.

Nosaurians speak their own native language whenever possible, a combination of barks, warbles, and hisses. Their written language relies heavily on metaphors related to nature, weather, and the seasons. Nosaurians are capable of speaking Basic, but prefer not to. One characteristic that distinguishes the personalities of most Nosaurians is that they hate humans, a holdover from their oppression under the

ONGREE

Very little is known about the Ongree, as they are not a prolific species. However, records indicate they are native to the Skustell Cluster in the Outer Rim. Ongree are bipedal, humpbacked, amphibious humanoids easily identified by their unique heads, which appear to most other beings to be upside down. They are sandy brown in color, with variations in shading among members of the species. Their mouths are on top of four nostrils, with their two eyes mounted on eyestalks coming out of the sides of their heads about halfway down their skulls, giving them a somewhat fish-like appearance. Ongree's eyestalks are flexible, and they can see

objects from many angles. Their hands have two thick fingers and opposable thumbs, so although Ongree don't have many digits, they are able to hold even small objects with ease. Surprisingly, given their somewhat awkward appearance, the Ongree are an agile species.

Ongree tend to weigh all possible perspectives before deciding on a course of action. They are accustomed to seeing things visually from all angles; perhaps this is a similar psychological trait. This tendency makes them particularly skilled

---

Empire. This deep-seated animosity may change, however, due to assistance offered by humans following the Imperial collapse; this is, of course, a slow change. The New Republic gave assistance to New Plympto to help the Nosaurians recover from their long years of occupation, although it could not repair all the damage done to the planet. Later, the Yuuzhan Vong released a life-consuming virus on New Plympto in retaliation for the Nosaurians' resistance. This virus rendered the planet uninhabitable and the subject of an ongoing quarantine. Most Nosaurians were able to flee the planet before the virus struck, and are being resettled on new worlds by the New Republic.

DESIGNATION: SENTIENT
HOMEWORLD: NEW PLYMPTO
AVERAGE HEIGHT: 1.35 METERS
PRONUNCIATION: NŌ-SĂ'-RĒ-ĂN

NOTABLE APPEARANCE: EPISODE I: THE PHANTOM MENACE

diplomats, politicians, and negotiators. Ongree served the Old Republic as best their numbers would allow. At least two Ongree Jedi served during this period, taking part in the Battle of Geonosis. However, their ability to see all sides of an issue also lead many Ongree into less-than-legal activities, consorting with crimelords and gangsters as quickly as they would influential members of mainstream society.

DESIGNATION: SENTIENT
HOMEWORLD: SKUSTELL
AVERAGE HEIGHT: 1.8 METERS
PRONUNCIATION: ÄNG-RĔ

OPEE SEA KILLER

Opee sea killers are large, aggressive aquatic monsters native to the deep seas of Naboo, although a specimen is the largest animal on display at the Royal Icqui Aquaria on Coruscant. They are a combination of evolutionary traits of various animals. Growing to an average length of twenty meters, they have the large maw of a fish, but the eight limbs and thick armored body plates of a crustacean. Sightings of dwarf opee have been reported. Extremely territorial, opee sea killers are also very resilient, and on occasion have survived fights with much larger colo claw fish, most likely by using their sharp teeth as weapons. In fact, there are local reports of young opee sea killers even gnawing and clawing their way out of the stomachs of colo claw fish.

Opee sea killers hide among ocean rock formations while hunting, as do colo claw fish. Opees lure in prey, then chase it down, ensnaring it with their long, adhesive tongues. Opees get their great speed by using a propulsion system unseen in other animals. They take in water through their mouths and channel it outward through openings beneath their plates, creating an almost jet-like effect. In addition, opees are mouthbreeders: the female lays her eggs near a male, and the male takes the eggs into his mouth after fertilizing them. The eggs remain in the male's mouth for safekeeping until they hatch three months later.

DESIGNATION: NON-SENTIENT
HOMEWORLD: NABOO
AVERAGE LENGTH: 20 METERS
PRONUNCIATION: Ō'-PĒ SĒ KĬL'-LŬR

ORRAY

Geonosian beasts of burden capable of hauling heavy loads, orrays are large, tame animals that are also used as mounts by the picadors in the Geonosian arena combats. Omnivorous, with leathery skin, four legs, and great strength, speed, and stamina, they are well suited to the Geonosian environment. In addition, an orray's coloring allows it to blend in with the Geonosian landscape to hide from predators. Prior to their domestication by Geonosians, orrays hunted Geonosian eggs, which had been laid to begin new hives.

The orrays would push their long snouts into egg chambers and consume thousands of larval Geonosians in a single meal. As a holdover from that time, an orray's teeth are blunt enough to crush hard objects such as their eggshells. Orrays have potent tail stingers that they use as defensive weapons, but these are amputated when they are domesticated. The removal of the stinger makes orrays docile and much more manageable for their handlers.

DESIGNATION: NON-SENTIENT
HOMEWORLD: GEONOSIS
AVERAGE HEIGHT: 1.52 METERS
AVERAGE LENGTH: 3 METERS
PRONUNCIATION: Ō'-RĀ

PACITHHIP

Natives of Shimia, located in the Outer Rim Territories near the Corellian Run, Pacithhips are plump humanoid pachyderms with wrinkled gray skin, long trunks, and thin, elegant tusks. Pacithhips have two eyes situated on the sides of their head, allowing a full 360 degrees of vision, and the back of their skull is protected by a bony ridge.

Pacithhip society is ruled by a rigid caste system that dictates whether an individual will be a scholar, a warrior, or a farmer. Membership in a given caste is determined by the shape of a Pacithhip's tusks, and because the tusks do not reach their full size and shape until a Pacithhip's adulthood, it is not known until then what caste they will belong to. Education and the law are the responsibility of the scholar caste; warriors enforce the law and defend the populace, and farmers provide food, clothing, and manufactured goods.

Starting with the era of the New Republic, Pacithhips were seen throughout the galaxy in increasing numbers, as their society supports and encourages those who wish to "find their own path." Pacithhips are innately rational and tolerant and enjoy meeting members of other species. In addition to their own language of Shimiese (a combination of snorts, trumpets, and intricate vocalizations), Pacithhips speak Basic easily. Also, they are able to adapt to a variety of climates and customs, making travel to new worlds trouble-free. Encountering Pacithhips on planets as diverse as Tatooine and Coruscant is not uncommon.

DESIGNATION: SENTIENT
HOMEWORLD: SHIMIA
AVERAGE HEIGHT: 1.5 METERS
PRONUNCIATION: PĂ'-SĬTH-ĬP

NOTABLE APPEARANCE: EPISODE IV: A NEW HOPE (SPECIAL EDITION)

RAKATA

Extinct for nearly thirty thousand standard years, the Rakata have a historical significance that warrants mention. As hyperspace travel originated approximately twenty-five thousand years ago, evidence of a species predating such a time period is usually limited to a planet of origin. The Rakata are the exception, as evidence places them on countless worlds. Among the facts being considered are a Rakatan temple found on Honoghr and a strange world steeped in the dark side located far beyond the charted area of the Outer Rim that cannot be examined, as a powerful energy field surrounds it.

That evidence is so scarce suggests a concerted effort was made to purge the Rakata from the galaxy. It is believed that at the height of their power, they formed an empire, and built the Star Forge, a dark side sun generator that was also a potential superweapon. Having gone too far, their subjects rebelled. The Rakatan Civil War ended when the Rakata were struck by a virus that local populations were immune to, and their subjects slew the few Rakata who survived on their worlds. Furthermore, use of the Star Forge on the Rakatan homeworld caused their sun to wither and die. It is possible that to avenge themselves, their former subjects attempted to erase their oppressors from history, destroying all the technology they used to oppress them and leaving them in a primitive state. Left in dwindling numbers, they soon became extinct.

Although the Rakata have disappeared, it is possible their influence is still present in the galaxy. It has been hypothesized that the Rakata may be responsible for altering the orbits of the planets in the Corellian system. Furthermore, Rakata warfare or failed terraforming efforts could be the cause of the cataclysm that turned Tatooine from an ocean planet to a desert world. It has been speculated that such an ancient species was responsible for widespread similarities among beings on far distant planets, as the Rakata would have brought colonists or slaves with them as they expanded their control.

DESIGNATION: SENTIENT
HOMEWORLD: RAKATA
AVERAGE HEIGHT: UNKNOWN
PRONUNCIATION: RĂ-KĂ'-TĂ

NOTABLE APPEARANCE: KNIGHTS OF THE OLD REPUBLIC (VIDEO GAME)

RONTO

Rontos are huge, gentle pack animals commonly used as beasts of burden by Jawas on Tatooine. They are known for their loyalty and their strength, and can carry hundreds of kilograms' worth of equipment. Though large enough to frighten off most attackers, including Tusken Raiders, they are also skittish and easily spooked, especially in more congested urban areas.

Rontos are reptiles, much like the native Tatooine dewbacks that are also used as beasts of burden. Like their dewback cousins, they are easy to train and often become quite fond of their masters. They exhibit a superb sense of smell—they can detect a krayt dragon as much as a kilometer

on a regular basis. Rontos, who are easily motivated to track scent—especially when mating is involved—will immediately be attracted to a Rodian if they encounter one. Needless to say, several ronto heads have garnered prize trophies for Rodian hunters upon their return to Rodia.

DESIGNATION: NONSENTIENT
HOMEWORLD: TATOOINE
AVERAGE HEIGHT: 4.25 METERS
PRONUNCIATION: RŎN'-TŌ

NOTABLE APPEARANCE: EPISODE IV: A NEW HOPE (SPECIAL EDITION)

SANDO AQUA MONSTER

A frightening predator, the sando aqua monster is native to the depths of Naboo's core. It is tremendously strong and has an incredible ability to conceal itself, which for many prevented verification of its existence, until one beached itself. Zoologists hypothesize that the sando evolved on land, later moving to an aquatic environment, due to its unique physiology. The sando has gills and webbed hands as would be expected from a sea animal, but the rest of its body and head does not appear to be optimized for life in water. The sando's tail is the exception, as it allows the creature to swim very effectively. The sando's great speed and aggressive nature make it difficult to study, as it will appear suddenly and attack without warning.

A very successful predator, the sando aqua monster dines on other predators of the oceans such as colo claw fish and opee sea killers. It holds victims in its large hands, until the meal is quickly eaten in the monster's powerful jaws. It would seem that a creature of the sando's size would require a great deal of food, but we can surmise that its success at hunting makes the amount it receives sufficient. Sando aqua monsters have been spotted near Otoh Gunga on occasion, and it is rumored that the Caves of Eleuabad host them on a regular basis. Visitors to the Royal Icqui Aquaria on Coruscant are able to see the tooth of one of these beasts, and are said to be chilled by the very thought of seeing one on a live specimen.

DESIGNATION: NONSENTIENT
HOMEWORLD: NABOO
AVERAGE LENGTH: 160 METERS
PRONUNCIATION: SĂN'-DŌ ÄK'-WÄ MÄNS'-TŬR

NOTABLE APPEARANCE: EPISODE I: THE PHANTOM MENACE

away—but because of their poor vision, sudden movement often takes them by surprise. They will rear, throw off any burdens or riders they are carrying, and run for a distance until they feel the threat has passed. Usually they trample over whatever it was that frightened them in their flight.

Rontos need plenty of water, but their thin, leathery skin easily sheds excess heat, allowing them to function well in desert surroundings. Despite their usefulness, they are rarely exported, because offworlders feel their skittishness makes them unreliable.

Even so, rontos are the favorite pack animals of Jawas, who enjoy working with the kindly animals. Sadly, Jawas are often not strong enough to keep a rearing, frightened Ronto in control. In the towns of Tatooine, rampaging rontos are commonplace, as are injured, cursing Jawas who try to keep them calm.

During mating season, female rontos give off a powerful, musky scent. While attractive to male rontos, it is repulsive to most other species, and females in heat have to be isolated. Many have likened it to the scent that Rodians exude

SARKAN

Sarkans are bipedal saurians native to Sarka in the Mid Rim. Tall creatures, they have thick green-scaled hides, yellow eyes with slit pupils, and thick tails. Sarkans have razor-sharp fangs in tapered snouts. Often, they will decorate their claws with multicolored varnish and clan symbols, and wear brightly colored baggy clothes decorated with gemstones. A Sarkan's tail is used for balance and stability, but it can also be used as a weapon by those trained in traditional Sarkan martial arts.

Sarkans speak Sarkese, an intricate mix of words and body gestures. Sarkan diplomats and explorers will learn Basic, but average Sarkans will not—they are not travelers. On the rare occasions when they do leave their planet, they tend to travel in groups of three, a remnant of the time when Sarka was ruled by a strict caste structure. Solitary Sarkans encountered in the galaxy are often outcasts. Other species who interact with Sarkans often find it a trying experience, as Sarkan culture is based on arcane codes of conduct that outsiders are expected to know. Violators are treated as barbarians and physically removed from the presence of high-ranking Sarkans by well-trained bodyguards.

At the height of the Empire, Sarkans reluctantly allowed humans and those who had the Emperor's favor to insult their strict cultural norms as a matter of necessity. As soon as they learned of the Emperor's death, they stopped the practice. As a result, representatives of such major galactic corporations such as SoroSuub find themselves on the outside of Sarkan trade, as they are unable (or unwilling) to speak Sarkese. Once snubbed, it is difficult to impossible to regain entry to their world.

DESIGNATION: SENTIENT
HOMEWORLD: SARKA
AVERAGE HEIGHT: 2 METERS
PRONUNCIATION: SÄR'-KĂN

NOTABLE APPEARANCE: EPISODE IV: A NEW HOPE (SPECIAL EDITION)

SELONIAN

Selonians are furry, bipedal mammals native to Selonia in the Corellian system. They are taller and thinner than most humans, with slightly shorter arms and legs. They have long bodies and are comfortable walking on two legs or four. Retractable claws at the ends of their paw-like hands give them the ability to dig and climb efficiently, while half-meter tails counterbalance their bodies when they are walking upright. Their bodies are covered with glossy short hair that is usually brown or black, and they have long, pointed faces with bristly whiskers and sharp teeth.

Selonians have a matriarchal society, as their population is largely female due to genetic factors, although the ratio of females to males is currently unknown. They are a thoroughly grounded, serious-minded people, primarily concerned about the safety of their family "dens" and their people as a whole. In their society, the needs of the entire group are more important than those of an individual. Because Selonians believe their actions could affect the entire den, they refuse to lie, considering it as terrible a crime as murder.

Select Selonians are trained to deal with humans and other aliens. While Selonians appear outgoing, friendly, and charitable, most have no interests beyond the den. Selonians have mastered shipbuilding technology, constructing ships that they use within their own solar system. Since they have no desire to travel beyond the boundaries of Corellia, their ships do not have hyperdrive capabilities.

DESIGNATION: SENTIENT
HOMEWORLD: SELONIA
AVERAGE HEIGHT: 2 METERS
PRONUNCIATION: SĔL-Ō'-NĒ'ĂN

NOTABLE APPEARANCE: AMBUSH AT CORELLIA (NOVEL)

SHAAK

Shaaks are large, four-legged herbivores native to the grasslands of Naboo. They usually wander the plains freely, with owned herds usually intermingling with the nondomesticated variety. They have thick woolly coats that are shaved at the beginning of the warm season to weave into warm fabrics. As pachyderms, shaaks have thick, leathery skin, and their bodies are plump with blubber. Shaaks serve as the primary source for meat on Naboo, particularly because of their large rumps, which contain half their weight in extra flesh.

Shaak meat can be stored and prepared easily, and giant cooling warehouses on Naboo serve this purpose.

Given their weight, most shaaks avoid wetland areas—they sink easily. Younger shaaks are light enough to swim, and are often seen dousing themselves with water in the cool lakes or mud banks of Naboo. The fatty ambergris that makes the younger shaaks extremely buoyant is used as a base for expensive perfumes for which Naboo has become famous. In addition, their hides are used to make a variety of excellent leather goods.

Shaaks are gentle and plodding, and while they are sometimes used as pack animals, they do not usually serve as mounts. When they do serve as mounts, they must frequently rest since they are not generally strong enough to carry passengers.

DESIGNATION: NONSENTIENT
HOMEWORLD: NABOO
AVERAGE HEIGHT: 1.5 METERS
PRONUNCIATION: SHĂK

NOTABLE APPEARANCE: EPISODE II: ATTACK OF THE CLONES

SHAWDA UBB

The Shawda Ubb are a squat, green-skinned, potbellied amphibian species native to the planet Manpha, which is located in the Outer Rim. Their spherical bodies are accentuated by twiggy arms and legs, which have three digits apiece. They have small heads, and their faces are topped by heavy brow ridges. A thin row of bumps runs from their foreheads down their necks. Like the Quarren and other water-born species, the Shawda Ubb need to remain moist to keep their skin from drying and cracking, and in extreme heat conditions they become mostly listless. Though small, members of this species have several inborn defenses, the most notable of which is their ability to spit a poison that will immobilize an opponent for a quarter of a standard hour.

One of the better-known Shawda Ubb is Rapotwanalantonee (known by his stage name Rappertunie), who played a native instrument called a growdi, a combination of a water-organ and flute.

DESIGNATION: SENTIENT
HOMEWORLD: MANPHA
AVERAGE HEIGHT: 1 METER
PRONUNCIATION: SHÄ'-DA ŬBB'

NOTABLE APPEARANCE: EPISODE VI: RETURN OF THE JEDI (SPECIAL EDITION)

SHI'IDO

Hailing from the Colonies region planet Lao-man (Sh'shuun in Shi'ido, their native language) Shi'ido are a species rarely seen around the galaxy. In natural form, Shi'ido are roughly humanoid, with large craniums, thick limbs, and no hair. Like Clawdites, they are born with the ability to mimic the form of any species that is approximately the same mass as themselves. Younger members of the species can only manage to take the form of other humanoids. Unlike Clawdites, however, this physical limitation disappears when an individual reaches the age of around 150 years, allowing older Shi'ido to shift and enlarge their shape to mimic more complex beings. If Shi'ido attempt a form that is beyond their normal limits, however, they may be forced to stay in that form until their body can recover, which can be several weeks.

Shi'ido physiology is extremely flexible. Their thin bones are very dense, allowing support even in the most awkward mass configurations. Their physiology includes a series of tendons that can release and reattach themselves in different formations. They also have a great deal of hidden fleshy mass that they can access and use to enlarge their shapes. Shi'ido transformations are made complete by the use of telepathic suggestions imposed upon viewers, painting the image of what they want the observers to see in their minds. This helps cover over any inaccuracies in the Shi'ido's transformation, but it is extremely difficult to maintain. Older Shi'ido have more mastery over this talent.

Shi'ido are a long-lived species: some of the oldest members of the race are five hundred standard years old. For this reason, they've developed an acute interest in learning about the universe and all the people in it—learning something new makes traveling from their solitary world worthwhile.

DESIGNATION: SENTIENT
HOMEWORLD: LAO-MAN (SH'SHUUN)
AVERAGE HEIGHT: 1.8 METERS
PRONUNCIATION: SHĒ-Ē'-DŌ

NOTABLE APPEARANCE: GALAXY OF FEAR (NOVEL)

SKAKOAN

Skakoans are mammalian humanoids native to the highly pressurized, methane-atmosphere world of Skako in the Core World region. This world is a teeming metropolis much like Coruscant, though its architecture is not as aesthetically pleasing. Visitors to Skako must wear a special pressure suit

tainment units of the medium- and heavy-pressure suits are not. Methane cells are located within the containment unit, and connect to the faceplate via alloy encased tubing. All the suits are fitted with a vocalizer that allows a Skakoan to be heard, but the result is a very distorted speech pattern. Skakoan pressure suits are known to come with certain dangers, primarily that the suits will explode if punctured. Due to the methane gas the suit contains for the Skakoan to breathe, such an explosion can cause a great deal of damage to the surrounding area and anyone in the vicinity. As a fail-safe, however, all Skakoan pressure suits are self-repairing to prevent ruptures. Skakoan pressure suits are only manufactured on Skako, as the Skakoans will not trust their production to offworlders.

Skakoans rarely leave their homeworld, fearing an accidental death from suit depressurization. When they are seen offworld, it is a demonstration of the strength of their belief in their undertaking. Because Skakoans are usually encountered in their pressure suits, other peoples rarely if ever see physical manifestations of their emotional reactions, such as body language and facial expressions. This leads to the misconception that they are passionless robots. In fact, their emotions are the one thing that truly controls them; in particular, their hatred and xenophobia keep them in virtual isolation from the galaxy at large.

Skakoans are shrewd, manipulative, severe beings bent on self-preservation at all costs. They are supremely logical, expending most of their creative energy on scientific and engineering endeavors. Any other problems they face are met with logical, calculated solutions. They are so engineering-minded that they speak in a formulaic machine language called Skakoverbal, which is similar to Bocce and also contains elements of Binary. Their written language is called Skakoform; it is often mistaken for engineering schematics or circuit diagrams.

The Skakoan people are known for their technological and engineering prowess, though they have not been a part of the galactic trade scene since the time of the Old Republic. During that period, they were the principal members of the Techno Union, a galaxywide association of megacorporations that had representation in the Galactic Senate. The Techno Union met its end when it joined the Separatist movement led by Count Dooku. It was expelled from the Senate at that time, and the Skakoan government decided to leave the Republic as well. Through the Clone Wars, Skakoan technology was pivotal, but when the Empire rose, the Techno Union and its nonhuman leaders were crushed. The Techno Union's member companies were put under Imperial control and the Skakoans returned to their world, angry and spiteful toward the humans who'd spawned the new galactic government. When the Empire fell and the New Republic was born, the Skakoans did lit-

to survive because of the harsh environment there. Likewise, a Skakoan must wear a pressure suit to survive offplanet. Skakoans cannot breathe oxygen or survive in the standard air pressure of most planets, but they are acclimated to most high-pressure worlds. As a result, few outsiders have seen what a Skakoan really looks like. However, some exobiologists have discovered, from obtained research specimens, that under their pressure suits Skakoans look like gaunt humans, with folds of grayish white skin draped over slight skeletons. Their faces are sunken with leering eyes, a flattened nose, and a toothless, scowling mouth.

Skakoans wear three varieties of pressure suits, depending on their work or the outer environment they must visit. Generally, a Skakoan pressure suit consists of two pieces: a full-body membrane layer (including a head carapace), and a durasteel containment unit for the face, neck, and torso. The membrane layer is flexible, but the required durasteel con-

tle to leave their seclusion. Having little trust for humans, they rejected any overtures the New Republic made to encourage them to return to galactic society. They also flatly refused to share any new technological advancements they'd made with the business community.

DESIGNATION: SENTIENT
HOMEWORLD: SKAKO
AVERAGE HEIGHT: 1.75 METERS
PRONUNCIATION: SKĂ-KŌ'-ĂN

NOTABLE APPEARANCE: EPISODE II: ATTACK OF THE CLONES

SKRILLING

Originally nomadic herders, the Skrillings of Agriworld-2079 on the spinward edge of the Mid Rim are stocky humanoids with wrinkled gray skin, stubby fingers, and deep-set eyes. They have multiple rows of needle-like teeth and a bony crest starting at the top of their bald heads, descending to the napes of their necks. Skrillings do not have nostrils, instead breathing through a series of eight tubes that vertically line the fronts of their faces. Skrillings are slow-witted, sulky, greedy scavengers. Most are bright enough, however, to know when they have pestered another being to the point of violence and will at least temporarily leave that person alone.

Skrillings are typically avoided by other sentient species for their unusual habits, most of which violate the galactic norm for civilized beings. They are known, for instance, for stealing battlefield corpses, with an unusual talent for appearing on worlds where battles have been fought and unclaimed bodies can be found. They are regarded as whiners who feed on carrion and uncooked, spoiled meat that would make other beings deathly sick. If Skrillings have decided they want something, they will repeatedly and unceasingly request the item from its owner, even following that individual to other worlds and star systems to obtain the object of their desire. However, this behavior is in fact the result of oppression. When the M'shinni colonized the Skrilling homeworld, they fenced in the Skrilling herds and claimed their lands, leaving Skrillings desperate for a way to survive. They managed to integrate themselves into M'shinni colonies as beggars.

Skrillings now travel the galaxy in starships they piece together from derelicts. They can often be found among criminal organizations and on planets of tyrants—which so often provide reliable supplies of corpses and carrion—although many were valuable spies for the Rebel Alliance during the Galactic Civil War, passing unnoticed to gather information.

DESIGNATION: SENTIENT
HOMEWORLD: AGRIWORLD-2079
AVERAGE HEIGHT: 1.7 METERS
PRONUNCIATION: SKRĬ'-LĬNG

NOTABLE APPEARANCE: EPISODE VI: RETURN OF THE JEDI

SPACE SLUG

Space slugs are large, toothed, silicon-based gastropods that survive in the cold vacuum of space, feeding on stellar energy emissions, minerals from asteroids, and small vacuum-breathing creatures such as mynocks. They primarily inhabit asteroid fields, where food is plentiful. Most space slugs measure less than ten meters in length, although they have been reputed to grow large enough to swallow small spaceships whole. In cases such as this, the mynocks they swallow are more likely to become internal parasites, rather than nourishment.

These creatures have a highly developed, genetically endowed spatial sense that allows them to calculate the trajectory and speed of every moving body in their area. This primal sense helps them to target food and to move between planetary bodies.

Like most gastropods, space slugs reproduce asexually. They will carry the young for a few months, then give birth. The newborn slug inherently knows how to survive on its own, and will leave the parent to seek out its own life.

Space slugs are prized by sentients for their organs and body parts, which industrial manufacturers use to produce special lubricants and fibers. Some space stations and shipyards also keep space slugs on hand to reduce the mynock population, though their size is carefully regulated.

DESIGNATION: NONSENTIENT
HOMEWORLD: HOTH ASTEROID BELT
AVERAGE LENGTH: 10 METERS
PRONUNCIATION: SPĀS' SLŬG

NOTABLE APPEARANCE: EPISODE V: THE EMPIRE STRIKES BACK

SWAMP SLUG/ NOS MONSTER

The giant swamp slug of the planet Dagobah in the Outer Rim is a gastropod that eats nearly anything it can pull into its wide, lipless mouth, animal or vegetable. Growing to a maximum length of eight meters from head to toe, this beast uses its size as a key natural defense. It has six small legs that enable it to move along the bottom of swamps, rivers, and lakes. Its large, orange eyes can see clearly beneath the murky waters, while two antennae on the top of its head act as sonar, sending signals around the creature's body to determine its distance from the bottom and banks.

These creatures possess a minimal number of vital organs, making it difficult to kill them. As a result, swamp slugs do not fear many predators, and enjoy their position at the top of the Dagobah food chain. Their only two concerns are feeding and reproducing.

Like most gastropods, the swamp slug is a hermaphrodite, and it reproduces without external fertilization. The creature will simply become pregnant and bear a child, which is born completely aware of how to survive. Although it can survive on its own, the baby swamp slug will usually stay with its mother for several months while it gets accustomed to its environment.

Because swamp slugs can eat practically anything, they have no trouble finding food. Anything pulled into a slug's maw is pulverized into digestible pieces by the thousands of tiny grinding teeth that line its throat.

Swamp slugs are closely related to nos monsters, an aquatic monster from the Utapaun depths. These beasts live in low-light to pitch-black grottoes, where their eyes have adapted to the conditions. They are fascinated by any lighted object that passes nearby. Capable swimmers and surprisingly fast on land, they are typically able to catch what interests them.

DESIGNATION: NONSENTIENT
HOMEWORLD: DAGOBAH / UTAPAU
AVERAGE LENGTH: 8 METERS
PRONUNCIATION: NŎS-MŎN'STĔR

NOTABLE APPEARANCE: EPISODE V: THE EMPIRE STRIKES BACK AND EPISODE III: REVENGE OF THE SITH

TIN-TIN DWARF (TINTINNA)

Tin-Tin Dwarfs are actually known formally as the Tintinna, a species from the little-known, rarely visited, primitive Outer Rim world of Rinn. They are a rodent-like species very similar to Ranats, and are considered to be distant relatives.

Unlike their cousins, whose incisors emerge from their bottom jaw, the Tintinna have simple, small, rodent incisors that emerge from the tops of their mouths. They have black, mouse-like eyes, small round ears, and soft brown fur. Small pink paws sport nimble digits, and they look, simply, like giant mice. Because of their environment, they often give off a pleasant, wood-chip smell.

Tintinna live in underground burrows that they dig out without the benefit of tools. They line their earthen homes with wood chips, leaves, and other natural materials that serve to keep them warm and dry. They chew the wood for this purpose, as well as to wear down their teeth, which otherwise may grow to uncomfortable lengths.

Because their planet is remote, Tin-Tin Dwarfs are rarely seen off their homeworld. Traders and smugglers use Rinn as a backwater hiding place, so some Tintinna have been known to befriend spacers and hitch rides offworld. This is an easy-going, pleasant, and curious species, always looking to learn new things about the universe. Tintinna are quick learners, and when exposed to technology, they begin to understand it almost immediately. Spacers have therefore found them useful as teammates and lookouts, because of their highly sensitive rodent hearing and eyesight.

DESIGNATION: SENTIENT
HOMEWORLD: RINN
AVERAGE HEIGHT: 1 METER
PRONUNCIATION: TĬN'-TĬN DWÄRF (TĬN-TĬN'-Ä)

NOTABLE APPEARANCE: STAR WARS EPISODE IV: A NEW HOPE (RADIO DRAMA, BBC)

TROIG

Troigs are a two-headed humanoid species native to Pollillus in the Vannell planetary system beyond the Koornacht Cluster of the Deep Core. Each head is capable of thought and speech, so it is most accurate to consider Troigs as two individuals who share a body. Troigs have four arms, two of which are controlled by each head. They have a primary hand and three off-hands. As such, they lack coordination unless the heads work together. In contrast, the personality and sense of identity of a Troig is a somewhat coordinated effort. The left head and identity is the Saprah (the source of "blood humors," or strong emotions such as love, anger, and passion), while the right head and identity is the Saprin (the source of "breath humors," or loyalty, faith, and cunning). The identities look out for each other, so they are not often caught unawares. Most Troigs have two heads, although when the rare Troig is born with more than two, it is a cause for celebration.

The names of each head of a Troig are said together on Pollillus (*FodesinBeed,* for example), but are commonly split by offworlders (*Fode* and *Beed*).

The concept of two individuals sharing a body has long been the subject of debate in the medical and ethical communities. During the years of the Empire, a Troig named DwuirsinTabb raised a controversy regarding what to do when the health of one threatens the other. Dwuir sought to be separated from Tabb, who was described as mentally disturbed and suicidal. As Troig technology at the time did not permit this, the Troigs appealed for assistance offworld. The ethical implications of the surgery were complex—it would have resulted in the death of one of the heads. There is no record that a surgery was ever performed, and the whereabouts of DwuirsinTabb are unknown.

DESIGNATION: SENTIENT
HOMEWORLD: POLLILLUS
AVERAGE HEIGHT: 2 METERS
PRONUNCIATION: TROIG

NOTABLE APPEARANCE: EPISODE I: THE PHANTOM MENACE

UMBARAN

The Umbarans are quiet, pale humanoids from the world of Umbara in the Ghost Nebula, one of the gloomiest systems tucked away in the farthest reaches of the galaxy. Their pale skin coloration is due to the world's limited sunlight. Their sunken eyes are also sensitive to bright illumination because of their world's eternal twilight.

Umbarans have been a political presence from the earliest years of the Old Republic, and yet they are never seen in great numbers. Their specter-like visages haunted the galactic political scene for generations. They have long been objects of fear and suspicion because of their subtle ability to influence others.

Umbaran society is built on a finely detailed caste system of nearly a hundred levels, and only those of the top ten castes are allowed to leave their world. Umbarans bear and raise their children as humans do for the most part, though from early childhood they are schooled in the ways of politics and intrigue to gain prestige among their class, with the hope of rising into the next class. Moving between caste levels is possible because they are so numerous; it is the ultimate ambition of every Umbaran. Through spying, political maneuvering, blackmail, subterfuge, and cool assassination, they move themselves from level to level. Umbarans of the highest caste are considered royalty (called Rootai), and they form a council that rules their world.

When a plot to move up in societal rank fails, however, the result can be devastating for individual Umbarans and their families. If, for instance, Umbarans attempt assassination and fail, they are imprisoned, and their family is dropped to one of the lowest caste levels. Depending on the rank of the individual they tried to kill, they may end up with a death sentence for themselves, and perhaps for their entire family.

As harsh as this may sound, assassination is attempted quite often because most Umbarans feel the attempt is worth the risk. Those able to kill and replace a high-ranking Umbaran are well rewarded with prestige for themselves and their families. If they fail and die, it is still better than dropping to the lowest of castes—which, to most Umbarans, is a fate worse than death.

When Umbarans attempt assassination, they prefer to do it through sly, hidden means. Attempting murder with such messy weapons as blasters or vibroblades is considered completely lacking in refinement. Umbarans will use more subtle, elegant means to kill someone, such as microscopic poison darts, nanotechnology, undetectable poisons, and small, stylish stiletto-like knives called vootkar. Umbarans will also wear, when spying or making such attacks, a special garment known as a shadowcloak that uses special sensors allowing wearers to blend in with their surroundings, making them virtually undetectable to those with normal vision.

During the rise of the Empire, Umbarans used their influence to secure favor with the new government. The Emperor found them extremely useful in carrying out his Jedi Purge, for Umbaran spies were skilled in tracking down Jedi in hiding. They were also good at weeding out Imperial officers who were out for their own agendas rather than those of their superiors. The Emperor chose an Umbaran to be one of his own top aides, finding Umbaran secrecy beneficial when hatching his plots. When the Rebellion became a threat, they were excellent at exposing Rebel sympathizers in the Senate and other levels of government.

When the Emperor was killed, Umbarans retreated quickly to their homeworld, fearing reprisals from members of the Alliance and the Imperial Remnant. Since the formation of the New Republic, they have rarely, if ever, made forays into galactic society, and galactic society prefers it that way. They are enigmatic, scheming, and unreadable beings who only desire power and prestige. Masterful at confusing and mystifying others, they never make known to others their agendas. Most Umbarans have a dark, cruel sense of humor—they enjoy seeing their victims bewildered, perplexed, or demoralized.

There is a great deal of debate as to whether Umbarans' ability to influence others is tied to some Force mind control ability, or if they are just really talented communicators. Since they are secretive, shunning any close ties with outsiders, in-depth study of this issue has been impossible.

Rumors abound of Umbarans taking control of, and/or becoming influential in, major underworld crime syndicates including the Black Sun and others. It's been suggested that they have offered their services to smugglers, influential corporations, mercenary organizations, pirates, and other nefarious persons and institutions. Their key motivation, of course, is power. Umbaran spies have also been noticed slinking around the many levels of Coruscant, no doubt keeping a discerning eye on galactic politics. Whether they will attempt a return to the Senate halls is anyone's guess, though they may wait a good long while in the hope that their reputation as conniving backstabbers fades with the passage of time.

DESIGNATION: SENTIENT
HOMEWORLD: UMBARA
AVERAGE HEIGHT: 1.8 METERS
PRONUNCIATION: ŌŌM-BÄR'-ĂN

NOTABLE APPEARANCE: EPISODE II: ATTACK OF THE CLONES

VRATIX

The Vratix are a highly intelligent insectoid species native to the world Thyferra in the Inner Rim. They are the creators of the miraculous healing substance known as bacta. Tall beings with greenish gray skin and black bulbous eyes, they stand upright on four slender legs—two long and two short. Triple-jointed arms extend from their shoulders, ending in long, three-fingered hands. At their elbow joints they have sharp spikes, which are often used in hand-to-hand combat. Two skinny, floppy antennae on their small heads give them very acute hearing. A thin, long neck connects the head to their scaly torsos. Vratix reproduce asexually.

Vratix excrete a chemical called denin that changes the color of their skin as an expression of emotion. This coloration is connected to their language, which is expressed in high-pitched voices, punctuated by clicking sounds. Because of their continuous trade relationship with other races, Vratix can speak and comprehend Basic. They also possess limited telepathic ability, allowing them to share thoughts with fellow Vratix whom they know well.

Bacta is a translucent solution of alazhi and kavam bacterial particles exuded from the skin of the Vratix themselves. Combined with a liquid called ambori, the solution acts like a body's own vital fluids to heal all but the most serious of wounds. Bacterial particles actually seek out the injuries and promote amazingly quick tissue growth without scarring.

Vratix culture centers on a type of hive mentality, and single Vratix usually refer to themselves with their hive name. They also use the plural when referring to themselves—preferring *we* to *I*, for example.

Like most worker insects, the Vratix are a very practical people. All industry and creative effort goes into producing items for everyday use. The concepts of art, music, and other forms of creative expression elude their understanding. They are very calculating, examining problems from every angle before proceeding toward a solution. They are somewhat detached from their emotions, and while they are natural healers, they see the practice of medicine as a mechanical or biological practice rather than one of compassion.

DESIGNATION: SENTIENT
HOMEWORLD: THYFERRA
AVERAGE HEIGHT: 1.8 METERS
PRONUNCIATION: VRĀ'-TÍX

NOTABLE APPEARANCE: X-WING ROGUE SQUADRON: THE BACTA WAR (NOVEL)

VULPTEREEN

The natives of the Deep Core planet Vultper are thick, barrel-chested, carnivorous reptiles with six tusk-like growths protruding from their long, tapering snouts. At the top of their heads, two pointed ears jut straight upward. They also have yellow-green eyes with snake-like black pupils that enable them to see in low-light conditions, but with poor depth perception. As a result, they use echolocation to sense where they are. Their two arms end in clawed hands, the amputation of which, uniquely, due to their lack of a central brain, will cause aphasia. They are otherwise very dexterous and hardy, considering that they are constantly subject to toxic environmental conditions. These traits give Vulptereens some degree of success at Podracing, a natural endeavor, as the planet is home to one of the galaxy's largest Podracer production facilities.

Although Vulpter was once a beautiful world of grasslands, forests, and other environments, it became a polluted wasteland during the Old Republic, the product of overindustrialization and exploitation at the hands of the Trade Federation. The world was for decades the dumping ground of the Federation, which saw the planet as only a factory and its inhabitants as inferior. One city was inhabitable for every five, there were no surface animals left, and the residents suffered from diseases caused by the toxic air they breathed and water they drank. Instead of leaving, however, Vulptereens held on to the world they called home.

The planet was considered so insignificant it was often left off star charts, first by the Trade Federation and then the Empire. After it came to power, the Empire blockaded the planet, not considering it worthy of even food shipments, causing widespread rioting and famines. However, the Rebel Alliance used the world as a safe haven and, after the Galactic Civil War, began successful reclamation efforts.

DESIGNATION: SENTIENT
HOMEWORLD: VULPTER
AVERAGE HEIGHT: 1 METER
PRONUNCIATION: VŬLP'-TĔ-RĒN

NOTABLE APPEARANCE: EPISODE I: THE PHANTOM MENACE

VURK

Vurks are nomadic, amphibious reptomammals native to the isolated planet Sembla in the Outer Rim, near the Tion Hegemony. Tall bipedal humanoids, they have a large, upswept headcrest that comes to a blunt, thin, tapered end above two deep-set dark eyes. Two arms end in large, three-fingered hands; their skin is a leathery gray-green. As befitting amphibious beings, female Vurks give birth underwater, and midwives are venerated in their culture for the service they provide.

As a planet, Sembla is in transition and has not yet been the subject of much study. Its warm seas are divided by volcanic ridges that are still slowly forming continents. Perhaps because their planet is still evolving, as a species Vurks are seen as doing the same. This world does not have heavy industry, and the species did not develop space travel on its own. Generally, Vurks are considered primitive by the rest of the galaxy, but this is inaccurate. The Vurks are highly intelligent and have a well-developed philosophical tradition that respects individual freedom, places a premium on integrity, and encourages self-reflective honesty about oneself. A Vurk will behave consistently with these beliefs in all matters. Given their calm, compassionate nature, Vurks are thus skilled diplomats and negotiators.

This is not to say they will not defend themselves. Vurks are worthy opponents—they see protecting themselves and their charges as extensions of personal integrity. In fact, a Vurk Jedi served the Old Republic.

And Sembla remains today much as it was during that time. Not receiving much attention on a galactic scale and being off most trade routes, it escaped the invasion of the Yuuzhan Vong. It had not yet sent sufficient numbers into the galaxy at large to be asked to join the New Republic or the Galactic Federation of Free Alliances.

DESIGNATION: SENTIENT
HOMEWORLD: SEMBLA
AVERAGE HEIGHT: 2.1 METERS
PRONUNCIATION: VŪRK

NOTABLE APPEARANCE: EPISODE II: ATTACK OF THE CLONES

WOMP RAT

Womp rats are a carnivorous, ill-tempered, and plentiful rodent species native to the desert world of Tatooine. There are a couple of different varieties of these creatures, but for the most part they all exhibit the same features. Depending on the breed, womp rats can grow to be upward of three meters long, and they frequently travel in packs to overwhelm their prey—which includes dewbacks and banthas. They primarily live in the caves of Beggar's Canyon and the Jundland Wastes.

Like most rodents, womp rats possess keen eyesight, hearing, and smell. Their fur is usually brown, tan, or gray, and their orange eyes refract sunlight. Womp rats have sharp claws and teeth that can easily slice through flesh, enabling them to kill and eat just about any creature they encounter. Their long, narrow tails are quite strong, and can be used to whip around their prey's legs to drag it off its feet. A ridge of spiky, dark fur forms a line down the length of their spines. They reproduce at an alarming rate in broods of sixteen or more at a time.

The most common womp rat is the variety that lives in the Beggar's Canyon region of Tatooine. These usually grow no larger than two meters, but are well known for attacking Jawas and raiding the storehouses of moisture farmers in the region. Another variety, larger than the Beggar's Canyon type, is sometimes called the mutant womp rat. Mutant womp rats are found in the Jundland Wastes, and are known for the long, wing-like ears growing from their heads. These creatures appeared mysteriously a short time after the Empire came to Tatooine, and rumors persist that they evolved from Beggar's Canyon rats that raided caustic substances in Imperial waste dumps. They are not as numerous, and do not reproduce as often as the regular Beggar's Canyon womp rats.

DESIGNATION: NONSENTIENT
HOMEWORLD: TATOOINE
AVERAGE LENGTH: 2 METERS
PRONUNCIATION: WŎMP' RĂT

NOTABLE APPEARANCE: EPISODE IV: A NEW HOPE

YODA'S SPECIES

Very little is known about this species. Exhaustive research by several groups of investigators has been unable to locate a homeworld for this species, or even more than three individual members. And yet the contributions of those three individuals have earned them mention here. Unfortunately, most of what we know is sketchy at best, leaving much room for conjecture. What we do know is that each of the three

was a Jedi Master. While they may not typify their species and there is no firm evidence to indicate that every member of the species is Force-sensitive, it is a considerable fact that must be mentioned.

This unnamed bipedal humanoid species is typified by a short stature, large pointed ears, and mottled green-toned skin. They have three gnarled fingers (one opposing) on each of two hands, as well as five-toed feet, with three toes in front and two in back. Two males and a female have been observed. Although they have hair, it is wispy for the males and thins as they age. Life span is unknown, but records indicate that they are extraordinarily long-lived. Jedi Grand Master Yoda is said to have been nine hundred standard years old at the time of his death, and Master Yaddle lived for more than four hundred years. The first recorded member of this species is Master Vandar, a Jedi Master four thousand years before the Battle of Yavin, but records could not be found confirming his age. This species was well known for its members' wisdom, deliberation, and compassion, as well as their mirthful sense of humor. However, they were also known for their strange tastes in food, often consuming meals that others could not even bear to smell.

DESIGNATION: SENTIENT
HOMEWORLD: UNKNOWN
AVERAGE HEIGHT: 66 CENTIMETERS
PRONUNCIATION: UNKNOWN

NOTABLE APPEARANCE: EPISODE VI: THE EMPIRE STRIKES BACK

YUZZUM

The Yuzzum of Endor, not to be confused with the Yuzzem of Ragna III, are an intelligent yet primitive species with round, fur-covered bodies, long, thin legs, and wide mouths that show protruding teeth. They often travel in groups, hunting down ruggers—the rodents that are their primary source of food.

Yuzzum actually vary widely in appearance. Some have sharp fangs, while others have blunt teeth. Some have thick, woolly coats; others, short fur. Hence, the term *Yuzzum* actually refers to a class of migratory, fur-bearing mammals on Endor. Developmentally they are at the same level as their diminutive Ewok neighbors, defending themselves from predators and outsiders with spears and other primitive weapons. Their livelihood depends upon their large size, which often intimidates predators and even drives them away.

The Yuzzum people communicate in a language made up of musical elements, and it is sung rather than spoken. For this reason, their voices retain a gravelly tone, and many

Yuzzum are hailed as excellent singers. Those Yuzzum who have managed to leave Endor—very few ever really do—often end up singing for their suppers.

DESIGNATION: SENTIENT
HOMEWORLD: MOON OF ENDOR
AVERAGE HEIGHT: 2.5 METERS
PRONUNCIATION: YŬZ'-ZŬM

NOTABLE APPEARANCE: EPISODE VI: RETURN OF THE JEDI (SPECIAL EDITION)

knowledge of medicine, particularly antibiotics. Because of their popularity, and because they spend their lives pursuing gratification, Zeltrons are quite common in the galaxy, particularly at spaceports, where they can find many prospective mates.

DESIGNATION: SENTIENT
HOMEWORLD: ZELTROS
AVERAGE HEIGHT: 1.7 METERS
PRONUNCIATION: ZĔL'-TRŎN

NOTABLE APPEARANCE: STAR WARS #70 (MARVEL COMICS)

ZELTRON

The extremely attractive Zeltrons are a somewhat near-human species native to the planet Zeltros, located on the edge of the Outer Rim and Unknown Regions. While they share some characteristics with humans, Zeltrons, like the Chiss, are now considered a distinct species from humans due to genetic differences. Their skin is bright pink, a special pigmentation that develops from a reaction to their sun's radiation. The Zeltron people have the ability to project powerful pheromones, much like those emitted by Falleen. These can be activated at will and can affect a specific individual or entire groups at the same time. Zeltrons will go to any length to please guests, and they get pleasure from being hospitable, holding massive celebrations for practically any event. They are extremely promiscuous, and extremely proud of their sexuality.

Zeltrons are also empathic, able to sense the feelings of others as well as project their own. For this reason, love and comfort are extremely important to them. Sharing positive emotions is deemed to be to everyone's benefit, while sharing negative emotions is not. In accordance with this, Zeltros's democratic government will go to great lengths to make sure no one on the planet is unhappy. Zeltros has had few tyrants or despotic rulers, because they cannot commit atrocities without experiencing another's pain. Zeltros has, however, been invaded twelve times in the past six centuries. But most invaders, because of Zeltrons' pheromones, have given up their hostile intentions and joined in the nonstop festivities. Hence, Zeltrons don't worry about such trivial matters as planetary defenses or military forces. They are able fighters, though, and they stay in peak physical condition at all times.

Zeltron technology is on par with that of most spacefaring worlds. They are capable of space travel, use advanced agricultural and industrial methods, and enjoy excellent

APPENDIX 1: PRONUNCIATION GUIDE

The pronunciation of a species' name will vary depending on the accent inherent to the speaker's home planet. The pronunciation guide below lists some key pronunciation symbols used in most standard dictionaries that will guide you in articulating the names of alien species. Note: an apostrophe (') is used after the emphasized syllable in each name.

Vowel sounds:

ă: short *a* sound as in the word *bat* and *act*.

ā: long *a* sound as in the word *age* or *rate*.

ä: open *a* sound used for words like *part, calm,* or *father.* It duplicates the short *o* sound of the word *hot*.

ĕ: short *e* sound used in *edge* or *set*.

ē: long *e* sound used in *equal* or *seat*.

ēr: this vowel sound before *r* may range from ē through ĭ in different dialects.

ĭ: short *i* sound used in *hit* or *pit*.

ī: long *i* sound used in *bite* or *whine*.

ŏ: short *o* sound used in *hot* and *pot*.

oi: a diphthong vowel sound that is a combination of an ō and an ē, such as in the words *boy* and *toy*.

ō: long *o* sound used in *moan* and *tone*.

ō̄: long *o* sound used in *toot* and *hoot*.

ô: relatively long *o* used in *order* and *border*.

ŏŏ: short double *o* sound used in *book* and *tour*.

ŭ: the short *u* sound used in *up* and *sum*.

ûr: the *u* sound used in *turn* and *urge*.

Consonants:

kh: a hard *k* pronounced at the back of the throat, such as *loch* or *ach*.

hw: a soft *w* sound used in the words *who* and *what*.

APPENDIX 2: A TIME LINE OF ALIEN HISTORY

As the varied peoples of the galaxies matured and headed for the stars, they charted trade routes, fought wars, made alliances, and established galactic society as it is presently known. This time line of pivotal events in the history of alien species movement and development demonstrates the formation of the panorama of galactic history and culture.

Circa 5,000,000,000 B.B.Y.

The galaxy is formed, many believe, by the gravitational collapse of an immense cloud of dust and gas spanning 1,000,000 light-years, made up of four hundred billion stars. Around half of these have planets that could support some form of life. Ten percent of those developed life, and one in a thousand of these worlds developed sentient life (about twenty million forms of sentient life).

Circa 3,000,000 B.B.Y.

An asteroid strikes Vinsoth, destroying most life on this planet. Surviving species evolve into the Chevin.

Circa 2,000,000 B.B.Y.

Wookiees begin to evolve on Kashyyyk, establishing dominance as climbers of the wroshyr trees.

Circa 57,000 B.B.Y.

Early humanoid settlements are established on Utapau.

Circa 35,000 B.B.Y.

A species known as the Rakata conquers much of the galaxy at the time, forming the "Infinite Empire." Rakata are credited with building Centerpoint Station, and reputedly turn Tatooine into a desert world through their special manipulations.

The ancient Killiks are driven from their homeworld of Alderaan and their colony on Alsakan (presumably by a species known as the Architects). They witness the creation of the Maw in the Corellian system.

Circa 27,500 B.B.Y.

The first human colonists arrive on Alderaan and its surrounding worlds.

Circa 26,000 B.B.Y.

The ancient Nikto discover the M'dweshuu Nova and form a religion called the Cult of M'dweshuu, which dominates the entire culture.

Circa 25,200 B.B.Y.

The Rakatan Empire falls due to a plague that affects only their people and a subsequent rebellion. The Rakata are driven to near-extinction.

Circa 25,100 B.B.Y.

The Klatooinians, Vodrans, and Niktos sign the Treaty of Vontor, binding them to the Hutts as permanent slaves.

The Hutts defeat Xim the Despot and take over his criminal empire.

Corellian scientists perfect their version of the hyperdrive based on the archaic Rakatan Force-powered device.

Circa 25,000 B.B.Y.

Galactic exploration begins on a wider scale, establishing the Perlemian and the Corellian Run trade routes.

A remnant of the Taungs, a militaristic, near-human, gray-skinned race from Coruscant, relocates to Mandalore and renames the world for their leader Mandalore the First—forming the basis for the present human Mandalorian culture.

Under the rule of benevolent Queen Rana, Duros scientists develop interstellar flight. They begin to explore the galaxy and build space cities. They establish a colony on Neimoidia.

Circa 17,000 B.B.Y.

The Arkanians take a sampling of six-armed Xexto to Quermia and, through experimentation, form a new race known as the Quermians.

Circa 15,000 B.B.Y.

The Aqualish (Aquala and Quara) fight a civil war, and an off-world exploratory vessel lands on their world. The two races unite to kill the visitors while taking their ship intact. After learning the secret of starship engineering, they cobble together an armada that leaves their star system to conquer other systems. They are defeated by the New Republic and are demilitarized.

The Hutts co-opt a planet named Evocar in the Y'Toub system, displace its citizens, and rename it Nal Hutta or "Glorious Jewel." They move their entire civilization to this world, abandoning their home world of Varl.

Circa 15,000 B.B.Y.

The Yuuzhan Vong are expelled from their sentient homeworld of Zonama Sekot and cut off from the Force, sending them on a search for a new homeworld and motivating their goals of conquest.

Circa 10,000 B.B.Y.

The Gran begin their recorded history.

Solar flares destroy most of the plant life on Kubindi, causing the (then) herbivorous Kubaz to feed on insects to survive, and launching their focus on insect farming and cuisine as a species trait.

8,000 B.B.Y.

The Gran found colonies on Hok and Malastare.

Circa 7,000 B.B.Y.

The Devaronians develop star travel.

Circa 4,500 B.B.Y.

The Barabels of Barab I are embroiled in a civil war that nearly destroys their species. An unknown Jedi mediates a truce that is never broken. The Barabels are consequently eternally indebted to, and respectful of, the Jedi.

Circa 4,030 B.B.Y.

Jedi Master Arca Jeth and a band of Jedi destroy the Lorell Raiders, and the women of the Hapes Cluster, freed from the Raiders' dominance, form a matriarchal society on Hapes.

Circa 3,970 B.B.Y.

The Lorrdians are subjugated by the Argazdans, who forbid them to speak with one another. They create a new language of facial tics, expressions, and hand gestures. They also become well versed in reading body language.

3,670 B.B.Y.

Jedi Knights free the Lorrdians from their slavery at the hands of the Argazdans. The Lorrdians later become very vocal critics of slavery.

Circa 3,500 B.B.Y.

The Iktotchi are discovered by the Republic.

Circa 3,000 B.B.Y.

Pioneer Freia Kallea establishes the Hydian Way hyperspace route, opening up new sectors of the galaxy to exploration and colonization.

Circa 1,500 B.B.Y.

As a means of preventing unending wars between their species and the Quarren, the Mon Calamari attempt a daring social experiment to civilize their opponents. They capture a million Quarren, take one generation of their children, and educate them among the Mon Calamari, making that generation more sympathetic to their enemies. While the experiment works, it creates lasting resentment on the part of the Quarren.

600 B.B.Y.

The first recorded domesticated rancors are reported on Dathomir.

Circa 500 B.B.Y.

Archaeological excavation begins at Polis Massa.

490 B.B.Y.

The Corporate Sector is formed, encompassing dozens of unexplored worlds.

350 B.B.Y.

The Trade Federation is established. Neimoidians serve pivotal roles in its formation and administration.

Circa 300 B.B.Y.

The Techno Union discovers Mustafar.

300 B.B.Y.

The Bothans start to master intelligence gathering, exploiting it for political gain.

The Bith engage in a civil war, destroying their planetary environment. Bith change their culture, repressing their emotions to prevent further wars.

200 B.B.Y.

The Dressellians are discovered by the Bothans, who, upon seeing their potential, leave them to evolve without interference.

120 B.B.Y.

Old Republic scouts come to Elom, and encounter the industrialized but not spacefaring Elomin. They subsequently set up trade and mining operations, which leads to the Elomin's first encounter with the other species on their world, the subterranean Elom.

100 B.B.Y.

The Gungans of Naboo fight off unknown invaders of their world, assembling their first Grand Army.

32 B.B.Y.

The Kaminoans of Kamino, at the behest of Chancellor Palpatine (and secretly Count Dooku), start the process of creating a clone army based on the template of Mandalorian Jango Fett. These clones soon make up the Grand Army of the Republic, serving as the basis for the Clone Wars and later becoming the core of the Imperial Army.

25 B.B.Y.

A group of Yuuzhan Vong land on the obscure planet Bimmiel, and begin surveying the surrounding sectors for the coming invasion.

22–19 B.B.Y.

A Separatist faction arises in the Republic, calling itself the Confederacy of Independent Systems. Forming a droid army that threatens the Republic, the conflict escalates to war, causing chaos and uprisings throughout the galaxy.

20 B.B.Y.

A space battle between a Republic cruiser and a Separatist science vessel named *Gahenna* (carrying a poisonous defoliant developed for the war) contaminates the world Honoghr. The native Noghri suffer in silence for several years as the vegetation on their world dies.

19 B.B.Y.

Palpatine declares himself Emperor, bringing about the rise of High Human Culture: the ideology that humans are inherently superior to aliens. Many aliens find their rights and freedoms restricted or revoked and face prejudice encouraged by the New Order.

The Empire enslaves the Wookiees and bombs their cities. The Trandoshans hunt those who escape the beleaguered world.

Caamas, a peaceful and noble world loved throughout the Empire, is completely ravaged by unknown attackers. Caamasi are relocated to refugee camps, one being Alderaan.

Darth Vader offers environmental aid to the Noghri people on Honoghr in return for their servitude. Vader then orders his staff to further contaminate the world to keep them enslaved.

Senior Anthropologist Hoole exiles himself from his homeworld of Sh'shuun, beginning his most famous studies of other species.

11 B.B.Y.

Imperials discover the planet Maridun, home of the Amanin, and establish bases there. They later take the Amanin for slaves.

10 B.B.Y.

Miners looking for valuable Lowickan firegems in the Lowick asteroid belt discover the Pa'lowick species. Not long afterward, their unique vocal talents become legendary.

9 B.B.Y.

A "death wave" (only the fifth recorded in Chadra-Fan history) occurs on Chad as ocean floor quakes create massive tsunamis. Hundreds of thousands of Chadra-Fan are killed.

7 B.B.Y.

On the planet Falleen, scientists under Darth Vader's orders develop a biological weapon that accidentally infects the Falleen populace. To protect the Empire from the virus, Darth Vader orders a bombardment of the planet. More than two hundred thousand Falleen die.

1–0 B.B.Y.

Mon Mothma issues a Declaration of Rebellion, distributed by holo to thousands of galactic worlds, which openly declare their allegiance to the Alliance. These worlds are quickly suppressed, but the event shines a new light of hope for oppressed species in the galaxy.

0 B.B.Y.

The world Alderaan is destroyed by the Death Star.

Firrerre is destroyed by Hethrir, a student of Vader. The Firrerreo people are either killed or enslaved.

4 A.B.Y.

Anakin Skywalker (Darth Vader) kills Emperor Palpatine ending his rule and persecution of all non-humans.

The Ssi-ruuvi Imperium attacks at Bakura, and is repelled.

7.5 A.B.Y.

Remnants of the Empire release a deadly plague, the Krytos virus, which targets nonhumans on Coruscant.

Rogue Squadron liberates Thyferra from rogue Imperial Admiral Ysanne Isard's control, and freeing up bacta production. The Vratix assume control of bacta production.

9 A.B.Y.

The Noghri pledge their service to the Alliance and help defeat Admiral Thrawn.

16–17 A.B.Y.

The Yevetha threaten the New Republic and are defeated.

19 A.B.Y.

The New Republic discovers that Bothans were involved in the destruction of Caamas.

23–24 A.B.Y.

A radical political movement called the Diversity Alliance is formed, which spouts alien superiority and the genocide of the human species. After an attempt to infect worlds with a plague, the Diversity Alliance is disbanded.

25 A.B.Y.

The Yuuzhan Vong begin their conquest of the galaxy.

The Yuuzhan Vong pull the moon Dobido down upon the world of Sernpidal, killing the famed Wookiee Chewbacca.

The Yuuzhan Vong decimate the garden world of Ithor to eliminate the bafforr trees that weaken Yuuzhan Vong vonduun crab armor.

26 A.B.Y.

The Yuuzhan Vong annihilate Nal Hutta, driving the Hutts from the system. In addition they attack Rodia, Druckenwell, Falleen, and Kalarba in an attempt to cut off the Corellian Run. In the end, they terraform Duro to use it as a launching point to attack the Core Worlds.

27 A.B.Y.

The Yuuzhan Vong conquer Coruscant and begin to terraform the world.

28 A.B.Y.

The New Republic wins a critical battle against Yuuzhan Vong at Ebaq 9, causing the invaders to begin stretching their resources.

The New Republic is restructured. Under a new constitution, the Galactic Federation of Free Alliances (or the Galactic Alliance) is formed, allowing a new federalism that clearly defines the balance of power among the judiciary, the Senate, and the planetary governments.

28.2–28.7 A.B.Y.

The Yuuzhan Vong conquer Barab I, Rutan, and Belderone.

29 A.B.Y.

Mandalorian Supercommandos led by Boba Fett drive the Yuuzhan Vong from the Caluula sector. This further defeat causes the Yuuzhan Vong to retreat to Coruscant in desperation.

35–36 A.B.Y.

Stirred from their obscurity by the arrival of three refugees from the Yuuzhan Vong War, the Killiks begin an expansion into territories decimated in the wake of the Yuuzhan Vong. Absorbing entire peoples into its hive mind, corrupted by a dark Jedi, the Colony threatens to succeed in its conquest where the Yuuzhan Vong failed.

The Killik expansion is repelled, when the core of the Dark Nest, Dark Jedi Lomi Plo, is defeated and Raynar Thul is removed from the hive mind.

BIBLIOGRAPHY

Coruscant and the Core Worlds • Wizards of the Coast, 2003

Agents of Chaos I: Hero's Trial • Star Wars: The New Jedi Order, Book 4, James Luceno, Del Rey Books, 2000

Agents of Chaos II: Jedi Eclipse • Star Wars: The New Jedi Order, Book 5, James Luceno, Del Rey Books, 2000

Alien Anthology • Wizards of the Coast, 2001

Alien Encounters: The Star Wars Aliens Compendium • Paul Sudlow et al., West End Games, 1998

Ambush at Corellia • Star Wars: The Corellian Trilogy, Book 1, Roger MacBride Allen, Bantam Books, 1995

Anakin • one-shot comic, Dark Horse Comics, 1999

The Art of Star Wars Episode I: The Phantom Menace • Jonathan Bresman, Del Rey Books, 1999

Assault at Selonia • Star Wars: The Corellian Trilogy, Book 2, Roger MacBride Allen, Bantam Books, 1995

The Bacta War • Star Wars: X-Wing, Book 4, Michael A. Stackpole, Bantam Books, 1997

Balance Point • Star Wars: The New Jedi Order, Book 6, Kathy Tyers, Del Rey Books, 2001

Before the Storm • Star Wars: The Black Fleet Crisis Trilogy, Book 1, Michael P. Kube-McDowell, Bantam Books, 1996

The Cestus Deception • Star Wars: Clone Wars, Steven Barnes, Del Rey Books, 2005

Children of the Jedi • Barbara Hambly, Bantam Books, 1995

Classic Star Wars • twenty-issue series, Archie Goodwin and Al Williamson, Dark Horse Comics, 1992–1994

The Courtship of Princess Leia • Dave Wolverton, Bantam Books, 1994

The Crystal Star, • Vonda McIntyre, Bantam Books, 1995

Dark Apprentice • Star Wars: Jedi Academy, Book 2, Kevin J. Anderson, Bantam Books, 1994

Dark Empire • six-issue series, Tom Veitch, Dark Horse Comics, 1991–1992

Dark Empire Sourcebook • Michael Allen Horne, West End Games, 1993

Dark Force Rising • Star Wars: The Thrawn Trilogy, Book 2, Timothy Zahn, Bantam Books, 1992

Dark Force Rising Sourcebook • Bill Slavicsek, West End Games, 1992

Dark Horse Presents Annual, 1999 •
"Luke Skywalker's Walkabout," Phil Norwood, 1999

Dark Journey •
Star Wars: The New Jedi Order, Book 10, Elaine Cunningham, Del Rey Books, 2002

Dark Lord: The Rise of Darth Vader •
James Luceno, Del Rey Books, 2005

The Dark Rival •
Star Wars: Jedi Apprentice, Book 2, Jude Watson, Scholastic, 1999

Dark Tide: Onslaught •
Star Wars: The New Jedi Order, Book 2, Mike Stackpole, Del Rey Books, 2000

Dark Tide: Ruin •
Star Wars: The New Jedi Order, Book 3, Mike Stackpole, Del Rey Books, 2000

Darksaber •
Kevin J. Anderson, Bantam Books, 1995

Destiny's Way •
Star Wars: The New Jedi Order, Book 14, Walter Jon Williams, Del Rey Books, 2003

Droids •
ongoing series, Dark Horse Comics, 1995

Edge of Victory I: Conquest •
Star Wars: The New Jedi Order, Book 7, Greg Keyes, Del Rey Books, 2001

Edge of Victory II: Rebirth •
Star Wars: The New Jedi Order, Book 8, Greg Keyes, Del Rey Books, 2001

Empire's End •
two-issue series, Tom Veitch, Dark Horse Comics, 1995

Enemy Lines I: Rebel Dream •
Star Wars: The New Jedi Order, Book 11, Aaron Allston, Del Rey Books, 2002

Enemy Lines II: Rebel Stand •
Star Wars: The New Jedi Order, Book 12, Aaron Allston, Del Rey Books, 2002

The Essential Guide to Planets and Moons •
Daniel Wallace, Del Rey Books, 1998

The Ewok Adventure •
"Caravan of Courage," MGM/UA, 1984

The Final Prophecy •
Star Wars: The New Jedi Order, Book 18, Greg Keyes, Del Rey Books, 2003

Force Heretic I: Remnant •
Star Wars: The New Jedi Order, Book 15, Sean Williams and Shane Dix, Del Rey Books, 2003

Force Heretic II: Refugee •
Star Wars: The New Jedi Order, Book 16, Sean Williams and Shane Dix, Del Rey Books, 2003

Force Heretic III: Reunion •
Star Wars: The New Jedi Order, Book 17, Sean Williams and Shane Dix, Del Rey Books, 2003

Galaxy Guide 2: Yavin and Bespin •
Jonathan Caspian et al., West End Games, 1989

Galaxy Guide 4: Alien Races •
Troy Denning, West End Games, 1989

Galaxy Guide 12: Aliens: Enemies and Allies •
C. Robert Carey et al., West End Games, 1995

Galaxy of Fear •
Books 1–12, John Whitman, Bantam Books, 1997–1999

Geonosis and the Outer Rim Worlds •
Wizards of the Coast, 2004

Han Solo and the Corporate Sector Sourcebook •
Michael Allen Horne, West End Games, 1993

Han Solo and the Lost Legacy •
Star Wars: Han Solo Adventures, Book 3, Brian Daley, Del Rey Books, 1979

Han Solo at Stars' End •
Star Wars: Han Solo Adventures, Book 1, Brian Daley, Del Rey Books, 1979

Hard Contact •
Star Wars: Republic Commando, Karen Traviss, Del Rey Books, 2004

Hard Merchandise •
Star Wars: The Bounty Hunter Wars, Book 2, K. W. Jeter, Bantam Books, 1999

Heir to the Empire •
Star Wars: Thrawn Trilogy, Book 1, Timothy Zahn, Bantam Books, 1991; six-issue comics adaptation, Mike Baron, Dark Horse Comics, 1995–1996

Heir to the Empire Sourcebook •
Bill Slavicsek, West End Games, 1992

Hero's Guide •
Wizards of the Coast, 2003

The Hidden Past •
Star Wars: Jedi Apprentice, Book 3, Jude Watson, Scholastic, 1999

The Illustrated Star Wars Universe •
Kevin J. Anderson and Ralph McQuarrie, Bantam Books, 1995

The Jedi Academy Sourcebook •
Paul Sudlow, West End Games, 1996

Jedi Search •
Star Wars: Jedi Academy, Book 1, Kevin J. Anderson, Bantam Books, 1994

Jedi Trial •
Star Wars: Clone Wars, David Sherman and Dan Cragg, Del Rey Books, 2004

The Joiner King •
Star Wars: Dark Nest, Book 1, Troy Denning Del Rey Books, 2005

The Krytos Trap •
Star Wars: X-Wing, Book 3, Michael A. Stackpole, Bantam Books, 1996

Labyrinth of Evil •
Star Wars: Episode III Prequel, James Luceno, Del Rey Books, 2005

Lando Calrissian and the Mindharp of Sharu •
Star Wars: Lando Calrissian Adventures, Book 1, L. Neil Smith, Del Rey Books, 1983

Lando Calrissian and the Starcave of Thonboka •
Star Wars: Lando Calrissian Adventures, Book 3, L. Neil Smith, Del Rey Books, 1983

The Last Command •
Star Wars: The Thrawn Trilogy, Book 3, Timothy Zahn, Bantam Books, 1993; six-issue comics adaptation, Mike Baron, Dark Horse Comics, 1997–1999

The Last Command Sourcebook •
Eric Trautmann, West End Games, 1994

Lightsabers •
Star Wars: Young Jedi Knights, Book 4, Kevin J. Anderson and Rebecca Moesta, Berkley Books, 1995

Lyric's World •
Star Wars: Junior Jedi Knights, Book 2, Nancy Richardson, Berkley Books, 1995

The Mandalorian Armor •
Star Wars: The Bounty Hunter Wars, Book 1, K. W. Jeter, Bantam Books, 1998

Medstar I: Battle Surgeons • Star Wars: Clone Wars, Michael Reaves and Steve Perry, Del Rey Books, 2004

Medstar II: Jedi Healer • Star Wars: Clone Wars, Michael Reaves and Steve Perry, Del Rey Books, 2004

The Movie Trilogy Sourcebook • Greg Farshtey and Bill Smith, West End Games, 1993

The New Essential Chronology • Daniel Wallace, Del Rey Books, 2005

The New Essential Guide to Characters • Daniel Wallace, Del Rey Books, 2002

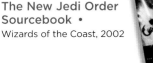

The New Jedi Order Sourcebook • Wizards of the Coast, 2002

The New Rebellion • Kristine Kathryn Rusch, Bantam Books, 1996

Outbound Flight, • Timothy Zahn, Del Rey Books, 2006

The Paradise Snare • Star Wars: The Han Solo Trilogy, Book 1, A. C. Crispin, Bantam Books, 1997

Planet of Twilight • Barbara Hambly, Bantam Books, 1997

Prophets of the Dark Side • Paul Davids and Hollace Davids, Bantam Books, 1993

Rebel Dawn • Star Wars: The Han Solo Trilogy, Book 3, A. C. Crispin, Bantam Books, 1998

Rogue Planet • Greg Bear, Del Rey Books, 2000

Rogue Squadron • Star Wars: X-Wing, Book 1, Michael A. Stackpole, Bantam Books, 1996

Secrets of Tatooine, • Wizards of the Coast, 2001

Shadows of the Empire • Steve Perry, Bantam Books, 1996; six-issue series, John Wagner et al., Dark Horse Comics, 1996

Shadows of the Empire Sourcebook • Peter Schweighofer, West End Games, 1996

Shatterpoint • Star Wars: Clone Wars, Matthew Woodring Stover, Del Rey Books, 2004

Shield of Lies • Star Wars: The Black Fleet Crisis Trilogy, Book 2, Michael P. Kube-McDowell, Bantam Books, 1996

Showdown at Centerpoint • Star Wars: The Corellian Trilogy, Book 3, Roger MacBride Allen, Bantam Books, 1995

Specter of the Past • Star Wars: Hand of Thrawn, Book 1, Timothy Zahn, Bantam Books, 1997

Splinter of the Mind's Eye • Alan Dean Foster, Del Rey Books, 1978; four-issue series, Terry Austin et al., Dark Horse Comics, 1995–1996

Star by Star • Star Wars: The New Jedi Order, Book 9, Troy Denning, Del Rey Books, 2002

Star Wars • ongoing series, Marvel Comics, 1984–1987

Star Wars • National Public Radio dramatizations, Brian Daley, 1981; published by Del Rey Books, 1994

Star Wars Adventure Journal • twelve-issue series, edited by Peter Schweighofer, West End Games, 1994–1997

Star Wars Battlefront • video game, LucasArts Entertainment

Star Wars: Behind the Magic • CD-ROM, LucasArts Entertainment, 1997

Star Wars— Clone Wars • animated, Volume 1, 2003

Star Wars— Clone Wars • animated, Volume 2, 2003

Star Wars Encyclopedia • Steven J. Sansweet, Del Rey Books, 1998

Star Wars Episode I: The Phantom Menace • film, Lucasfilm Ltd., 1999; novelization, Terry Brooks, Del Rey Books, 1999

Star Wars Episode I Insider's Guide • CD-ROM, LucasArts, 1999

Star Wars Episode II: Attack of the Clones • film, Lucasfilm Ltd., 2002; novelization, R. A. Salvatore, Del Rey Books, 2002

Star Wars Episode III: Revenge of the Sith • film, Lucasfilm Ltd., 2005; novelization, Matthew Stover, Del Rey Books, 2005

Star Wars Episode IV: A New Hope • film, Twentieth Century Fox, 1977; novelization, George Lucas, Del Rey Books, 1976

Star Wars Episode V: The Empire Strikes Back • film, Lucasfilm Ltd., 1980; novelization, Donald F. Glut, Del Rey Books, 1980

Star Wars Episode V: The Empire Strikes Back • National Public Radio dramatization, Brian Daley, 1983; published by Del Rey Books, 1985

Star Wars Episode VI: Return of the Jedi • film, Lucasfilm Ltd., 1983; novelization, James Kahn, Del Rey Books, 1983

Star Wars Galaxies • video game, LucasArts Entertainment

Star Wars Jedi Knight: Jedi Academy • video game, LucasArts Entertainment

Star Wars: Knights of the Old Republic • video game, LucasArts Entertainment

Star Wars: Knights of the Old Republic II: The Sith Lords • video game, LucasArts Entertainment

Star Wars Monopoly Game • Parker Brothers, 1996

Star Wars Republic Commando • video game, LucasArts Entertainment

Star Wars: The Roleplaying Game • second edition, Bill Smith, West End Games, 1992

Star Wars Sourcebook • Bill Slavicsek and Curtis Smith, West End Games, 1987

The Swarm War • Star Wars: Dark Nest, Book 3, Troy Denning, Del Rey Books, 2005

Tales from the Mos Eisley Cantina •
edited by Kevin J. Anderson, Bantam Books, 1995

Tales of the Bounty Hunters •
edited by Kevin J. Anderson, Bantam Books, 1997

Tales of the Jedi •
five-issue series, Tom Veitch, Dark Horse Comics, 1993–1994

Tales of the Jedi: Dark Lords of the Sith •
six-issue series, Tom Veitch and Kevin J. Anderson, Dark Horse Comics, 1994–1995

Tales of the Jedi: The Freedon Nadd Uprising •
two-issue series, Tom Veitch, Dark Horse Comics, 1994–1995

Tales of the Jedi: The Golden Age of the Sith •
five-issue series, Kevin J. Anderson, Dark Horse Comics, 1996–1997

Tales of the Jedi: Knights of the Old Republic •
five-issue series, Tom Veitch, Dark Horse Comics, 1994

Tales of the Jedi: The Sith War •
six-issue series, Kevin J. Anderson, Dark Horse Comics, 1995–1996

Tales of the Jedi Companion •
George R. Strayton, West End Games, 1996

Traitor •
Star Wars: The New Jedi Order, Book 13, Matthew Woodring Stover, Del Rey Books, 2002

Triple Zero •
Star Wars: Republic Commando, Karen Traviss, Del Rey Books, 2006

The Truce at Bakura •
Kathy Tyers, Bantam Books, 1993

Tyrant's Test •
Star Wars: The Black Fleet Crisis Trilogy, Book 3, Michael P. Kube-McDowell, Bantam Books, 1997

Ultimate Adversaries •
Wizards of the Coast, 2004

Ultimate Alien Anthology •
Wizards of the Coast, 2003

The Unifying Force •
Star Wars: The New Jedi Order, Book 19, James Luceno, Del Rey Books, 2004

The Unseen Queen •
Star Wars: Dark Nest, Book 2, Troy Denning, Del Rey Books, 2005

Vader's Fortress •
Star Wars: Junior Jedi Knights, Book 5, Rebecca Moesta, Berkley Publishing Group, 1995

Vector Prime •
Star Wars: The New Jedi Order, Book 1, R. A. Salvatore, Del Rey Books, 1999

Vision of the Future •
Star Wars: Hand of Thrawn, Book 2, Timothy Zahn, Bantam Books, 1998

Wedge's Gamble •
Star Wars: X-Wing, Book 2, Michael A. Stackpole, Bantam Books, 1996

The Wildlife of Star Wars: A Field Guide •
Terryl Whitlatch and Bob Carrau, Chronicle Books, 2001

X-Wing Rogue Squadron •
ongoing series, Dark Horse Comics, 1995–1999

Yoda: Dark Rendezvous •
Star Wars: Clone Wars, Sean Stewart, Del Rey Books, 2004

ABOUT THE AUTHORS

ANN MARGARET LEWIS began her career writing children's stories, comic book stories, and activity books for DC Comics. She has contributed to several media magazines, books, and websites, and is the author of the first *Star Wars: The Essential Guide to Alien Species*. She inhabits a section of our universe known as the Bronx in New York City with her life mate, Joseph Lewis, her toddler offspring, Raymond Allen Lewis, and a member of a feline species whose name is Camille.

HELEN KEIER has had a varied career, including advanced training as a research psychologist and statistician. She currently works as an online learning specialist and technical trainer and writer. Helen has written for several genre and media websites and is a past contributor to *Star Wars Insider,* the official Lucasfilm magazine. She lives in New York City with her son, Vince Skrapits, and two cats, Wedge Antilles and Aurra Sing.

ABOUT THE ILLUSTRATORS

CHRIS TREVAS grew up playing with lightsabers and Wookiees in the suburbs of Detroit, Michigan. He attended the College for Creative Studies before beginning his official *Star Wars* career in 1995. Since then he has created artwork for a multitude of *Star Wars* projects, including books, magazines, games, trading cards, packaging, and toys. Chris is also a writer and illustrator for *Star Wars Insider* magazine. Visit him online at www.christrevas.com.

WILLIAM O'CONNOR was born on Long Island, New York, in 1970. He began studying art formally at the age of ten. After receiving a BFA from Alfred University in 1992, he continued his studies as an illustrator in Manhattan, where he quickly became a familiar face in the gaming and publishing field. Working with clients such as Wizards of the Coast, Hasbro, HarperCollins, AEG, The History Channel, and Doubleday Books, William has created thousands of paintings and drawings for hundreds of projects. The artist now keeps his studio in New Jersey, where he illustrates and paints, and also teaches in his free time. You can visit him at www.wocillo.com.